Also by Antoine Volodine
Published by the University of Minnesota Press

Solo Viola

MEVLIDO'S DREAMS

A POST-EXOTIC NOVEL

Antoine Volodine

Translated by Gina M. Stamm

A UNIVOCAL BOOK

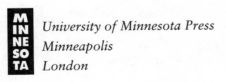

University of Minnesota Press
Minneapolis
London

CONTENTS •

In *Mevlido's Dreams*, the world is ending, not in fire or ice (or nuclear disaster) but in a heavy, humid heat, within the shrinking boundaries of the livable surface area of the planet, under torrential rains that, instead of relief, bring a more oppressive atmosphere. This universe may not seem as far from our own in the Global North as it did when the book was first published in 2007; I write this following the hottest week ever recorded on Earth, a record that will surely not take long to be broken. I first read *Mevlido's Dreams* in 2018 when looking for material for a class I was teaching on contemporary francophone science fiction and found it to be much more than that. While it is a dystopia, set a number of centuries in the future, it is also a detective story with tones of film noir, a revenge thriller, and a tragedy of love and attempted redemption. But it was only when I returned to the book a few years later that I realized that, without realizing it, Mevlido's world had taken up permanent residence in my own dream world, with its nocturnal urban landscape glistening under constant rain and sticky with humidity. It's appropriate that the novel lives rent-free in my dreams, as the narration itself passes back and forth between dreams and a waking life scarcely less strange; dreams are also the medium that characters use to communicate with each other across space and time. This oneiric atmosphere is not unusual for the work of Antoine Volodine, for those readers who may have read other books by the prolific author and his other pseudonyms (Elli Kronauer, Lutz Bassmann, Manuela Draeger, etc.). *Mevlido's Dreams,* however, is unique in the intensity of its atmosphere and the psychological and emotional depth of its protagonist, perhaps matched only by the Medici Prize–winning *Radiant Terminus.*

Civilization in Mevlido's world is gasping its way to an end in the petty corruption of a government both authoritarian and incompetent, in a theater of politics that carries only distant echoes of the ideological convictions of a bygone era. As the character Deeplane observes, humans are deeply alienated: "They no longer believe in themselves, or in society. They inherited political systems to which they've lost the keys; for them ideology is a prayer devoid of meaning. The ruling classes have become criminalized, the poor obey them. Both classes act as if they were already dead. And as if, on top of that, they don't even care." With writing often compared to the bizarre yet compelling plots of Samuel Beckett or Franz Kafka, Volodine is unique in his ability to depict the physical and cultural environments inhabited by his characters with great specificity. Sometimes he is in the Siberian taiga, the Central Asian plains, the South American jungle, Lisbon, Macau; this time a decaying city somewhere in East Asia, a capital called Oulang-Oulane, surrounded by sprawling slums crowded with refugees: Koreans, Chinese, "Ybür." This is not our world, even if climate and political crises make it seem nearer than ever. But it is a world that we can recognize from popular media: Kowloon Walled City or Bangkok from action movies; the retrofuturism of Ridley Scott's *Blade Runner* or an anime like *Cowboy Bebop* without the technological advances; a hot, wet world of people making do by any means necessary; a city's grimy and ramshackle underbelly populated by mutant birds and junkies. The character of Mevlido self-consciously references the "golden age" of cinema and its Hong Kong action movies.

This situation presents a unique set of challenges to a reader and translator. It requires not only a knowledge of French but a familiarity with the media universe from which the imagery can be recognized, as well as an understanding of how those media are received by anglophone audiences. How is the content of anime or Hong Kong action movies presented to a Western audience (anglophone or francophone), and how would it change if that were the original language, not calqued on another language's structure? This connects to one of the more unusual characteristics of Volodine's overall project, which he has dubbed the "post-exotic." Although the name was originally a joke in response to a journalist's question, this genre (of which Volodine claims to be the "spokesperson") posits a postnational literature that would be "a foreign literature written in French." The stylized prose verges on a staccato poetic rhythm, characterized by frequent use of hypotyposis, anaphora, and parataxis, especially when reporting speech or thought or when free, indirect discourse is being employed. Although these are "French," they also indicate a distance from the French spoken in our own time. How can this distance be rendered into yet another language without sounding too strange? In addition to these stylistic differences, the post-exotic allows different perspectives, human and nonhuman, to be occupied by a narrator who may or may not correspond to a character in the book or to the putative author, who is always also a character inside the post-exotic universe. In *Mevlido's Dreams*, an unidentified "I" will occasionally intrude into the otherwise third person narration, bringing into question the status of the narrative as a whole.

Mevlido's Dreams is made up of seven parts of seven short chapters each. In that way it corresponds to the post-exotic project as a whole, the forty-ninth and final planned book of which is forthcoming in the next few years. This auspicious number—seven sevens—already points to the kind of syncretic spiritual traditions more or less explicitly underpinning most of Volodine's work. Here Buddhist and Korean shamanic traditions facilitate the transition between life and death, between one life and another, between life in different worlds. Volodine imagines a supernatural organization invested not in the preservation of humanity as a species or as a collective of individuals but in a principle of so-called humanism, proletarian morality, or egalitarianism, values that humans as a species have betrayed. The agent they have sent to gather information to ease the transition from "hominids" to spiders (who supposedly represent this morality better) is Mevlido. Readers of the novel *Solo Viola* will perhaps recognize the spider as the insignia of the fascist thugs from that book and thus sense the ambivalence of the author toward the replacement of humans by a supposedly better-ordered society of arachnids.

Despite his supernatural origins, Mevlido somehow becomes fully human, perhaps more so even than the people he is meant to be watching. This novel stands out among Volodine's works for the rich interiority afforded the protagonist and the profound sense of duty to memory and promises he both feels and inspires. Mevlido, when we meet him on Earth, is a sad, mediocre man, described physically and mentally as rather average; he used to fight in the recent wars on the side of the forces of egalitarianism and the proletariat but has now given up political engagement. But unlike those around him, who are mostly portrayed as having surrendered to the end times or maintaining hope only in madness, Mevlido is anchored to his life on Earth and motivated by his connections to the women he has known: his murdered wife, the trauma-shattered woman with whom he shares an apartment, a young anarchist assassin, a mysterious woman who falls under the tram one day before he can save her, a psychiatrist who reminds him of a Hong Kong cinema star, a shaman, a no-nonsense talking crow who is sometimes also a woman. His desire to be near them, to protect them or to avenge them—impulses he is ultimately incapable of carrying out—tie him to life but also submerge him in a kind of survivor's guilt, as he feels not only that he has sinned by omission in not managing to rescue them but that his presence in their lives has somehow put them in danger. What is necessary for him to come to any kind of resolution or closure? Is it possible? What does such personal attachment mean at the end of the world? These questions are not exclusive to such dystopian fiction but rather can be asked by any one of us who witnesses the fate of someone else without being subjected to that same outcome—especially when we might see ourselves as participating in the harm that befalls them by our position in an unjust system.

The structure of the book allows for a range of narrative perspectives. From chapter to chapter the temporality and mood of the narration also change, alternating between the past and present, the indicative and the conditional. Our perception of reality, along with Mevlido's own, is challenged: are events we are seeing waking life or a dream, reality or supposition? The first part of the book introduces us, through a series of episodes going into and out of waking life, to Mevlido and his world. We learn that he is a somewhat duplicitous policeman in a society that goes through the motions of maintaining law and order and some kind of political ideology, but only for show. Closest to the protagonist are his boss, Berberoïan; his flatmate, Maleeya Bayarlag; the young assassin Sonia Wolguelane; and the talking crow Gorgha, who visits him in his dreams to give him instructions from some mysterious organization. In the second part, Mevlido's job-mandated visits to a psychiatrist reveal more of his internal life to us but also establish him as an unreliable narrator. The trauma he reveals to the psychiatrist is immediately compounded when, after leaving his appointment, he witnesses a political assassination and the death of a woman whom he believes looks like his wife, killed twenty years before. He is ordered to investigate her identity in Part III, but he will do so while trying to keep his progress secret from his colleagues and superiors. In Part IV, however, we will see that Mevlido belongs to another kind of hierarchy—an ascetic organization called the Organs, which surveils Earth from what seems to be another dimension. Mevlido is being sent to gather information about the end of humanity and will have to undergo a painful process of reincarnation as a human, but his superior Deeplane promises that he will bring him back safely when his job is done. When we return to Earth in Part V, Mevlido learns where to find his wife's murderer and goes to take revenge. Mortally wounded in the process, he is visited one after another by friends who bid him goodbye, and he leaves for the Shambles, a ghetto that seems to be suspended between life and death. The following part is devoted to Mevlido's existence in this kind of limbo, wandering in and out of situations that echo the previous life he remembers more or less well, until he comes across a shaman (Korean: *mudang*) trying to contact his spirit. Finally, in the seventh and last part, when Mevlido has crawled in his half-alive/half-dead state through centuries, maybe millennia, of decaying Earth, Deeplane comes with a *mudang* to try to keep his promise of rescue. What that promise is ultimately worth is left ambiguous, as three alternative endings for Mevlido's life are proposed to the reader.

In some ways, the plot has the elements of a fairly classic tragic romance: man and woman are in love, the world prevents their being together, man descends into tragic circumstances, intervention of a deus ex machina brings resolution. And in this case, Deeplane literally comes in a machine, in the carcass of a burned bus, to ferry Mevlido to the conclusion of his story, whatever that conclusion may be. This allows us not only to think about what the resolution of a story at the end of the world would look like but also to consider the perspective of the deus ex machina himself. What can motivate that kind of action, and what is the cost for the rescuer? Ultimately, it is easy for us to see ourselves in the various characters that populate *Mevlido's Dreams* as climate catastrophe and political crises accelerate. Do we become apathetic or ineffectively nostalgic for a time when action had meaning? Do we continue to fight for a better outcome, and what would that look like? What are the commitments, personal or political, that keep us engaged with the world around us and one another? What is our help worth to those around us?

1

Mevlido raised the brick a second time, and Berberoïan, who detested being hit on the head by a subordinate, hastened to continue his self-criticism.

"Yes," he admitted, "peccadillos. Until now I've only acknowledged those, peccadillos. But now . . . now I'm going to . . ."

He cleared his throat and straightened up a bit.

"Now, I'm going to be truthful."

A curtain of blood flowed over his eyes, and, on the other side of that red mist, he saw the representatives of the masses who were witnessing his humiliation and being bored by it. What he was confessing had nothing original about it; regarding the violence of the scene, there was nothing that would have disturbed police officers used to taking part in beatings. Besides, Mevlido wasn't really taking advantage of the situation. He was striking with restraint, continuing to treat Berberoïan as a superior, and, even if he had laid open his scalp, it was after softening the blow. The clerk of ideology, Balkachine, was no longer there to check the ferocity of the impacts, and in the end, the interrogation was playing out without any great damage being done. Because of the accused's rank, which was after all that of commissioner, Balkachine had made the trip over, but only to slip away after a quarter of an hour, after a speech on proletarian morality that had put everyone to sleep. It was yet another failed self-criticism session: a theatrical moment that had had a reason to exist in the past—two or three hundred years earlier, during an era when the wars against the rich had not yet all been lost—but nowadays, at the end of history—if not at the end of everything—it had degenerated into pure ritualistic foolishness.

"I understand the extent of my abjection . . . I don't deserve to be trusted with responsibility," said Berberoïan in a murmur.

In reality, Berberoïan knew that after the censure that the assembly would bestow upon him, everything would return to how it had been before. He would put some mercurochrome on his wound, and he would regain his place behind his commissioner's desk—perhaps smoke a cigarette in Mevlido's company, for example—and they would both return to studying the criminal dossiers abandoned since earlier that morning. Nothing would have changed in society, nor in the habits of the police. They would simply have progressed a little further together in the ongoing disfigurement of revolutionary values. They would have reluctantly taken another little step toward barbarity and the extinction of all hope.

"I have betrayed the confidence of the working class," Berberoïan exhaled once more.

He hiccuped.

"That's why I consider myself to be a foul vermin . . . and . . ."

"Louder! We can't hear you!" shouted Mevlido.

The afternoon was oppressive. In the conference room floated a tropical gloom, like that before a storm. On his way out, Balkachine had reached out his arm to turn off the lamps as if, without his presence, energy-saving measures were necessary. No one had gotten up to turn them on again. On the dais at the front of the room, Mevlido and Berberoïan gesticulated with distaste and so little spontaneity that, if they had been charging admission for this spectacle, they would have deserved to be booed.

The "masses" comprised only four people, who, since Balkachine's departure, shouted no more slogans: Petro Michigan, Mackie Jiang, Bapos Vorkouta, Adar Maguistral. Berberoïan studied them for a moment with a despondent eye, then his vision clouded over once more. He blinked several times to get rid of the blood that kept him from seeing. Under normal circumstances, the four inspectors were under his charge, and now displayed a sullen attitude. Over the course of months, of years, each one would find himself alternately in Berberoïan's role, babbling inconsistent confessions, or in that of the spectators, or in Mevlido's place, obliged to beat up a colleague; no one was thrilled with this system of rotation.

Berberoïan shook his head. He spluttered something incomprehensible.

"Louder!" Mevlido insisted.

He bent and struck Berberoïan's left arm without using the brick. The blow was almost a friendly pat.

The commissioner was on his knees in the posture of a man condemned to death. He slumped forward and moaned, then he once more gave a little force to the litany of political transgressions he was accusing himself of, among which there figured

- illegal writing of insulting reports on the highest directors of the police
- clandestine consultation of their paystubs
- the aborted preparation of a series of attacks on the moon

- a culpable indulgence of the Bolshevik beggars of Henhouse Four, that uncontrollable ghetto, that parallel world without law or religion, where the subhuman and the insane took refuge
- tactical support for terrorist networks whose names and agenda he did not know
- misappropriation of small change from the police station's community chest
- and also, to complicate the picture of his misdeeds, a nightmare that had visited him the night before—vague visions of sodomy with a giant bird

"What bird? What did this bird look like? Who did it look like?" Mevlido demanded in a hoarse voice.

Berberoïan's breath retuned. He was soaked with perspiration. Blood and sweat mixed together on his face, giving him a haggard look.

"What color of bird?" Mevlido insisted.

"Black," stammered Berberoïan. "You might say a giant crow."

"And its name?" asked Mevlido, brandishing the brick in front of Berberoïan's face. "Do you remember its name?"

"No one was talking," said Berberoïan. "It was a giant crow. I had never seen it before, up to that point."

"Who was assaulting it?" asked Mevlido. "Was it you assaulting it? Or someone else?"

"No one assaulted it," Berberoïan claimed. "It consented."

"How can you be sure of such a thing?" Mevlido demanded indignantly.

"I don't know," sniffled Berberoïan. "The dream was confusing. I hardly remember it."

"No," contradicted Mevlido, "you remember. You should

pour your heart out in front of the masses who have the patience to listen to you, but you are lying."

"I can confess to other crimes?" proposed Berberoïan.

"It's all right," Mevlido relented. "We'll come back to this story about the crow."

"Shall I confess other crimes?"

"Go ahead," said Mevlido. "If you express yourself openly, the masses will show you indulgence."

He stood over the commissioner, not knowing what to do with the brick. In addition to a trickle of a reddish color, Berberoïan's cut-up skin wouldn't stop oozing liquids, some of which, for obscure biological reasons, appeared to be a dirty yellow. Beneath the commissioner's short hair, the wound looked nasty. Mevlido brandished the brick with manifest disgust.

"The masses are listening," he threatened.

Berberoïan pulled his head down between his shoulders, then began to list his crimes again in a whisper:

- theft of confidential documents, passing these documents to armed groups whose names and agenda he didn't know
- *sympathy for the assassins of important people, whether these people were of primary or secondary importance*
- giving munitions to unknown persons
- nondenunciation of wrongdoers, understanding that wrongdoers must have all been friends of Mevlido, and doubtless Mevlido himself
- poor management of the double game played by Mevlido, an agent undercover with the Bolsheviks while simultaneously serving as a spy for Henhouse Four within the police

- theft of toilet paper belonging to the collectivity, three rolls last month
- lacking effort in improving the stormy relationship he had with Balkachine, the clerk of ideology

"The list isn't complete," he commented.

"Well, if the list isn't finished, go on," said Mevlido.

Berberoïan now accused himself of love affairs with women much younger than himself, in particular with a completely irresistible anarchist young enough to have been his daughter. She would sometimes come by the police station, disguised as a cleaner, to rifle through drawers. She had a copy of the keys to the armory, and she probably used them to pilfer a few light weapons. He had seduced her by relying on the authority his position conferred upon him. He was in love with her, she had gotten under his skin, but he wasn't sure it was reciprocal.

Mevlido glanced in the direction of the masses, to see if they were shocked by Berberoïan's confession. The four inspectors were feigning the greatest of indifference. However, Bapos Vorkouta, who was naturally of a pale complexion, was red in the face with indignation. The scene revolted him, as it did all of us.

"Shall I give you her name?" murmured Berberoïan.

"What name?" Mevlido panicked.

"That girl's name," said the commissioner.

"No!" yelled Mevlido, "That's none of our concern! The masses don't care! Do as you did with the crow! Don't say her name!"

To shut up Berberoïan, he began to kick him arbitrarily. Beneath his shoes the commissioner's body had the consistency of a sandbag. Berberoïan collapsed forward, hands clasped together behind his back as if his brains had just been blown out.

"No!" bawled Mevlido again.

Then he awoke.

"What's the matter? Why are you yelling like that?" murmured Maleeya Bayarlag, the woman who lay next to him.

"Nothing," he said. "Go back to sleep."

He rose. The bed groaned. Maleeya Bayarlag turned toward him without saying anything. In the dark he couldn't tell whether her eyes were open or closed. The sheet had slid down to her ankles. It was very hot, stifling. The room had no windows.

He took three steps, crossed the hall, went to the kitchen, and, without turning on the lights, drank a few swallows of lukewarm water. He used his hand as a cup. On the wall above the food cupboard the spiders moved about, provoking in their webs the vast vibrations that they prefer to keep for the darkest hours of the night, and which, according to some controversial specialists, corresponded to a sort of language. Mevlido wiped his mouth and face. He didn't feel like engaging in conversation with them.

Now he found himself in the living room. The reflections from the street lightened the shadows. The window was wide open. He stayed still for a moment as he breathed in all the world's smells, then went toward the light.

The night was scorching hot.

"Is that true? There's really nothing wrong?" said the woman behind him.

He pulled her close. Shoulder to shoulder, hip to hip, they took their place at the window. They dozed there like that for a moment, listening to the habitual murmur of Henhouse Four: echoes of brawls, music from the rituals organized by the Ybürs and Koreans to speak with their dead, the nocturnal cries of the psychotics, the Bolshevik slogans shouted by crazy old women, the incessant squawking of the birds, their clucking.

Soon it began to rain.

The sound of the enormous raindrops bursting against the ground covered up all other sounds.

With the humidity, the heat increased.

"We should go back to bed," said Mevlido.

Maleeya Bayarlag declined the invitation. She had no desire to lie down on the damp mattress.

The rain pattered on the street.

They didn't move.

They perspired, pressed up against one another.

They watched the night drip with water.

They were naked.

2

Suddenly there came a piercing metallic whine and a jolt. Mevlido's head struck the window. He must have dozed off.

I must have dozed off, he thought.

He sat back up in his seat.

The tram raced along, all its lights extinguished, sometimes agitated by strong jolts as if it were about to derail, sometimes rolling along without a bump, and then one could hear the electric silence of the motor with the basso continuo of the volts and the brusque, incomprehensible clacking of circuit brakers followed by no effects.

Mevlido rubbed his head, let eight or nine seconds go by, and curled up against the window again. Darkness reigned inside the car. The streetlights outside were not enough to illuminate the passengers. It was a part of the journey that Mevlido disliked. The avenue had been cleared after the war, but the houses lining it remained too damaged to house any tenants. They passed by kilometers of uninhabitable buildings with their black openings and rotten facades that exhaled the stench of mildew. According to some rumors, some child soldiers had found refuge there, former actors of the last, of the nth genocide. Wandering from ruin to ruin without ever showing themselves, incapable of growing older normally into adulthood, they hid behind the walls their obstinate absence of remorse, the cold memory of atrocities they had committed. Until, one day, one of their old victims flushed them out and took their vengeance.

It was after midnight. It was very late. As with every summer night for the last fifteen or so decades, the feeling of suffocation had not lessened with the arrival of the evening. They were going to have to wait until dawn and a brief moment of cool air to recover their breath.

In the tram the passengers had closed their eyes and were being jostled about on their seats. Besides the conductor and Mevlido there were six of them. All men, or at least male, or at least mostly not female. Under the influence of miasmas exhaled by the insalubrious houses, each dozed or agonized as far away as possible from his neighbors. I remember the scene very well: I was a part of this group, and, all the while applying the recommended procedure for living or for sleeping, I was observing from between my nearly closed eyelids. We were all dressed in the same style, a white dress shirt with a greasy collar or a T-shirt smudged with motor oil, pants in military drab, flip-flops or tired old shoes. You couldn't expect anything else, at this hour, from those taking the circle line and going to their homes in the second-tier worlds, in the havens for refugees, and in the ghettos.

Then the tram headed into a curve and started down Macadam Boulevard. I knew that, from then on, we would continue with no detour until Marachvili Gateway, the station where Mevlido would have to get off. The orientation of the track changed, the moon came out and spilled its wan white light through the train's windshield. It was a gigantic moon. It took up half the sky, canceling out the stars and transforming the roofs and treetops—because now there were trees—into brutal silhouettes.

The light was powerful and milky. On our faces, drops of sweat glistened along our hairlines. The metal poles seemed to shoot fire. The six passengers and Mevlido had slid from a shadowy nightmare to a brighter nightmare. Now we plunged ahead toward the full moon. As if we were sitting in a bizarre cable car, we were headed straight toward it.

As Mevlido looked aimlessly around himself, he noticed a very black crow underneath the seats hopping up and down, its rump heavy, its feet thick, its feathers disheveled: like the bastard of a giant crow and a mutant chicken. Its massive beak was slightly open. Its eye couldn't be seen. It shifted its weight with the rhythm of the lurching tram, and, to keep its balance, it would spread its wings from time to time with a majestic laziness, then shrink them back up again into the intimate shadow of its body.

The tram stop was approaching. Mevlido stood up, pulled the cord to signal to the conductor. At first, he stood by the doors in the middle of the car, but then, since the crow was staring at him, revealing an amber yellow and inquisitive eye surrounded by a ring of blood red, he became apprehensive and walked to the rear door. The tram braked and screeched to a halt; the windows clattered, then an absolute silence set in for two interminable seconds. And at last, the doors in front of Mevlido angrily opened, as they always do in machines where the pneumatic system was designed in periods of turmoil, revolution, or war.

Mevlido got out. In accordance with the tradition that demands one follow the vehicle one has just exited with one's eyes, he turned toward the tram, which had already started off again with its load of sleeping or dead passengers.

The tram accelerated. It was once more a dilapidated train car ready to take off in the direction of the moon.

On the platform of the station, a meter away from Mevlido, stood the enormous crow, also interested by this departure for outer space. It had exited the tram through the middle doors.

In the light, the crow appeared less sinister. Its eyes had a golden tint that could have given them a banal or even agreeable expression, if it weren't for the sort of red wound that surrounded them, evocative of a contagious disease.

"They didn't drop us off any too early," squawked the crow. "It seemed to me that we were going to spend the night in that awful box."

Mevlido uttered a low sound of agreement without looking at his interlocutor. He wasn't enthusiastic about the prospect of talking with this individual.

"Are you going into Henhouse Four?" the bird asked.

"Yes," Mevlido let out.

"You must be brave," said the bird. "It has a very bad reputation."

"Bah," said Mevlido, "no more than anywhere else."

"The police won't set foot in there," insisted the bird. "They're too afraid. There are witches on every corner, and it's swarming with mental patients and Bolsheviks. Do you know what Bolshevism is?"

It cocked its head toward one shoulder. It had a shaggy back and unclean wings. It stared at Mevlido; its red-rimmed eyes seemed to examine his insides; they looked him over with insolence.

"Well, it's where I live," explained Mevlido.

The bird had begun to hop up and down again. It succeeded in contorting its beak in such a way as to express mistrust. It was hard to tell whether that mistrust was mixed with disapproval or, on the contrary, a cautious complicity.

"You sympathize with Bolshevism?" croaked the bird. "Are you part of their gang?"

"I'm a police officer," Mevlido explained.

"Ah." The bird seemed startled.

It let another second go by.

"At any rate, it has a bad reputation," it began again.

"Yes, so it has a bad reputation," Mevlido agreed. "But you know, when you compare it with the rest . . ."

"The rest of what?" croaked the bird.

From the nearest houses came an awful smell of dirty feathers and guano, arriving just at nostril or beak height.

Mevlido coughed and cleared his throat.

The two interlocutors scowled at each other.

The conversation just didn't seem to take. It might have managed to give something, but here, manifestly, it wasn't taking.

3

The next day, or rather, the following night.

In those days, every night was like all the rest, in Mevlido's life and in our own.

Mevlido was heading back to Henhouse Four after a day of work at the central precinct.

Again, the backdrop was the tram, with its sleepy travelers, noises, and shadows.

Seven or eight hundred meters farther on, the moon was barring the way, as it often did. It barricaded Macadam Boulevard with all its yellowish ivoryness. It was sprawled heavily on the rails and filled the view halfway up the sky. Not knowing too well how to respond to this display of arrogance, the city hesitated between collaboration and defeat, with pitiful attempts at resistance here and there. To outwit the invader, the city counted on a few unextinguished lightbulbs, which in reality emitted only wan, pitiful light. No one was visible in the ruins. Whole sections of walls disappeared, canceled out by the abyssal darkness.

Such was the general ambiance again that night.

The tram rocked side to side as it made its way forward. Once started on the straight line running the length of Henhouse Four, the car began to accelerate, as if it were gathering momentum to crash into the lunar obstacle. Inside the tram, the lightbulbs were burned out. The passengers swayed, reproducing the rhythm of the train's lurching with a slight delay. They bore the opaque expressions of dead people. It was obvious that they had delegated one of their number to take command of the machine, requesting that he smash it against the first available giant satellite, onto its white rocks, dust, and terminal silence. And apparently this imminent end gave them no anxiety.

Mevlido stood; soon they were going to pass by his stop. He walked among the crumpled forms and pulled on the cord that communicated with the conductor's cabin. In front of his control panel, the conductor was nothing but a black silhouette, flat like a cardboard target in a shooting gallery. You couldn't make out his movements. Mevlido was going to repeat his signal when everything screeched and groaned: the brakes' jaws, the wheels, the rails under the wheels, the framework, the windows, the grab rails, the metallic floor, the seats.

Then the train came to a stop. After two seconds of inertia, the doors parted in front of Mevlido and into the opening rushed a breath of torrid night. A plaque announced their arrival at the Marachvili Gateway. While not having succeeded in rendering it illegible, someone had gone to the trouble of smearing the inscription with shit or mud.

Mevlido got out.

He was the only one to exit the tram. The air of the neighborhood enveloped him at once, and he closed his eyes to better fight the nausea that often seized him at that moment when he abandoned the relatively sealed-off space of the tram to enter the universe of Henhouse Four. The nocturnal breeze carried the stench of guano, lingering odors of the barnyard and human and animal excretions of all kinds. It was an abject odor of the ghetto, fibrous and damp, dark, unhealthy, an odor of preinsurrectional despair and mass graves.

The odor of our future and our past.

The odor of the real world since time immemorial.

Then he reopened his eyes.

At the stop, under the shelter built to hold travelers when it rained, a shape stirred, feminine and graceless.

"You were here? You were waiting for me?" Mevlido sounded surprised.

Maleeya Bayarlag detached herself from the shadowy corner where she had remained hidden, seated on the cement bench, doubtless for hours. Her shoulder rubbed against the side wall of the shelter, a rectangle of corrugated iron that had been riddled by bullets during a period of social tension. The iron shuddered. She took two steps forward and emerged suddenly into the acid light. She seemed to have trouble keeping her balance, as if she were going to topple heavily backward and sit down again.

She wore black trousers and a blouse made from garish old fabric. She was a woman whom madness had rendered ugly, with a worn, sallow face, which had perhaps had great charm in the past but now no longer expressed anything but stupefaction and anxiety. Her gaze did not flee yours, but it passed through things, manifestly without really understanding them or seeing them. Her hair was in disarray, her skin was shiny, beads of sweat formed around her mouth. Her teeth were almost all in place, but they were gray. She went to Mevlido and slipped her hand into his. She moved slowly, breathing loudly. The physical effort, in this too-humid atmosphere, cost her. She did not answer Mevlido, but she seemed content to have found him and to now be able to go home in his company.

"It's after midnight. You must have waited for me for hours," he lamented.

"How long?" she asked, confusedly.

Her voice was mutilated by asthma.

"Hours," he repeated.

They left the platform, going forward in the direction of the Marachvili Gateway; they passed through it. Hand in hand they made their way without hurrying, two middle-aged lovers, on a stroll in the moonlight: a medium-sized man, solid, with the look of a policeman—because he worked for the police—and a woman a bit shorter than him, stout, poorly dressed, with the look of a patient in a hospital courtyard.

She didn't part her lips except to smile aimlessly, or to repeat the last words he had said. He was used to that and didn't take offense at it. He told her about his day. He spoke of an upcoming self-criticism session, scheduled for the following week. His turn had come to enumerate his crimes before the masses, and he had no desire to do so. He then brought up Berberoïan, who was accusing him of no longer being in his right mind. Five sentences were enough. She wasn't listening.

As soon as they were on the other side of the Marachvili Gateway, the bleaching effect of everything under the lunar rays lessened. The streets had narrowed. The municipal lighting was failing. They had to go tens, sometimes hundreds of meters in the dark, taking their chances. The sidewalks and pavement were strewn with bodies. Often, they brushed against junkies of either sex, slumped in their vomit and their dreams. Where the darkness was deepest, birds colonized it: obese, gigantic gulls, monstrous crows, owls, chickens; they covered large sections of the ground, making up compact groups that protested against intrusions and barred the way with their pecking. They walked through cackles and screeches.

It was a night like any other night. Mevlido and Maleeya bumped against semicorpses; they had their calves attacked by poultry; they felt their way forward. When they emerged into the moonlight, they squinted, dazzled.

They were covered in hot droplets of perspiration.

They swallowed feather debris.

They choked.

From time to time, Mevlido mulled over his nightmare from the night before. He had argued with a crow on the subject of Henhouse Four. The crow was running down the neighborhood, calling it ill reputed and gangrened with Bolshevism. Mevlido had claimed that it was a ghetto like any other, neither better nor worse than the others. The bird was trying to sound him out, it wanted to know what his political opinions were. Not having any confidence in his interlocutor, Mevlido had been evasive. He had made no pronouncement on Bolshevism. As Mevlido was avoiding the conversation, the bird became aggressive. They had parted on bad terms.

"How are you doing, Maleeya?" Mevlido asked again and again.

They tacked between miserable bodies; they skirted the vociferating flocks of gulls. Maleeya Bayarlag was glued to him, up against his right hip.

She said she was all right. Her legs felt heavy, and her lungs had difficulty breathing the dust-filled air, but she was all right.

She stopped for a moment to catch her breath, then they went back to walking.

"It's not going too well in your dreams," she pointed out.

"That's true," he said.

He was happy to hear her react with a commentary rather than by the simple sleepy repetition of his last half sentence.

"They're crazy dreams," Maleeya said again.

They laughed together. She was appreciative of the tenderness he was showing by talking to her, guiding her through the obstacles. She took pleasure in the affectionate nonchalance of their stroll. Mevlido himself also liked this complicity encouraged by the shadows.

Time and the difficulty of living had almost frozen around them. They weren't in a hurry.

The ghetto night caressed them.

It pacified them.

Later they climbed the stairs of a small building on Factory Street. It was their house. It was no more decrepit than any other. On the fourth floor landing the hall light was working. Mevlido pushed open the door, and, once inside the apartment, he didn't turn on the electricity. They were in the shadows diluted by the streetlights. The moonlight also played its part. They could move from one room to another without running into the furniture or a wall.

"Have you eaten?" asked Mevlido.

He went into the kitchen and explored the contents of the pantry. Maleeya had picked over the food. She hadn't put back the covers that were meant to prevent the food from spoiling too quickly, but she had shut the wire mesh door. Two cockroaches lay in wait at one of the hinges, tempted but kept at a distance. They couldn't care less about Mevlido's presence. They waved their antennae, waiting for an opening; they knew that one day they would get into that cage. They would get in, they would gorge themselves, and they would die. It had manifestly become the principal objective of their existence.

"Well, you've snacked a bit," said Mevlido.

"Snacked a bit," said Maleeya.

He removed from his belt the small bag that contained his business cards, two meal tickets, a little money, and two clips of ammunition. He laid it on the table and sighed. The day was ending as it did every evening, with gestures as ordinary as could be. Soon he would make himself a cup of tea, and he would eat a handful of industrial-grade pemmican or hardtack. He wasn't hungry. He wanted to sit down, but not sleep.

"Bayarlag," said Maleeya, as if she were calling him.

"What did you . . . ?" said Mevlido.

"Bayarlag," repeated Maleeya, "Yasar Bayarlag. It's not getting any better for him."

She swayed back and forth in the half shadow, a meter from the window. The soles of her espadrilles rasped against the tile floor. The bulb of the streetlight attached outside, just across the way, lit her hair a dark red.

"He is going crazy," finished Maleeya.

"Yasar Bayarlag?" asked Mevlido.

Maleeya assented.

"There's nothing we can do about it," said Mevlido.

"He's sinking into madness," said Maleeya.

Yasar Bayarlag, the man with whom Maleeya Bayarlag had previously lived, was dead. He had been killed next to Maleeya, fifteen years before, in a terrorist attack on a bus. Maleeya had recovered physically, but her mind had been permanently damaged by the explosion. Mentally, she had difficulties now. Every now and then she would recover her intelligence, her certitude of judgment, and her imagination, but the rest of the time she remained on the margins of reality, locked up in a sometimes sullen, sometimes garrulous somnambulism. She frequently brought up Yasar, often went out looking for him in the depths of Henhouse Four, in the sector referred to as the Shambles, in the alleys where, it's true, one could find the dead, but where she did not find him and where she lost her way, walking over debris for days, weeks. She would claim afterward to have spoken with him and confided her troubles in him, even to have extracted from him a promise that he would come back soon. She saw everything as through a fog, a deceptive veil of memory, and she confused Yasar with Mevlido, giving Mevlido details of the small pleasures they had recently shared, Yasar and herself, muttering that Yasar had given her a gift, or that they had gone to bed together, or that he had made her a mushroom omelet or a chicken curry, or that they had watched the flight of the bats at twilight—the two of them standing in front of the Factory Street house.

Mevlido sat down. He was leaning on the table, his arms next to the little bag containing his police things, the tiresome and useless life of a policeman. They sat there for a minute without saying anything.

"We're all going to sink into madness," Maleeya began again.

"Yes," said Mevlido, "that's certainly the direction we're headed in. It's natural."

"That's the direction we're headed," repeated Maleeya in a neutral tone.

"There's nothing to be done. Toward madness or toward death. Everyone is headed there."

"Everyone," said Maleeya.

"Well, yes," said Mevlido.

"Toward madness or toward death," said Maleeya.

She was rocking her torso back and forth. She had unbuttoned the collar of her blouse; she was dripping with sweat. Suddenly her face was deformed by an angst-filled rictus.

"And you, the same," she said. "You're going mad as well."

"Don't worry," said Mevlido. "The two of us, you and me, we're together. We will stay together until the end. We'll get through this."

"It's because of me that you're going mad," said Maleeya.

"Of course not," said Mevlido.

"I'm contagious," Maleeya insisted. "I know I'm contagious."

"Of course not," Mevlido assured her.

"Of course I am," said Maleeya. "You're going mad, Yasar. May I call you Yasar?"

"If you like," said Mevlido.

"I can call you Yasar, right?"

"Of course," said Mevlido.

"You're foundering, Yasar. It's because of me."

She ran her hand through her hair. Beneath the light coming from the street the strands seemed colored. Her fingers were also tinged with red.

"It's the two of us," she began again after a silence. "That's why. Because the two of us are together. Exactly. That's why we won't get through this."

4

Mevlido reached out his hand to gently touch her cheek, and she fled from him, already retreating toward the shadowy humidity of the bedroom as if she wanted to disappear. It was a dark place where ordinarily she settled in alone or with Mevlido to sleep or to wait for sleep or to copulate, a stifling room without a window. She had closed her eyes. She had just closed them, doubtlessly because she preferred to no longer see the metallic bed, its mattress dotted with stains, and because she longed to forget the spider webs that covered the wall and branched out onto the bedposts. But above all because she wanted to focus all her attention on the phrase she was formulating inside her head. To better concentrate on it. It was a prayer, and, that prayer, she addressed it to the man she loved who was not Mevlido, because, even if she often communicated with Mevlido by calling him Yasar, or giving him Yasar as a name of love, she knew deep within herself that he was not Yasar Bayarlag. She knew he was only Mevlido—a companion of disaster, but not the essential man whom she had known during another time when she wasn't mad: in a time when buses didn't explode, ripping apart Yasar's body and, simultaneously, Yasar's wife's mind—that is, hers, Maleeya Bayarlag's, own mind. Her own mind. Maleeya Bayarlag.

The prayer murmured and shouted in her head, uncoiled in an elsewhere of her memory, behind and in front of her memory and in the throbbing silence of her own body; she wandered there with buried words and buried images:

- Touch me, Yasar.
- Go through me, Yasar.
- Take my flesh with your arms, with your head.
- Go through me, shake me.
- Take my entrails, my organs, to the last one.
- Take my heart between your fingers and go through it.
- Touch me with your vertebrae, Yasar, with the inside of your vertebrae.
- Whisper to the inside of my bones.
- Inside my bones go from zero to one.
- Whisper to me, murmur to me, and go through me so that I can verify the reality of my existence, touch my existence, Yasar.
- Moan in my moans.
- Hollow out the existence of my voice.
- Sink into me so that I know that somewhere else exists and that you have come back among us, among those we call living.
- Caress the inside of my heart and the inside of my existence.
- Move my face against your face, with your face come back from the elsewhere of the dead.

- Enter my head with your head to build me.
- Touch my skeleton to build and rebuild me.
- Touch the inside of my skeleton to rebuild yourself then as if we were still living you and me.
- Count our two existences by counting from zero to one.
- Put your shoulders on my shoulders again.
- Inhabit my feet and my hands and all my limbs one by one.
- Inhabit my blood and my drool.
- Inhabit the intimacy.
- Hollow out in me the existence of intimacy.
- Inhabit my breath, Yasar.
- Inhabit the existence of my silence with your silence.
- Come back, Yasar.
- Come, come back in force.
- Leave the elsewhere of the dead and learn the else-where of the living, Yasar, learn the elsewhere of the living in taking hold of me.
- Act as if nothing in you had been destroyed.
- Act as if you hadn't been reduced into fragments of nothing.
- Settle into the elsewhere of the inside of my existence.
- Build us here, Yasar, rebuild us.
- Act as if nothing in us had been destroyed.
- Act as if we hadn't disappeared.
- Act as if we hadn't been separated together separated together separated together separated together in the elsewhere.

It was a breathless prayer; in some of its motifs it resembled a demand for physical love, and, if the man who was less than a meter from her had heard it, he would have believed it inevitable, or charitable, to melt into Maleeya's body sexually, in the heat and sweat of the night. But he didn't hear it, and it mattered little, because for her that silent cry, that violent desire to be possessed, wasn't associated with images of coitus.

Not *at all*, even.

Mevlido stood near the entrance to the bedroom. He came no farther. By experience or by instinct, he knew that she had distanced herself from him, and their pact of mutual affection had been temporarily shattered. He had trouble imagining what was happening inside her, he felt her to be foreign, he didn't understand her anymore, he no longer made any effort to understand her. With weariness he watched her eyes flickering behind her eyelids like during a REM phase of sleep, and her slightly open lips, her dingy teeth, her extenuated features, ravaged by the half-light.

She weakly babbled syllables with no meaning.

A few seconds of nothingness slipped by.

Suddenly they had begun to walk each on his or her own, at a great distance from each other. They were no longer communicating. In turn Mevlido withdrew into his own labyrinth. He neglected what tied him to Maleeya Bayarlag, his present life with her, that fatalistic sharing of the Fall. He had begun to think of Verena Becker, his wife killed twenty years earlier by child soldiers, during the racial violence in Zone 5 at Djaka Park West. Killed twenty years ago by child soldiers. Verena Becker. The image of Verena Becker was on the point of becoming clear; in his memory the doors began to part and threatened to open wide. The child soldiers were there, almost on the threshold, with their necklaces of human ears and their wigs of multicolored vinyl. Mevlido himself also hovered at the threshold. Only one step forward and he would be able to venture into the pain of mourning. Into the pain and the ashes. He was once again going to enter into it and fall into ruin, among the intolerable images. Then something blocked his way, shook him violently, a lifesaving reflex. And already he was looking away. It was a forbidden memory. He mustn't bring up past happiness, the loving life he had lived until the day Verena Becker was martyred. He mustn't show himself again the martyrdom of Verena Becker. It was better to come back to Henhouse Four, next to the bed, and to try to retrieve the contact he had lost with Maleeya Bayarlag.

The night rippled like the air in a furnace.

The night.

It rippled like the air in a furnace.

Light entered the main room and rebounded into the bedroom, creating here lighter spots, there black spots, brilliantly black.

Maleeya Bayarlag still hadn't said a word. She had ended up sitting on the bed. Since the month of November, they had been subject to an invasion of spiders. In some years they had terrifying territorial ambitions, and they multiplied to fulfill them. They were going through one of those years, the worst.

"You're hot," said Mevlido. "Do you want me to go get you a glass of water?"

"Hot," murmured Maleeya.

"Are you thirsty?" Mevlido asked again.

"Is that you, Mevlido?" she asked without opening her eyes.

She was surfacing into consciousness, vaguely aware that she had experienced a kind of trance. An impression of supplication remained on her tongue, but her memory revealed nothing more to her. She didn't remember any words.

"Yes. It's me."

"I was thinking of Yasar. We were together. I thought you were Yasar."

"No, you see," said Mevlido, "it's just me."

"Was I talking just now? Did I say anything?"

"When?"

"Just now, when I had my eyes closed."

"You muttered a little, I guess."

"Really? I didn't speak?"

"No. You were muttering. I couldn't understand what you were saying."

"You didn't understand?"

She was out of breath. Her legs were hanging over the edge of the bed. Like Mevlido, she was now wearing only a T-shirt.

In the building, the neighbors were sleeping; nothing could be heard through the dividing walls or the ceiling, but through the open windows in the main room came the noise of the street. Mutant or not, gulls, poultry, and crows fought ceaselessly and squawked. In the house across the street someone was listening to music on a hand-cranked phonograph, a song of disenchantment: Korean, monotonous, magical.

Sweat was running down Mevlido's cheeks. He sat down on the bed. Maleeya was gasping for air next to him.

"You're not lying to me?" she said. "You couldn't understand?"

"No."

"So much the better," she said.

At that exact instant a nocturnal procession began. Somewhere beyond the crossroads a demonstration was starting up. Slogans were chanted by old Bolshevik women reverted to a state of savagery, at the top of their voices. Usually, they were to be found in groups of two or three or alone. This time there were two. Their shouted demands began to rise above the city. And as with those who proclaimed them, the slogans were wild and insane:

ONLY KILL ADVISEDLY!

GO TO THE SHAMBLES AFTER YOUR DEATH!

DON'T GO TO THE SHAMBLES AFTER YOUR DEATH!
KILL THE DEATH IN YOU!
A THOUSAND YEARS LATER, REMEMBER, PARDON
  NOTHING!
FORGET NOTHING, ONLY KILL ADVISEDLY!

Mevlido wiped his face and wiped his hands off on the cloth of the mattress.

"I'm going to get you a glass of water," he said.

He felt drained. That evening, like every evening, the reunion with Maleeya Bayarlag had brought something exhausting with it. He felt great affection for her, they were a couple, he didn't dream of abandoning her, and he certainly had the intention of helping her through her daily anxieties, her madness; he had made once and for all the decision to cherish her and protect her until death, but the love that bound them was only animal and desperate, like between two survivors of a catastrophe. He did not love her like he had loved Verena Becker.

The old women were getting farther away. Their slogans became deformed by the increasing distance. It was less and less possible to decipher them; one received them syllable by syllable below the surface of consciousness, no longer trying to grasp their meaning:

BURY YOURSELF!
PUT YOUR LAST BLOOD IN A BAG!
REJOIN THE SUBTERRANEAN SHAMBLES, BURY
  YOURSELF!

"All right, I'm going to get you a glass of water," repeated Mevlido.

He waited several minutes before moving, but finally he got

up and went to the kitchen to fill a cup with water. He drank a mouthful, took the rest to Maleeya. She gulped the liquid eagerly and set the cup down on the pillow. Mevlido had gone back to sitting next to her. They spent a moment like that without speaking, from time to time smashing with a hand a drop of sweat that was irritating the side of their nose or the nape of their neck. They received the incongruous cries of the night. They didn't lie down. For the moment they had given up on the idea of sleep.

"I got into an argument with Berberoïan," Mevlido said at last. "You know, Berberoïan."

Maleeya assented with a nod.

"I know. The commissioner."

"He's accusing me of losing my marbles," said Mevlido.

"Ah, you see," reasoned Maleeya, "you're going mad. I'm not the only one to notice."

"He wants me to go see the police psychiatrist."

"So go," said Maleeya, "since he's telling you to go. He's the boss, isn't he?"

Mevlido started to reach out to her. He would have liked to be able to nestle against her and hope for her to comfort him, but he was reluctant to expose his weakness to someone weaker than himself in that way, and his arm, which he had barely begun to lift, fell back.

"Berberoïan is your boss, right?" she insisted.

"Yes," said Mevlido.

"So, he's in charge," murmured Maleeya. "Go."

"I don't want to," Mevlido objected. "I'm just worn out, that's all. I'm mentally worn out and I'm having bad dreams. It's my own business. What's the matter with him that he has to bother me with his psychologist?"

"His psychiatrist," Maleeya corrected.

The madwomen's demonstration could still be heard:

EVEN IN THE EVENT OF DEATH, CHANGE PLANS!
SHUT YOUR FACE UP IN A BAG!
GO UNDERGROUND FOR A THOUSAND YEARS!

They could no longer make out the speech itself; they had to reconstitute and reinvent the phrases from almost nothing. Above Factory Street once again the echoes of the gramophone dominated the voice of the singer across the street.

Maleeya's breathing made a whistling noise.

A bird came to perch on the windowsill in the other room.

A bird. On the windowsill.

It came to perch. It was fat, landing with the clumsiness of a pelican, its claws rasping against the zinc, the cement. Its wings sent a load of sour stench into the apartment. It didn't stay. From the bed, neither Mevlido nor Maleeya saw it, but they heard it thrash about like a thing deranged. It made as if to caw, they heard the splat of droppings splashing onto the linoleum tile, then it flew away.

On the wall, at the head of the bed, a trapped insect vibrated in a spider web, doubtless a fly losing its mind in horror. Life went on.

"I already went, in fact," Mevlido took up the conversation again.

"Already went, in fact," repeated Maleeya.

At the same time, almost inaudible, a last injunction passed by in the street and was snuffed out:

YOU ARE NOTHING NOW, DON'T SIT DOWN WITH THE
BEASTS!

Maleeya began to sway back and forth slowly. It's the best

thing there is to do when surrounded by spider webs, it's late, and yet somehow you have the vague certainty that life goes on.

Somewhere in the bed frame a spring squeaked.

"Went where?" she asked.

"To the psychiatrist," continued Mevlido, "the day before yesterday. For the assessment."

The spring squeaked, the trapped fly fought, taking pathetic pauses. The light from the street was refracted against the walls. The Korean song went on. It was a lament from after the defeat, after death, intended to give pride to the fallen warriors or their companions still alive. The singer's voice was harsh, hardly tuneful. When the mechanism weakened and the music began to degenerate grotesquely toward the lower pitches, the guy listening to it would turn the hand crank to reenergize it. It was endless.

In the bedroom floated the smell of bird.

Maleeya Bayarlag was rocking and breathing heavily.

She was sweating heavy drops.

"You're nothing now, my Yasar," she stammered. "You sit with the beasts."

5

It's three o'clock. Maleeya Bayarlag went to sleep. But not Mevlido.

Three o'clock, then four. Impossible to say if Mevlido is now deep in sleep or not. He himself doesn't know. He doesn't care to delve any deeper into the question and gets up. Behind him, Maleeya doesn't react. She is lying across the bed, totally uncovered, backside in the air. He gets dressed; he closes the apartment door carefully; he leaves the building and begins to walk the streets. Something is pulling him forward. He moves about like we do, as if in a dream. He goes at random, without questioning himself about that randomness. At random and forward.

Around him, Henhouse Four is quiet. Only the sound of his footsteps echoes against the walls. No more gramophone, no more subversive clamors, no more click-clacking of Chinese knives on cutting boards in the places where Chinese refugees congregate. No more bursts of the voices of insomniacs, the calls of the junkies who twitch in their excrement and fear. Everything has calmed down. The birds themselves are quiet too. They are sleeping together, in compact flocks, as if the temperature were very low or a terror of the end of the world obliged them to pile on top of one another. At certain points, a collective downy being spreads out across the road and blocks the way. Mevlido tramples this moving mass, with disgust he progresses to the middle of the flapping of wings.

The smell of poultry makes him feel like vomiting.

He gets pecked on the legs.

Above the city the full moon has diminished in volume.

It has hardened, sending a harsh light toward the earth.

Mevlido goes back up Factory Street, Gunmen Street, Palm Avenue, Market Street. After a few minutes of wandering, he chooses as his goal the disused train station of Container Avenue. In the past, in Henhouse Four and in the adjacent neighborhoods, there were hundreds, thousands of train stations. The one on Container Avenue is off-limits to the public because part of the concourse is threatening to collapse, but they haven't dynamited it like other official buildings, at the end of the war or after. You can get in. Mevlido likes the atmosphere that reigns there, especially at night. I do too.

He arrives in front of the train station. Everything is dark inside. Half the door has been torn off its hinges; he slides through the opening. The shadows of the hall engulf him. He tries not to suffocate, because animals and humans have been relieving their bladders and bowels here for countless decades. He walks through the stench and comes out on the other side, safe and sound, on the platform. Then he can fill his lungs with fresh air.

He freezes. Only his rib cage is moving.

The moon is pouring its acid onto the picture.

Mevlido breathes. He stays planted on platform number one. It's made of wood. All he would need to do for it to crack is to move a little bit. Mevlido lifts his head toward the moon and looks at it at length.

"It doesn't seem real," says a voice next to him.

"Ah, Gorgha," says Mevlido.

The other leaves the shadows that were hiding it completely. It's large, of an impressive size even.

I say "it" in reference to its status as a crow, but I should say *her*, because Gorgha is a female crow. With smooth, shining feathers, electric black—almost blue—and impeccably clean, it's even an exquisite female. One might also admire her smoke-colored, powerful beak, her eyes the color of dark honey ringed in black.

"I was just wondering if I was dreaming or not," says Mevlido.

"Well, you see," says Gorgha.

They remain silent for a few seconds.

"I didn't know that you hung out around here," says Mevlido.

"Which express train are you waiting on?" asks Gorgha in a sarcastic tone.

"I couldn't sleep," says Mevlido.

"Nothing has run here since the war," Gorgha reminds him.

"Bah," says Mevlido, "after all. You never know what—"

They both sit lost in reverie for a moment without saying anything. They contemplate a tank car rusting on the other side of the tracks. The train station is like a train station from a western; it reminds you of what you could see at the cinema in films made in the golden century of cinema, now a little less than three hundred years ago. Everything is made of wood, everything is deserted, the rails disappear in a straight line toward nothingness, and, on a platform made of old, faded boards, two characters stand, taciturn, like two hired guns before the action starts.

Two tight-lipped heroes. One of the two is an exquisite female crow.

It is the middle of the night; a cricket sings softly.

The dust gleams white. Footprints are stamped into it as if in snow. Above the platform are lamps hanging from wires, but no bulb is lit. The light comes from the sky. It comes from the dark sky that projects pitch, ink, pallor upon this picture.

They could have believed themselves to be inside a photograph, with no surprises, when suddenly two more sinister-looking figures appear. Until this moment they blended into the scenery—one glued to the wall, the other invisible behind a pillar—and here they are now in motion. They emerge noisily three meters from Mevlido, with the coolness of experienced soldiers. They show no sign of complicity with Gorgha, turn their backs, and walk away slowly. Mevlido has no time to make out their features; he doesn't even know if they, too, like Gorgha, have faces covered with feathers. Under their leather boots the planks groan. They have military uniforms, boonie hats. They reach the end of the platform and stop. In front of them is a small staircase, six or seven steps. You might say they're analyzing whatever is beyond the platform down below. They lean out over the shadows.

"Friends of yours?" Mevlido asks Gorgha.

"They're part of the team," Gorgha equivocates.

Mevlido acquiesces with a grunt.

"They're looking after my security," finishes Gorgha. "It's disreputable here, I've heard."

It's hard to understand what Gorgha's bodyguards are inspecting with so much attention. On the abandoned tracks, some scraggly shrubs are growing. There's no activity of any kind. Nothing is breathing or moving. The vegetation is totally gray.

The old soldiers aren't moving anymore. You'd think that they were two taxidermied bandits who ended up inside an antique photograph.

Silence.

The cricket sings.

After a minute when nothing happens, Gorgha heads over to a dilapidated lean-to, probably where in the past the station master worked, or an employee who answered travelers' questions. The miniscule facade is pierced by a small window in front of which a wooden shutter has been drawn. Gorgha puts her hand into a groove and lifts the board. Disturbed by this maneuver, a medium-sized spider scuttles away along the wall, at first very brightly lit and exaggerated by its shadows, then invisible under the roof ledge.

Now the booth is open.

In the confined space of the lean-to can be made out a chair and, just below the small window, a slab of cheap wood on which the employee must have propped themselves when giving information or making announcements. On the slab are still lying two receipt books, some pencils, a microphone.

"I have instructions to pass on to you," says Gorgha.

"Ah," says Mevlido. "From whom?"

"From Deeplane."

Mevlido utters an uncertain vowel. He makes no comment.

"Deeplane, that rings a bell, right?" confirms Gorgha.

"Well, yes," says Mevlido.

In reality, he's not sure. At the pronouncement of this name, he saw again a desk illuminated by a lamp and, behind it, an intelligent face, hard, austere features, and a gaze directed at him—probing, authoritarian, as only a superior officer or a doctor can project. But, almost at the same time, that picture began to dissolve and to melt. For a half second, it had seemed like a memory. But what memory? No, his memory couldn't contain anything like it, it's impossible. Deeplane doesn't exist, has never existed, he has never been part of Mevlido's life. They have never met. The criminal organizations to which Mevlido had belonged in his youth and later on never had such an institutionalized functioning, with bosses sitting under a desk lamp receiving their underlings without inviting them to sit down. Or maybe yes, Mevlido did recognize that, from a time when the global revolution still controlled some regions of the globe, in the time of Verena Becker, for example. Or after, in the period of civil war or dark war. He doesn't really know; he doesn't know anymore. It seems to him that he was never in a situation where a guy named Deeplane could examine him with severity in a dark room in the middle of the night, while giving him orders. And straight away, he drifts to the opposite certainty. He knows perfectly who Deeplane is. No, he has never heard of Deeplane. Or rather yes, they have worked together, they have plotted together. In the Deeplane column, his memory is swarming with stories. But in the end, no. In the Deeplane column, his memory is nothing.

"I say pass on, but it's more a question of reminding you of them," Gorgha explains.

"Do you think that's necessary?" falters Mevlido.

But it's obvious he's bluffing.

"In case you might have forgotten them. One never knows with your memory."

"What about my memory?" Mevlido protests.

"Deeplane told me to remind you whether you want or not," says Gorgha.

"OK. Fine. I'm listening," says Mevlido.

He concentrates. Deeplane now is only a scrambled blotch

among other confused archives in the middle of other confused stories, in the hodgepodge where he stores in bulk real and false memories, images from films, post-exotic rants, or fragments of dreams or past lives.

"First, don't make any contact with the spiders, no matter what the circumstances," Gorgha begins to recite. "Don't allow yourself any liberties in their company, don't talk to them. Act as if they didn't exist."

"Act as if they didn't exist," Mevlido agrees.

"That also goes for the child soldiers," adds Gorgha. "Don't talk to the child soldiers. Neither to the spiders, nor to the child soldiers."

"I know," says Mevlido.

"Two," Gorgha presses on, "respect proletarian morality. Don't breach proletarian morality for any reason. Stay firm on your class positions."

"What class positions—"

"These are the instructions," says Gorgha. "Don't interrupt me. Three, don't put yourself in the hands of psychiatrists. If inadvertently you find yourself in front of a psychiatrist, deny."

"Deny," repeats Mevlido.

"Deny until the end," insists Gorgha.

"Understood," says Mevlido.

"Do as you would in self-criticism," insists Gorgha again. "Talk about nonsense or approach sensitive subjects in an incomprehensible or grotesque way."

"All right," says Mevlido.

"Four," continues Gorgha, "Sonia Wolguelane."

"Sonia Wolguelane," repeats Mevlido.

"Only enter into contact with her as a last resort. She is not a very safe person."

"What do you mean as a last resort?" murmurs Mevlido.

"As a last resort," persists Gorgha. "The expression means exactly what it means."

Then, Gorgha falls silent. The two of them remain next to each other. They listen to the cricket that stridulates with regularity.

"Is that all?" inquires Mevlido.

"Yes," confirms Gorgha. "One, two, three, four. It's a reminder."

They listen a little while yet to the nostalgic song of the cricket, then Gorgha slides one shoulder into the opening whose shutter she had lifted shortly before. A pencil can be heard rolling on the slab and falling to the ground. She touches the microphone, finds the electric cable that feeds it; she feels around on the wall by the window. She gropes around for a good quarter minute. Then she finds what she wanted—a switch.

She presses it.

A sharp click.

As extraordinary as that might seem, the sound system is still in working order. The loudspeakers in the train station at once broadcast ruffling feathers and scraping noises, because Gorgha wants to unhook the microphone from its base and pull it toward the outside, but the apparatus resists, and finally she has to give up on speaking in conditions of optimal comfort. She stuffs her head and shoulders into the opening and now inclines her head toward the other, metallic head.

And so there rings out, in the stillness and emptiness of the station, above the rails devastated by rust lacework, a sentence. Then another. The echoes are clouded by magnetic sputtering, each syllable ricochets off obstacles or voids.

"Gorgha here, calling home base," says Gorgha. "Contact made. Message delivered. No loss of men or matériel."

The announcement takes time to die out. It reverberates in the angular space of the terminal; it floats above the dust, above the blackened planks and the chalky planks. It passes by the two bodyguards still frozen in front of the little staircase; it goes toward the termite mounds, toward the indistinct night beyond. After the announcement, Mevlido raises his arm and places his hand on Gorgha's left shoulder blade, on the very dark blue plumes, warm, crisp.

He touches them. They are warm, crisp to the touch.

He is touching them to get Gorgha's attention, without pressure, but, at the same time, his gesture resembles a caress.

Gorgha stiffens. She doesn't like these familiarities. Everything shows it.

She has straightened up a bit; she turns brusquely toward Mevlido.

"What now?" she asks.

"Besides those four points . . . ," begins Mevlido, then he stops.

"Would you mind finishing your sentence?"

"About Verena Becker, did Deeplane say anything?" Mevlido finds the courage to say.

"About whom?"

"Verena Becker," stammers Mevlido.

"No, he didn't say anything," Gorgha says impatiently, twisting her shoulder so that Mevlido will take his hand away.

Already she is leaning toward the microphone again.

"Fall back," she orders. "Fall back immediately to the positions prepared beforehand!"

"Does that mean me too?" asks Mevlido.

Gorgha says no with a shake of her head.

Then she turns off the electricity, abandons the microphone, tries to lower the shutter in front of the booth. The grooves are clogged with dirt. The shutter protests, it gets stuck halfway. It stays there, neither up nor down. Gorgha makes a gesture that is difficult to interpret—of weariness, maybe, or indifference.

She smiles at Mevlido and, without a word of goodbye, leaves him.

She hurries toward her companions.

She rejoins them at the end of the platform. One of the two goes ahead of her, the other follows her. They begin to go down the service stair, all three of them, then, with no transition, they disappear.

"Hey!" cries Mevlido. "The shutter . . ."

No one is there any longer to answer him.

"Hey!" he cries again. "The shutter! Do I close it, or doesn't it matter?"

6

Silence. No one cries, no one answers.

The pictures have been extinguished. The dark has now returned over everything.

Mevlido's sleep continues, now without any notable event.

If I might be allowed to speak here. No one has asked me to, and I don't even know if I will succeed in saying what I have in mind, but if you will allow me.

I would like to come back for a moment to Sonia Wolguelane, whose name was mentioned in Mevlido's dream.

Sonia Wolguelane is an important figure in our night, and at that time we—men and women—were all in love with her, in love unto death.

Silence. Something moves. Then the darkness, in turn, is extinguished.

For a picture, at present, the photograph is of a young non-conformist, a small girl with narrow hips and an unprepossessing chest, a very seductive girl, with very dark, very curly short hair, the face of a little Mediterranean goddess with white teeth, eyes capable of shooting you down or making you fall madly in love, and an admirable complexion, perfect but equivocal, of a texture so uncommon that we had a different perception of it depending on the circumstances, depending on the exaltations or frustrations we felt in her presence, depending on our fantasies, depending on our memories.

- First variant of the image: her bird's body, entirely velvet with ivory down, her limbs slender without fragility, solid, with joints softened by the troubling thickness of feathers, and her head with slightly angular contours which gave her an expression of energy and even of cruel independence, an inky gaze so intense that pupils and iris blend together.
- Second variant: her insolent young human's body, as if triumphant at the end of adolescence, whose small breasts and flat stomach she had kept, with a tanned complexion of a wonderful Asiatic bronze, whose beauty was elevated yet again by light brown eyes of blistering intelligence.

Freeze-frame on these pictures.

Pause.

Like many of us, Sonia Wolguelane roamed the ghettos of the failed revolution. She gave herself over to bloody revenge against the winners and pompous billionaires who had taken power after the war and who, to justify their gangster politics or to make us forget the exterminations they had plotted a few decades earlier or even to explain the present distress of nearly everyone, invoked sometimes a humanist morality, sometimes the ideological rags of the defeated in which they would drape themselves without compunction, sometimes continental drift and climate change. From time to time, when the occasion arose, she would kill a child soldier, but, in general, she reserved her ammunition for the former genocides and warlords who had reinvented themselves in independent wealth management or in the mafia, or in a combination of the two when they belonged to the circles close to the central powers. She killed a lot.

We all helped her to commit her crimes, we helped her with all our strength—from the positions we held in the police or the ghettos, or from our subhuman dreams, our infirm dreams, ill, defeated; from our lives of dead men walking, from our dreams of former or future prisoners and of former or future assassinees or assassins.

Without ceasing and without remorse we helped her from the reality of our dreams.

Silence.

From the reality of our survival.

Silence.

Sonia Wolguelane was one of ours, a heroine emerged from our night and known by all who lived in the mud, and we loved her, but not only for her sense of action. Not only for her hand that didn't shake when she pulled from her pocket a Makarov or a Browning stolen from the arsenal. We loved her not only for political reasons, not only because, upon leaving childhood, she had joined our old radical egalitarian movement, immediately founding a deviant branch whose audacity and efficiency often left us speechless—no, not only for that: she moved us also with the grace that emanated from her.

She was pretty: very, very pretty. Or rather, to adopt one of the expressions she had introduced among us, she was a knockout, a total knockout, with a style of beauty very different from that of the women of the first and second generations of the Organizations. And as soon as we found ourselves in contact with her, whether in reality or in thought, we adored her.

Silence.

For example, at the end of the night, it happened that we might repeat her name and spend a moment between sleep and waking, a moment that we hoped to prolong as much as possible, evoking her face and her body, her appearance of a deadly and adorable girl, ready for anything. Some of us, especially the males, especially the youngest, were aroused. We thus also forced her to roam in the muddy gutters of our consciousness, associated with our prehistoric moisture, the stifled genetic calls and the pulses of blood that dated back to the first vertebrates, from the Cretaceous or even further. So we also dragged her into the raw animal images of coitus that we had been taught not to judge pitiful or shameful, that we had been taught to humanize, to civilize by talking about eroticism or even about love. So she found herself involuntarily an actress in our sometimes very lyrical imagination of the sex act, and sometimes, on the other hand, without a lyre, reduced to a brief, raw, sordid frenzy, especially for the males. There you have the affective and not exclusively political dimension of the relations between us. For what the sexual in our relations is worth.

Because our encounters had only taken place in a dream.

Silence.

Because they took place. Not only in a dream.

Silence.

In Henhouse Four or elsewhere we had many occasions to cross paths because, not having a permanent address, she haunted the same subversive corners as those we were used to. She slept sometimes with one, sometimes another, changing lodging as a game more than as a security precaution. It's clear that she also had one or two secret hideouts, because it would come about that she would no longer be anywhere for months, during which, nonetheless, the government big shots would fall like flies.

She was often dressed like a worker who smelled vaguely of gunpowder or iron shavings, as if she had just worked ten hours straight in a metal warehouse, but sometimes she could appear dressed as a revolutionary student from the time of red Mongolia or decked out as a petit bourgeois princess from the suburbs, with a provocative miniskirt or too-tight jeans that didn't belong to our world. In any case, we melted in front of her. As conversation developed with her, we brushed—as if by chance—against the dark vivacity of her eyes, or we slyly admired the softness of her cheeks, her downy skin, the slightly elongated line of her brows, and we took advantage of the smallest space between two sentences to imagine what our fingers would feel if they lost themselves in the little curls that she often dyed and amused herself coloring straw blonde or very black, blue black, or very light mahogany. We took advantage of the smallest space between two sentences. Or even to think that we guessed, when we guessed nothing, the yield of her small breasts and the rich, intimate pliancy of her hips, when they were squeezed into a particularly skin-tight fabric.

She was still very young, twenty years old, hardly more, very young—much younger than us. She behaved like a comrade, she didn't play upon her femininity in an irritating way, she didn't express herself with pouts and whims. She could be tender; some of us could testify that she also knew how to abandon herself and come along, abandon herself and dance in their arms, against their body and around their body, then fall asleep.

Deliciously.

Silence.

And also, when we were close to her without necessarily thinking about expressing it, we understood that something essential had escaped us previously, and we felt nostalgic for an "elsewhere," as if, in the course of our existence made of bad trips and bad wars, of squashed insurrections and atrocious defeats, we had missed a clue that would have led us to her without pain, without scars, and without having grown old in the disaster.

Silence.

Without having grown old during the disaster.

That could have led us to her, to this girl who did not look like our past.

Silence.

That is the charm that Sonia Wolguelane exercised upon us. She asked us for weapons for her crimes, and we gave her weapons for her crimes. She asked us for information about the individuals whom she wanted to execute, and for her we would open the strongboxes of the police and extract envelopes containing confidential information. She shrugged at the theories that had illuminated us, she mocked the old long-term programs upon which we grafted some vestiges of revolutionary logic, but that didn't stop her from reviving, at the necessary moment, the political frenzy we had abandoned too soon. She gave us the courage that we had lacked after the defeat. She made us believe that some belief remained. She offered us the youth, the blaze of her beauty, she offered us the invincibility of mud and grime. She represented the last generation—the best of what it could contain.

She was young; after her there would be nothing more.

Silence.

But anyway.

7

Without having wanted to—because, like many of us, he was incapable of mastering his sleep to that degree—Mevlido awoke.

On a periphery of his consciousness, he had Sonia Wolguelane's name. He wanted to think of her.

Immediately a vision of Sonia Wolguelane coming toward him formed in his mind's eye. She wore a midnight blue dress, not very long, and, what's more, open to mid-thigh, revealing her legs covered with a very white down, wonderfully soft and alluring. He opened his eyes. The darkness surrounded him, and he didn't want the picture to fall apart. He had in his hips and hands an erotic languor, as if he had just left the young woman after having made love with her. He had not really seen her in a dream, but there she was occupying the absolute forefront of his immediate memory. He was hard. For at least a minute he fantasized about Sonia Wolguelane. He imagined that she had come to press up against him lovingly, favorable to his male initiative, putting herself at his disposition sexually, sensual, brazen, desiring to share with him the same frenzied movements of humans in rut. She undressed, she sighed in his ear, she trembled, she promised him everything. Men often pull themselves out of unconsciousness with such scenes.

At the same time, out of his night, out of that same periphery, a sentence was trying to take shape in his head. He couldn't manage to make it clear.

The sentence stirred, sounding more like advice or an order.

Only enter into contact with her if . . . No. *Don't enter into contact with Sonia Wolguelane if* . . . No, it was something else. *Enter into contact with her if* . . .

Then he remembered the female crow. It was her, Gorgha, who had uttered that.

From time to time, Gorgha emerged inside his dreams. She planned with him actions he should carry out in waking life, or she made sure that he was in control of his ambiguous role as a criminal infiltrating the official police, that he had the situation in hand, that he didn't contradict himself, that even during self-criticism sessions he didn't contradict himself, that even in his dreams he didn't let anything compromising or irreparable slip. She exerted a confident authority over him, and he—most of the time—obeyed. When he didn't obey, it was usually through clumsiness and only in small details, or else when the instructions she dictated concerned his love life and his relationships with women, with Verena Becker, Maleeya Bayarlag, Sonia Wolguelane, or others, as it seemed to him that, in that matter, Gorgha didn't need to intervene and, especially, that she didn't understand anything about it.

The sentence stirred.

Only enter into contact with her as a last resort, he thought suddenly. Much of the rest was already gone, forgetfulness reigned, but that recommendation from Gorgha had resurfaced, finally, in all its unpleasant brutality. He could still feel Gorgha's epidermal reaction under his hand, her stiffening when he had touched the feathers on her shoulder. What gave her the right to interfere? he thought.

The last elements of his dream frayed away. The sentence vanished. Gorgha, stiff and unfriendly beneath her black feathers, was becoming an insignificant trace. Then she was nothing. Inside Mevlido's skull, fragments of a less dreamlike reality already combined to reconstitute memories, real moments tied to experience and life. Sonia Wolguelane, again, was part of them. She reappeared in a sequence that this time had lost all phantasmatic character, a recent sequence. As if on a flickering reel of film, in black and white, she was walking down the street, becoming more distant. The slap of her shoes on the asphalt could be heard; she passed underneath a streetlight on Gunmen Street. It was a week earlier. They had just separated, she and Mevlido, after having arranged to meet in a dive bar. They had spoken of several high-up bureaucrats, in ideology and in the mafia. Mevlido had communicated to the young woman the schedule of their movements, their itineraries. Sonia Wolguelane, that time, had dyed several of her curls crimson. She wore Chinese trousers and a Chinese jacket in dark gray cotton, and in the street lit by a lone bulb she had no trouble blending into the wall.

It's true that she could knock anyone out, he thought.

He reopened his eyes.

Maleeya Bayarlag was no longer lying next to him.

The air was stagnant in the bedroom; the mattress gave off the smell of damp straw; the sheet was rolled around his ankles. From outside came the noise of a fight between mutant chickens and dogs. The chickens were winning.

The night wasn't over.

The night.

It wasn't over.

He listened to find out if Maleeya was still in the apartment, if she was moving around or breathing in the next room.

"Maleeya," he said softly.

No answer.

"Maleeya," he said again, "are you there? It's too early, you should go back to bed."

Seven days a week, Maleeya got up before dawn and, when the water wasn't cut off, got washed up in the kitchen and went out. She had a job in a co-op, and she spent an hour stocking the shelves with the products missing from the display, going back and forth between the adjoining stock room and the shop; then she washed the floor before the doors opened. Then she went to a waste management company. She crossed the yard strewn with scrap metal and rags, piles exuding a suffocating odor, as often vagrants or cadavers would sleep in the middle of the detritus, and she entered the little administrative building she was supposed to clean. She swept hallways and stairs, she chased out the birds who had gotten in through the broken windows or the ventilation shafts. She had the ground floor and two upper floors to clean. Then she was free. Doing this, she earned three dollars a day—two at the co-op and one for cleaning the building.

"It's still too early," murmured Mevlido again. "You haven't slept enough."

Nothing and no one moved in the apartment. Outside, the dog and the mutant chickens had finished tearing each other apart. Calm returned for a minute, then a drunk bellowed out the beginning of a song at the end of Temple Street, then there was a water hammer in a pipe behind the wall, the sound of running water. Someone was urinating.

A woman shouted in the house next door. She was arguing with her husband.

"Leave me alone, you son of a bitch!" she roared.

Mevlido sat up straight.

The bed frame creaked. On the walls, the spiders panicked, then froze. It had been agreed with Maleeya Bayarlag that they wouldn't kill them. According to her, other specimens would replace those killed, and at least those already in place had understood that they shouldn't run across the sleepers' faces or spin webs in the places where the humans circulated. Mevlido mostly agreed. He could hardly stand spiders, like me, like all of us, but he preferred to have a reason not to fight with them. There are adversaries so repugnant that even the idea of destroying one turns your stomach.

He left the bed and arrived in the kitchen, the corner that had been arranged next to the sink to resemble a shower stall. As always at this early hour, the tepid water carried with it scales of rust that he could feel crumble at the touch of his fingers. Once washed, he dressed, attached his policeman's bag to his belt, and went down into the street.

The lamps were still lit. At the intersection, surrounded by birds of prey that hesitated to peck them, lay a man and a woman in derelicts' clothing, drugged or dead. He stepped over them and started down Temple Street, the little street of restaurants. There were already people in the cafeteria, at least ten. Mevlido sat and began to devour a bowl of porridge and two dumplings. Inside the spongy dough he could detect the traces of a filling, made of vegetables maybe, or gull gizzards.

He had almost emptied his bowl when Sonia Wolguelane came to sit at his table. She carried the standard meal on a tray with a glass of tea. She was dressed in work clothes only slightly less foul than those of the junkies agonizing in front of the door. It was not a day of elegance for her. She seemed not to have shut an eye for two or three nights, but she wasn't swaying and was in control of herself. She had the efficient movements of a killer.

"I knew I would find you here," she said. "You're always up at dawn."

"Yes," said Mevlido. "And you? How are you?"

"Not bad."

"In fact, you won't believe me, but I dreamed about you last night," said Mevlido.

"Cut the bullshit," grumbled Sonia.

She set to inhaling her meal, a bowl of noodles onto which the cook had crumbled dried shrimp and peppers. She ate with a spoon, and messily.

"I'm going to leave soon," announced Mevlido. "You wanted to ask me something?"

"I'm out of ammunition," said Sonia. "I thought you'd be able to . . ."

"No," Mevlido said firmly. "I know what you want to do with it. Don't rely on me."

Sonia Wolguelane interrupted her meal and lifted her head. She opened her eyes wide and stared at Mevlido. She stared at him with theatrical astonishment. She stayed there, spoon in front of her mouth, and suddenly, despite her filthy clothes, she appeared as what she was: a splendid creature with an intelligent, very young face, a very slightly lascivious smile, lips that you had an intense desire to kiss, and a gaze that sparkled with audacity.

If in the past Mevlido and Verena Becker had had a child, their daughter would have been now about the same age as Sonia Wolguelane.

"And who do you want me to rely on?" she asked.

"I don't know. On someone else. Ask the old women?"

"What old women?"

"The Bolshevik beggars. They have arsenals in preparation for the big night. In their cellars there are vintage Molotov cocktails, machine guns from the Tchapaïev cavalry. That could work for you."

"Seriously, Mevlido?"

"Of course I'm kidding."

Both of them relaxed.

The room was filling up. As always at that hour the conversations were rare and quiet.

"Honestly, you don't expect the police to supply you with cartridges?" Mevlido continued, lowering his voice.

He didn't want to have those eating nearby participating in their conversation.

"But what? You've given me some before," protested Sonia Wolguelane, spraying a flake of red pepper onto the table. And not just once.

Mevlido reached for the bowl sitting in front of him and turned it around between his fingers as if it were a museum piece. Then he raised his eyes to her.

"I know you have some on you," she said.

"Oh yeah? I have some on me? . . . And what makes you think that?"

"In your bag. On your belt. You always have a clip or two."

Mevlido put the bowl back on the tray.

"I've already told you that these executions lead nowhere," he said.

"There are some you approve of," said Sonia.

"A few, yes," said Mevlido. "That doesn't stop it from leading to nothing."

Sonia Wolguelane shrugged her shoulders, and for two seconds in his imagination he explored her back and the nape of her neck under the striped shirt that the worker's jacket gave a glimpse of. He knew that she had tattoos at the base of her arms and elsewhere. It was exactly what subversive organizations hated and forbade, since the beginning of the revolutionary era, for practical reasons—you could change your identity, but tattoos stay—and for ideological reasons—scarifying one's body, marking one's skin, was to readopt practices from the Stone Age. But she had a few tattoos here and there, and Mevlido imagined them, and he found that it suited her marvelously well, that the ink drawings were adorable and arousing and that, in the end, no one cared about the Stone Age, now that the worst of barbarous human or subhuman history had been reached and even surpassed.

"We have lost," Mevlido began again. "It's only you and the madwomen who hold on to some semblance of hope. What good is it to cut down one of the guys in charge every so often? Nothing. It's criminal."

"But sometimes, you approve?" insisted Sonia.

"It depends on the guy you take out," said Mevlido.

"Ah, you see," Sonia gloated, "it depends on the guy. It's criminal, but it depends on the guy."

Mevlido smiled foolishly. He was thinking more about Sonia Wolguelane's tattoos than about the fate of the enemies of the people she intended to eliminate.

"Go on, don't be an idiot," said Sonia. "Give me those fucking cartridges."

8

That same day, a Thursday. Let's say Thursday the nineteenth of that same month. If one watched attentively, one could see the drop of sweat that was trickling down Mevlido's temple, then his cheek. He was in a building on Memorial Avenue, the longest street in the city, on the fourth floor. In a doctor's office. Specialty: nervous illnesses, behavioral problems, professional anxieties. The afternoon was wearing on. On the other side of the window, the sky was motionless, stuck on a violent slate color.

Mevlido was no longer speaking. He could feel the progression of the droplet that had formed at his hairline trickling slowly toward the bottom of his jaw.

After a moment, the psychiatrist reminded him that he should talk, that talking would bring him relief, that talking was healthy, especially in his case. Then she went silent. She had an unusual face, like those pretty women who had once been foxes or weasels in a previous life. Her name was Maggie Yeung.

"Especially in my case . . . ," muttered Mevlido, stunned by all that was contained in that expression.

He had returned to the psychiatrist more as a personal challenge than on the advice of Maleeya Bayarlag, and now he was regretting it. He had been on the defensive since the beginning of the session.

He shook his head.

During the previous session, the Monday before, she had asked him to talk about his problems. You can say everything that's weighing on you, she proposed after she had asked him to take a seat. No one will judge you. I don't count. She had begun listening to him without interrupting, and Mevlido, impressed by her carnivorous face, had been weak enough to tell her straight off that his wife was dead, martyred by child soldiers, and that he was currently with a mentally ill woman who often confused him with her former husband, a man who had been blown to bits by a bomb in a bus. Then, realizing that he had revealed a number of intimate details better left in the dark, he had chosen to turn toward the realm of dreams, in his mind a less sensitive topic, but, unfortunately, he had gotten muddled up. There again, he had said too much. For example, he had explained that he always had trouble establishing whether a memory was derived from an actual experience or a dream. He had added that in his dreams, people often died so that he could go on living. Women, in particular. There are moments when I feel responsible for their death, he had said in a muffled voice. Objectively, I played no role in their death, in my dreams or anywhere else for that matter. But I have the impression that I'm to blame for their deaths, I mean . . . because they had the misfortune to meet me . . . one day they had that misfortune . . . their mere contact with my existence did that . . . He had at least managed not to return to the topic of Verena Becker's demise, he had skirted the mention of that horror, the enumeration of the abuse, the laughter of the adolescents around their victim, the agony. In his haste to talk about something else, he had blurted out some general observations about death, insisting on the fact that he didn't have a morbid fascination with death, or with his own death in particular, and that, quite the opposite, he constantly had to suppress this idea in remote zones of his consciousness, so that he didn't just start screaming in terror. He then realized that he had once more strayed into an area of conversation where he didn't have much control and had sharply changed the subject— falling back on the monotony of his daily life, his professional life, the precinct and the ritual of self-criticism in front of the masses. I'm coming to see you as a sneak preview, he had tried to joke. I have to practice. In a week I will have to do my self-criticism in front of my colleagues again. Then he mentioned his fatigue, his lack of appetite, and after that he didn't change the course of his monologue. But it was already too late; watching her take notes without emitting any commentary, he knew that during the first part of the consultation he had opened up more than was reasonable. To finish with, he had questioned the judgments that Commissioner Berberoïan had made on his situation. He's afraid I'm losing it, he had grumbled. He watches me with a wary eye, as if I've become unpredictable or dangerous. When really, I . . . Don't tell me that . . . after all don't tell me that . . . The psychiatrist had let him wonder. She had neither affirmed nor denied Berberoïan's opinion. And it was also for that reason that he had come back to see her so quickly: to hear her say what she thought of him.

And her: "It's healthy. Especially in your case."

Above Maggie Yeung, a ceiling fan stirred the heat without modifying the temperature. The window was cracked open. A mosquito-netting screen added its grayness to the darkness of the sky. It blocked the insects, but not the noise of the city, nor the music of the shopping arcade at the bottom of the building. Maybe it had been put up there to keep suicides from performing their morbid theater on the ledge of the building.

Mevlido was quiet. He took refuge in the bursts of noise coming from outside; he tracked, for example, the squealing of the trams on their rails or the faraway sirens of ambulances. He concentrated on them to lessen the mental pressure he was under. Maggie Yeung had propped her elbows on the table. She was turned toward him, she watched him with a total absence of a smile. She waited for him to put an end to his silence. Her head was really quite thin, pointed and carnivorous, and, at the same time, had a stupefying Chinese perfection.

A new drop of sweat left Mevlido's temple and began to roll irregularly downward. Open your mouth, imbecile, he thought, or else she is going to convince herself that you are hiding something from her, something dirty and unmentionable that is making you perspire from fear. And she's going to end up thinking you're some kind of dangerous guy.

His policeman's white dress shirt stuck to his chest. He felt damp from head to toe, and, in front of this pretty woman, the dampness seemed shameful to him.

He didn't move.

A minute went by.

The space was impersonal. A table, two chairs, white walls. Behind Maggie Yeung, a door led to a more comfortable office where she received her patients after the first few sessions, when she had established a trusting relationship. Today, the door was closed, but at the beginning of the week, Mevlido had seen it open. He remembered the decor—furniture from the first People's Republic, shelves collapsing under books. And a cage with a bird, a gleaming black mynah that hopped every so often and whistled.

"I don't seem to be able to talk," he said effortfully. "Nothing comes to mind. Nothing interesting for you. I already told you about the main thing the last time."

"Oh, really? The main thing?" The psychiatrist's interest was piqued.

She didn't smile, but one could sense, in her question, something at once mocking and inquisitorial. With her fascinating fox's features, with her very white little teeth you could barely see, Maggie Yeung had gotten a hold of him and wasn't letting go.

He scowled even more. He felt he was in a position of inferiority, like during the self-criticism sessions, when he was on his knees in front of his colleagues, with his name written backward and crossed out in red hanging around his neck.

The "main thing" passed through his mind again, everything he had not managed to repress, everything that, the previous Monday, he had more or less well camouflaged or mixed up:

- the horrible death of Verena Becker, his soulmate
- all the women who had died around him, in reality or in dreams, all those affecting women who passed away and whom he left behind him, whom he abandoned, as if their sacrifice was systematically necessary for him, Mevlido, to continue his semblance of an existence
- the daily life in the ghetto with its mix of dead people, birds, and the living, with its atmosphere of nocturnal catastrophe, with the madness of Maleeya Bayarlag, who, most of the time, confused him with someone else and gave him a dead man's name
- his laughable, grotesque (when you thought about the difference in their ages) attraction for Sonia Wolguelane, a girl who could have been his daughter
- the horror that seized him when he thought about how

he was fifty years old already and the void was
approaching rapidly

He felt like screaming out a series of indistinct sobs.

The unacceptable infinity of that void, he thought.

They die one after another, and I, I keep living, and I'm terribly
afraid to go join them there, he thought.

No sound left his mouth.

The ceiling fan snorted and grunted. Outside, a storm was
brewing, but no lightning was zigzagging between the clouds. The
sky was a formidable mass, dark and motionless.

"Listen, Mevlido," said the psychiatrist, "you came last Monday on the advice of one of your superiors, we could even say on
his orders. But, today, it's not the same situation. You're here of
your own free will."

She leaned forward toward him, elbows propped on the table
where there lay only a pad of paper and a ballpoint pen. She wasn't
sweating. Her lips expressed no tenderness, and she was absolutely
not playing upon her natural charm to seduce Mevlido, but her
face was overwhelming. Two or three centuries before, in the time
of the first People's Republic of China, she could have been on the
posters for movies from Hong Kong, next to Maggie Cheung, for
example, another Maggie. She had that kind of beauty.

In the next room, the mynah let out a few trills.

"You feel bad," continued Maggie Yeung. "You're sitting
calmly on your chair, but it could be that you feel like crying. Or
screaming. Deep down, if you came back, it's because you feel like
you are on the edge of a precipice. Am I right . . . ?"

Silence.

"You know you need help. But you're hesitating . . . For you,
talking means displaying one's weakness."

Silence.

"We'll need time to get results, Mevlido. Weeks, months. But when you start talking, really talking, that will be a good moment for us."

Mevlido was bathed in sweat.

The mynah had begun another series of trills.

"I say we, Mevlido," continued the therapist, "because we're in this together. Do you understand?"

Of course, I understand, thought Mevlido, without budging a millimeter.

He knew it by heart, that old police trick. Establish subjective ties with the suspect, make him believe you have something in common with him, for better or worse.

He was in front of Maggie Yeung, able to clearly see the image he was presenting of himself—a sick policeman, stubborn in his silence, short hair not long enough to move under the breeze of the ceiling fan, head and arms covered with disgusting drops of sweat. The groan he was suppressing, the howling that the slightest thing could have made break free, rumbled in disorder between his temples. Fragments of intimate phrases, deferred whimpers.

No, honestly, it would have been obscene to pour out such misery out loud.

"Maybe another day," he said at last.

"Now would be better," insisted Maggie Yeung.

Mevlido let her finish her sentence. He then counted slowly to ten, even to eleven, so as not to give the impression of being panicked or impolite. Then he pushed back his chair and stood up.

"Listen, Maggie," he said, "no. I prefer another day."

Maggie Yeung's gaze followed him, serious, as if distanced in principle from any practice of smiling.

Mevlido swallowed. He gestured as if to wipe the sweat beading between his nose and mouth. He stopped his arm halfway.

"It doesn't bother you if I call you Maggie?" he asked.

9

The psychiatrist picked up her telephone, hung up, then, having lit a cigarette, leaned back in her chair and remained pensive. She had gone back to her office after Mevlido's departure. The session had broken off in disastrous fashion, and even if they had separated on friendly terms afterward, with an informal promise to see each other soon, she was not at all sure that he would make the effort to come back.

Through the cloud of smoke, she examined the mynah bird swinging on its perch, jumping to the back of the cage to rub its orange beak against the bars or against its porcelain water dish, then returning to its perch to swing again. The cigarette tasted like moldy tea, as was often the case with the tobacco bought from street vendors. The mynah jumped from one corner to the other without spreading its wings, sometimes whistling three joyful notes at the end of a movement.

When she had finished the cigarette, Maggie Yeung stubbed it out in an ashtray next to a previous cigarette butt, then dialed the number of the precinct. Berberoïan had given her his direct line.

"Yes? I'm listening."

"It's Maggie Yeung."

"Ah, yes," said Berberoïan, "Doctor Yeung. So, our Mevlido? He's come to see you?"

"He just left my office. I've already seen him twice this week."

"How is he? I mean, in your opinion, is he . . . ?"

Berberoïan hesitated.

"He is very disturbed," said Maggie Yeung. "You were right to insist that he come see me."

"What's the matter with him?" asked Berberoïan.

Maggie Yeung paused. Even if she had a professional relationship with the police, she didn't willingly communicate information about her patients to them.

"He needs to take care of himself, and he knows it," she said.

"Yes," Berberoïan agreed, "he knows that he's become too emotional. He told me that himself, in those terms. Too emotional. I believe he's begun thinking again about a woman who died twenty years ago. A dreadful story. She was massacred by child soldiers. And now he lives with a madwoman. That doesn't make his life any easier. Did he tell you about that?"

"We talked about a lot of things," said Maggie Yeung.

The bird behind the bars whistled. Two notes. Then three notes of unmixed gaiety.

"Don't worry, Dr. Yeung; I'm not asking you to break professional confidentiality . . . What I want to know is if he is still in any condition to carry out his work as a policeman. In our profession, we can't allow ourselves to have low spirits . . . What if you gave him a couple weeks of rest and relaxation?"

"In my opinion, it would be better for him to keep working normally," said Maggie Yeung. "There's no reason to put him on leave."

"I'm worried that he'll crack up on assignment."

"That would surprise me," said Maggie Yeung. "He controls himself well. He's on the edge of a precipice, it's true, but he doesn't want to jump."

There was a short silence on the line.

"And besides, we are here to keep him from falling," said Maggie Yeung.

"All right," said Berberoïan. "OK, I'll trust you, Dr. Yeung. But I'm going to arrange not to have him directed toward dossiers where he might have to make delicate decisions."

"What kind of decisions?"

"Oh, I don't know. Decisions that need to be made quickly. To draw his gun or not. To shoot or not. Often we have to . . ."

The commissioner had gotten tangled up in his speech. He could be heard making a gesture of powerlessness.

"Don't change his assignments at all," Maggie Yeung added, "so he doesn't feel that he's being sidelined."

"In any event, I will stay in contact with you," said Berberoïan.

At that moment, the mynah went to hit its beak against the water dish and whistled again. It was a blue-and-white water dish from the Qing dynasty, an exquisite antique that Maggie Yeung's father had given his daughter for her birthday, shortly before his death. The bird's whistling expressed an intense joie de vivre, the joy of drinking water, the joy of being in a cage.

"Is that a bird calling behind you now and then?" inquired the commissioner so as not to have to end the conversation too abruptly.

"Yes," said the psychiatrist, "a mynah."

"Mynahs are pretty," said Berberoïan. "I had one, in the past. But it was like yours; it sang too sadly."

"Ah," said Maggie Yeung.

"Yes, too sadly," Berberoïan continued. "It really brought me down. I got rid of it."

10

The elevator remembered at the last second that there was no basement and froze suddenly, with a screech.

The doors opened.

Mevlido got out.

Now he found himself in the little shopping arcade occupying the ground floor. A commercial tune crackled out of the loudspeakers on loop. With a wave, Mevlido acknowledged the security guard whose job it was to bar intruders from accessing the elevator. The guard was settled in against a pile of packing crates, on the remains of a stenographer's chair. He was wearing shorts; he had removed his sandals and was massaging his right foot. He didn't respond to Mevlido's greeting.

After having passed by a discount clothing store and a drug-store/stationer, Mevlido found himself in the street. He raised his head toward the fourth floor. His gaze wandered among the air-conditioning units sticking out of the facade. He thought again about the session with Maggie Yeung. A sketch without dialogue:

- In a bare interior, a man is seated, dazed by reality, overcome by the weight of his dreams.
- Across from him, a woman waits for him to crush his horrible present and past, his absence of a future with his words.
- The woman is beautiful; she looks like an actress from Hong Kong from the era of Hong Kong cinema.
- And him, the man, soaked in sweat and silent.

At that moment he was hit by two drops of water, as big as bird droppings, fallen from the sky or spat out by an air conditioner. He moved a step away. The sidewalk was also constellated with water drops. A smell of earthy dust had begun to spread. Above the city, the clouds were made of pitch, with electric fires, mad lightning that as yet produced only the hint of thunder.

Mevlido went into the pharmacy and picked out an umbrella, a little telescoping rag for a dollar. He wanted to put his ideas back in order before presenting himself to Berberoïan. The precinct was located near Continental Plaza, twelve tram stations away. He would be there in an hour on foot.

He was less than two minutes into his walk when he noticed an old woman sitting on a folding chair in front of the entrance to a building.

Cornelia Orff, he thought. She was a Bolshevik beggar from Henhouse Four, come to spread propaganda downtown. He knew her well; he frequently went to meetings of the cell she organized at her place, not very far from Factory Street, or in even more lugubrious spots, warehouses reeking of spiders, old slaughterhouses, ruined shops. The heat wasn't keeping her from wearing a long military raincoat draped over her shoulders. She had on a black dress that barely revealed her ankles; she hid her feet in filthy clodhoppers. Dressed like that, with her sparse and very white hair, her thick glasses on her nose, she waited for customers. The left earpiece of her glasses was wrapped in a bandage made of duct tape. You could see that her impoverished appearance didn't bother her at all; on the contrary, it was a source of pride.

She had attached a sign around her neck. In front of her enormous shoes, she had unfolded a handkerchief upon which lay four books and some badges. A poster was tacked up behind her, with slogans calling for the punishment of the wealthy in general and for the constitution of a people's army of liberation. She sat bolt upright on her folding chair, ready to answer any question about strategy or dogma in the event that someone spoke to her. No one was paying attention to her.

"Hello," said Mevlido.

The old woman turned her ruined face toward him, her eyes spotted with gray leukomas.

"Oh, it's you, Mevlido?" she asked. "What are you doing here?"

"Oh," said Mevlido evasively, "just hanging around. And you?"

"Oh, you know," said Cornelia Orff.

They said nothing to each other for a good fifteen seconds. Mevlido was wondering if he would like to be seated like her one day among the passersby, without really seeing them or being seen by them, become at last a simple biological object, no longer having anything to answer for to society or to himself.

"It's going well today." He finished by uttering, "Sympathizers? Contacts?"

The old woman straightened the sign, which had slid down.

THE OLD BOLSHEVIKS, it read, HAVE SURVIVED CENTURIES OF ABOMINATION. IT IS FORBIDDEN TO SHOW THEM HOSTILITY, TO HUMILIATE THEM, TO MAKE FUN OF THEM, OR TO COMMIT ANY VIOLENCE WHATSOEVER AGAINST THEM.

"No, today, it's dead," said the old woman. "People are afraid of getting caught in the storm. They don't stop. They don't buy anything. There are days like that."

"Of course," said Mevlido.

He had crouched down in front of the display.

The smells of exhaust, motor oil, and rotten food were stronger near the ground.

The thunder was growling in the distance.

Furious motorists honked their horns.

"There's a sale on the badges," announced the old woman.

There were eight badges, all in very bad condition because they dated from the first decades of the proletarian revolution and had not been designed to last so long in a hostile environment. Most of the revolutionaries displayed on them disappeared under patches of dust and rust. Collective memory had forgotten their names. Mevlido pretended to examine them one after another with interest, then he lined them up again on the dirty cloth.

"Three for two dollars," the old woman offered.

You could hear a trembling at the bottom of her voice.

"I already have them all," Mevlido apologized.

"It's a steal," the old woman argued. "A chance like this won't come around again in a long time."

"I know," Mevlido said with an apologetic but firm expression.

His interlocutor muttered. Now he examined the books—reports on historical congresses held in clandestinity or in indifference, in Ulan Bator, Iquitos, Zone 2, or here even, quite nearby, in Henhouse Four. There was also a post-exotic *romånce*. The book was in shreds. The cover was missing.

"It's by Djohnn Infernus," said the old woman, noticing that Mevlido had started to leaf through it. "His best book, it appears."

"You don't happen to have a copy in better condition?" Mevlido asked.

"No," said the old woman, "in literature, that's all I have left."

"And in your back stock?"

"Congress reports—I still have some at home, but I've sold all the Infernus."

Mevlido shrugged. After such an extended conversation, he couldn't now avoid buying something from her. He picked up three badges at random and got up.

"I'll take these three," he said.

"There's a big one in that bunch," quibbled the old woman all of a sudden. "It wasn't part of the sale. You'll need to add a dollar."

"Say, you're really killing your clientele," Mevlido protested.

"We're in a society of commerce," the old woman exclaimed, irritated. "You think this is fun for me? Go on, three dollars for the three. It's not for me, as you well know. It's for the Party."

The old woman took the sum without thanking him. But she was happy. Her voice had softened.

"So that one day everything will be free," she added.

11

Memorial Avenue buzzed away on his left.

A tram passed by, sounding its alarm, a metallic instrument with the timbre of a ceremonial bell.

Traffic on the avenue was dense. Mevlido saw it out of the corner of his eye without paying it much attention. The contrast with the atmosphere of the ghettos was stark, and, even if the prosperity of the downtown represented only an island in the middle of a sea of misery, here you could have the sensation of having entered a world that could claim to incarnate reality, a world that had turned the page on the disasters and the dark war, and where civilization had been reestablished, along with justice, the end of utopian ideals, and the industrious tranquility of which humans and even subhumans are capable in times of peace.

Transported by his reverie, Mevlido slightly clenched his right fist. The badges pricked his palm.

Put your purchase in your bag, Mevlido, he thought. Three portraits of dead men. Betrayed egalitarian leaders, betrayed red leaders, erased anonymously, forgotten and betrayed. You don't even know if they are men or women.

He walked beneath the trees, which came one after the other on the edge of the sidewalk, trees from after the war that had already had the time to reach adult size, mutant linden trees, mutant pagoda trees with long, pendulous leaves, fig trees. The smell of pollen fell heavily toward the ground, heightened by the proximity of the rain.

What . . . , he thought. I'm suffocating.

He stopped. His forehead was shiny with sweat.

Without warning, the malaise that had weighed on him in front of Maggie Yeung, and that he had believed had dissipated, swelled again within him and took away his breath. Distress overran the limits of his consciousness and expanded to his whole body. He felt that he couldn't go a step farther.

I should never have sat down in front of that psychiatrist, he thought. She made me stir up what I had no desire to stir up. And all for nothing. I have absolutely no need of her. I won't go back to see her. He grumbled like this internally for a minute, then the malaise grew stronger. He was obsessed by the fear of venturing once again into the martyrdom of Verena Becker. Don't take that forbidden path, he thought.

Drops of sweat ran down his face. He wiped them off.

A new tram glided by on his left, announcing its passage with peals of a ceremonial bell.

You can't take this sticky heat any longer, Mevlido, he thought. But get a hold of yourself. Don't let the horrors of the past spill over into your present. Avoid thinking about the past, only consider the present in the most favorable light. Calm down. Look at reality as it is downtown, get a grip on yourself. Look at Memorial Avenue. You are in the center of civilization, in the center of what hasn't been destroyed; it's true that that doesn't mean much anymore on a planetary scale, because almost nothing has been spared, but all the same, it's the center. The city has withstood the massacres, it holds those who have stood fast, those who remain, it's now called Oulang-Oulane. Begin your walk again in Oulang-Oulane; you can see that everything is reassuring in the reality around you and that you, you as well, have stood fast. You, too, have remained after the misfortune, after all. Begin your walk again and look at the avenue, Memorial Avenue. It was reconstructed according to the plans of the old metropolis, rectilinear, impressive in width and length; it was designed by architects who imagined their masters to have the features of invincible titans, it was designed to astonish foreigners, in the time when there were still foreigners or tourists. The wars and genocides have put humanity in its place, the titans have disappeared, the foreigners have rejoined other worlds. The tourists sleep forever in mass graves. No one bothers to think of either group anymore. You see, Mevlido, you are crossing the domain of impermanence. Don't jump to any disastrous conclusions. It's the disastrous conclusions that take your breath away. Not the burning humidity, not a physical defect in your lungs. Don't stop here. Start walking again. Stop ruminating pointlessly on the past or the future. Look at the trees that line Memorial Avenue. Fig trees, frangipani with heavy green leaves, lindens. Breathe. The trees are not old. They were born after you, after the end of the war; they will outlive you. Don't be afraid of that.

He paused. He could reason with himself all he wanted; he was still suffocating.

Look at the pedestrians moving in rows on the sidewalks, he continued. Look at the normal people who get by with no problem in the rebuilt society, in the center of Oulang-Oulane, far from the ghettos and the camps. Leave aside the others, the ragged communists, the flea-bitten refugees dying under the vermin, and the junkies. They've slipped into the real world for a few hours, but after dusk they will return to their parallel chasms. You will extract no comfort from the contemplation of these wrecks. You are among them like a fish in water, and it's for that reason also that you are suffocating. Look instead at the anonymous passersby of Oulang-Oulane, those who feel in place in the reconstructed reality. It doesn't matter that you don't respect them. It is they who will act out the end of the catastrophe, otherwise they would be wandering in Henhouse Four, in the ghetto where more than anywhere else you feel at ease and where each night you rejoin your peers. Go forward among them, among the ordinary citizens of Oulang-Oulane, as if you were like them. These men and these women no longer think of extermination, of past barbarity, of the ignominy to come. Be like them; don't be terrorized by the present, by what it is built on and by what it foreshadows.

Look at the faces of the crowd. The crowd moves without nervousness; it doesn't care about anything. It is clear that the people whose paths you cross have managed to dispense with the fear of death and in particular with the idea of the death of others. Follow their lead. No one is trembling. No one is suffering. No male or equivalent individual is breaking down suddenly, tears in his eyes, broken down by his memories or his shame. No female is sobbing or staggering in front of a building's entrance, not knowing how to manage her body and her mind, suddenly horrified by the unpardonable state of the world.

Walk, Mevlido, thought Mevlido.

Keep going.

Breathe.

Breathe in the dust, the pollen, the smell of smoke, motors, trash bins, shabby clothes, masculine smells, feminine smells, the smells of dirty cardboard, beggars, linden flowers, the smell of the frangipani along the gutters, the smells of food near the fast-food restaurants, the smells of the storm. The city has its own way of breathing before the storm, it will outlive you, it too. It will last. It will still be stirring up its stale and vile smells when you no longer exist. Don't be afraid of that.

Sweat is running down your face, Mevlido, it is running down your face and your bare arms. From head to toe you're dripping as if you had a high fever. Once more, instead of making your way naturally along the sidewalk, you feel yourself moving along that corridor of death to which life, according to you, is reduced—a stretch of road made hideous by its brevity and by the echoes of tragedy that are stirred up with each step. *Dead man walking.* You're not wrong, Mevlido, you may be right all the way along, but it's better if you consider things otherwise. Follow the example of the people whose paths you cross. Take refuge in their ignorance. Appreciate as they do the sleep that the victors have brought. Imitate these people.

Let idiocy and blindness enter you.

Look at these faces coming toward you, observe them as best you can, with sympathy, fraternally, with impartiality, with compassion, with charity, with softness. Breathe in, Mevlido, breathe in several times; fill your lungs. Breathe in idiocy and blindness. Maybe like that you will find a semblance of serenity.

Maybe you will find that, he thought.

But he found nothing.

His legs carried him along reluctantly. The palms of his hands throbbed like when you lean over the edge of a precipice.

People moved about close to him.

Look at the faces, he thought. See the faces. Don't lose consciousness. Don't desire to reach unconsciousness. Don't envy the insane. Adapt yourself to reality. Examine the faces. They are full of riches, they tell stories that hold together, and, sometimes, they are beautiful.

Sometimes, they are beautiful.

Keep yourself in the crowd in the middle of the faces, on the middle line between total forgetfulness and cretinism.

KEEP YOURSELF IN THE MIDDLE OF THE FACES!
TRANSFORM YOURSELF INTO A FACE, FORGET
   EVERYTHING!
DON'T FORGET YOUR IDIOT FACE, FORGET
   EVERYTHING!

He recalled the slogans heard in Henhouse Four. None of them fit the situation. None of them was useful to traverse the real world. But it was necessary to hold on to something.

swim among the faces, he thought. forget
nothing, forget everything!

12

He moved a few steps forward, then he approached the edge of
the sidewalk and stopped again. Lassitude filled all his movements.
He wasn't really out of breath, but the desire to walk had left him.

Sweat soaked the nape of his neck. It ran from his armpits to
his belt.

For a minute, he watched hazily what was in front of his eyes.
The avenue stretched for kilometers from east to west, without
a curve, up to Continental Plaza and its administrative center.
The part of the roadway reserved for the tram marked out a dry
riverbed, with four rails that allowed the cars to pass each other
without touching and, on the gray ground, a multitude of black
marks, streaks of motor oil. Above the rails, a raised cement platform held, every three or four hundred meters, transparent shelters under which travelers could wait for cars heading for Peesch,
for Ingra, for Henhouse Four, for Managony. The others, going
toward Continental Plaza, had to wait under the trees. The peak
hours for public transit were over, and there weren't many people
on the platforms, but behind them the flow of traffic was intense.

It was noisy and intense.

What are you waiting for, Mevlido? he thought. Have some
courage. It's that conversation with the psychiatrist that has you
depressed.

He filled and emptied his lungs without conviction, planted
under a fig tree, near a pillar where the stop was listed—Iyim Garden West—as well as the numbers of the trams and the places they
stopped.

Don't let yourself be knocked down, he thought.

The sky couldn't have been darker.

Isolated raindrops burst here and there, but, for the moment, the rain was letting itself be desired, and it was mostly insects falling to the ground or onto passersby and landing softly, mostly winged ants that the fall in atmospheric pressure had immobilized. The little bugs bounced onto Mevlido's cropped hair, his shoulders. He brushed off the top of his head with a grimace and went to stand farther on, away from them, that is, not under the branches.

Behind the neighborhood of the Iyim refugees, thunder growled.

The traffic on the avenue wasn't smooth. Despite the width of the lanes, traffic jams formed constantly.

A tram for Continental Plaza braked in front of Mevlido with a squeal, took on two people, and took off again.

On the other side of the cement platforms where two or three travelers were waiting, some official cars had made their appearance, as they often did at that hour—five limousines full of ministers and enemies of the people with government jobs, sated after their midday citizens' banquet. Impeded by the congestion, the convoy sometimes moved at a snail's pace, sometimes stood still. It slowed again, then broke in two. A car had lagged behind, blocked between two pickup trucks carrying a load of vegetables.

Without attaching any importance to them, Mevlido examined the bunches of green onions, the clusters of peppers, the cabbage, the fresh pandan leaves, when his gaze was attracted by an individual standing on the platform of the tram for Managony, about five hundred meters away. The individual had all the characteristics of a casual proletarian, with a military jacket spotted with plaster and a cap that hid whether its wearer was a man or a woman. Mevlido squinted. What . . . , he thought. You'd think . . .

No. But yes. Of course, yes.

Sonia Wolguelane.

On the lookout. Surveilling the avenue.

And obviously she had a weapon on her. A pistol. The pistol that . . .

With the ammunition that this morning . . .

She's going to use it right now, here, he thought.

Sonia Wolguelane, however, wasn't giving the impression that she was up to no good. She was leaning against the glass shelter and showed no nervousness. For the unsuspecting spectator, she was simply one of these young beings of interchangeable sex, unemployed or not, who emerge from a jobsite or a ghetto with music and misery in their head, and, among a jumble of other inexact ideas, the desire that everything end as soon as possible. From time to time, artlessly, Sonia Wolguelane crushed a mosquito or a bead of sweat on her cheek.

You absolutely wouldn't have said a killer before a political assassination.

She's really someone, after all, that girl. Mevlido was moved.

He was wondering who she was going to fire on this time, and whether he would approve of her choice, when he sensed a presence on his right.

A stranger had come around the trunk of a fig tree and walked down the edge of the sidewalk, and she was heading toward Mevlido as if he didn't exist, as if she couldn't imagine an obstacle in her way as mediocre as a policeman in a shirt soaked with sweat. She must have been about thirty. She had black hair that fell to her shoulders, a slightly angular face with an energetic expression and intelligent, shining, blue-black eyes. She wore a green dress, of the Asiatic green that in the past had been designated by the term *shocking green,* in the era when Asia was exotic for those who monopolized the language, and when there were still English speakers who determined if a color was or wasn't shocking to Western tastes. In any case, it was a rich green. She walked holding herself very straight and with a slight flexibility, which gave her body the ease of a ballerina.

She brushed past Mevlido without seeing him. Mevlido got a whiff of her perfume: simple, of bitter almond; powerful, as if she had just come out of her bathroom on Memorial Avenue.

That perfume didn't remind him of anyone in particular, but as she was already turning her back to him, he felt his heart contract painfully and then change rhythm.

That woman looked like Verena Becker. It wasn't really the same way of holding herself, nor the same haircut, nor the same color of skin. Nor the same size. But she resembled her tremendously, by some trait that he would have been unable to define. The perfume didn't match either. But it was her.

Verena Becker twenty years earlier, he thought.

At the moment when we were happy, at the moment she was going to die. Twenty years ago.

My little Verena, my dear little Verena.

He hesitated a few seconds, then, without forming the slightest plan, began to follow her. She had a fifteen-meter head start. Now he had turned back in the direction of the psychiatrist's office. She continued to walk along the very edge of the sidewalk, unthinkingly crushing winged ants in the last stage of their personal stories. To her left, the sparse crowd; to her right, the rails. She had a purse slung across her body and held a plastic bag upon which Chinese characters appeared along with their transcription in Latin characters: May Chow, Shoes Co.

It couldn't be Verena Becker, he thought abruptly. I'm going mad. It couldn't be her.

I'm going mad, but it is her, he thought further.

At this same instant, a bolt of lightning divided the world into two pale halves. The thunder was only a sharp crack, and, with no transition, a cataract fell from the heights and hit the ground. Just then, lightning struck again, and this time, a deafening roar shook Memorial Avenue from top to bottom. Finally, the storm broke, with its fury and its sheets of water. The city became blurred, the surfaces bristled with black, with silver, with mercury; a cyclist passed by on the sidewalk raising a spray as if, between two blinks of an eye, puddles had had the time to form on the asphalt. The beggars finished disappearing into the entrances of buildings. People were running. Most of them weren't headed under the trees, which offered insufficient protection. They zigzagged in a frenzy to reach the shops, the porches. Some yelled or called out to each other. Some were laughing; they had been instantaneously soaked to the bone.

Mevlido had begun an argument with his umbrella. The ribs were not in the mood. He saw himself again putting a dollar on the counter of the pharmacy. He should have chosen a more expensive model.

The rain was hot and stinging, but at the same time it was a welcome shower that washed him clean of sweat and insects.

He continued to reconnect the rebellious segments of his umbrella one by one.

The gutter was already boiling. He raised his eyes to see what had become of the woman who looked like Verena Becker. In the distance, through a sizzling curtain, a tram coming from Managony left its stop. It took off and began to gain speed. The rails could no longer be seen, nor the difference between the street and the sidewalk. The ground was frothing. Verena Becker had gotten down onto the rails, as if trying to forge the stream. She was rifling through her bag while hurrying to reach the glass shelter that stood on one of the platforms. Water splashed around her ankles. She bent her head toward her bag; she was having trouble getting her umbrella out of it; her plastic May Chow bag was in the way, and all of a sudden, she slowed down, seeming to wish to stroll under the raging torrent. There was no one between her and Mevlido, only the whistling, translucent crosshatching of the rain. Toward her came the car coming from Managony, but especially, little, frantic, androgynous, the silhouette of Sonia Wolguelane.

A gray silhouette. That of Sonia Wolguelane.

Sonia Wolguelane had just reemerged into Mevlido's field of vision. She ran the length of the indistinct rails, like a madwoman, in the middle of splashes.

She was fleeing. She was bolting after having done justice. Mevlido hadn't seen her act, but now he realized that something had taken place on the other side of the platform, between the pickup trucks of vegetables. The attack had taken place. The limousine had broken windows, a man wearing a brimmed cap was slowly extracting himself from the car with the movements of a sleepwalker. Sonia Wolguelane must have fired her pistol during the thunder. She must have fired on the passengers, sparing the driver, as is customary among killers with style.

During the seconds following an assassination on a public road, the conventional rules of the universe are broken. No need to look very far back into your memories, we have all known this phenomenon. The actors move with a supernatural fluidity, the scene is a photograph upon which the onlookers are temporarily inert, the rain falls noiselessly, the witnesses perceive with acuity tiny, useless details. Before Mevlido's eyes, everything played out inside a compact time that would have been impossible to measure in sixtieths of a minute or even in sixtieths of any unit whatsoever.

Sonia Wolguelane ran along a line that led her toward Mevlido, and on her trajectory happened to be an incongruous obstacle in *shocking green*. We don't know why—maybe because she was blinded by the rain—the young murderer insisted on not changing her course, and we don't know why Verena Becker behaved as if she wanted to bar her way. In reality, bent toward her purse, she was fighting with a miniature umbrella and wasn't paying attention to anything else. She had just gotten the cover off and was desperately looking on the handle for the place she had to press to open the mechanism. The tram was approaching; it was continuing to accelerate because the two women were thrashing about well away from its path.

Mevlido stayed still, without moving, thirty meters or so away. At some point he had stepped down off the sidewalk. He felt the water coming over his shoes.

He witnessed the scene with a vacant mind.

Sonia Wolguelane was going straight forward at top speed, claiming a sort of right of way over the woman in green; it's true that when you have just shot an enemy of the people at point-blank range, you generally like people to get out of your way. Then, about this stranger who was in her way, her opinion changed: she wasn't an ordinary passerby; it must be a plainclothes officer, a policewoman getting out her service weapon. Both of them had their heads pulled down between their shoulders: Sonia Wolguelane in order to crash into her adversary before being riddled with bullets, Verena Becker because the rain was pouring down on her and deafening her.

Intending to shake it open, Verena Becker brandished her still-closed umbrella, and, at the same fraction of an instant, she saw the brilliant eyes of the runner about to throw herself onto her. There was only a meter left for Sonia Wolguelane to go. Verena Becker made as if to move to avoid the collision, a dancer's leap; she tore herself from the water with a cry that the din of the storm swallowed up.

Now she had lost her balance. While Sonia Wolguelane passed

by her without touching her, she started to slide sideways. She tried to grab on to an invisible wall, to imaginary helping hands.

Her bag from the shoe store flew behind her.

May Chow, Shoes Co.

And so, she slid, almost slowly, toward the rails, toward the monstrous front of the tram, the metallic shield, the couplings. She threw out an arm to protect herself, then was sucked underneath.

Lightning crackled again above the avenue, immortalizing the city in a sodium flash. Everything began to shake.

The tram stopped alongside Mevlido.

Nothing more moved except Sonia Wolguelane, who was sprinting a mile away from Mevlido, with a psychotic grimace and eyes that looked full of tears. She met Mevlido's gaze and pretended not to recognize him. The rain no longer made any noise, only the splashing of the fugitive's rapid feet could be heard. The spray she kicked up didn't fall back to earth.

Then the conductor and a militiaman who had been among the passengers jumped out of the car, ran toward the end of the train, and everything took on a normal rhythm.

The rain once more furiously showered down over everything.

The thunder echoed from facade to facade.

The conductor and the militiaman were hurrying. They raised spray that came up to their mid-thighs and then fell back down.

Stunned, Mevlido observed what was happening under the deluge. The militiaman and the conductor ran beyond the tram, along the rails. There, in the foaming water—shining, black, in that ink whipped with rain—in the mercury, in the foam, and in the nearly nocturnal reflections of the sky, lay at present a shapeless mass, ragged, whose *shocking green* color had been darkened by water and blood. The two men reached her and froze. They did not bend over her, they stayed standing nearby, as if they wished for the rain to dissolve the horror of the spectacle. The rain dissolved nothing.

A certain distance away, up against the sidewalk, the floating plastic bag was visible.

Some centuries earlier, just after the beginning of the First Soviet Union, one of our favorite Russian novelists, Mikhaïl Bulgakov, had described the decapitation of a young man by a tram. The conductor of the car in that case was actually a conductress, she was a member of the Communist Youth, and, taking Brunnaïa Street at full speed, she treated herself nonchalantly to the decapitation of whoever fell across the rails. The head of the victim rolled across the ground elegantly. That's what it's like in fiction, but here one was in the heart of reality, and the head of the woman in green had not been prettily severed—quite the contrary. The iron wheels had mashed it ignobly after having dragged and chewed up the body. As for the conductor, it was not, as in *The Master and Margarita,* an elegant worker en route to the radiant future. It was a man of about fifty, and, if he had ever had any sympathy with the Komsomols, he hadn't bragged about it for a very, very, very long time.

13

The storm went on.

Mevlido did not mix with the gawkers who, before the arrival of the militia, came to tremble with horror near the *shocking green* corpse. He hadn't made his presence known as a witness or as a policeman. He threw his shapeless umbrella into the trash; he went back into the river that flowed between the rails; he walked under the driving rain to the place where the woman in green's purse had fallen, bent and picked it up. He searched it with enough assurance not to be noticed. He extracted a wallet, an envelope of dripping identity papers, then he put the purse back down where he had taken it from—at a distance, under the water. And then he turned his back on the scene of the accident and hesitated for two or three minutes, as if indifferent to the brutal torrent that was hammering his skull, and finally, he went into a fast-food place. He went up to sit on the upper floor.

He is now seated in a spot that benefits from a plunging view onto the avenue. He has open in front of him the wallet that he had sneaked away, he has taken out the documents, the laminated cards that he has wrapped in paper napkins without having the courage to examine closely. There is water all around him, his clothing continues to drip, his policeman's trousers and shirt. He seems shocked. He seems like a desperate man rescued after he tried to drown himself.

He leans his right shoulder against the glass.

The breath of the air conditioner makes him shiver.

He grips his hands around his second cup of boiling tea. He has goosebumps.

The room is almost empty. Two tables away from him, high school girls in uniform chatter over vocabulary homework, with moments when they bicker, when they laugh, others when they copy in silence the result of their collective cogitations. When the flashing lights of the militia began to appear, they showed a certain excitement, but, as the spectacle is blurred by the rain, they return to their exercises.

It's a calm moment. The loudspeakers of the establishment aren't playing any music. The space smells like wet socks, damp tropical sandwiches, genetically modified potatoes for the lower middle class.

Mevlido inhales a swallow of liquid through a straw and burns his tongue. The tea doesn't seem to be getting cold; Mevlido doesn't seem to be getting warm. He keeps repressing the images that are born and reborn behind his brow with damning clarity. He puts them off until later. They refuse to disappear:

- The woman in *shocking green* loses her balance between the rails turns toward the tram her umbrella not unfolded she tries in vain to escape the fall to the screaming metal to her fate she puts out a hand the metal screams.

- He checks that no one is paying attention to him he plunges his hand underwater to find Verena Becker's purse no one is watching him he moves aside the thick bubbles on the surface of the water, wondering if they are bubbles of blood.

- Sonia Wolguelane is running among the splashes a girl disguised as a proletarian leaving a demolition site a dirty jacket spots of plaster on the front on the sleeves a cap pulled down to her eyebrows she raises her face toward him their gazes cross she recognizes him he meets her black eyes drowned in rain she doesn't blink she shows nothing she goes through him mentally as if he didn't exist she doesn't slow down.

- The tram brakes, screaming strident notes it screams strident, indescribable notes; the conductor never rang his bell anyway no one heard him the brakes yes this howling yes but not the bell.

- Near the gutter floats the May Chow, Shoes Co. bag, big fat bubbles near the surface of the thick and brownish water.

- Sonia Wolguelane is panting a meter away she splashes him the water sprays up to shoulder height she passes close to him a few centimeters her face deformed by the effort the cap making her head seem strange as if underneath she were bald and already she's no longer in front of him she's not looking at him anymore she goes past him without knocking into him she gets up on the sidewalk she vanishes.

- He puts the purse back under the water after having emptied the contents he left the makeup and keys inside.
- The militiaman pushes open the doors with his elbow the doors that aren't opening fast enough he bursts out he runs toward the back of the tram he freezes he's sturdy you might say a fifty-year-old gymnast after having run the length of the rails he doesn't move he doesn't bend down he takes no initiative he doesn't do anything else the conductor joins him.
- The lightning freezes everything for a hundredth of a second.
- The rain sometimes a thousand war drums sometimes a silent image.
- The woman in green is hit by the front of the tram then brutally dragged under she is sucked under she disappears.
- As if the tram were a hovercraft when it stops it is surrounded by ripples the ripples disappear at this moment the door opens the militiaman bursts out.
- A scrap of *shocking green* cloth is still caught between two wheels.
- Big fat bubbles that the impact of the raindrops don't burst float toward a sewer drain don't burst one bigger bubble more resistant browner he wonders if it is blood.

"What does 'dolichocephalic' mean?" asks a schoolgirl in the silence.

She shows the word to the others. They examine it from every angle. It makes them laugh. They see something obscene in it, it makes them think of a phallus. Cochinea-cephalic, with a bright-red penis? Colico-cephalic, with a penis that has diarrhea? Oligo-cephalic, with an oily penis? . . . Each in turn, they invent possible meanings, then they realize that Mevlido hears their salacious teenage jokes and quiet down. They start giggling in a whisper.

Mevlido barely notices them.

He drinks his tea.

He looks outside. Militiamen in yellow raincoats are directing traffic around the site of the attack. The limousine with smashed windows hasn't moved. The victims, wounded or dead, have already been transported elsewhere. The driver spared by Sonia Wolguelane is no longer to be seen anywhere. For the first statements, the militia sent two inspectors, but for the last half hour, the number of investigators has only grown. Petro Michigan can be recognized—with his two meters of height he can be picked out of the crowd easily. The others remain anonymous behind the water. The red reflections of the flashing lights multiply on the inundated asphalt, in the borderless lake that has replaced the roadway and the sidewalk. In front of the fast-food place, several trams are motionless, one behind another. All the passengers have left the cars.

A perimeter has been established with plastic ribbon around the limousine and the tram that ran over the woman in green, and when I say the woman in green, it's so as not to have the sadness of recalling yet again that she looked like Verena Becker. The mutilated body now lies in a van that looks like a small, refrigerated truck, which is parked there waiting for other human debris to be collected. In the vast diamond whose ribbon borders shake beneath the rain, the militiamen continue to explore the tracks. They are looking for clues hidden under the water. From time to time they bend down.

Near the van the search and rescue workers take a break before going back to scrape remains of the head off the wheels. Not knowing what to do with their hands, they stare at the eddies of the gutter. The river that is running over the rails has taken everything away, blood and fragments of flesh. A little farther on, in front of the murderous tram, two policemen are talking. Bapos Vorkouta and Adar Maguistral. They have the air of seabirds. Their feet disappear under the water. Lightning crackles above them. They don't react.

Memorial Avenue, this afternoon, was marked by violence and death, but, upon reflection, no one would be able to tell in detail how the scene took place, or even what really happened. The coincidence of the event with the beginning of the storm has destroyed all possibility of objective testimony. The people present on the sidewalk had their gaze occupied elsewhere. They felt assailed by the sky's brutal fall, they ran to take shelter, they heard nothing but the din of thunder and raging water, they noticed nothing in front of them but the deafening avalanche and the lightning. It's improbable that anyone was able to see the shots on the limousine transporting the enemies of the people and, a few seconds later, the horrible decapitation of a young woman beneath the rain.

Witnesses will be few and imprecise, thinks Mevlido. And, at any rate, they won't come forward.

He finishes his tea, he collects the dead woman's documents, the case of warped leather, the plastic card holder, the wallet, he stuffs them into the bag at his belt, then he goes down to the ground floor. Next to the restroom is a pay phone. He slips a quarter dollar into the slot and dials the number of the precinct.

"Hello, Berberoïan?"

"Oh, it's you, Mevlido. How's it going?"

"Well, not great. I'm in a fast-food place. It's raining cats and dogs. There are cops all over Memorial Avenue. A terrorist has been decapitated."

Silence.

"You're on Memorial Avenue, Mevlido?"

"Yes."

"There's been a terrorist attack there, near Iyim Gardens. You're on-site?"

"Is it serious?"

"What?"

"The terrorist attack."

"Three dead. Balkachine the director of Ideology, and two ministers."

A whistle from Mevlido.

"Ministers?"

"Yes. Müller, of Fuel, and Batyrzian, from Food and Agriculture."

"And the driver?"

"Not a thing. A little rattled in his nerves, but not a scratch."

"Good. Clean work."

"We can do without your commentary, Mevlido."

"Listen, Berberoïan, I saw everything. The woman had her head crushed under a tram. She was sucked right under. They are scraping her off the rails."

Silence.

"Speak up, Mevlido, I can't hear you. Which woman?"

"The terrorist. I saw everything. She fired on the car and ran away. She fell under the tram a few seconds later. You know, she actually looked like Verena Becker."

"Verena Becker . . . ," Berberoïan repeats in neutral, pensive voice.

"I was thirty meters away," explains Mevlido. "She was running at top speed. The rain must have blinded her, deafened her, or maybe she was in an altered state, after having fired on her targets. At first, I thought the tram would pass by her without hurting her. I didn't intervene. I could have."

"You have nothing to reproach yourself for, Mevlido. Or rather, save it for next week. When you do your self-criticism."

"I could have thrown myself at her if I'd thought it out. I could have stopped her in her tracks. I didn't."

"We'll see about that when you do your self-criticism," Berberoïan promises. "You haven't forgotten, hmm, Mevlido? We'll do that next week, Tuesday or Wednesday. Late morning so that afterward we can go eat together."

Silence.

"Her resemblance to Verena Becker was uncanny," Mevlido began again. "Same look. Same size. It struck me."

His voice is trembling.

"Verena Becker," Berberoïan reflects. "I've heard that name before. An actress?"

Another silence.

"My wife," Mevlido finally says. "You know, twenty years ago . . ."

"Oh, but of course . . . I'm sorry," Berberoïan apologizes immediately. "I should have remembered, you're right. I . . . really, I'm sorry. It slipped my mind."

"Not mine, no," says Mevlido.

"Forgive me, Mevlido," says Berberoïan.

He's not a bad man. His embarrassment is visible.

"The way she looked, just like her, it sounds crazy," says Mevlido.

"Yes," says Berberoïan, "that's crazy."

Silence.

14

After the rain, Mevlido wanders along the glistening avenues.

Commissioner Berberoïan has encouraged him to go give

his testimony to Petro Michigan. He has asked him to join the team that had begun the work of investigation. His colleagues. At the moment they are looking for the murder weapon. The woman in green must have lost it just after emptying it on the ministers or right before being knocked down by the tram. They are probing holes in the pavement, the gutters. They aren't finding anything.

Berberoïan reminded Mevlido who the victims of the crime were:

- Iagor Balkachine, fifty-five years old, deputy director of the Office of Ideology, as a general had directed operations in Zone 2, pursued after the end of the hostilities for having destroyed masses of unarmed Auguani, Jucapira, and Golsh people. Amnestied, redeployed in Ideology and pharmaceutical laboratories, sudden and enormous fortune, numerous decorations, high-profile media figure, numerous works of philosophy published in his name. Over the course of several self-criticisms, he accused himself of having embezzled twenty-eight dollars from the community chest.
- Jakko Batyrzian, forty-seven years old, minister of the Food and Agriculture communities, director of the Department of Solidarity. Civilian responsible for the extermination of Zone 1, organizer of columns of child soldiers in Zone 2, suspected of having tortured 700,540 Ybürs in Zone 3—but exonerated, not bothered after the end of hostilities. Industrialist, enormous fortune, deputy director of the grain trusts in the remaining zones, numerous honorific titles, member of the Supreme Commission for the integration of refugees, high-profile administrative career. Several

times during legal self-criticism, he admitted to having cheated at poker when he was a teenager.

- Toni Müller, forty-nine years old, delegate to the Office of Fuel, policy officer during the final project of pacification of the remaining zones, initiator of the so-called *controlled genocide* practice, threatened with legal action after the disappearance of the Wongres, the Spanish, and the Myrzes, sued for not having been able to provide an explanation for the mysterious annihilation of the inhabitants of the Philippines. Amnestied. Director of the petroleum trusts in the remaining zones, billionaire, numerous books of economics published in his name, numerous honorific titles. During his last self-criticism, he admitted having constantly hidden from the masses the fact that he didn't share the household chores with his wife.

Mevlido made note of these elements, which for him were nothing new, and he promised Berberoïan that he was going straightaway to join Michigan on Memorial Avenue. Beneath the rain, which had lost all its force, he chatted for half a minute with Michigan, and, as the latter didn't seem interested by what he was telling him, he withdrew, avoiding all contact with the police team, and began to wander aimlessly.

The dead woman's name was Linda Siew.

Now he knew her name. After having talked with Berberoïan, he opened his bag and glanced at the woman in green's documents. He examined them, but very briefly, because he didn't wish to linger over the face that Verena Becker had twenty years earlier. The resemblance is actually striking. It is unbearable. Linda Siew. He didn't try to find out more. The wallet held nothing but a ten dollar bill, almost new but still very wet.

The sky has not cleared, the afternoon is still dark, and, around five o'clock, it becomes even darker. Tricked by the twilight, large bats are already soaring from one public garden to the next. The diurnal birds croak in the frangipani and fig trees, on the giant pagoda trees, the plane trees, the catalpas. They are sorry that the rain has decimated the flies, and they are croaking. The trees provide no coolness. Anyway, Mevlido is avoiding walking under the trees because of the water drops and falling guano. He wanders into the old rich neighborhoods, no longer enclosed by barbed wire fences and spikes. He walks in circles; from time to time he reaches the river's edge. In the past there were luxury residences there that enjoyed an unobstructed view of the estuary. The buildings underwent the ravages of centuries, their mirrored facades are chipped and irregular. Some units are uninhabitable and uninhabited since the ethnic cleansing of the last war. At the foot of the buildings, the water is moody, smooth and splendid. Without a ripple it runs to the ocean. Mevlido doesn't lean on the cement parapet. He doesn't daydream over the gutted shipping containers, he isn't interested in the boats made of reeds or in the comings and goings of the Lak refugees who squat in the ruins of the port facilities. The beauty of the spot does not hold him. As soon as he gets within view of the water, he turns in his tracks. He begins his wandering again; he joins the main roads radiating out from Continental Plaza. He mixes again with the crush of the crowd, because here there are many people. He inhales the smells. He receives the fragments of sentences uttered by the people as if they are coming from a great distance. Then it is evening again.

It is evening again, so he returns home to Henhouse Four.

15

And, very quickly, night falls. In the packed tram heading toward Henhouse Four, the light is even dimmer than outside. Bodies are packed together unseeing, or at least scarcely taking notice of one another. Hair smells like unhealthy feathers, clothes reek of mud. All the shoes exude wet-shoe smells—especially those of Mevlido, who is standing a meter away from me. The hours following a rainstorm always remind us with a cruel insistence that we live in a reality permeated by stench.

And that too—this pestilential reality, like the final triumph of barbarity—must be accepted without complaint.

We cross Martyr Hog Road, then Dahaliane Street. Soon we will begin to go along the wall of Henhouse Four. Soon Macadam Boulevard will begin. Everything is very dark. The streetlights have not yet been lit. We can hear the hissing of water under the wheels. Every so often the car crosses puddles that look like black ponds.

Shadows of the ruined houses loom on either side of the road, but on our right, they form a craggy dividing line, one final curtain of fallen rocks before the world of the ghetto. Our weary gazes follow it, the fissures and opacities of this rampart, and suddenly someone spots a furtive ghost.

"Hey! Look, over there!" yells an excited voice. "A child soldier!"

The passengers wiggle around and glue themselves to the windows. No one sees anything at all. The passenger who had let out the exclamation admits that he was perhaps wrong. He is sheepish, he perspires in the darkness, he flounders.

"I'm not very sure anymore," he mutters.

For my part, I continue to observe Mevlido without being distracted. I don't bother to scrutinize the darkness. Even if a child soldier has been surprised while sneaking into a collapsed house—which would be astonishing—the apparition couldn't have lasted more than half a second. Child soldiers carefully avoid revealing the places where they hide. Some manage to camouflage themselves under a borrowed identity, and they live on borrowed time among us until someone unmasks them, but the others prefer to live and roam far from our gaze, taking the most extreme caution not to be noticed.

As the brouhaha in the tram dies down, let me share with you a few words on the topic of the child soldiers:

- They've grown up, they've stopped being torturers, and they think they've turned the page on the atrocities and ethnic cleansing; sometimes they've even managed to readapt themselves to the postwar world, but on their path they meet only deserved hostility and vengeance. The monstrosity that afflicts them is irreversible. They

drag the past with them and they drag it until their
dying breath.

- Even those who didn't have to undergo their violence
directly can't stand the contact or sight of them. Or even
simply the idea that they existed and that they exist.
- The brutes who recruited and manipulated them were
already adults at the time. They were amnestied after
the war. They were recycled like other criminals into
commerce and industry, or today they occupy positions
in the senior administration. They govern the world
in the company of those that they brought to power.
These brutes are not child soldiers and don't live in the
ruins like them.
- These brutes are cut down one after the other by an
anonymous military group of which, in the depths
of the ghetto and of our memory, we approve 100
percent, always without proclaiming it openly; we approve the actions of Sonia Wolguelane 100 percent.
- (1) It's good that this elimination is taking place, even
if it restores nothing to anyone. (2) Doing justice has
no meaning, but it has to be done. (3) It is desirable
that those in charge of the racist carnage outlive the
shortest time possible the abomination that they ini-
tiated. (4) Even those with the smallest responsibility
must be unmasked and killed. (5) The child soldiers are
not priority targets, but, when the occasion presents
itself, there's no hesitation. These are the principles
according to which this military group acts.

Sometimes the sides of the tram catch low branches of fig
trees, plane trees, acacias, and drops of water spray into the car,

onto the already-soaked clothes smashes the spittle of these mutant trees, coming in from the night—onto Mevlido's left cheek, onto his neck.

Mevlido gags. He's just let himself think about these prepubescent warriors, these laughing torturers and mad killers. The spasm keeps him from developing the pictures that could come, a succession of taboo images, images showing Verena Becker fallen into the hands of girls and boys wearing rosaries made of ears and scalps on their chests. But, even if these pictures remain undeveloped, they are nevertheless there.

He lets go of the handle he's holding on to and wipes his cheek.

He's suffocating. He has to get out of the tram.

Rather than get out at Marachvili Gateway, he chooses Leonor Iquitos Station.

No one else gets off the tram with him besides me, and I don't count.

The vehicle lets us out and moves on into the distance.

The air around us is hot and very humid. The place seems deserted, and, if you don't count a lamp on the facade of a little wooden shack standing in the middle of the ruins, there is no lighting. Just after the mass of rocks, Henhouse Four begins. Leonor Iquitos Gateway is nothing more than an alley between some collapsed houses. Scarcely a hundred meters separate the gateway from the tram stop, and halfway there is that shack. No light is shining onto the street. Like everywhere in Henhouse Four at this hour, you can hear conversations of animals taking possession of the shadows: cackling, bats' high-pitched cries, croaking.

The lamp is projecting yellow stripes onto the tram platform. Besides that, in the surrounding darkness, there are no signs of life.

Mevlido remains still, he waits for the asphyxiating hideousness of the memories to dissipate. Revolting scraps still rise to the surface of his consciousness. The laughter of the child soldiers.

The masks they wear. Their way of squabbling while they torture. Their filth. The nauseating grime that encrusted their knives.

At the end of a long minute, the nightmare fades. So he begins to walk toward the lamp. The ground is potholed, with plastery puddles turned anthracite gray by the darkness. He avoids these puddles. He takes about fifty steps, stops in front of the hut. A man there has a telephone business. The little house has only one opening through which the customer and shopkeeper do business. The man is sitting behind the plank that serves as a counter, half hidden by a hanging slate that proclaims

- Alban Glück's Place
- Last telephonic station before Henhouse Four
- Communication with faraway speakers
- Night service
- Sending and receiving in all languages and all dialects

"Can I make a telephone call?" asks Mevlido.

"Do you have a dollar?" grumbles the shopkeeper.

He's a thin man, Alban Glück. Thin and ageless. Bent, an uncombed balding head punctuated with miniscule dirty tufts. Little watery eyes, surrounded at the center of his cheeks by coarse-grained skin. His whole appearance is that of a vulture.

"Here," says Mevlido.

The other man picks up the dollar and throws it into a metal box, then gets up. He agitates his narrow, vulturelike shoulders and starts rummaging around in the shadows. Mevlido sees him walking around a massive machine the size of a cement mixer. He pulls down a lever, he pulls it up, he pulls it down a second time. He doesn't insist.

"It runs on lunar energy," he says. "You have to wait until the moon rises."

"I don't have the time," says Mevlido. "Can't you plug it into a battery?"

"I can," says Glück, "but that will cost you another dollar."

"Now you're taking advantage," protests Mevlido.

"Of what?" asks Glück. "What am I taking advantage of?"

Mevlido puts another coin down on the counter. The vulture takes possession of it with an angry gesture. He goes back to his equipment grumbling. He proceeds with an elementary connection. Then he holds out an old country telephone to Mevlido, like those that existed during the war to communicate from the trenches—during one of the wars; it's not too clear which one.

After half a minute, a voice crackles in the earpiece.

"Berberoïan?" asks Mevlido.

"Ah, it's you, Mevlido? Michigan told me that you checked in with him on Memorial Avenue but that after that you were nowhere to be found. Where have you hidden yourself? We need witnesses of the terrorist attack. I believe you're the only one. You should have stayed at Iyim Gardens to help the team."

"I didn't have time. I'm leading the investigation on my side."

"Have you identified the woman?"

"What woman?"

"The terrorist. The one crushed by the tram."

"No. But I think I have a clue."

"From Henhouse Four, eh? Is it related to the Bolsheviks from Henhouse Four? The old women?"

"No. I have my eye on them. We can leave them out of the picture. If they had planned something, I would have known. I would have told you."

"Look around in that crowd anyway, Mevlido. Go to all their meetings and listen well."

"It's useless," objects Mevlido.

"You never know," insists Berberoïan.

"And the weapon?" Mevlido enquires.

"What weapon?"

"The pistol that killed Balkachine and the ministers."

"Vorkouta and Maguistral went over the crime scene with a fine-toothed comb. There was a lot of water. They had a lot of trouble. They didn't find anything."

"Someone must have picked it up and kept it."

"Yes. Otherwise, I wonder where it could be."

"And the bullets?"

"According to the preliminary analyses, they come from a police arsenal. But that doesn't mean anything. Any cop could have sold them or given them to anyone in the course of the last ten years."

Silence.

"We have to identify that woman," says Berberoïan.

"Who?" asks Mevlido. "What woman?"

Silence. Berberoïan clears his throat.

"That woman, under the tram," says the commissioner. "The killer in the green dress. She was in a horrible state, it seems. The top of her body was ripped off. Her head seems to have been completely crushed."

"I know. I saw it. I could have stopped it."

"Stopped what?"

"I don't know. It could have ended differently."

"You don't have to feel responsible, Mevlido, I already told you. Every day there are women who fall under trams. Some of them have just committed an act of terrorism, others haven't. The police can't do anything about it. Forget it."

"I should have intervened," sighs Mevlido.

"Intervened how? She would have taken you out; she surely still had bullets in her clip."

They meditate for two seconds, each for different reasons.

"She looked like Verena Becker," says Mevlido. "She was crossing the tracks, blinded by the rain. The tram was coming at full speed. She threw herself under it."

"A kamikaze. We're dealing with a kamikaze, Mevlido. She chose her fate. Once the ministers turned into sieves, her life had no meaning, and she threw herself under the wheels."

Silence.

"You wouldn't happen to have a photo of her?" the commissioner continues. "That would help us in our investigation."

"A photo of whom?"

"Your wife. Verena Becker."

Silence.

"Why are you asking me for that?" says Mevlido. "I don't see the connection."

"Because you said she looked like her," explains Berberoïan.

"She looked like whom?" murmurs Mevlido. "Who looked like whom?"

Silence.

"Forget it, it doesn't matter," Berberoïan finally says. "It could have been useful to us, but it doesn't matter. I merely ask because the wheels went over her face. Over the terrorist's face. That's going to slow down the identification process."

"I didn't keep any photos of Verena Becker," Mevlido announces in a flat tone.

"OK," says Berberoïan, "forget it, Mevlido. I shouldn't even have brought it up."

"I prefer to keep the pictures of her in my head," insists Mevlido.

"You're right, Mevlido. It's . . ."

"That way I can avoid looking at them," continued Mevlido.

"But yes, of course. Forget I asked, Mevlido. We'll figure out how to identify the victim in some other way."

"What victim?"

"The kamikaze in the green dress. We'll interrogate her cadaver. We'll end up knowing where she comes from, who she is. And you, on your end, make inquiries, but . . . stay centered on your main mission."

"Which is?"

"Your mission in Henhouse Four, of course. Spying on the Bolsheviks and company. Infiltrating the organizations of beggars. Listening to rumors."

"Sometimes I think it's an idiotic mission," grumbles Mevlido. "Those old women are harmless. They're crazy. The slogans they yell are meaningless."

Berberoïan shakes his head on the other end of the line.

"Who knows what they're capable of, under their guise of wizened witches. It's not a glorious mission, the future of the world doesn't depend on it, but I'm counting on you to see it through."

Silence. No one is shaking his head anymore. If they hear anything, it's the noise of the magnetic current along the wires.

"I'm telling you solemnly," continues Berberoïan. "I'm counting on you."

Mevlido lets out a breath.

"It's an idiotic mission," he says.

"No, it's not," Berberoïan pushes back.

His sincerity doesn't sound very genuine, maybe because of a distortion of the sound.

They say goodbye. Mevlido hangs up.

Alban Glück retrieves the receiver. He wipes it with a rag, as if Mevlido had been spitting disgusting germs onto it.

"I recorded the conversation," he says. "Just following the police's orders. For a dollar, I can erase it."

Mevlido shrugs his shoulders.

Beyond the yellow rays projected by the shop's lamp, the

location is dark, desolate, formed by piles of rubble and by walls. It's difficult to believe oneself to be in the real world. The shop itself seems to have emerged from a dream.

"Or even for half a dollar," bargains Glück.

He's a vulture with a human face. That is to say, that's how great his ugliness is. He has placed his forearm or a bit of wing on a protuberance of the lunar energy machine. Mevlido has hung up, but something can still be heard turning and humming, probably the spools of a tape recorder.

Mevlido looks at the shopkeeper, barely visible in his den. He feels like killing him, but he doesn't do it. He gives him a half-dollar and leaves.

16

Then he returns.

"You want something else?" asks Glück, the vulture Glück.

Mevlido puts a coin on the plank that serves as a counter.

"The moon is up," he says. "You can cut the battery."

Unwillingly, the thin man leans on his counter and stretches half his carcass to look at the sky. The bulb attached under the roof makes him blink his eyes. Above the ruins, the clouds look like thick smoke, but, behind the mist and the folds of dark blue velvet, they can see a milky presence. The moon is up. It's undeniable.

"OK," creaks the vulture, pulling his half-bald head down between his shoulders in a somewhat human fashion, then sticking it out. "You put down another dollar, and we'll get going."

"Are you kidding, Glück?" Mevlido is outraged.

"I'm giving you the night rates," says the vulture. "Two dollars per call."

"That's theft," says Mevlido.

"No one is making you talk at night," replies Alban Glück.

Mevlido takes a second coin out of his pocket.

"And the recording for the police?" he asks.

"I'll erase it for you for free," the shopkeeper softens.

"I wonder why that is," murmurs Mevlido.

"Glück's Telephonic does that for our good customers," explains the vulture.

Then he sits down on a stool half a meter from the telephone, looking at the ceiling with a feigned air of indifference, but showing by his whole posture that he's ready to spy on the conversation.

Then Mevlido dials the psychiatrist's number.

"Hello? Dr. Yeung?"

"Yes?"

"This is Mevlido."

"Ah, Mevlido. I'm happy to hear from you."

Silence.

"So, we're seeing each other tomorrow, right?"

"I'd like to see you right away, Maggie. I can call you Maggie?"

"If you want."

"This afternoon, after our session, a woman died because of me."

Hesitation on both sides. Silence on both sides.

"I'm listening, Mevlido."

"She died very quickly. I could have spoken to her, but I . . . She was decapitated."

Silence. Each of them is seeing images dominated by the ripping apart of bodies, violence, and blood, but these images make up fundamentally different cinematic sequences. The scenarios have nothing in common, nor do the gestures that Mevlido is making in them. Maggie Yeung sees Mevlido holding a knife or a saber.

"Wait, Mevlido. But why . . . ?"

"Excuse me?"

"But what came over you, Mevlido? Why did you . . . ?"

A pause. The sentence remains suspended.

"It was raining," Mevlido tells her. "It was the start of the storm. You couldn't see ten meters away. The tram was going full speed. She disappeared under it."

"Oh, I prefer that. That's better."

"Excuse me?"

"No, nothing, I thought that . . . I thought it was you who . . ."

Maggie Yeung gets a hold of herself again. She lightens the voice that emotion had made hoarse and regains her professional tone.

"And this woman, you knew her?" she asks.

"No."

"You told me a minute ago that you could have spoken to her."

"She passed by me. Yes, I could have spoken to her. But she died."

"She maybe reminded you of someone?" suggests the psychiatrist.

Mevlido lets a second go by.

"No. Absolutely not," he tells her. "I don't know who she could have reminded me of. She passed me and then I randomly looked in her direction at the moment she was crossing the rails. She was trying to open an umbrella. She was alone."

"You told me she died because of you."

Mevlido inhales abruptly. Sobs swell up and suffocate him, in an irrepressible spasm of his imagination.

"It's my presence that accelerated everything," he breathes. "Often, all it takes is for me to be present for people to die in a horrible way."

Silence. The psychiatrist is listening.

"It's enough that I'm present, yes," continues Mevlido, "or absent. It's enough that . . ."

Silence.

"Continue, Mevlido."

Silence.

"I feel like I'm going mad, Maggie."

"But of course you're not. It's just a feeling. It will pass."

"I can call you Maggie, right?"

"If you want."

"I can't hear you. Can you hear me?"

No answer.

"You hear me, Maggie?"

Mevlido moans into the phone. He turns toward Alban Glück and interrogates him with a look, showing him the earpiece.

"It's not working," he says.

Alban Glück walks the tip of his wing over his coarse-skinned face and pushes his stool back noisily. He gets up and takes the telephone. He puts it to his ear.

"Hello? Maggie?" he says shamelessly.

Mevlido clenches his jaw.

"She's not answering," says the vulture. "It's the moon. The clouds. There was an interruption."

"Will the connection come back?" asks Mevlido.

Alban Glück grimaces doubtfully. He stretches out his neck, his featherless neck. He has begun speaking into the nonfunctioning receiver again.

"Hello? Can you hear me?" he screeches. "Maggie, can you hear me?"

Then he turns toward Mevlido.

"Can I call her Maggie?" he asks.

17

As Mevlido walked along the rails, the moon remained hidden, then revealed itself a few seconds later, and, just as he was going to pass through the Marachvili Gateway, it enveloped him in a strong, vibrant white light. A spider crossed his path and disappeared into a crack, two isolated gulls dragged themselves heavily up onto a pile of rocks and followed him with their eyes at the exact moment he was walking by at their level. Not wishing to lose his way in the uninhabited labyrinth accessible through Leonor Iquitos Gateway, he had preferred to return to his neighborhood by following the rails along Macadam Boulevard, with, on his right, the dark piles and, behind him, soon invisible in the distance, the telephone shop and its vulture, Glück.

The moon had taken on its dimensions of the hot season, where it knew no other phase than plenitude and occupied a good third of what we call the celestial vault in an imperial fashion. As soon as it had torn the curtain of black mist that had previously kept it hidden, the moon began to shine with no softness or restraint. In an instant the lunar light flooded our spirits with its mercury and its ribbons of lead gray, of pewter gray, of silver gray, pearl gray. As on every other evening, this light seemed to transform the ghetto into a dreamlike netherworld. Instead of thinking of the class struggle and of actions meant to punish the fortunate and powerful of this world, here we were again, preoccupied by our somnambulism, by our tentative wandering through Henhouse Four, and by our survival from second to second. Then, like every evening, we were possessed by a great mental confusion: it was impossible to say what part of reality we had gotten ourselves into—a nightmare or just the horribly banal corridor of life we must walk end to end if we wish to reach death. From time to time, giant tropical bats would fly across the moon's immense surface in groups of four or five. I wasn't the only one who saw in them a hallucinatory resemblance to winged dinosaurs, pterodactyls, pteranodons, etc., you understand. We didn't even know which geological era we belonged to, from the secondary to the end of the quaternary, or after the genocides in Zone 2.

Mevlido left Marachvili Gateway and slowed his pace, because he had entered a territory that the moon was ignoring. The vivid light struck buildings forming a barrier that kept it from penetrating further, and, as if seeking revenge, it managed to leave abnormal shadows across certain passages. Mevlido advanced, taking precautions not to crush gulls or beggars. He passed us without seeing us.

After a curve, the street became a canyon in which the already-dense shadows became increasingly harsh and oppressive. On the sidewalk where Mevlido walked, nothing could be seen. The mutant poultry clucked in front of him, swerving at the last second, beating their wings in anger. He could smell the nauseating odor of their feathers soaked with sweat. Often his calves felt a peck. He didn't respond to these attacks.

It was a night like any other: overwhelming and cloying.

Next, he was traversing Rainbow Street. On the other side of the block of houses, a procession had formed. The protesters weren't walking yet. They were doing vocal warmups. There must have been four or five.

COUNT THE SOLDIERS RAG BY RAG!
COUNT THE SOLDIERS MOB TO MOB!
COUNT THE SOLDIERS ONE TO ZERO!

"Isn't this beautiful, do you hear it?" a breath next to Mevlido whispered, almost against Mevlido's shoulder.

Sonia Wolguelane's breath.

Mevlido froze.

"I didn't see you in the dark," he said.

He put out his hand and brushed the young woman's face. Physical contact between them was rare. His fingers had settled on the roots of her hair. He felt the curls, the imperceptible rasp of down under his ring finger. They were very close together, and the night brought them closer still. He moved to caress her forehead and her ear, but then he withdrew his arm for fear that Sonia Wolguelane might perceive his emotion, his laughable old-man emotion, or that she might be repelled by the dampness of his skin.

"Yes, it's beautiful," he said.

"It's dreamy," she said.

They listened to the slogans that pierced the darkness from the neighboring street. The birds were disturbed by the stridency of the Bolshevism, and they answered by cackling.

INTERPRET THE SCREAMS!

IMAGINE THE ENEMY!

ENTER THE FOREIGN IMAGE!

TRANSFORM YOURSELF IN A FOREIGN IMAGE!

SLEEP, DON'T FORGET YOUR FOREIGN IMAGE!

They crossed the intersection and turned into Old Street. The noise subsided a little. The roadway was once more bathed in the moon's rays. Upon this light, that of the streetlamps was superimposed. Birds abounded on the sidewalks. All of them had monstrous shapes and proportions.

Sonia Wolguelane was going in the same direction as he was.

"You're going to Factory Street?" she asked.

"Well, yes. I'm going home. Maleeya is waiting for me."

"By the way, were you on Memorial Avenue today?"

"When?"

"This afternoon. I have the impression that I saw you."

"Yeah? You saw me there?"

"Yes, I think so."

"When?"

"Just before the storm broke."

"Well, I was on Memorial Avenue, near Iyim Garden West."

"And so you saw me?"

"I was walking. I had to buy some clothes."

"You could have let me know. We could have walked together."

"You were too far away. And then it began to rain on the people who were running in every direction. And what were you doing?"

"Me what?"

"What were you doing at Iyim Gardens?"

"Nothing. I was looking for a fast-food place. I was hungry."

They crossed another intersection. Sonia Wolguelane was sporting the same jacket that had given her the appearance of an androgynous proletarian during the attack, but she no longer had her cap, and her hair was loose, with half-long locks and very dark and shiny little curls that contrasted with the slightly brassy hue of the down that covered her cheeks. The pistol shots and the frantic race beneath the rain had left no trace on her face. Doubtless she had been able to rest and wash up in one of the hiding places put at her disposal on the days of the assassinations by the organizations whose plans or name we were few to know. In any case, in this third-rate clothing, she was pretty again, a real knockout. Mevlido began a nostalgic sigh. Her curls, in particular, troubled him. They awoke within him a desire to plunge his fingers into them; he would have liked to softly grab those curls as he often did in a dream, to pull the young woman's head against him. Whisper her name, Sonia, Sonia Wolguelane. Reach out his arms, pull her toward him, hold her, seek her lips, kiss her. Melt into her lovingly. Forget himself in her.

All of that was present in his sigh, melting together lovingly, forgetting themselves, but, this evening, his imagination wasn't working very well. He was too disturbed. He had accumulated too many tensions, too many lies. He needed to free himself from them.

"On Memorial Avenue, I saw a woman who looked just like Verena Becker," he confessed suddenly.

"Verena Becker, your first wife?"

"Yes."

"She looked like her?"

"It was uncanny. Same appearance, same look. She was wearing a *shocking green* dress. She was walking like a dancer, with flexibility, with elegance. She smelled like bitter almond. She passed right by me."

"And then?"

The moon had begun its fight with the clouds again. It shone less. They slowed their pace. On this part of the street, most of the streetlights were out.

"Then nothing," said Mevlido.

"What do you mean, nothing?"

"Not much. I followed her."

"And then what? After that, what? Did you try to catch up to her?"

"No. It started to pour."

"And then?"

"She disappeared."

"It was during the storm?"

"Yes, right at the beginning. Near Iyim Garden West. She disappeared."

They had arrived on Factory Street, in front of Mevlido's house. Under the streetlight, the light was enough for each to make out the other person, and, farther along, the shadows and the moon invaded everything.

They separated.

Mevlido watched her grow more distant in the night, slight, dimly lit; but it was taking time for her to turn back into an androgynous and anonymous creature. She could have been his daughter leaving for a clandestine meeting, she could have been his regular mistress, just leaving him after a tryst, or the furtive lover of a single sordid occasion, or, why not, a single but not sordid occasion—touching, unforgettable—she could have been a political murderer unaware of the presence of the police at her back, about to be killed by the police, she could have been a junkie who hadn't yet succumbed to the last injection, going to look for a dose, zigzagging between the turkeys and chickens and degenerate gulls, she could have been the reincarnation of a red proletarian from some proletarian society of bygone times, the reincarnation of an unusual red guard, without the braids that go with that uniform. She was ravishing.

"Sonia!" he cried out, while she was still within earshot.

She stopped, turned her head to look back, and, when she had seen that he was walking toward her, she turned and then leaned her back against the closest wall. She was now enfolded in shadow, but the moon illuminated the building across the street. The picture was violently pale in places. In the middle of the street, two bodies lay curled up on the asphalt as if bound together by interlacing rags and garbage. They had attracted large birds: toucan buzzards, phosphorescent gulls, hunchbacked snowy owl–guinea hen hybrids, fattened chickens. I'm naming them at random. They were essentially scavengers. They glided low over the sidewalks, landing near the cadavers, quarreling, jumping a few meters farther without spreading their wings completely. They paid no attention to the human shapes that appeared near them. Some were the size of a dog. Mevlido made a detour to avoid them and reached the spot where Sonia Wolguelane was waiting for him.

He was now two steps from her. Her eyebrows raised, she surveyed him with a slightly inquisitive look. He quickly lost his composure. He had called out to her for no reason. He urgently had to invent a pretext so as not to confess that his shout had been a simple expression of want, of animal sadness at having to leave her.

"I forgot to tell you," he began, clearing his throat.

She watched him without smiling. Her captivating face registered sudden fatigue. Then she detached herself from the wall with a very feminine movement, an involuntarily voluptuous undulation that clashed with her clothes, which seemed to have just worked a shift at the factory. Her shoulders stretched and then returned to their place; under her too-long jacket you could make out her body, her bust, her hips. No one could have resisted wanting to fold her in their arms. Mevlido met the sparkle of her dark amber irises, practically black, and he couldn't bear her gaze. He had to fight against himself not to close the distance between them, not to pull her to him, caressing the nape of her neck, her back, not to begin to breathe who knows what idiotic words of affection into her ear.

"Suppose you need a guy . . . ," he babbled.

"Cut the bullshit, Mevlido," she sighed, disappointed.

"Wait . . . no. I meant . . . a guy who knows how to use a gun."

"Why do you say that?"

"A guy for your organization," he said more boldly.

"What organization?" she asked.

She tossed her head with a slight frown.

I could eliminate the distance between us, he thought. I could eliminate it. But not the age difference. Even if she didn't push me away, the scene would be ridiculous and embarrassing. Try as he might, he couldn't manage to really look at her directly. Respect proletarian morality, he thought. Don't impose on women comrades with your own disastrous male instincts. Don't impose on women comrades with demands dating from bygone geological eras. Don't breach proletarian morality for any reason. Stand firm on your class positions. He turned his head slightly, as if he were interested by what was happening a few meters away, in the direction of the corpses and the birds. The toucan buzzards screamed, they were claiming their priority in the pecking order for the eye sockets of the cadavers at threatening the less-noble birds, the deformed poultry.

"Whatever," he said, "your organization or another. The name and the agenda aren't important."

She scrutinized him strangely, then the strangeness in her eyes vanished. Two or three seconds went by without words.

"I'm maybe not a world-class shot," Mevlido continued, "but I can make guarantees. And I know how to fight in close quarters. I learned hand-to-hand a long time ago, but it's stayed with me. So, if you need an accomplice. If a target presents itself."

"What target?" she asked.

He had the impression that she was holding her lips out as if expecting a kiss, and immediately he reasoned with himself. Get a hold of your wits, he thought. Her lips aren't waiting for yours. You're projecting your fantasies onto her. She's not expecting anything. It's her natural way of moving her mouth, or it's because of the questions you're asking. The questions that you're asking are disturbing her, making her pout.

"You know," he said.

A new silence came between them. The birds were surrounding them, fighting, pushing and shoving each other on the stomachs and faces of the corpses, less than ten meters away, agitating their tousled, deplumed, very ugly wings. Some of the losers hopped up and down out of the way; others came back belligerently, only to get pecked by the strongest ones. All of them exhaled the smell of wet down feathers, feverish selfishness, and shit.

She began to laugh noiselessly, then she reached out her hand and brought it up to Mevlido's head. She touched his right cheek at the height of his ear. It was an affectionate, fraternal gesture. In it there was no sexual overture. Mevlido moaned an indistinct soft sound. He would have liked to have seemed relaxed, to show that he was receiving her caress as a comrade, but he only managed to clench his jaw, and his whole body was on alert, like before a fight. She felt it and immediately pulled her hand back.

"Sometimes I wonder if you're not insane, my Mevlido," she said.

"Bah," he breathed, "insane. Who isn't."

"I mean, deeply insane," she said, "with a dark insanity. Like the old women. A dark and incurable insanity."

"I've started seeing a psychiatrist," he said. "The police psychiatrist says I'll get through it."

Sonia Wolguelane shrugged.

"We all get through it," she said.

She made a fatalistic sign with her hand. She gestured toward the moon above the roofs, the enormous moon, and already her arm was falling back to her side.

Who knows why, the birds seemed to have obeyed her suggestion to raise their heads toward the sky. They seemed to have ended their disputes, and, beaks full of food or open, they looked at the star with its outsized diameter that transformed the night into a dream. They had golden eyes, often shot through with yellow or red. Three clouds had begun to shade the gigantic surface, but what remained uncovered was still considerable. For several seconds the scene was motionless. Mevlido, Sonia Wolguelane, and the birds seemed under a witch's spell of petrification. Then everything came back to order, that is to say, to the brouhaha and usual nocturnal chaos.

She has a tattoo, thought Mevlido. She's the last of the last generation. And then, no one will take over from her. She has a tattoo, her skin is covered with extremely fine down, she has a maddening gaze, everyone is in love with her, the Bolsheviks pardon her anarchist tendencies, she shrugs her shoulders in an enchanting way. She is the last one, and then, me, I'll be dead.

18

No lamp was lit in the apartment, but the moon and the streetlights were helping. Mevlido didn't even bother to flip the light switch.

The instant he closed the door, a film of damp shadow fell over his face. Drops of sweat immediately started to roll down his skin under his shirt. His legs were damp as well, his arms.

"Maleeya," he said in a worn-out voice, "I'm here."

Maleeya Bayarlag was sitting on the edge of the bed, wearing only a sort of white T-shirt and underpants of the same color. She didn't smell like bitter almonds. She smelled like night, sleep drenched in sweat, madness, hopeless flesh. She wasn't sleeping. Her gaze empty, hands on her bare thighs, she noisily breathed in the mist that floated inside the apartment.

"Do you want to drink a little water?" he offered.

She continued to breathe heavily.

He stayed next to her for a minute, waiting for her answer, then kissed her forehead and went back to the main room.

He sat down at the table.

He had unhooked his bag from his belt. He now extracted from it the woman in green's identification papers. He spread them out in front of him, remnants of existence that had dried in the wrong position and now smelled of the sewer. A moment passed. The investigation has to begin, he thought. Then he swallowed a large gulp of hot air and decided.

The investigation began.

He was already leaning over the documents, picking out those that were still decipherable; then he sat back up and examined one after another in the trickle of light that came from outside. The shadows didn't allow him to see the photographs clearly. He was thus able to avoid the painful confrontation with the dead woman's face. He concentrated on what might still be gleaned from her personal information: name, date and place of birth, home address, military status, juridical and ideological status, sector of employment in the case of ethnic conflict, professional activity, expiration date of her visa. Not all the columns were filled out; the water had blurred most of the others.

- Linda Siew was born twenty-nine years earlier.
- She lived on Waddell Street.
- She was a singer, with curious specifications, according to the notes written here and there. On a permit, she was a *songso singer*; on her employment certificate, the officer in charge had written *may also perform the gut, sing and dance the uga.*
- According to the offices that had registered her, she must have arrived in Oulang-Oulane with the Iyim refugees and the Korean and Chinese survivors.
- Neither her visa nor her military status was in order.

Mevlido set the papers back on the table. He sat several minutes without bending over them. He watched the darkness through his closed eyelids and tried to bring together several ideas. Hunches. Often an investigation started like this, with hunches. He kept his mind open, then, as nothing took shape, broke the silence.

"Maleeya, can you hear me?" he asked in a low voice.

In the adjoining bedroom, Maleeya didn't react.

"Berberoïan put me in charge of an investigation," announced Mevlido. "An investigation into a woman. Linda Siew. A singer. She sang *songso*."

Maleeya didn't answer. Mevlido imagined her, on the other side of the dividing wall, suffocating next to the spiders, damp, legs bare to the hips, worn out by her own madness, shut up in her amnesia and her memories.

He was sure, however, that she could hear him.

"*Songso*, does that mean anything to you?"

No answer.

"She could also sing the *uga*. She was barely thirty years old. She was decapitated today on Memorial Avenue. She was blinded by the rain. Decapitated and crushed. She didn't suffer."

He spoke slowly. He had raised his voice a bit so that Maleeya could participate in his monologue.

On the other side of the wall, Maleeya inhaled and exhaled regularly.

"And the *uga*, do you know what that sounds like?"

There was silence again, and outside, without warning, all the streetlights went out. The outage had hit several sectors. A few lamps gleamed beyond the rooftops, very far away. In Factory Street, the abrupt intensification of the shadows hadn't provoked any particular reaction. As always, a basso continuo could be heard, made of cries, flapping wings, collisions, falls, breaks, with, above all that, human voices going back and forth. Everywhere in Henhouse Four, residents of all species continued to grumble or be silent in small groups. Over by the restaurants, the clatter of dishes had not stopped.

Someone had lit a candle in a house near the intersection.

The flame illuminated nothing.

The moon was now hiding. The stars had given up, the mountains of tarry vapor gathered together in the middle of the sky.

A revolting damp sensation invaded Mevlido's lungs. The oxygen was too full of water to bring with it any freshness.

He returned to his seat. He had to open his mouth to catch any vital gas. Drops of sweat trickled down his forehead, under his shirt.

"It's going to rain," he murmured.

He let a minute pass, maybe two.

"She was staying on Waddell Street," he continued.

Maleeya Bayarlag was still breathing heavily on the other side of the wall. She gave no other sign of life or intelligence.

"I wonder where that is, Waddell Street," remarked Mevlido.

"Yasar," said Maleeya.

Behind the dividing wall, she was suddenly coming out of her lethargy. Two trailing syllables.

"Yes?" said Mevlido.

He had thought she was calling him, giving him, as she often did, the name of her murdered husband.

"Bayarlag. Yasar Bayarlag," said Maleeya.

"Yes," Mevlido encouraged her, "I'm here."

"Waddell Street. Near the border. In the Shambles."

Mevlido got up. He went into the bedroom. Now, without the light from the street and after the disappearance of the moon, it was very dark.

He sat down next to her, on the bed. The springs creaked. All around him, the panic of the spiders must be at its height.

"It's in the Shambles?" he asked.

"Near the border. You're in the Shambles. You're looking for Yasar in the Shambles, by looking you come to Waddell Street."

Maleeya slowed her speech, then interrupted herself. She gave the impression of wanting to continue but of not having the strength to do so. Mevlido encouraged her.

"Waddell Street," he said.

"Farther on, it's the border," continued Maleeya. "You can't breathe. You cough. Then you find Yasar Bayarlag. You find him. Yasar Bayarlag."

Mevlido put his right hand on Maleeya's knee. Their flesh was feverish and sticky with sweat.

Maybe a Waddell Street that Maleeya knows exists over there, he thought, but Linda Siew couldn't have lived in the Shambles before her death. No one could stay for a long time in the Shambles before they died. It's impossible.

Or Linda Siew was there visiting, like Maleeya.

"And Linda Siew?" he asked.

Maleeya hesitated.

The silence in the bedroom grew.

It was much too hot.

"A woman, a Ybür or a Korean. She sang," continued Mevlido.

"Yasar," said Maleeya, "he's there, at the border. One day he calls. He asks me to go meet him on Waddell Street. I go there, I meet him. We hold hands. We walk together in the Shambles. We're together. Sometimes we go into a house. There are people. A singer. She lives downstairs or next door. She sings magical songs. She sings the *uga*. We are together in a room with Yasar. We make love. I don't like to make love, but, with Yasar, I like it. From time to time, we leave the house. We walk down Waddell Street. We hold hands and walk down the street. Waddell Street smells like charcoal. It's like that everywhere near the frontier. A very strong smell. It stings your lungs. We cough. We come back to the house. The singer sings the *uga*. While she sings, Yasar and I make love. I don't like to make love, but with Yasar it disgusts me less. Everywhere the smell of charcoal is in the air. Then you get used to it. With Yasar, you get used to it."

Maleeya's voice fell to a murmur. The murmur got lower still.

"The singer. Did you see her?" Mevlido cut in.

"I don't remember," said Maleeya.

"I remember," said Mevlido. "She was thirty years old. She was beautiful. She looked like Verena Becker."

"Verena Becker?"

"Yes."

"Her body looked like hers? It was the same body?"

"Yes. She was beautiful, young. She danced as she walked. She was wearing an elegant dress, *shocking green*. She was elegant. She smelled like cleanliness, like perfume. Bitter almond. She smelled like happiness. They crushed her in front of my eyes. On Memorial Avenue."

They were both quiet for a moment.

"If she looked like Verena Becker," said Maleeya, "she isn't dead. Her name was Linda Siew?"

"Yes," said Mevlido.

"Then her name is Linda Siew as the body of Verena Becker. She lives in the Shambles with Verena Becker's body, or right nearby. She lives there near Yasar Bayarlag, on Waddell Street. She isn't dead. Or in any case, if she is dead, she's like us."

"I don't know," said Mevlido, "I'm not sure."

"You have to go there," said Maleeya. "She's your wife."

"Yes," said Mevlido.

"She is like us. She wants us to be together her and you. She asked you. She asked you to go there, to the Shambles," said Maleeya.

Mevlido raised his arms, drew Maleeya close to him. Words were lodged in his throat, but he didn't say them. He wanted to sleep or to cry against her, shoulder to shoulder, breathing hard, forgetting the spiders, the darkness, the grim present, the ongoing investigations, ongoing life.

"She is like Yasar," said Maleeya. "Sometimes he asks me to join him. I go there, to his house. We listen to the songs. There is someone who sings the *uga*. We listen, each individually. Then we are together. We make love. Even with him I don't like it so much, but we do it."

In the street, it had begun to rain. The rain fell straight down, with force. At first its noise covered up all the other noises, then the voice of a Bolshevik could be heard. Perhaps she had taken shelter in a corridor so that her slogans would echo better, or maybe she was screaming at the top of her lungs, bareheaded and headstrong, indifferent to what fell on her from the sky.

DREAM A THOUSAND YEARS, DREAM A THOUSAND
YEARS WITHOUT BELIEVING THAT DREAMS EXIST!
WANDER A THOUSAND YEARS, WANDER WITHOUT
BELIEVING THAT SPACE EXISTS!
LOVE A THOUSAND YEARS, LOVE WITHOUT BELIEVING
THAT LOVE EXISTS!

19

Around three o'clock, Mevlido awoke with a jolt, with the certainty that he hadn't been breathing for days and days. His heart was racing. He threw himself out of bed. Maleeya Bayarlag kept sleeping. Anxiety cut his legs out from under him, and he tripped over the threshold of the main room. Air rasped in his throat. In the apartment, everything seemed calm. The power outage in the sector was over, but the bulb in the streetlight across the way had burned out, and it was dark. A bird was perched on the windowsill, with the massive silhouette of a giant owl. With its wings folded, it didn't move. One could make out its enormous black back. The rain could be heard falling—a violent rain that had begun at midnight and not stopped since.

Mevlido went to drink a glass of water in the kitchen. Only

approximate shapes were visible. He felt his way around. His hands caught a spider web that had been woven between the faucet and the piping. He tore it apart with disgust. He was naked, and on his arms he felt the threads that stuck like glue, strands of monstrous silk. He moved away, grimacing; he was afraid of trailing the occupants of the sticky trap after him, the arachnids he imagined frantically climbing up their destroyed ladders, attacking his testicles and stomach.

He left the kitchen and went to the window. Disturbed, the bird spread its wings and let itself fall out into the void. Mevlido reached the window, stretched out his head a little to follow its flight and saw nothing. In the street, the roadway had disappeared under the flowing water. Some living or equivalent bodies huddled under tarpaulins. Mevlido counted five on the sidewalk across the street. Two had taken refuge in the carcass of an automobile from which they must have ejected the probable inhabitants— monstrous gulls and chickens, or other junkies. The combat had left no trace, but, lower down, toward the alley of restaurants, near a sewer drain that no longer drained anything, the floating shapes of dead birds could be seen.

The rain pattered on Henhouse Four.

The rain hissed on all the surfaces of Henhouse Four.

The rain roared. The rain murmured witches' prayers.

The rain drummed.

Mevlido wiped away the sweat rolling down his sternum. His heart continued to beat hurriedly. He might well observe that his lungs were filling and emptying normally, his anxiety had scarcely diminished. He leaned half his torso out the window. Raindrops burst against his skull, his shoulders. He would have liked to have calmed himself down by contemplating the deluge, but his mind wandered. He began to think about Sonia Wolguelane, trying to determine in what place and position she found herself at that moment, in which clandestine hideout, miserable or not; anxious to know if she was sleeping alone, or curled up next to a man or an *Untermensch* or a woman, then he imagined that he was holding her tight and that she was burrowing into his arms, then after half a minute of erotic reverie he made himself change the subject, embarrassed to have an erection in front of an open window. Then a new anxiety pierced through him, and he remembered that he should be preparing for his self-criticism, planned for the next week at the precinct.

The rain showered Henhouse Four like bullets.

The rain made the metal roofs vibrate.

The rain crosshatched the night.

A raindrop splashed into his left eye; he took a step backward and rubbed his eyes. At the same time he became aware that the inside of the apartment smelled like a mixture of rotten sponge and urinal algae, and he wondered if these were bad smells encrusted in the house since long ago or if the stench came from his own fingers; then his sense of smell became numb once more, and he wasn't bothered. He went to the kitchen and, with a cautious gesture, made sure that the spiders had not begun patching up their webs again around the faucet. The tap whined as he opened it. He soaped his hands under the trickle of water that ran in the shower. Then he placed himself entirely in the middle of the ceramic square and washed himself head to foot, taking his time and trying to cool himself off. The water was lukewarm, not plentiful, it lapped meagerly at his feet, scarcely audible because of the din of the rain that reverberated in the apartment. It wasn't cooling him down. He closed the tap and waited a minute in the shower without drying himself, then wrapped a towel around his waist and returned to the window.

He was leaning out the window again, the drops from the sky hitting him continually on the ears, the eyes. He began to list the elements around which he could organize his self-criticism. He imagined that Commissioner Berberoïan or his colleague Maguistral was hitting him with a brick, he felt the water and sweat inundate his face, and he didn't need to make an effort to persuade himself that these liquids tasted of blood, that around his neck he had a sign declaring him a scapegoat, a fetid right-winger. His name was written backward and smeared with shit. He stammered out serious crimes, and, when they beat him, he was silent. He looked at the floor of the platform just in front of his knees. His colleagues were abusing him with moderation, but droplets of currant red had still spattered the ground around him.

He blinked his eyes and continued the list of his crimes.

He was at the window, and he murmured:

- took shelter in a fast-food place while my colleagues worked selflessly under the downpour
- profited from my authority as a police officer to obtain preferential prices at the telephonic station run by a certain Alban Glück
- exposed myself at night at the window of my apartment without wrapping a towel around my waist
- took ammunition again for myself by forcing the door of the police arsenal, then lost it again
- procured propaganda materials sold illicitly by an old woman on Memorial Avenue
- offered, by ideological and amorous indulgence, tactical support to terrorist networks whose name and agenda I don't know
- neglected to attend the meetings of Bolsheviks the surveillance of whom was entrusted to me
- rejoiced in the assassination of Iagor Balkachine, Jakko

Batyrzian, and Toni Müller, all three suppressed rightly
by a terrorist whose name and agenda I don't know

The rain intensified.

The list was already a reasonable size, but without someone to
lead the interrogation, he couldn't know whether it was finished.

Mevlido leaned on the windowsill.

He had pulled his head back in to stop being hit by raindrops.
He had stopped muttering.

The rain made the noise of gravel thrown onto an iron plaque.

The rain fell in ropes—sometimes silvery, sometimes blackish.

The rain emitted a monotonous melody.

The rain absorbed the available oxygen.

The rain was boiling.

The rain exuded the smell of hot water.

"And the recording?" said someone behind him.

It was not the voice of Maleeya Bayarlag. Mevlido turned
around all at once.

In the room where almost everything was dark, an intruder
had appeared. He was between the armoire and the chest where
Maleeya Bayarlag put the linens. He was settled there, hunchbacked, motionless, and black. There was no reason to believe that
his intentions were friendly. He had entered the apartment who
knows how, noiselessly, and now he was not coming toward Mevlido, as if, from his shadowy corner, he was up to no good.

"Do I erase it, or not?" said the shadow in an evil voice.

I should answer, thought Mevlido.

I have to come up with an answer, he thought.

An animal sound formed between his noise and his throat,
then stopped. He felt that he had all of a sudden forgotten the
basic techniques of language.

"The recording for the police," continued the intruder.

An intense physical despair unfurled onto Mevlido. The wind was knocked out of him. None of his muscles obeyed him. From his feet to his mouth, he felt transformed into a mass of inert flesh. He didn't see the individual who addressed him, but he had identified him. The vulture telephonist. His silhouette, his insolent evil. Alban Glück.

"So do I erase it, or do I send it?" rasped Glück.

Mevlido had begun to moan. For the moment it was the only way he had found to argue. Words melted away in his mouth, becoming only an inarticulate and ineffective bellow. It's not real, he suddenly thought. I am elsewhere than in reality. His fear grew. He had realized that he was dreaming, but he couldn't leave this elsewhere, nor could he chase Alban Glück out. He would have needed to pronounce some conjuring formula. But his tongue had unlearned speech and was no help to him anymore.

"Don't scream," said someone. "Don't scream, my Yasar. You're scaring me."

He had goosebumps. He felt the hand of Maleeya Bayarlag on him. A nightmare, he thought. Nothing more than one more miserable nightmare. He was lying down, he still seemed to hear the echo of the complaints by which he had expressed his violent desire to change worlds. He crawled on the mattress and went to huddle against Maleeya. His hair was still on end. Maleeya rubbed his back, then stopped. She didn't ask him to tell her what he had seen.

Their breaths mingled together and calmed each other.

The spiders on the wall were still trembling. They are like us; they hate someone moaning near their webs.

The apartment was plunged into darkness. The outage in the sector continued. No light came from the street.

Outside it wasn't raining.

The rain wasn't pattering down on Henhouse Four.

The rain wasn't showering down on the roofs like bullets.

The rain wasn't dancing, drumming on the tin roofs.

The rain wasn't showing itself.

The rain was elsewhere.

20

The next day was a Friday. Mevlido attached little importance to the date. He only knew that the week was ending and the next one would bring with it his self-criticism. Each new day brought him nearer to the torture, humiliation, and absurd litany of errors and crimes imagined or committed. He woke up with this idea in his mind, imagining the kicks, the pain of the kneeling position, the bawling of the inquisitor and the hate of the audience, but very quickly, all of that faded. Very quickly, the perspective of this horrible session became at once more banal and foggier and gave way to other horrors, and, as he got up and got ready, he was already only thinking of the death of Linda Siew, the meticulous false investigation of this woman he had promised to carry out, the hodgepodge of lies that he had already accumulated on that subject, and the painful relationship that he had established between Linda Siew and Verena Becker. Maleeya Bayarlag had already left for work, and, as he washed himself with the lukewarm water from the kitchen, he remembered the sentences that Maleeya Bayarlag had uttered during the night, and many sinister visions that put Maleeya Bayarlag in the Shambles, wandering on Waddell Street, perhaps listening to Linda Siew singing songs for the dead, coughing amid the smells of charcoal of Waddell Street, and miserably making love with Yasar Bayarlag. To make matters worse, mixed with these visions were those of a nightmare in which the vulture Glück appeared. Mevlido dried himself off, went to get a bowl of porridge for breakfast in the alley of restaurants, and left Henhouse Four. The images kept returning endlessly in his mind's eye, obsessive, with dreamlike variants that made them even more painful.

Mental illness prowls too near me, he thought. It's everywhere.

I'm losing my grip, he thought.

Soon you will be dragged down to the bottom, Mevlido, he thought.

Now he was standing in the tram that stopped in front of Continental Plaza, three hundred meters from the precinct.

You have to find something to hold on to, he thought. If you want to get through it, you have to grab on to something or someone foreign to all these bad dreams, someone really exterior to Henhouse Four.

Maggie Yeung, he thought, the psychiatrist.

He got out on Memorial Avenue before Iyim Gardens and telephoned Maggie Yeung from the shopping arcade downstairs from her office. She could see him. He went up to the fourth floor and sat down across from her. He had decided to confide some of his anxieties to her, to talk to her about Linda Siew, about Verena Becker, about the birds that poisoned his nocturnal hallucinations, and also about some dangerous certitudes that had taken root in him, leading him to confuse existence in death with existence in reality and in dreams. As he pressed the button of the elevator, he had in mind a clear and well-structured account, but as soon as he was under the ceiling fan—and perhaps because this superb woman was disposed to listen to him out of professional reasons and not friendship—he lost all confidence and desire to speak openly. He babbled banalities about the tram accident the day before, brought up the subject of his difficult nights full of bizarre comings and goings and specters. And then, in contrast to what he had planned to do, he clammed up. The words just weren't coming.

"It doesn't matter which one," she insisted. "Tell me one of your dreams, Mevlido."

The fan spun. In the office next door the mynah whistled. It hopped, rubbed its yellow beak on a bit of cage, whistled two notes. Outside, beyond the window screen, the morning clouds were contorting themselves slowly.

"An image from a dream that struck you. Start with that. With a static image. The rest will come."

She did everything she could to put Mevlido at ease. She had even put a well-meaning smile on her lips, but like in the previous sessions, like the day before, her physiognomy was too strangely beautiful, too bewitching. Again, Mevlido, troubled, watched her as if she were the reincarnation of a fox. He had the impression that he was being questioned by a supernatural creature, which counteracted his wishes to be sincere.

"Stop hesitating," the psychiatrist encouraged him. "Dive right in."

In one second, dozens of dreams rushed into Mevlido's mind. A number of them were long and well structured, sometimes rich enough to constitute real former lives, full of tragic choices, poor choices, defeats.

"I don't know how to talk about my dreams," he said, avoiding looking her in the eye. "I can't manage it."

"You don't need to tell me everything, Mevlido," said Maggie Yeung. "Even a fragment can be enough. The main thing is for you to get started. We'll figure out how to keep going afterward, the two of us together."

Mevlido shook his head, as if concentrating on his memories. In reality, he was trying to distance himself from the mass of biographical and dreamlike information that cluttered his memory, at the same time choosing the beginning of a lie that would allow him to hold up several minutes in a row in front of the psychiatrist without giving up anything personal. He thought about the women in his life, about the women whom he had lost, like Verena Becker, or whom he accompanied in their madness, like Maleeya Bayarlag, or whom he'd never had the chance to embrace until orgasm, like Sonia Wolguelane. That wasn't the area that he should explore. He had to invent a dream with fantasies. Whose elements wouldn't lead him too far astray, wouldn't push him to betray himself. At that moment, one clear image rose above the others, an inspiration that immediately seemed good to hold on to.

"The *gut* ritual," he said abruptly.

"Yes. For example," said Maggie Yeung, "the *gut* ritual. Yes."

One could detect, in her intonation, a certain caution. Korean shamanism was perhaps not totally familiar to her. The *gut*—the ceremony during which the shaman dances and sings to speak to the dead and to calm them—is not necessarily the subject matter taught in psychiatry.

And, if I can say it in passing, that's too bad. But oh well.

"The song of the *mudang* during the *gut*. The *uga*," Mevlido proposed.

He let the scene come to him, characters appear. The image gained clarity. He didn't know where it would lead him, but it seemed to him that in setting off from that point, he could tack about without risk at a safe distance from any hazard.

"Yes," the psychiatrist encouraged him, "the *uga*. Yes."

Mevlido felt the breath of the ceiling fan on the roots of his hair. He knew that his forehead was shining, that between his mouth and nose, many drops of sweat were growing. He stared at an irregular patch of plaster on the wall.

"First, it's a woman who calls," he said, "a woman on Factory Street. She has a powerful voice; you realize immediately that she is talking to the dead more than to the living. Before the ceremony she was petite, elegant, and here she is, nothing but a voice. A voice that hails the wandering dead nearby. She bends toward the earth, and for several minutes she dances with gestures I don't understand. Then she begins her call again. She sings in the language of the dead. She is dressed in a long *shocking green* dress tied high on the chest with a pale green ribbon. After a moment I hear her name being spoken. People are watching the ceremony. They are gathered in the entrance of a hallway that opens to the street. They are whispering. *Mudang*, I recall, is the Korean word for shamans. According to these people, exchanging opinions in low voices, she is an exceptional *mudang*. They say her name, they say that her name is Linda Siew. Everyone is listening to her voice calling on the dead. There are cries, tragic cries, then chants. She addresses the dead already here or to come, she addresses us. She sings beneath the rain. The person beating a drum to accompany her is invisible. We are in a very dark street. People have taken shelter in doorways; they are pressed up against each other. Linda Siew is alone beneath the rain. She sings and she dances. The cloth, even though it is soaked, doesn't stick to her body. Her voice is stronger than the noises of the falling water. The universe is transformed into an enraged waterfall, but Linda Siew's voice is stronger. There are too many people in the threshold, at the entrance of the corridor where I'm standing. I'm not in the first row, and I don't see very well. I distance myself from the group of spectators. I climb the staircase of the building to look at Linda Siew from my apartment, through the window. As I climb the stairs, I think about what Linda Siew is trying hard to accomplish outside. She would maybe want us to have a better dialogue, so that the distances between us disappear."

"Between us," says Maggie Yeung. "Between us who?"

"Between the dead," says Mevlido. "She wants a dialogue to be established. I think while I climb the stairs, but I don't come to any conclusion. At any rate, since the beginning of this dream, I feel mentally diminished. My movements obey forces I scarcely control, the thoughts and the words that I formulate don't really belong to me. Mentally diminished and a stranger to myself. Upon arriving on the fourth floor, I push open the door of my apartment. The electricity doesn't work. It's night, but there is enough light remaining to make movement possible. In the bedroom the bed is empty. I go stand at the window. I lean out to see what is happening on Factory Street. I don't see anyone. Neither the *mudang,* nor the musician who accompanies the *mudang,* nor the people who a moment ago murmured her name. The rain is falling harder. Henhouse Four seems deserted. In the building across the way a window is lighted and wide open. A curtain of rain blurs the picture. Through the opening can be heard a centuries-old ethnographic recording; in the forefront is the sound of the gramophone needle blazing a trail into the past, in the dust that clogs the record's dark grooves. The sounds are syrupy, regular, most of the time they mix with the flow of the rain. Sometimes, in the middle of that and far in the distance, you can catch the vibrations of the head of a drum. I'm not a musician, but I know enough about music to know the difference between a Tungusic or Korean rhythm. I listen with great anxiety. I have the feeling of an irreparable loss. I have the impression that this drum used to speak to me in the past but that it's much too late for its effect to be useful to me or even understandable. I close my eyes; the image of Linda Siew, who danced and sang beneath the rain a few minutes earlier, comes to mind. Now the memory of Linda Siew and the recording combine harmoniously. Linda Siew sings the *uga,* the drum gives the rhythm for the *uga.* The rain sizzles. I open my eyes to see what the night offers us. On the other side of the street, I know that a man has the habit of playing a gramophone at night. He always leaves his window wide open . . . The lamp in his place is lit . . .

The rain draws vertical striations over everything . . . But I already said that I think."

"Yes, you did," confirmed Maggie Yeung.

Between them, between the psychiatrist and her patient, a silence was born. Maybe she shouldn't have intervened.

Mevlido stared at a point on the wall. He was a bit slumped over; for a minute he was speaking without intonation as if he were hypnotized or totally disgusted with himself.

A serpent of lightning was reflected across part of the sky. Seconds later, the roll of the thunder arrived over Memorial Avenue.

"I shouldn't have interrupted you," said Maggie Yeung. "I apologize."

"I don't remember what came next," Mevlido realized.

"You were looking at a window of the house across the street," recalled Maggie Yeung. "The room was illuminated. A gramophone spat out faraway drumbeats."

"Yes," said Mevlido.

Then he was quiet.

"It was raining," said Maggie Yeung. "You told me that the rain was falling. You were listening to the music through the murmur of the rain. You were looking at the window across the street through a curtain that kept you from seeing."

"No," said Mevlido, "the rain wasn't keeping me from seeing. It blurred the image, but I could see. I saw well enough. In the apartment across the street, a woman was dancing. She wasn't moving much. She moved slowly, standing in one place. It was a ritual movement. She wasn't wearing anything that I noticed in particular. I had the feeling that it was Maleeya Bayarlag. She was wearing a T-shirt and a very loose pair of shorts. She is fifty years old; she neglects herself; she isn't all there. She sank into madness long ago. I recognized her by her way of holding herself. You know, I feel a great deal of affection for her. We are each other's support system. We're together. We're going together through what is left to be gone through. I recognized her by her slightly plump arms, her exhausted heaviness, her stomach. She no longer has the flat stomach of her youth. She was dancing the *uga*."

He paused. He must have thought he'd lied enough, muddled the story enough so that the psychiatrist doesn't have any clue that might help her reach him.

Now, he relaxed, he sat upright in his chair, his gaze came back more openly to Maggie Yeung.

"She was dancing the *uga*," he repeated.

"Wait, Mevlido," said Maggie Yeung, as if she were, more than anything else, interested in this detail. "Who was in the apartment across the way, dancing? Maleeya Bayarlag or Linda Siew?"

"I don't really know anymore," said Mevlido in a dreamy tone. "Maleeya Bayarlag or Linda Siew, I don't remember. Or someone else."

The psychiatrist moved her hands. An evident disappointment veiled the beauty of her animal-like face.

"At any rate, it was her," said Mevlido.

21

After leaving Maggie Yeung's office, Mevlido called the precinct. They told him that it was good he was calling because there was a message for him. Berberoïan was expecting him today at noon for a work meeting near the crime scene, in the fast-food restaurant across from the Iyim Garden West stop. Mevlido made a note of it and hung up without asking what crime they were talking about. He began to stroll aimlessly on Memorial Avenue, particularly investigating a covered market where the new society's wealthy furnished themselves with unpolluted food and toiletries that hadn't been tested on animals. Then, a hundred meters farther on, behind the flashy facades that hid the Iyim ghetto, he wandered among the small retailers' displays, in the shade impregnated with the smells of gas and filth. The heat of the morning was crushing. He walked slowly, saving his energy, stopping frequently in air conditioning, under ceiling fans. In a pastry shop where he stopped without buying anything, a guard insulted him and kicked him out.

It was time to go meet Berberoïan. He pushed open the door of the fast-food place and went upstairs. Besides Berberoïan, there were two inspectors there who were investigating the attack, Petro Michigan and Bapos Vorkouta. He set his tray down next to Vorkouta's. The policemen sat at the table where, the day before, he had sat like a zombie to drip dry far from death, far from the police and far from himself—far from everything.

As he took his place, he remembered the burning of the tea on his tongue the day before. Shivers were running down his legs. He had immense survivor's guilt. He had difficulty keeping the cup near his lips without dropping it. High school girls were twittering obscenities at the next table. On the glass the falling water split into a thousand moving veins and rivulets. Again, he heard the roll of thunder. Then he had a vision of the brownish bubbles resisting the endless arrows coming from the sky. Again he saw the bubbles floating, not bursting, holding up to the rain, and, once more, he wondered if they were or weren't bubbles of blood or bloody mud.

And then, abruptly, he reemerged in the present. The room in the restaurant was empty. Berberoïan was watching him with a concerned look. Outside, the heat bore down on the world. Memorial Avenue hadn't disappeared under the deluge. The leaves on the trees were dark green, bronze. The outlines of the buildings stood out as if traced in charcoal. The atmosphere was stormy, with a few raindrops, but it wasn't raining. The clouds didn't burst.

"You have any results on the terrorist's identity?" Michigan asked him immediately. "The commissioner told me you were making inquiries. Did anything come of them? Did you find anything?"

His tone was half-mocking, half-aggressive.

"And you?" counterattacked Mevlido, biting into his soy sandwich.

"We made a little headway," Berberoïan summed up. "Not much, but a little. The lab confirmed that she was a woman. Thirtyish, according to what remained of the body. The features couldn't be reconstituted. Natural black hair, that's all we know. In her purse, nothing useful for us. No papers. She had taken everything out; she didn't want us to be on her trail after her death."

"Or someone stole them before we got there," suggested Bapos Vorkouta.

"Stole what?" said Mevlido.

"Her papers," said Michigan.

"Why would someone have taken that risk?" asked Mevlido.

All four of them frowned doubtfully at the same time. The police collective reflected. Petro Michigan glanced out the window. The afternoon had started. Raindrops were falling with great irregularity, giant and sparse, promising rain soon. A lost bat, with its meter wingspan, soared across the avenue, glided heavily, and disappeared into the density of a lime tree.

"She had been shopping in a shoe store," Berberoïan began again, "but Jiang and Maguistral interrogated the salesgirl, and she doesn't remember the woman in green coming through."

"What store?" asked Mevlido.

As if against his will, Bapos Vorkouta glanced at an open notebook near his hamburger.

"May Chow," he said, "fifteen hundred meters from here, on Memorial Avenue."

"Shoes Company," said Mevlido.

"What?" Michigan made him repeat himself.

Michigan didn't hear well. He was bothered by the blowing of the air conditioning.

"May Chow, Shoes Company," enunciated Mevlido, raising his voice. "There is another, closer store with the same name."

"Closer how?" asked Berberoïan.

"In the Iyim ghetto," said Mevlido.

"You know it?" asked Michigan.

"What?" asked Mevlido.

"This store, you know it?"

"Of course, that's where I went for information."

"That one's not cataloged," grumbled Vorkouta. "It's not on our lists."

"Our files on the ghettos aren't up to date," commented Berberoïan. "We say that every time. We have to update everything."

"Jiang and Maguistral went to the wrong store," said Mevlido. "They didn't interrogate the right saleswoman."

"A shoe store in the Iyim ghetto," said Bapos Vorkouta. "That must be worse than pathetic . . . It must be more like a cobbler's shop?"

"It's tiny and in a cellar," confirmed Mevlido, "in the middle of the ruins. I had trouble finding it."

"That doesn't fit," muttered Michigan.

Mevlido was immediately on guard. There was a short silence, but, as Michigan wasn't developing his thought, Mevlido continued his own.

"The saleswoman had sold a pair of shoes to a woman with a *shocking green* dress," he said.

"We're still looking for them, by the way," remarked Berberoïan.

"What?" asked Mevlido.

"The shoes," said Berberoïan. "In my opinion, they were washed into the sewers."

"Or else, someone . . . ," began Mevlido.

"It doesn't fit," interrupted Michigan.

This time he wasn't muttering.

"What?" asked Berberoïan. "What doesn't fit?"

"The girl is planning to execute three enemies of the people, and she does her errands before heading to the scene of the crime? That doesn't bother you?"

"She maybe wanted to hide her gun in the store's bag," suggested Bapos Vorkouta. "It's more practical to transport it like that. More practical and less noticeable."

"Fair enough," said Berberoïan. "Speaking of which, I'll remind you that you are talking about a weapon that has also simply disappeared as well."

"It must have been picked up by some thug," said Vorkouta.

"One of these days, it will be used in a robbery," continued Mevlido.

"OK," said Berberoïan, "it's no good to speculate. It disappeared, it disappeared."

He turned toward Mevlido.

"And so, at May Chow's in the Iyim ghetto, did you get anything solid?"

"Yes," said Mevlido. "The woman in green said several things. For example, that she lived on Waddell Street. She was relaxed and talkative. She stayed at least a quarter of an hour in the store, trying on shoes and chatting. The saleswoman is pregnant, so they talked about several names for the baby. The woman in green said her name was Linda."

"Linda, Waddell Street," reflected Berberoïan.

"It all fits together," said Michigan.

"What fits together?" asked Vorkouta.

"Everything fits together," Michigan repeated in a sarcastic tone. "Everything fits together remarkably well. The girl is getting ready to go gun down three guys, she knows she might not get out of it alive, and she's trying on shoes. She's so relaxed and unworried that she gives her name and even her address to an unknown saleswoman. That story really holds up. Solid."

Mevlido made a gesture of powerlessness. There's often a lot of irrationality in the actions of assassins. Sometimes you run into that, a total absence of logic.

They all marked a pause.

"And Waddell Street, where is that?" someone finally asked.

"It's in Henhouse Four," explained Mevlido. "On the outer limits of the world. Near the border. In a sector called the Shambles."

"Ah, the Shambles," Berberoïan said sadly. "That's all we needed."

"And you went there to investigate?" asked Vorkouta.

"Where?" asked Mevlido.

"To the Shambles."

"Why?" Mevlido sounded astonished.

"Well," said Vorkouta.

"To continue your work on this woman," intervened Michigan. "Your personal investigation of this woman."

"OK, boys, you must be joking," said Mevlido. "That trip can take days, and if it goes badly, you may have to stay there for weeks."

Outside, a bolt of lightning shot across the sky. The thunder took four seconds before shaking the windows. No one was talking anymore. Mevlido let the last echoes die out.

"I have a self-criticism session Tuesday," he continued. "I can't disappear like that, what are you thinking, Michigan? I'd be accused of abandoning my post."

"We don't care about your self-criticism," said Berberoïan. "It's not a priority. We can put it off until after you get back."

Mevlido tossed his head. He had red on his lips, like his

colleagues, because the soy sandwich was slathered with a thick layer of ketchup.

"Look for the traces of this woman in the Shambles," continued Berberoïan. "That's your priority. Waddell Street, Linda, thirty years old, excellent shot with a pistol, with a face that only you can describe. You have enough elements to follow the trail back, Mevlido. And there's also a point on which I insist. Don't forget to keep an eye on the Bolsheviks. Sound out the old women in your cell. They have maybe heard of a Linda who likes to wear green."

"I already questioned them," Mevlido claimed with assurance. "I got nothing."

"I have a hard time believing that there is nothing to be gotten from those old women," objected Berberoïan. "Question them again. I'm sure they're hiding something from us."

"In fact," said Michigan, "it would seem that you could give a physical description of the murderer."

"What murderer?" said Mevlido.

"Linda, the kamikaze who tells her life story in fashion boutiques," said Michigan.

All four of them wiped their mouths with a ball of cellulose passed from hand to hand and slowly losing all form. Originally, this disgusting mass had belonged to Vorkouta, the only one to have thought that he should take a napkin from the dispenser downstairs.

"Right, a fashion boutique," corrected Mevlido. "A woebegone little shop in the Iyim neighborhood. With no sign outside. If I hadn't talked to one of my informants . . ."

"Yes?" encouraged Michigan.

"Without the advice of my informants, I would have gone astray in the store on Memorial Avenue, like you."

"Like Jiang and Maguistral," corrected Vorkouta.

"What informant?" Berberoïan asked with interest.

"Cornelia Orff," said Mevlido. "A beggar. She sells Bolshevik badges on the sidewalk. I spoke to her about the shoe store bag. She indicated the May Chow boutique in Iyim Gardens. According to her, it's lower quality . . ."

"I knew that there was a Bolshevik angle in this story," Berberoïan cut him off with a half-triumphant voice.

"A minor angle," observed Michigan sagaciously. "Up to this point, minor."

"Yes," said Bapos Vorkouta, "minor."

"It's lower quality, but much cheaper," Mevlido continued.

All four of them remained pensive for eight or nine seconds, then Petro Michigan broke the silence.

"And so what did she look like?" he asked no one in particular.

"Who?" asked Vorkouta. "The beggar?"

"No," intervened Berberoïan, "I suppose Michigan is talking about the terrorist? That's right, Michigan? You're talking about her, right?"

"About whom?" asked Michigan.

"About the terrorist," said Vorkouta.

"Yes," said Michigan in a nasal voice, "I was talking about her."

They were silent for a little while longer, then, as Mevlido wasn't saying anything, Petro Michigan broke the silence again.

"You know," he said, this time addressing Mevlido unambiguously, "you saw her. You saw everything. The commissioner repeated your description of her to me. It seems she was a pretty woman?"

"Yes," admitted Mevlido, "a very pretty woman. The storm had broken. In an instant the road was flooded. She fired her pistol, then threw herself under the tram. She wanted her death to be a sort of apotheosis. She wanted to control her final minutes right up until the end. She was like us."

"Bah," said Michigan.

"I should have stopped her," sighed Mevlido.

"Of course not, Mevlido," said Berberoïan.

"In what way could you say that she was like us?" wondered Vorkouta.

"Well . . . ," Berberoïan hesitated.

"She showed a hell of a lot of courage, that girl," said Vorkouta. "The same couldn't be said for us."

"Everyone does what they can," objected Berberoïan. "We're not kamikazes, but all the same, we're not a bunch of pansies."

"Well, we . . . ," said someone, trying to weigh the pros and cons but not succeeding in formulating a commentary.

All of a sudden, all four of them were kneading the remains of their empty paper cups or tapping their fingers on them. They reflected. Then Michigan raised his head.

"In any case," he exhaled, "there is a heroic side to her death."

"And she spared the driver," Mevlido pointed out.

The afternoon was torrid. The mist of a short shower smoked for a minute above the roadway that now sizzled like a griddle, then the storm moved toward the northwest without having emptied itself out. The sky almost immediately returned to its menacing, oily slate color.

Before dismissing his team, Berberoïan had called for another round of questioning of the saleswoman from May Chow and had asked Mevlido to guide Bapos Vorkouta to the shoe store in Iyim Gardens. Mevlido and Vorkouta crossed Memorial Avenue and headed toward the concrete barrier that forever forbade the entrance of vehicles into the refugee camp. Since they had left the fast-food restaurant, Mevlido had been trying to recreate out loud the route that led to the shop. He explained to his colleague that he didn't remember which way to go. He searched his memory, but his recollections were vague.

"It was after the rain," said Mevlido. "Everything was soaking wet and dark. We're going to have a hard time getting oriented."

After going ten meters into the ghetto, Vorkouta shrugged his shoulders.

"After all, it's useless for me to come with you," he decided.

"Wait," said Mevlido, "at an intersection we should pass by a row of gutted houses. That's what we have to find first. Then there was a little street. I think it was on the left. Left or right. A little street with a sort of ford through the mud. Then I had to go through a mezzanine floor with a fire door. There was a slogan painted on the door."

"We're going to trudge for kilometers in the middle of the ruins," said Vorkouta. "In the Iyim ghetto, there are slogans on all the doors. We're going to walk kilometers for nothing."

"We can always try not to get lost," said Mevlido.

"So you go ahead," said Vorkouta. "Look all by yourself. You don't need two people for that."

They split up. Mevlido watched him go. Behind the barrier you could still see the trees of Memorial Avenue. You could still hear the hum of the traffic.

Then, very quickly, Mevlido was surrounded by the silence of Iyim misery, death, and Iyim desolation.

He walked aimlessly.

The fluidity of the air diminished.

The thunder rumbled in the distance.

Children were playing basketball in a courtyard. For a long time Mevlido watched the game without thinking of anything.

After the basketball he wandered for a good hour inside the Iyim labyrinth. He could feel presences behind the walls, but he didn't encounter many people. The potholed streets all looked alike, the rubble piled high to the upper floors, no building had been spared by the hail of machine gun fire during the battle that had marked the end of the extermination. The refugees or survivors had been encouraged to take possession of the still habitable houses, but the wounds from the military and social clashes had not healed over. Mevlido climbed over the debris, and, from time to time, he would glance into the buildings and go in. For a minute he would listen to the echoes of his own footsteps in the empty space. Sometimes he would intrude into an apartment being squatted, try not to look too closely at the mattresses or the cardboard that was being used as a mattress, and would back away, babbling excuses, and leave. He stuck his nose into a few ground floors open on all sides, then abandoned his search. I can't find that shoe store, he thought. I'll have to talk about it during my self-criticism:

- didn't even wait until evening to give up exploring the false trail I had voluntarily started down
- let discouragement invade me
- showed neither class tenacity nor professional conscientiousness
- clung to the absence of truth like a buoy

The rain had started to fall. After a moment of uncertainty it became violent and showed its intention of staying around for a while.

He sat down in the doorway of a building to escape the raindrops. In that shelter the hot air was unbreathable. His arms were dripping. For a moment he contemplated the movement of the sweat on his skin, then succumbed to sleepiness. The dreams he hadn't mentioned to Maggie Yeung took advantage of the occasion to reemerge. He invented others, with variations, with other women, with other women's names. Behind him the piles of rocks formed an impenetrable gray mass. In front of him was a black pool in which the sky was not reflected. The rain whipped the surface of puddles. The water roiled. From time to time, wrapped in a shower curtain or a tarp, a human being passed by the length of a wall, avoiding the basins full of mud, the streams. Then the twilight climbed over the lightless houses, and the rain stopped.

Night was coming.

Mevlido got up.

This evening, I have to go to a cell meeting, he thought.

His shirt clung to his chest.

His shirt was glued to his chest as if he had been hit by a bullet at the top of his rib cage.

22

Forty-two years or so before his death, Mevlido pushed open the
door of the Organs, threw his convocation down in front of Deeplane, and, as he had not yet said anything, continued to be silent.

Deeplane, who directed Action Branch at that time, was bent
over a report. He was reading it with sustained attention, and,
from time to time, he circled a half sentence in red or scribbled an-
notations in the margins. The fact that Mevlido was sitting across
from him hadn't disturbed him at all, and, for a minute, one might
even wonder if he had even noticed his subordinate's presence.
The pen squeaked against the paper. The nib stopped moving in
the middle of a word, perhaps because of a difficulty with spelling,
then crossed out a syllable and took off again. The pen again produced a slight scraping sound. There was no noise from the hallway, and, except for the discrete complaining of the metal, nothing
disturbed the silence.

The space housed several more or less identical workstations. Only Deeplane's was occupied for the moment. On top of a small brass column to Deeplane's right a half globe glowed. The light formed a crisp little patch around his hands and, beyond that, renounced its battle against the shadows. The lamps at the other three desks were extinguished. As always, when he came to see one of his bosses, Mevlido felt like he had somehow ended up in a subservice employing second-rate bureaucrats. It's obvious that the Organs, to the extent that the outside world was unaware of their existence, weren't required to pay attention to public appearances, but, if one day it had been necessary to publish a document conveying an idea of their activity and their power, it would be better to choose something besides a photo of this kind of administrative cul-de-sac, radiating energy efficiency and petty paperwork.

Mevlido crossed his legs and coughed and, after a moment, uncrossed them.

"You aren't waiting for me to tell you what you have to do, are you, Mevlido?" Deeplane suddenly asked.

Without looking at Mevlido, he vaguely indicated a direction. His hand pointed toward the directories, to an ashtray full of paper clips, to the remains of a newspaper from which articles had been cut out, but the gesture was imprecise and also indicated what lay noiselessly dormant a little farther away: a television set with, on the screen, the still image of a gigantic bird.

Mevlido moved the ashtray and turned the screen to counteract the glare from Deeplane's lamp onto the picture, pushing the command button so that the image would move.

That was what he had to do.

The bird's wingspan was about two meters. Perched next to a puddle, it flapped its wings. Had its feathers been white or dirty yellow, the bird might have called to mind a pelican, due to the animal's considerable size and the hint of a pouch visible hanging below its beak, but the hypothesis didn't hold up more than a second. No, pelicans have a different shape. A less massive silhouette. And anyway, on a pelican, the feathers wouldn't have been this color. From the prominent forehead to the tip of the tail, the body was black; it radiated blackness. If we make an exception for the grayish beak, only the eyes brought any light to the ensemble. Set very far apart and very large, they had a golden and seemingly autonomous existence. The bird closed them, and, once more, its wings flapped with the loose sound of a bedsheet on a clothesline abandoned to the wind.

Slow motion would have shown the violence of the blow that stirred the air and then folded itself back up again. But the film didn't have the educational mission of a wildlife documentary, the film was live, and on the screen, they saw the form rise up, take flight above the water, and, after a moment of effort, skim heavily over a first palisade topped with barbed wire, then a second, then approach a lookout post whose lookout was absent. On the second palisade appeared a slogan: "SURVIVOR, PREPARE TO ATTACK THE MOON!" The sun was not shining anywhere, and the light was mediocre, but the humidity gave an exceptional clarity to the contrasts. Drops of water pearled along the wires, the roof of the lookout post shone. One had the feeling it must be very hot.

The bird brushed by all that and uttered a cry, a brief croak.

Deeplane had finished correcting the document that he had in front of him. He turned his seat to be able to observe the bird at the same time as Mevlido.

"It's a virtual image, obviously," he said.

"I can't identify that animal," Mevlido remarked.

"Me neither," said Deeplane.

They had begun to scrutinize the screen again. The bird flew at medium speed, sometimes opening its mouth halfway to caw.

Stumps of horns could be seen on its head, emphasizing its prehistoric nature.

"It's like a pterodactyl with feathers," said Mevlido.

"A pterodactyl!" protested Deeplane. "We're not in the secondary era."

"But that fog, all of that hot humidity looks like it," Mevlido justified himself.

"It's after the global revolution," said Deeplane, "a long time after. It's not the same thing. Not really the same geological era, you know."

The camera was working to follow the bird and was now using a higher-powered telescopic lens. The operator was getting superb pictures—in his youth he must have worked with teams specializing in zoological reporting; he managed to get frames that satisfied the eyes and didn't wobble, despite the growing distance. The bird was being filmed from the side, most often from starboard aft. It flew over barely smoking factories, railways overgrown with shrubs, barracks, working-class suburbs, streets lined with frangipani of a dusty, unhealthy green. Here, flying low on the horizon, it was the only one of its kind. The other birds seemed like dwarves next to it and hastened to change their aerial corridor as soon as they saw it, as one does when one realizes the risk of getting in the way of a bird of prey.

The streets were wet. They crisscrossed at right angles, and a postwar atmosphere of economic archaism reigned. Cars were only present as wrecks. From time to time one could see a pedestrian standing in front of a deserted construction site or urinating on a brick wall.

"A pterodactyl," muttered Deeplane, "what nonsense."

He was no longer looking at the screen. He had removed his glasses and was wiping them on his pullover. It was a brown wool pullover patterned with small diamonds in a broadly oatmeal tone.

For the next minute, Mevlido continued to examine the bird, whose size, in the picture, was diminishing. He already couldn't see its eyes or hear its call, supposing that it was keeping its eyes open and uttering any more cries.

"Listen, Mevlido, this is what . . . ," said Deeplane, "this is where you are going. So you will have all the time necessary to study them up close, these strange, web-footed birds. We haven't had anyone left in this region for the last half a century. We must reestablish contact with reality. We need something besides virtual images. We are going to . . . we are going to organize a disengagement to transfer you to the zone."

There was an extended moment of silence. It lasted longer than the four seconds ordinarily allowed between interlocutors for one of them to swallow their own saliva.

"Well, I've heard of even more idiotic missions," Mevlido finally let fall from his lips, "but, all the same, an ornithological investigation . . ."

He was no longer watching the flying creature, which, at that moment, was circling to land between a truck with no wheels and a pile of stones. He was no longer interested in the bird, he was trying to catch the gaze of Deeplane, who, without the protection afforded by glasses, had a guileless expression on his face. Then Mevlido paused on Deeplane's well-groomed, very intellectual hands, and, after a moment, he let his attention float along at random over the jumbled storeroom where the hierarchy of the Organs flourished.

In recent years, advanced technological equipment had been introduced in the offices—high-definition visual monitors and computers—but the graft hadn't really been successful, and, to be truthful, no one had said farewell to the world of handwritten files, press cuttings, and colored folders, one thousand times more comfortable. So the paper archives were piled up everywhere in the room, blocking access to most of the keyboards and burying the printer shared by the directors.

Deeplane settled his glasses back on his aquiline nose and reached an arm toward one of the piles, with the goal of harpooning a file folder, a currant-red dossier he wanted Mevlido to read. At the wrist, the sleeve of his pullover was the worse for wear and had begun to unravel. Like Mevlido's other superiors, Deeplane wore clothes that harmonized with the spartan morale that inspired the actions of the Services in general and the Organs in particular. He was dressed in a mix of functional wools and modest fabrics, and, when you were close to him like this, waiting for him to extract a bright-red bundle swollen with documents of military or oneiric origin from the Archives, you realized that the digitization of his department hadn't changed Deeplane. It would never change him, would never transform him into a vulgarly secular character, a vulgarly intemporal character, would never spoil him or mutilate him or break him.

"The observation of birds will not be your number one priority," said Deeplane.

"Ah," replied Mevlido, "I had thought . . ."

Deeplane had placed the currant-red folder in front of him, and now he could decipher its title, a coded reference that we won't reproduce here and that looked more or less like an organic chemistry formula. The folder was thick. It must have contained a variety of intelligence, a list of directives, and objectives to be attained.

"Those aren't the animals that are causing us a problem," said Deeplane.

"Is it the hominids?" asked Mevlido.

"Yes," answered Deeplane, "they're the ones, yes. Despite the global revolution, they have sunk to a level of barbarity and idiocy that has astonished even the specialists. They've become an inexplicable species. They are just getting out of multiple wars of extermination, but a new conflict is already in sight. The population has decreased by a hundredfold, even more. Entire continents are currently uninhabitable. Those who have survived remain socially organized, but they no longer believe in themselves, or in society. They've inherited political systems to which they've lost the keys; for them ideology is a prayer devoid of meaning. The ruling classes have become criminalized, the poor obey them. Both classes act as if they were already dead. And as if, on top of that, they don't even care."

"Maybe they've mutated," suggested Mevlido.

"Excuse me?"

"Maybe they've been the victim of some kind of mutation," Mevlido said again.

"Maybe. Something in them has changed. You'd think that they no longer have the ability to differentiate between life, dreams, and death."

Mevlido hadn't yet opened the folder. He walked his fingers over the organic chemistry formula as if examining a braille inscription. A shirt cuff with a pattern of brown checks on a red background protruded from the sleeve of his track jacket. He also seemed to dress himself at the army surplus or discount stores.

"For us, that makes any intervention problematic," continued Deeplane.

"And what if we continued to calmly let them degenerate, without intervening?" suggested Mevlido.

Deeplane nodded. Yes, humanity was a detestable species that had systematically betrayed all the hopes that had been placed on it. Yes, the Organs had ended by leaving it to its abominations and chaos. But now humanity had entered its extinction phase, and the Organs had decided to reactivate their former program of compassion and support. And once again, Action Branch had been asked to intervene. It was necessary to create conditions that would make the long phase of coming agony less atrocious. Before anything else could be done, that meant the work of intelligence gathering. They were going to send agents on-site. Just a few. The best. Their task would be to immerse themselves in the barbarity so as to work out a few ways to move forward. So that maybe afterward, for the generations to come, they might understand how to promote a slightly more peaceful end for humanity. It was in view of this last crossing over that the Organs set themselves to work.

Mevlido expressed his lack of conviction by a concerted movement of his lips and his eyebrows.

He had a round and austere head, thick lips, thick eyebrows, a face that made you think more of brawling than of yogic meditation and self-control.

They were silent for fifteen or sixteen seconds.

Mevlido had opened the dossier. He flipped through it.

"Henhouse Four," he said.

"It's a gigantic ghetto," Deeplane explained, "but it will grow even more after your birth."

"That's where you're sending me?"

"Once you're reincarnated, we don't really know what will happen to you," said Deeplane. "There are too many variables, and it's total war there. We don't know where you'll end up. We don't control those things."

"At no point in my training have I taken a class on Henhouse Four," he said. "It's practically unexplored territory for me."

"Yes," said Deeplane, "I know. We have technicians who know the territory better than you. Mingrelian or Gorgha, for example."

"I thought Gorgha was dead," said Mevlido.

"They will stay here, in a support roll," said Deeplane without taking the bait. "Here is where they are the most useful. In a way, they will be right beside you. Us too."

"In a way," repeated Mevlido.

His tone was bitter.

On the screen, the bird walked and pranced. It walked a meter and froze near a charred jerrican. It was photographed in close-up, like at the beginning of the film. The lens caught its impenetrable golden eyes, absolutely beautiful.

"We would prefer to infiltrate with an agent whose mind is not weighed down with too much information," said Deeplane, "someone pragmatic and solid, with a powerful memory for dreams. That's you, Mevlido."

Mevlido let out a discrete, low groan. It was not a demonstration of enthusiasm.

"We'll organize your incarnation into a good guy," Deeplane continued.

Mevlido again moved his tough pugilist monk's face. He continued to flip through the numerous sections and subsections of the currant-colored dossier. *Don't contact the spiders,* he read. *Don't talk to the rats. Neither to the rats, nor to the spiders. Don't participate in the ceremonies where the deads' souls are invoked. Refuse any one-on-one with a psychiatrist.* He turned the pages. *Accept your destiny no matter what it is. Accept your difference no matter what it is. Hide your difference.* There were hundreds of instructions. Most of them seemed sensible. *Always betray the conquerors,* he read further. His fingers brushed dividers that were straw yellow or canary yellow, or blue, or cardboard gray.

"Hmm," he said, "I see that there's been a dissection."

"Dissection isn't the word," said Deeplane. "One of these . . . pterodactyls. It got caught in a cluster of barbed wire. The lab took the opportunity to film it with a special lens."

Mevlido skimmed the report and let out a whistle of consternation, then he read aloud the paragraph that discussed the digestive system. In the digestive system, no food had been discovered.

The stomach was scarcely different from a vacuum cleaner bag, containing only dry, granular, black dust.

"You see, Mevlido?" said Deeplane. "You'd think it was an accumulation of weirdness inside a dream. Something is changing their reality. And watched from here, it's hard to see what doesn't fit. One of us has to . . ."

The bird was spreading its wings to take flight again.

"There's no other solution," said Deeplane.

"Bah," objected Mevlido.

The bird began to beat against the air powerfully again. Its enormous wings occupied the whole picture; you could see the details of its wings, and, all of a sudden, you had the impression that the camera had gotten too close and the bird had detected its presence. It had just stabilized itself after its flight. Suddenly, it ducked behind a hangar and disappeared. The cameraman immediately tried to follow it, but with no success.

On the screen there was now only a not-very-animated industrial landscape, made up of warehouses locked with padlocks, empty garages, and the promise of rain.

"OK," said Mevlido, "how much time will I have?"

"For what?"

"For my mission."

"Oh," said Deeplane, "you'll have to stay on the ground for quite some time. The time to . . ."

As if he had run out of words, he turned toward the window, toward that rectangle of night that had until now not contributed to the lighting, because behind the glass the night was very dense, but also because the chemically treated glass did not reflect the lamp that was shining on the desk.

On the other side, it was the outside, a mass of compact, abyssal, black space in which you couldn't even imagine someday seeing the beginning of light appear. Deeplane had raised his hand; he traced against this background, onto these depths, a lazy arc that could mean anything, then his hand fell back, struck by a kind of apathy.

"Be more precise, Deeplane," insisted Mevlido.

"Listen, Mevlido, it will last a lifetime. You are going to be reborn there, you are going to grow up and become an adult there. You will wait for death there. We need an observer who experiences things from the inside. We will collect information through your dreams."

There was a new silence. It was heavy.

"You are going to be reincarnated as a good person, Mevlido."

"A good person," grumbled Mevlido. "And me? You anticipate pulling me out when, exactly? Once my job is done?"

"Please, Mevlido, don't act as if you don't know the procedure," Deeplane said irritably. "You've been receiving training here for more than forty years to be sent there or somewhere else; you're not just learning your working conditions today."

He had adopted a tone that wasn't really brusque but lacked warmth. In the minds of directors like Deeplane, Mevlido had been prepared for action over a very long period of time—several decades—and, now that the action was taking shape, he didn't need to be showing his reluctance like this. He had received enough compassion during the training sessions, and asking for more, here, had something inappropriate about it.

"You could maybe shorten my stay," said Mevlido as if he had the right to negotiate the length of his mission. "You could maybe not force me to live through everything, up to and including death."

"We'll try to extract you before," promised Deeplane. "You know that we always try. But most likely we will have to fall back on the only moment that is really 100 percent certain—your death throes. We will pick you up during your death throes."

"During my death throes . . . ," repeated Mevlido.

"During, yes. If they are long enough. Or shortly thereafter."

Deeplane wasn't avoiding Mevlido's gaze, and his voice was more fraternal than it had been a minute before.

"We'll try," he said.

His glasses gleamed beneath the lamp.

He gave another few somber details. No other ways to get reliable information existed. He had to penetrate human society without being suspected of double-dealing, belong to their society right from birth, lead an ordinary life among the inhabitants there, know their suffering and their fears from the inside. Walk with them the path that leads to death.

"Contact with us will be extremely poor," said Deeplane, "a few dreams. And a slight feeling of duplicity that may bother you a little when you reach adulthood. It will be with you until the end."

"The end," murmured Mevlido. "I hope it will come quickly."

"No," said Deeplane, "it will not come quickly. It will come in its own time. You'll have to wait, Mevlido."

Mevlido was no longer facing him. You might even say that he was turning his back on Deeplane. He had gotten up and taken a few steps. He was now standing near the window, and he pressed his forehead against the glass; he dove in his imagination toward the black depths; he rushed toward them; he spread his wings, enormous colorless wings; he went forward toward a forgetfulness of everything; he inhaled darkness, dust. He was fully conscious that he belonged to the Organs, and he was a soldier of the Organs, at its chiefs' disposition for eternity. He had been trained so that one day they would announce his departure to him, and he would leave. He wasn't protesting. He wasn't protesting against anyone or anything, maybe because, ultimately, besides the darkness, there was no one and nothing. The glass had no temperature, neither warm nor icy. No ring of mist indicated that Mevlido was breathing.

"We can't speed anything up," Deeplane continued. "You will have to wait."

"All right," said Mevlido, "I had thought that . . . one always hopes that . . ."

23

When he had learned by heart the 356 pages of instructions that Deeplane had given him, Mevlido went to deposit the currant-red folder and its entire contents in the Archives, he ate a sandwich in front of the Archives' automat, then he went to a fitness center where he had promised to stop as soon as possible for a last session. For the last twenty years he had gone there every morning for three hours of classes.

The instructors were waiting for him. They had been informed and they knew they would never see their student again. They surrounded him, but without excessive joviality or seriousness, which he appreciated, and he received practical recommendations from them that they had previously abstained from giving him, not because they wanted to keep them secret but because the philosophy of certain elementary principles is only understandable on the eve of the voyage. Earlier, he would only have retained empty sentences, while now, urgency gave to the aphorisms their full usefulness and their meaning.

He thanked his teachers and took his leave, and then he was free.

You always have several hours before a departure of this kind, for a mission of this kind. Precious hours that you feel you are wasting because all of the final nuisances have been gotten out of the way—blood drawn, scans, voice imprint, discharge, return of all professional equipment, solemn declarations in front of the Control Commission, closing your cafeteria account, closing your medical and sports files—and it's hard to know how to give a positive character to the miniscule amount of private life that still remains to be lived.

Sleep is out of the question. It would be useless to start a book because you won't finish it. It's not recommended to tire your body out with an *n*th session of close-combat training. You have had, moreover, the decency not to organize, with your colleagues and comrades, a goodbye ceremony. As for kneeling in front of a wall to meditate, you willingly deny yourself that, since it seems so imbecilic this evening to struggle to see illusory shadows, when before the end of the night you'll be effectively and very concretely thrown into the heart of black space.

You see yourself thus confronted with loneliness, in an idleness like that of a tourist in transit in an airport. And you try to gain time by wasting it. And you fight not to do the only thing that you really want to do: telephone your best friend.

Hear your best friend's voice.

Tell her that you have been chosen, that the crossing is imminent. And that after that, there will be nothing, no shareable or tellable scraps, nothing but an outsized silence, only that.

Only that.

A chasm.

No bridge.

You have received the order though, for that night, to avoid emotions, and you have sworn to keep yourself indifferent: detached from beings and things. But the nostalgia of past sentimental affairs and sexual or sexed complicities reopens an old scar below your consciousness. And you are gnawed by the idea of talking one more time with a woman, with the woman you love, who you loved and still love. You want to communicate with her one more time, even if, in anticipation of this delicate moment, the hierarchy has taken her away, even if for years Action Branch has arranged to keep her out of reach and treacherously take any real character away from her, disincarnate her, make her phantasmatic, transform her in a pure amorous hypothesis.

You approach the public telephone on the landing of the fourth floor, and you hesitate. You aren't completely detached from things and people, and you hesitate even more because nearby, in the hall or in the offices, there is no one else.

Mevlido hesitated. His movements slowed.

He had started down the stairs that led to the third floor. He went down two more steps, then turned around and went back up. On a corner table an ordinary black telephone was at his disposition, and, around him, nothing moved, like in an office building outside of business hours, when all the doors are locked and only the fluorescent lights are on.

He unhooked the receiver. He dialed a number, his best friend's number.

"This is Verena Siew," said Verena's recorded voice. "If you wish, you can leave a message after the beep."

"It's me," said Mevlido. "I wanted to hear the sound of your voice."

There was a change in the electronic silence, an imponderable weight of mutism. Someone was spying on the other end of the line, near the answering machine, or from a bug installed on the line.

Mevlido suppressed a sigh.

"I wanted to talk to you one-on-one," he said. "Someone is listening to us. I'll call back when we are alone."

Three seconds passed, followed by an electric click. The answering machine had been shut off.

"Is that you, Mevlido?" asked a masculine voice.

"Yes," said Mevlido.

"You want to speak to Verena Siew?"

"Yes."

"You know very well that that is impossible. She is no longer reachable. You'll have to be content with your memory of her. She won't answer you, Mevlido, not this evening, nor any other day."

"Where is she?" asked Mevlido in a tone he thought was neutral. "Where have you . . . is that you, Deeplane?"

"This is Schumann," immediately answered the voice. "I'm replacing Deeplane at the switchboard."

"Ah, it's you," said Mevlido.

"Yes."

"Where is Verena Siew right now, Schumann?" Mevlido insisted stubbornly.

"She won't answer," repeated Schumann. "Listen, Mevlido, once and for all, you have to consider her dead to you. If she survives, it will be inside your memory. And that's the only place you can still find her."

"I would like to leave her a message," said Mevlido, "in case she may be accessible elsewhere, in spite of everything."

"No problem. Dictate it to me."

"It's personal," protested Mevlido.

"Enough childishness, Mevlido. Privacy hasn't existed for you for ages. Nothing has been personal for you since you started working at Action Branch. We've never hidden it from you, don't say we did."

The conversation paused.

"Several dozens of us will hear your message to Verena Siew," Schumann continued. "There's nothing to make a fuss about."

Mevlido didn't react. Regular breathing could be heard on the line; perhaps it was his.

"Go ahead," Schumann encouraged him, "I'm making a note."

"I'm thinking of you," murmured Mevlido after a new silence. "I miss you. I will think of you until the end. Whatever the end is, I will miss you."

On that note, brutally, and without saying goodbye to Schumann, he hung up.

Action Branch often succeeded in this: provoking in its agents eruptions of repressed hatred, unspectacular but visible, for which they didn't apologize.

It wasn't necessary to change buildings to get to the library.

The reading rooms were open twenty-four hours a day, but, in the evening, a clear drop in activity could be observed. Mevlido wandered from one room to another. The place looked deserted, or nearly so. His goal wasn't to find familiar faces. He simply wanted to spend a few moments in a place that had always been for him the equivalent of a friendly shore on the edge of the world. He had no research to do, and he walked about as you might stroll along a beach.

As you might stroll along a beach:

- when your eyes are dazzled by the immensity
- your soul under the spell of the distance
- and you are at peace with the present
- at peace with your own insignificance

For about forty minutes, he circulated among the shelves, without a plan, rifling through the encyclopedia section, opening and reclosing the volumes according to whatever fell under his hand, from time to time looking up the translation of a verb in a dictionary of Quechua, Blatnoï, or Korean, reading here an article on the bacteriological wars, there a page consecrated to the poems of Leonor Iquitos, there again a chapter of a grammar book explaining the order of words in the sentences of existence and in the sentences of disappearance. Then, after a stop in the restroom, he left.

He left the vicinity of the library and walked about three hundred meters under the concrete and under the ground, and then, as he passed by the sports facilities, he crossed the threshold of one of the martial arts clubs, the kung fu club, and entered the locker rooms. The space was brightly lit, like before or after a training session, but no garment hung from the hooks. The evening students had already dispersed. The recently scrubbed floor was finishing drying. Mevlido went to help himself in a cupboard, taking a bath towel and a bar of soap. He undressed; he went to the closest shower stall.

For a long time, hot water.

For a long time, he allowed the hot water to flow over him, at a very pleasant temperature. Steam surrounded him, more and more dense. The drops pattered, the static of the cascade became the most important thing in the world, became the center of the real world, the noise of rain imposed itself on the foreground of his consciousness. The rain was his consciousness. He was going through the motions of scrupulously washing, but at the same time he was cleansing himself of that irruption of impotent rage that had polluted him just before. After the deplorable Schumann incident, the vocabulary verification in the library had helped him to reconstitute his natural serenity, but only this boiling water helped him get rid of the residue of his bad mood. The soapy foam wound between his feet. It branched out into complex alphabets, and, as the minutes passed, it dissipated.

In a stall situated at the other end of the locker room, a newcomer had settled in under a showerhead, and, like Mevlido, he was relaxing and splashing around without being able bring himself to shut off the tap. It must be an athlete who liked to perfect his skills in the evening, without witnesses, far from the collective gaze, and who was recovering after a series of exhausting exercises. He could be heard singing a repetitive melody, a graceless tune with the rhythm of an incantation.

Mevlido turned off the water and walked barefooted to the

place where his things were folded, then dried himself, pulled his clothes back on, buttoned what needed to be buttoned. Fifteen meters away, the anonymous larynx continued to trace dismal circles of sound, and the water ran and ran and foamed. Across from the stall hung a kung fu outfit soaked with sweat; on the bench were black jogging pants and underwear, an undershirt, a white shirt. Elia Fincke, the technical expert, dressed like that. Mevlido approached, and, loud enough to be heard through the splashes and the door, he let out:

"Fincke, is that you? I'm saying goodbye."

The flow of the water was immediately interrupted. The technical expert had turned off the tap.

"Is that you, Mevlido?"

"Yes."

"They said you're leaving soon?"

"Yes. Tomorrow. Tomorrow morning."

There were three seconds of heavy silence. Fincke tried to find an ordinary sentence but found nothing, and, already, he was already engaging with Mevlido's memory.

"Are you ready?" he ended by saying.

"I think so," said Mevlido.

"Well, then . . . good luck, Mevlido, yeah?"

"Thanks."

"We're with you," said Fincke.

"I know," said Mevlido.

He had to traverse a second silence. The technical expert was no longer moving in the shower stall. Then the tap grated, and, immediately, the waterfall began again.

The splash of water took over the space again.

Mevlido moved away.

The water hummed.

Elia Fincke had not begun his song again.

24

Mevlido left the kung fu locker room behind him and started down a long, deserted hallway. He had decided to put an end to his wanderings and find the little studio he had occupied for almost seventeen years. The gallery that led him to the residence had no opening to the outside and had the atmosphere of a prison fortress, with the light gray and dark red that military architects recommend for their postcataclysmic complexes. Mevlido's steps echoed under the vaults of reinforced concrete. No one else's heels clicked in front of him or behind. He had the impression of being a lone soldier doing a three-kilometer routine inspection.

Now he was returning home. He was going there directly, to his room. He would await the disengagement there—that moment whose horror was minimized when you called it that, with a technical term, almost abstract, when, concretely, it was a painful operation, with all the characteristics of a pure and simple murder.

That is what he went to wait for there.

Mevlido's apartment was situated above the space where the central heating furnace rumbled, and, because of this proximity, a muffled vibration haunted the walls night and day, a feeble trembling that was not always perceptible but that sometimes, on the other hand, evoked the shivering of a cargo ship a thousand miles from any coast, when the ocean is oily smooth and the engines run full throttle.

He pushed open the door and felt around to find the light switch. The wall shook familiarly under his palm. Half a second later, the switch let out a proud and decided click, as light switches do, but the lamp itself also made a noise, and, after a brief flash of lightning, stopped radiating. The filament had just burned out.

Mevlido produced a distressed vowel. Out of austerity concerns, the lighting of the apartments was limited to a single central lamp. As he didn't want to walk the subterranean corridors for the next hour to ask, at the accessory storeroom, to be given a new bulb, the only thing left for him was to be content in the darkness until his departure time, or to beg light from a neighbor.

He went back out again and took a few steps. On the nearest door to him was a sign. He bent his index finger and knocked next to the plaque that announced "1157 Mingrelian."

Mingrelian was sitting in front of his worktable. He was writing.

"Can I borrow your lamp?" asked Mevlido. "Mine's burned out."

"Wait," said Mingrelian, "one paragraph to finish."

He blackened another twelve centimeters of paper, then put down his pen and got up. He already had a rag in his hand to be able to unscrew the bulb without burning his fingers. He pulled over a chair to bring it under the ceiling light, which, as in Mevlido's room, was the only source of light. Already he had climbed onto the chair and stretched his arm upward.

"They should give us candles," said Mevlido.

"Yes, candles, that would be good," said Mingrelian.

His leanness gave him the look of a starving beggar, and his angular face had the bluish tint characteristic of graphomaniacs—those who stay shut up in front of a text for months, hour after hour, without ever inhaling anything other than the dubious fragrance of words, with for an outcome nervous and nonreparative sleep, the reading of inextricable glossaries, and dreams.

The socket squeaked, and, without transition, shadow invaded the room, tempered by the light from the corridor that came from the slightly open door.

"I'm leaving tomorrow," said Mevlido.

Mingrelian had gotten down from his perch.

"I know," he said. "It's been maximum alert since yesterday. Everyone has been warned."

"Deeplane told me: Mingrelian will stay here in a support role."

"Yes. I'm the one who will write up the report on your mission."

They were now in the hallway. Mevlido smiled approvingly.

"At least, with you, there will be adjectives," he said.

"Bah," said Mingrelian, "for as much as they take any notice."

"Your style isn't like the others'," said Mevlido.

"Oh," said Mingrelian, "apart from you, no one appreciates my efforts here. For Deeplane or Schumann, all the reports are equal. It lands on their desk, and, once they've summarized it, they archive it."

They pushed open the door of Mevlido's cell, and they left it open behind them so as not to have to move about blindly. Mingrelian flicked the light switch several times, as if in that way he was evaluating the size of the outage.

"And the guy who I'm going . . . ," interrupted Mevlido.

"What guy?" Mingrelian said, astonished.

"Deeplane claims that I'm going to reincarnate as a 'good guy.' This guy, do you know anything about him?"

"I do," said Mingrelian reluctantly, "but I'm keeping it for myself. I don't have the right to influence you. There could be unforeseen events."

"What unforeseen events?" said Mevlido.

"We don't have all the puzzle pieces," said Mingrelian. "In half a century, a man named Mevlido will be the age you are now. Half a century, that's thousands of possible bifurcations. Fundamental bifurcations. What if the child is born into a family of delinquents? What if, instead of following the trajectory laid out for him by the

Organs, he goes completely off course? If he joins bands of criminals? If he goes crazy?"

"Bah," breathed Mevlido.

"Don't worry," said Mingrelian, "everything will be fine. At any rate, once you're there, you won't remember anything. Or almost anything. You won't even be aware of having a previous life."

Mingrelian had placed a stool under the ceiling light. He pulled himself up on it. Now, he stretched with all his lean body to get on with the exchange of lightbulbs.

"And besides, there's the question of sending another agent to the same zone," he said, "a little later. In addition to you."

"What agent?" asked Mevlido.

"A woman," said Mingrelian.

"Do I know her?"

Mingrelian hesitated.

"If you really need to get to know each other, you'll do that there," he said.

"Deeplane didn't say a word to me about that," Mevlido said regretfully.

At that instant the newly installed bulb received the current sent to it. It blinked for a second, then sizzled and went dark.

"There's a short somewhere," said Mingrelian.

"It certainly seems like it," said Mevlido.

"That one is burned out too, now," said Mingrelian.

"Bad luck," said Mevlido.

Mingrelian stepped back onto the ground, put the stool back in its place under Mevlido's little desk, and, for about ten seconds, he rocked back and forth in front of Mevlido, then he sighed.

"She won't remember anything either," he said.

"Who?" asked Mevlido. "The bulb?"

They exchanged a smile.

"I wonder what she'll be like, this woman," said Mevlido after the smile.

"Deeplane always says as little as possible to those who go," said Mingrelian. "He counts on chance for their missions to go well. On destiny."

"Bah, me too," said Mevlido. "It's safer than counting on the Organs or even on Deeplane."

In reality he cared only moderately about having details about his future life.

Mingrelian opened Mevlido's desk drawer, put the burned-out lightbulb in it, and closed it again.

"We're both going to have to stay in the dark," he said.

"I had originally thought that it would bother me to spend the last hours without light," remarked Mevlido. "That's why I went to you looking for a lamp. But, after all, it's not important."

"It rests the eyes," said Mingrelian.

"You were writing the beginning of the report," asked Mevlido.

"Yes," said Mingrelian, "but it's really tomorrow morning that I'll begin."

"Should we make some tea?" asked Mevlido.

"Sure," said Mingrelian.

Mevlido went to rinse the teapot in the sink, lighted the gas, poured the boiling water onto the leaves, and, when the leaves had brewed for a minute, came back over to Mingrelian and served the tea.

The door had stayed ajar, and they were taking advantage of the light coming from the hallway, but they couldn't see very well. Around them, the walls vibrated softly.

"Strange goodbye party," said Mevlido.

"They're all like this," said Mingrelian.

Then they drank their tea.

They drank, they exchanged a few more insignificant sentences,

Mevlido gave Mingrelian a suitcase where he had thrown together clothes and books, and, around midnight, they separated.

The walls and the ground shivered.

The furnace growled on the floor below.

It growled like that until Mevlido dozed off, and, even then, the vibration went on, the music from the flames didn't stop, that melody of destruction and of travel that is in all of us anyway, since always, and which everyone, at the moment they fall asleep, confuses sometimes with their own existence, sometimes with their own death.

The music of the flames didn't stop, Mingrelian wrote in his report later on, that melody of destruction and of travel, that guttural, harmonious, regular song, apt to make you understand the unknown and the unconscious, that somber clamor that is in all of us anyway, in us since always, like a shamanic song from an immobile, oily, heavy, unvisitable, sorcerous, deaf sea, without shores, without odor, shining, black, without any architecture but infinity, without color and without softness, a completely black original sea that Mevlido, closing his eyes, saw in red, orange, and at the moment he fell asleep—as all consciousness, all intelligence vanished—he saw it really and truly friendly and orange, hospitable, seductive, and red, welcoming and orange.

25

For forty years you train yourself for reincarnation and the voyage. But in reality, no departure is like the others. And you never know ahead of time who will come, or what will happen exactly.

The agents of disengagement, a man and two women, presented themselves at Mevlido's room earlier than expected, around 4:30 A.M., at a moment when the whole building was plunged in torpor.

They hadn't made any noise walking in the corridor. They didn't knock on the door that no bolt held closed; they pushed it open, avoiding making it creak, and they slipped one after the other into the opening, then softly closed the door behind them. The man then flipped the light switch. As the overhead light did not light up, they stayed quiet for a few minutes as their eyes became accustomed to the darkness. The light from the hallway filtered in under the door. Quite soon, it was enough for them to act and to move in Mevlido's direction.

Mevlido hadn't heard them arrive. Just the minute before, he had fallen into a pit of slumber. They found him stretched out on the still-made bed, in traveling clothes, well protected, despite the heat emitted by the radiator, by a navy-blue woolen pullover and wearing walking shoes. Overall, he looked like a hiker who had fallen asleep in a waiting room. He emerged from unconsciousness and saw them suddenly above him, ghostly, practically not moving, and examining him with a professional gaze.

For the moment they were content standing around his bed and weren't trying to touch him.

They were all three as naked as earthworms.

Earthworms, yes, or like babies who had just been born, but it doesn't matter, because deep down, we're describing a very simple reality: no garment covered them. They were going, effectively, to lead Mevlido through nothingness, where the possession of the slightest artifact handicaps living creatures, weighing them down and barring the way back. That's why they had already taken everything off, keeping no article of cloth or fabric on them, going so far as to refuse the least fig leaf, and thus exposing themselves to the loss of the dignity proper to executioners as they do their sordid tasks. At any rate, because their immediate function had nothing to do with eroticism, and had no connection, as tenuous as it might be, with any sexuality, they accepted this exhibitionism with absolute indifference.

The two women were thin. Part of the shorter one's chest was hidden under a cascade of hair that, even if the shadow reduced contrasts, appeared violently black, that brilliant black that can have a blue sheen, in the sun, for example, or under theater lights. She was less than thirty years old, with features that revealed Manchu or Korean heritage, and yet, from an aesthetic point of view, neither her body nor her face was very remarkable. Emanating from her was an impression of solidity and a threat. One suspected she might be brutal. A week earlier, Mevlido had eaten dinner next to her in the cafeteria, without guessing, of course, that he would see her again this morning, undressed, near his bed. He had judged her to be unpleasant.

The second was taller, and she also had a Far Eastern appearance. Her black hair covered her ears but didn't reach her shoulders. She couldn't have been forty years old. She had an elegance and a beauty incomparable with those of her companion. She was superb. It's true that her face scarcely smiled, but she reminded one of a fearless goddess, and not, like her companion, of a sullen student.

As for the man, nudity took away all his imposing presence and reduced him to the rank of a simple mammal, stocky and clean shaven, but, at the same time, he looked like a robust soldier, surely an expert in judo and blessed with sangfroid in any ordeal. One might have guessed him to be forty-five or fifty years old. He occupied the position of the eldest in the group.

Mevlido had already run into them several times, in meetings or in the cafeteria, and he knew their names:

- Tatiana Outougaï, the unlovable young woman with long hair

- Samiya Choong, the magnificent forty-something
- Sergueïev, the man

He greeted them with a gesture and sat up on the edge of the bed, not showing the slightest inclination to rebellion. He had put his hand on his belt buckle. He didn't know how to act in front of them.

"It's unnecessary to get undressed, Mevlido," said Sergueïev. "For you, all of that doesn't count."

"All of what?" said Mevlido.

"The precautions," said Sergueïev. "The precautions to be taken."

"Against what?" asked Mevlido.

He felt the futile need to make the sound of his own voice exist.

"Against death, as well you know," said Tatiana Outougaï, shrugging her naked girl's shoulders.

At that moment, the hallway light went out, relieved by the night-lights that signaled, every fifteen meters, the presence of a junction in the electrical network. The darkness thickened by several degrees in the bedroom. The images, around Mevlido, became less legible.

By applying oneself, one could still make out the light surfaces of skin, the curve of stomachs and legs, the inelegant mass of Sergueïev's genitals, and a few splotches of ink—hair, mouths, areolas, triangular tufts of pubic hair. But one had to rely on imagination to see more than that, for example, to determine what the gazes were turned toward.

Mevlido turned toward Samiya Choong, regretting not having heard her speak yet. He was sorry that he could hardly make out her silhouette now, when it was with her that he would have preferred to establish a dialogue. Something about her reminded him of Verena Siew, her vertical grace, her way of breathing, of being, or, quite bluntly, her beauty. He concentrated for a few seconds on the hope of a mental contact with her, intelligence to intelligence, and then, as the shadows drowned his efforts and the time passed, he gave up.

He relaxed and settled his eyes on nothing.

"I'm ready," he said.

Without a word, Samiya Choong abandoned the close surveillance of Mevlido to her companions. With assurance, she took four steps in the direction of the corner kitchen, whose composition, from one cell to another, didn't change: a sink, a drain board, a cupboard, a hot plate fed by bottled gas, a stool, a tiny table attached to the wall. Mevlido reconstituted her movements from the noises and smells. She moved, the darkness had swallowed her up, and, in her wake, the air was agitated. A wisp of perfumed air reached Mevlido, of recently used soap, with elements of cloves and rose.

In the kitchen, Samiya Choong began to move around the items that Mevlido had assembled so that Mingrelian could inherit them after his departure. Invisibly, she rifled through the silverware, shook a packet of scouring powder, dropped a spoon that she did not pick up. She was looking for something. The box containing the tea was opened, it was closed, the lid sighed as it met the opening. Then Samiya Choong's hands could be heard feeling the wall above the sink. Her hands walked insistently over the wall, pressing on the concrete, and, after half a minute, she said:

"We'll go through the window. That will save us walking for an hour in the basement corridors."

Her voice was rather ordinary, which disappointed Mevlido. It didn't have that quality of huskiness and theatricality often attributed to femmes fatales, and which one likes, in general, to discover at the end of a sentence, at night, in reality or in a dream.

It was the ordinary voice of a woman of action who was feeling about on a wall.

The furnace continued to purr on the floor below.

The night was peaceful, the hallway silent, no one had turned on the light again, no one in the neighboring cells was moaning in their sleep or talking. Very far away, in the bathroom located on the landing, someone flushed a toilet. A door closed, then no exterior sound could be heard.

"There's no window," said Mevlido. "In this part of the building the walls are two meters thick, and they have no windows."

Samiya Choong did not answer.

The furnace purred.

"There's not the smallest opening, the rooms are like caves," added Mevlido.

Above the sink, the teapot clinked against a glass.

Samiya Choong pushed aside the stool, which was in her way. A second spoon fell onto the floor.

Then, in who knows what groove, a metal plate slid with a sharp screech. A metal plate that Mevlido would have claimed never to have seen in his kitchen if one had questioned him on the subject.

"What are you talking about, Mevlido, no window?" said Samiya Choong.

"But after all," protested Mevlido, "you're in a position to see that . . ."

He lifted himself from the mattress and stood up, unhappy not to be taken at his word.

Tatiana Outougaï and Sergueïev immediately glued themselves to him, as if he were getting ready to make a hostile move or wanted to escape toward the hallway. Tatiana Outougaï blocked his way on the left; her skin gave off a more springlike fragrance than that which accompanied Samiya Choong, a more grasslike and greener perfume. The young woman had washed her hair with citronella shampoo. Sergueïev, also, smelled clean. He must just have gotten out of a bath and slathered his armpits with menthol deodorant.

Tatiana Outougaï grabbed Mevlido's left sleeve and twisted his arm, forcing him to keep his numbed hand between his shoulder blades, separated from pain by a fragile millimeter that could be broken at any moment.

"Don't be a fool, Mevlido," she murmured in his ear. "I won't hesitate to tear you limb from limb if necessary."

Mevlido was a head taller than she was, and heavier, but she was controlling him perfectly, and he noticed and even appreciated, against his own interests, her specialist's determination, her knowledge of the skeleton and the intimate morphology of limbs. He recognized the economy of effort and hesitation that belongs only to the best. He could sense her serene breathing, the muscles that she hadn't even contracted to dominate him; he inhaled her bare, warm skin, her wildflower perfume. She tightened her grip imperceptibly. He was in pain.

"I didn't want to . . . ," he stuttered.

"Come on, let's go," said Sergueïev.

Sergueïev hadn't grabbed his other arm, but he stayed on his right side, very close, and, to indicate to Mevlido that he needed to go forward, he gave him a little pat on the back.

They reached the kitchen corner. Thanks to the hold that made his arm useless, Mevlido walked docilely, bent over. Beyond Samiya Choong's silhouette, the wall was black. No opening penetrated it.

"All the same," said Mevlido, "a window. You can see perfectly well that the wall . . ."

Tatiana Outougaï loosened her hold and shook her head, as girls with long hair tend to do. The extremely black mane swept across Mevlido's pullover, first from right to left, then from left to right, then vanished. The smell of citronella shampoo had strengthened. Sergueïev had still not grabbed Mevlido, but he might have been demonstrating his technical superiority, simply by holding himself very nearby, and, one could tell, very vigilant, with his dangling penis and massive testicles and mentholated armpits, ready to intervene to counter Mevlido's least unexpected movement.

Samiya Choong then came forward and rejoined Mevlido. She touched his right shoulder.

"This way," she invited him.

Mevlido didn't understand what was expected of him. He didn't see what the "here" was that Samiya Choong's voice was talking about.

In place of explanation, Tatiana Outougaï pulled his wrist upward. Vicious suffering ran through the tendons in his forearm, then further into his body.

"I won't hesitate," she reminded him.

At the same time, Sergueïev slid behind him and, kicking him in the back of the knee, made him lose the support of one leg.

Though he had the build of a fighter and enough martial arts skill to react, he went along with them. He bent toward the sink and toward Samiya Choong.

He had never intended to resist. He was mentally prepared for this episode, and, even today, in his solemn declaration before the commission, he had reaffirmed that he would submit without balking to the trials of the passage, and then those of the voyage and those of the rebirth. He wasn't ignorant of the fact that the disengagement always took hateful forms and that, to pass through the first gate, he would be psychologically mistreated, dispossessed of his combativeness, and, on the physical level, deconstructed, emasculated, reduced to a mass of disordered rags. He had accepted it. He had said that he accepted it.

He suppressed a whimper, and, guided by Samiya Choong, he slumped his rib cage over the edge of the sink.

The fall hadn't hurt him at all, but he now found himself off balance, in a lopsided and humiliating position that had something grotesque about it. Tatiana Outougaï made him bring his legs closer to the cabinet under the sink. She was trapping him by the knees, hips; she had increased the torsion of the joints she controlled. The thing that protruded from Mevlido's shoulder had no more autonomy than a dead chicken wing, scrawny and horribly bent. Sergueïev now immobilized his other arm and pulled it backward, moving aside to leave room for Samiya Choong, who was going to need to get closer. Tatiana Outougaï shook her perfumed hair, she spilled it onto Mevlido, she was stuck to him, behind him, she clung to him like an octopus.

The tip of someone's toes hit the little spoon that had fallen to the ground shortly before.

And then there was a pause difficult to measure.

One second. Or two, maybe. Or ten.

A glass shook on a shelf.

They could feel their breath and the beating of their hearts and, very far off, in other depths, the regular purring of the furnace.

Above the basin, near the aluminum draining rack, Mevlido who couldn't see anything thought he saw a flash. A silvery blade, gray. It occurred to him that Samiya Choong was holding a cutthroat razor under the tap, but he wouldn't have sworn to it, because, in reality, his eyes weren't transmitting anything trustworthy. There was no longer any distance between he and Samiya Choong, but, for the moment, she was barely brushing against him. She was right next to him, on his right, and, unlike the others, she was barely brushing against him. It was impossible to understand what she was doing, she was moving her hands maybe, right there, above the sink.

By arching his neck as well as he could, he made out in front of him the faucet, a sponge, dish soap, a piece of soap. The slightly fetid humidity of the pipes entered Mevlido's nostrils, immediately combated and conquered by the emanations from Samiya Choong's body. The magnificent forty-year-old suddenly pressed against him, put her arm around part of his back, around Mevlido there was a surge of honey touched with cloves, a wave of full-blown roses, and he felt on his right ear and cheek the provocative elasticity of a breast, because she was abruptly leaning against him, and he imagined Samiya Choong's very beautiful face, now extremely close, that Asiatic tragedian's or goddess's face, her very brilliant eyes, capable of love, which, by weakness and lack of time, he confused with those of Verena Siew, with what he remembered of Verena Siew's eyes.

"No matter how much I look, I still don't see what window . . . ," he blustered in a livid voice.

"And that? What is that?" said someone.

Tatiana Outougaï made herself very heavy, she was tangled up in his legs and twisted his wrist with more and more pronounced ferocity. Sergueïev had a way of crushing his fingers one against the other that completely petrified his arm. He moved the angle of his grip by one centimeter, and all of Mevlido's right side was, in turn, paralyzed.

Samiya Choong's left hand crawled through Mevlido's hair to pull his head backward, but, as its length didn't allow for an effective grip, she continued her way the length of his skull, until his forehead, until she could hook onto his brow bone. Then she could pull Mevlido's head up so that he could glimpse the invisible window.

Everyone at that exact moment was in close contact with Mevlido, pressed against Mevlido, as if compactly solidary with Mevlido.

He kept his eyes open, but his retinas neither received nor sent any more messages. The time of comprehensible messages had reached its end. He had become incapable of truly understanding the nature of the events in course. He wondered what the others were doing, if they had or had not already started the disengagement, if they were opening a window or a trapdoor or something else.

At the risk of snapping his neck and destroying his eyelids, because that's where she was gripping his head, Samiya Choong continued to hold his head up. And yes, it was a razor that . . .

A cutthroat razor.

It was of course a razor that she was moving beneath Mevlido's chin, above the sink's drain, like a bow.

26

After that they went out the window.

Pushed by Samiya Choong, Mevlido went through the opening first, followed closely by Sergueïev. Tatiana Outougaï followed them. They clung as well as they could to the vertical outside wall, and they remained motionless at first, flattened against the bricks, having beneath their feet a drop of twenty meters or a little more. Samiya Choong was the last of the group. She crept out backward, head held in the shadows of the building until the last minute, as if she wanted to breathe as long as possible over the sink and its horrors. Instinctively, Mevlido understood that they had to wait for her before starting off. He didn't budge until she was in turn glued to the wall, in precarious equilibrium over the void.

No one spoke.

Bathed in darkness and cold, all four began to proceed toward the frozen earth. Between the bricks were plenty of bumps and cracks, and sometimes pieces of pipes stuck out, wrapped in sleeves of fiberglass that defended them from freezing. They were constantly finding handholds. Even for someone who wasn't a mountaineering ace, the descent presented no major difficulty.

Mevlido moved with a certain ease, because he had shoes, and especially because rock climbing was one of the disciplines that he had practiced for thousands of hours. His companions, on the other hand, had trouble. Above Mevlido they could be heard groaning. For them, who had not changed organic status, immersion in black space meant fear and suffering that special training had not been able to teach them to completely overcome. They were going naked into a hostile environment, subnatural, subreal, and, to escape it, they were obliged to undergo the embrace of a hideous thing that enveloped them and that, through every pore and orifice, second after second, without respite, penetrated them. It's impossible to harden oneself to the point of placidly accepting such a dreary ordeal.

Mevlido, himself, hadn't had to fight to stay alive, and, since the scene at the sink, he faced the nothingness with a sangfroid of which even zombies and golems are not always capable. Now that Sergueïev and Tatiana Outougaï weren't twisting his arms behind him, now that Samiya Choong wasn't excavating his throat with a razor, the future seemed less somber. The disengagement had ended, the journey had started, and at the moment he had in view another passage, crossing the border—that is, the moment when he would finally be able to begin living again. It wasn't as anxiety producing as the previous stage.

To reach that, his new goal, it even seemed to him that he didn't need help. When, guided over the sink by Samiya Choong, he had put his head through to the other side of the window and felt his skin absorb the reinvigorating humidity of the outside, he had almost turned around to say to the others that he would be able to get along by himself, that he would find the way to the border without anyone having to escort him in pain and distress through the black space. But all of a sudden, he was afraid of appearing presumptuous, and, so, beyond the border, the glacial night surrounding him and flowing over him, he hadn't said a word. He hadn't tried to pull his head back through toward the kitchen to speak. And he had obeyed Samiya Choong's hands, which pushed his body through the opening.

Protected from scratches by his clothes, he let himself slide down the length of a vertical pipe, and, under the soles of his feet, he finally felt the contact of the earth. Above him, in the position of mountain climbers, their movements lacking assurance, his naked companions maneuvered.

Sergueïev in turn reached the ground, then Tatiana Outougaï. They separated. Mevlido continued to follow Samiya Choong's movements. She had no more than four meters to travel. She moved slowly, pausing frequently. She stretched to reach a pipe that stuck out to her right. The fiberglass sleeve tore; she let go and fell. She collapsed at Mevlido's feet.

Without a cry she rolled on the hardened clay.

Her head hit a frost-covered ridge of mud.

One can imagine what Mingrelian had been able to write after this fall. Her head hit a frost-covered ridge of mud, he would have written. She was still very beautiful in an Asiatic way in body and face, and she was more and more naked.

A meter away, Tatiana Outougaï and Sergueïev were panting, backed against the brick. The atmosphere—if there was an atmosphere—carried along substances that shouldn't suit their respiratory systems.

Mevlido, himself, was no longer concerned by the nature of the gas circulating in his lungs. Until the moment when he reincarnated in a hominid embryo he didn't have to worry about any physiological problem. It's true that, at moments, he could be seen inflating and deflating his chest, but it was purely a matter of simulation: he was maintaining the theater of breath first of all to furnish the flow of air necessary for words and, besides, because he didn't want to show off his difference with anyone else. For the others, he was pretending to have a life.

The nocturnal cold was penetrating.

Samiya Choong had just hit her head against the frozen ground.

She was more and more naked.

A few stars twinkled between the clouds, giving out a sparse light. They could locate each other in space a bit better than in front of the sink, but not much more clearly.

Mevlido bent toward Samiya Choong and helped her up. She was shaking in all her limbs. He saw her small breasts tighten, her stomach take on a gray color. Her knees were bleeding. Again, he inhaled from her the smell of cloves and rose that she had broadcast in the bedroom just before, that is, one thousand years before. To that known fragrance was now added a salty scent of anxiety and hurt.

"It's hard for you too," he said.

"Yes," she admitted.

She didn't loosen her jaw. She spoke through her teeth.

"Can I do anything for you, Samiya?"

"No."

"Does it bother you if I call you Samiya?"

"No."

"Did you scrape yourself?"

"No. Well, yes, a little."

He pulled her to him, to his chest, to the warm pullover that he was allowed to wear and she wasn't; he held her, he embraced her fraternally, and she let herself go a little, nestling a bit against him, seeking the compassion he was offering, and the heat.

She stayed like that for about ten seconds, her shoulders shaken as if by tearless sobs.

"What if I went alone?" he said.

"No," she said.

"For me," Mevlido insisted, "it no longer means anything in particular. I only have to go straight ahead."

"No," she said, "we have to . . ."

"Even if it's far," he continued, "I only have to go straight ahead."

"No," she said. "Without us, you wouldn't succeed at all."

Then she freed herself. She went to join Sergueïev and Tatiana Outougaï again. Already, the stocky military man and the unsympathetic girl had closed ranks with her. They were trying to share their energy, and they were going to need it, to get Mevlido to the assigned spot and make it back. They were trying to do that, but what they succeeded in doing more than anything else was shivering together and suffocating, gasping. Waiting for the three companions to regain their strength, Mevlido raised his eyes to the building they had left behind. No lamp shone there.

An immense wall with no opening loomed in the night, very vaguely divided into stories by clues such as the branches of external pipes or the horizontal lines in the brick. The height of the stories was enormous and did not correspond, at any rate, to any normal architecture. Mevlido examined this giant surface to find the first gateway, the place where they had started their descent. He saw nothing. The window seemed to have been walled up immediately after their passage; no fresh scar of cement or new bricks indicated its placement. After the second floor his gaze became lost, with the black of the wall blending into the black of the celestial vault. It was impossible to have a complete vision of the structure, and he gave up trying to imagine that, behind it, lived a world that had known or knew heat and light, a society constituted of men and women who were working or had worked, slept and dreamed in the cells and gyms, weight rooms, testing rooms, study rooms.

The calm was profound, and it went on and on, then was broken by a faraway rifle shot. Despite appearances, the night also hid certain forms of collective action.

Mevlido neared the small group. His eyes fastened on Tatiana Outougaï's tense face. Her long hair was currently falling in disorder; it was tangled and made her look like a young witch.

"Did you hear?" he asked.

For several seconds, no one said a word.

"I don't think we should delay," Mevlido went on.

"No one asked your opinion, Mevlido," said Tatiana Outougaï.

Mevlido refrained from answering. He judged it ridiculous to fight with Tatiana Outougaï. He had had a bad relationship with the girl from the beginning, and, going forward, nothing would change.

"All right," said Sergueïev, "now let's go."

They walked away from the wall and, on Samiya Choong's initiative, began to move forward in single file.

In the distance, other rifle shots rang out. The shots came from a part of the night situated in front of him. They punctuated long, quiet intervals, and, if someone absolutely had to say something about the silence surrounding the travelers, they might have said that, despite everything, it reigned.

Mevlido, with his big shoes, made the most noise. In front of himself he could make out a meter of poorly lit path and, immediately after that, Samiya Choong's very pale legs and buttocks. She went a third of a kilometer without turning around, then she entrusted the task of leading the way to Tatiana Outougaï; after that they changed places frequently. Their nudity hampered them. They were slowed down at each moment, on the icy mud that had trapped pebbles with sharp edges, or when, in the potholes, the water broke and cut them like glass, or when they stepped on snail shells and detritus.

Plants were infrequent and dead.

Like this, in single file, they skirted several fields of garbage, which the lack of shoes made uncrossable.

From time to time a flare shot up over the horizon, but not high enough and in any case too far away to usefully illuminate the place where they were walking. Of the landscape he could see almost nothing. What he could see evoked a flooded, monotonous plain, devoid of trees.

Despite their episodic nature, the shots didn't stop. At the end of a quarter of an hour, they echoed with an increased clarity, and the intervals between the shots grew shorter.

Suddenly, a second after a detonation much closer to them, Mevlido heard the whine of a projectile.

They increased their pace. There was gravel on the path, which ceaselessly bruised the soles of bare feet. All three of Mevlido's companions began to sigh more and more strongly and chaotically. Finally, hoarse vowels emerged from their throats, horrible to hear.

"We're coming to the edge of the water," announced Sergueïev.

"What if we made a stop?" asked Samiya Choong.

"No, not yet," said Sergueïev.

"I can't . . . I can't take it anymore," confessed Samiya Choong.

"We have to keep going," said Sergueïev.

Their voices resembled tattered murmurs.

"I think I see the truck on the embankment," said Tatiana Outougaï, throwing all of her hair back.

"Ah," said Sergueïev, "in that case, yes, we can stop."

The two women came close to him, and they immediately formed a group with shoulders and arms mixed together, a pitifully animal trio, as they had earlier at the foot of the wall, like blind baby birds stuck together at the bottom of a nest. They rubbed each other's limbs. They exchanged short plaintive sounds, an affectionate camaraderie, breath. One could only have a very vague idea of what was gnawing at them, the terrors that were beating inside their bodies and destroying everything.

Mevlido kept himself at a distance.

Unexpectedly, given the circumstances, his brain was suddenly visited by a literary reminiscence. His memory projected before his mind's eye a chapter of a novel related to their current ordeal, a scene with which Mingrelian was finishing one of his works of fiction. Because Mingrelian also wrote that kind of text, narratives that didn't correspond to what the Organs expected and demanded from him. Poetic narratives. He wrote them for himself, without dreaming of publishing them, and, if he allowed them to be read, it was only because his neighbors on the floor appreciated them and demanded insistently to read them.

Mevlido remembered the final episode of this book, whose title he had forgotten. An invulnerable being, condemned to death, was executed in the only place he could be reached—inside one of his dreams. In a deep sleep, he opened his eyes, and he saw before him executioners who had come to him without weapons or clothes, assassins poisoned and almost killed by the traversal of dream worlds: a man and two women, specifically. Asphyxia slowed their movements, their skin was bluish, they shivered at the door of his room. The slumbering man, the being who no weapon could harm, left his bed. He approached the assassins, he examined them as if he were going to violently settle the score with them, and yet, toward these three individuals whose job it was to destroy him, he felt compassion. Such was the infernal mechanism of the nightmare. Disdaining the fact that the aggressors were at his mercy, he consoled them, leaning over them and talking to them. And thus the trap of pity that had been set closed upon him. One by one his defenses fell, his capacities of resistance and annihilation. Sympathy, empathy, dissolved his shell, and, finally, in contradiction with the principles that had until then governed his existence, he lost all desire to escape and went philosophically to meet death.

That passage from the novel floated before him the length of a snap of the fingers. Then it was no more.

Then Mevlido came back to Samiya Choong, Sergueïev, and Tatiana Outougaï. They continued to huddle together with pathetic little movements. Beyond the group, the night remained opaque, and despite his efforts, Mevlido couldn't manage to locate the truck that Tatiana Outougaï had claimed to see. The shore was certainly very close. If he listened very carefully, he could hear the sound of a waterway that gleamed several times in the light of the flares. Little waves lapped between the grasses and reeds, and, a little farther on, pieces of ice grated as they tumbled over and bumped into each other in the current. The magnesium flares had revealed a broad expanse, the flashes of light running over immense, oily swells. A river ran there, and it was breaking free. The debacle of springtime had begun.

While Mevlido reflected on the debacle, a burst of automatic fire crackled nearby, less than two hundred meters away.

"Get down, Mevlido!" ordered Tatiana Outougaï.

Mevlido obeyed. He crouched down.

"Quick," said Sergueïev, "we'll run to the truck."

The compact interlocking of naked bodies dissolved.

Tatiana Outougaï rushed to Mevlido. He felt her hair flying above him. She had grabbed a sleeve of his pullover and was tugging on it.

"Go!" she ordered him again. "Stay low!"

Already she was dragging him behind her roughly. All of them, all at once, were running over trash, tin cans, shards of glass, woody stems of climbing plants. They went forward bent over, as if broken in two, quickly, without thinking about the uneven ground or its pitfalls. They had taken the direction of the river.

After about fifty paces, they came upon the vehicle waiting for them—an ordinary military truck, small but robust, with a narrow cab and a bed set up to transport ten or so people sheltered under tarpaulins. The front looked like a pig's snout.

Sergueïev opened the driver's-side door, climbed up, and sat behind the wheel. Samiya Choong had arrived at the passenger door. She unlocked it, grabbed on, and, after some painful contortions, fell onto the unoccupied front seat next to Sergueïev. Both were panting the way soldiers or human guinea pigs pant when they've been exposed to gas containing 100 percent chlorine.

There was a new burst of gunfire. Bullets shrieked past nearby. You could hear their desire to bite, to throw themselves as fast as possible into the earth or into flesh.

"Go, Mevlido, hurry up!" Tatiana Outougaï said impatiently.

She wanted Mevlido to get in the back. The tarp was untied, and they could slide into the opening, but first they had to get over the tailgate, which was up. Mevlido hung suspended from it, steadied himself, and fell into the bed. Without asking for his help, and with the promptness of an acrobat, Tatiana Outougaï climbed up after him.

The truck smelled like wet tent fabric.

Mevlido felt around and sat down right behind Sergueïev.

He heard Tatiana Outougaï stumbling in the dark.

There was no separation between the cab and the back, where two lateral benches were formed of wooden boards. Tatiana Outougaï took another step and fell onto the floor, behind Samiya Choong's seat. She was now in front of Mevlido. Limbs spread out oddly to try to counter the suffocation, she had adopted a pose that in another place might have been judged pornographic, and that didn't do her any favors. She could no longer catch her breath.

After a few seconds of vain effort she gathered her legs to her chest and wrapped her arms around them. With her back against the bench, her folding herself up evoked Aztec or Nazca mummies, but not perfectly, because here the idea of physical distress and torment was superimposed on that of the tomb. Now, her hair fell all the way to the ground. She curled up, bent over at the abdomen, tortured by horrible cramps and waves of death. Maybe she had also taken one of the bullets that, a minute before, had shrieked their desire to bury themselves in flesh.

She hiccuped, then was silent. She remained immobile for two seconds, then contorted herself as only a tormented Nazca mummy can, and, once more, she hiccuped and was silent.

In the front seat, Samiya Choong was experiencing similar suffering. In turn she gathered up her body in an awful fetal position and froze. Her mouth let out an empty sound that collided with the silence—a mix of coughing, vomiting, and prayer.

As for Sergueïev, he wasn't shriveling up or contorting himself, but he wasn't in any better shape than his companions. He started bent over the steering wheel like the victim of a car accident, his breathing rapid and shallow, his head touching the windshield. After a minute, he managed to sit up normally, but the poisons of the black space continued to carbonize the inside of his organism and his consciousness. He was sighing convulsively at the same time that he was trying to hold his breath the longest possible time. His lungs could be heard searching for a way not to suffer so much, and one wondered, in his condition, how he could drive.

Mevlido glued himself against the front seat and was holding his head as if to tell Sergueïev a secret. The absence of a dividing wall between the passengers being transported and the driver allowed such a thing.

He could make out Sergueïev's shaved neck, a round, solid shoulder, a smell of mentholated sweat. A flare went up very far away on the other side of the river and slowly tore apart a bit of the sky. At that point he noticed that Sergueïev's skin was drenched with gray droplets. Some of them had clumped together and were running down his skin.

"Sergueïev," said Mevlido, "we have to leave right away. If you . . ."

"I know," said Sergueïev.

"If you want, I can get behind the wheel," continued Mevlido. "You'll tell me the way, what it looks . . ."

Sergueïev's ear moved next to Mevlido's mouth. His whole head moved. It was to indicate a refusal.

"Listen, Mevlido," rasped Sergueïev, "you have your mission, we have ours."

He sat up on his seat.

"When it's your turn to act, you'll act. But, in the meantime . . ."

"I could maybe . . ."

"No, you can't do anything," interrupted Sergueïev.

He was bringing the gearshift to neutral. The shifter moved, then there was a contraction and a relaxation of springs, then a silence.

Sergueïev didn't start the ignition, he wasn't even trying to turn the key, supposing that there was such a thing under the steering wheel.

Outside, the flare had just faded out.

A rifle shot echoed from one of the refuse warehouses they had just passed. On Sergueïev's left the side mirror exploded.

Sergueïev hadn't let go of the gearshift. He changed the position again, then brought it back to neutral. The vehicle shuddered. There had been no noise of combustion and no odor of gas or any other kind of fuel. Slowly, the truck headed to the right, onto the ice-covered water. Sergueïev corrected his route and began to drive along the bank, at a very slow speed and without turning on the headlights. He must have trained himself to drive like that, desperately naked and sick, in the enemy darkness, over uneven terrain, through potholes and debris.

They jolted along for ten minutes, following the course of the river slowly. The truck tilted and groaned, listed, righted itself. Sometimes the wheels spun on marshy surfaces. Sometimes the ground seemed like corrugated iron covered with ice. Sometimes a passage had to be opened through the thicket of reeds that totally barricaded the route. The stalks cracked. They scraped along the tarpaulin. Drained of color by the night, dried plumes scattered themselves over the windscreen or swept across it with a squeak.

Not a single sound came from under the truck's hood.

Sergueïev's training program evidently must have also had a course on how to drive a vehicle with no motor.

The two women kept their eyes closed. From their mouths escaped a very feeble lamentation. The jolts shook them from one side to the other, and every so often they unbent, abandoning their Nazca posture and sitting with their feet on the ground, but, as soon as the pain and the anxiety became too strong again, they bent over completely. They curled up again.

"Is it far?" asked Mevlido.

"We still have one hundred fifty kilometers to go," said Sergueïev. "One hundred fifty and then some."

Mevlido contemplated what he could see of Samiya Choong on the front seat, then he looked at Tatiana Outougaï, who, after having been on the floor, had ended up pulling herself onto the bench in front of him.

He crossed the width of the truck and went to sit down next to her. He touched her knee, her hand. Her flesh was like cardboard. She was horribly cold.

"Do you want me to warm you up, Tatiana?" he asked. "To put myself against you to warm you up?"

"No," she said in a dying voice.

"Can I call you Tatiana?"

"No."

He returned to sit behind Sergueïev.

"Will they survive?" he asked.

"And you?" said Sergueïev. "And you, Mevlido?"

27

As soon as the truck had begun to roll with difficulty along the riverbank, the shots stopped. The world became as calm as it had been in the first minutes of the trip. One last magnesium flower illuminated the waterway whose ice was breaking up on their left. The flare revealed the expanses of reeds surrounding them, the frozen puddles, the lack of a track, then it went out. No other flares followed. Only the meager twinkle of the stars cut through the darkness after that. Images became rare. The images were monotonous. The images were uniformly black. Even when it had undergone special training, the human retina had trouble accepting them as images.

They advanced slowly. Sergueïev seemed to be driving from memory rather than as a function of what he could actually see coming toward him. Sometimes he would turn the wheel violently, as if to avoid, at the last second, a terrible obstacle that he alone suddenly saw. Branches knocked against the underside of the chassis. The wheels crushed slabs of ice, piles of mud. There were still scratches on the hood and the tarpaulin from the reeds.

A while later, the terrain evolved. The tires were supported by something that must have been a passable road. The vegetal murmurs stopped. They had left the vicinity of the river. The truck accelerated.

As there was still no noise from the motor, a sort of coarse nocturnal silence began to press down around Mevlido and his companions. The rushing wind blew through the chinks in the doors and the gaps in the tarpaulin covering the back. Besides these humble melodies and the creaks of the suspension, nothing disturbed the shadowy quiet of the trip. Neither the passengers nor the driver opened their mouths to speak. The cold was harsh. It must have been cruelly attacking the two women and the man that no garments protected.

No one complained.

Mevlido was sitting across from Tatiana Outougaï, whose obscene postures he could guess from time to time. She changed tactic against the pain often, sometimes trying to curl up on the bench or under it, sometimes stretching in all directions as if trying to mime being quartered, sometimes slouching, her face hidden under her long hair. It was a horrible dance of horrible suffering. Not having any means of attenuating such torture at his disposition, Mevlido tried to look away. He turned away and tried to figure out what lay beyond the windows and the windshield. His gaze went no farther than Sergueïev, who, at intervals, let out a sigh of fatigue, and it moved over Samiya Choong, who seemed frozen and dead. On the other side of the windshield the darkness wasn't penetrated by a single light, as tiny as it might be.

The night remained indecipherable.

Mevlido would have liked to calculate the number of kilometers they had already covered.

He would have liked to know how many hours still separated him from the border.

He would have liked to understand what, exactly, they were passing through.

But he didn't understand it, and he withdrew into himself, his eyes half-closed across from Tatiana Outougaï.

After three hours without incident a grayish tone began to appear. It had neither a cardinal direction nor the sky for origin.

It was as if a dirty froth had oozed out of the earth, with the ridiculous intention of imitating the dawn. They discovered little by little a panorama of hills and thickets, made ugly by destroyed farms and spiked fortifications. The light was increasing, but at the end of five minutes it stopped progressing and stagnated at the level of a sub-marine dawn, but that was enough for the eye to take in a battlefield several generations old, extending for kilometers on all sides, where the memory of primordial global butchery and explosive murders or mutilations was preserved in the clay.

The sky itself had not gotten any lighter, quite the contrary. It was infinitely tarry and colorless. It had the blackness of black pitch, now empty of any star, or even of the notion of a star or interstellar space. And, if it remained a vault, the qualifier of "celestial" suited it less and less well.

Sergueïev had a spasm of pain and slumped over the wheel. He clenched his hands so violently that the skin of his knuckles burst. Blood accumulated on the edges of the wounds, and, when it reached the necessary mass for the phenomenon to occur, it left the surface of his skin, collected into bubbles, and began to float around the cab. There were now a series of small, elastic, unruly spheres floating between Sergueïev and Samiya Choong. It's like something you would see if you killed a monkey in zero gravity: if, in an experimental space station (for example) orbiting the earth or any other comparable sphere, you eviscerated a chimpanzee or a laboratory dog, to see what would happen (for example), or even to advance science, or research, or surgical techniques. The blood wanders globulously around the murderous -nauts (whom the paid commentator will continue to call cosmonauts), and, pushed by a force that is not the principal objective of the study, it goes bit by bit to stick to what, in this scenario, takes the place of the sky. It forms a strange little flock on the spaceship's wall, just above the sacrificial table. I've seen that—maybe you have too—and nausea still overwhelms me at that thought. Here they weren't in a space shuttle, they were in an atmosphere of total darkness, but, after a period of wandering, those vermilion globes that, in the light of dawn or false dawn appeared more or less the color of anthracite, acted as if they were in zero gravity. They were obeying some residual forces, and they slowly moved to the top of the windshield, behind the rearview mirror or to the edge of the roof, then, without melting together, they bumped against each other and danced to the rhythm of the jostling truck.

Even if his body was losing its substance and, intimately devastated by the night, felt dead all over, Sergueïev was holding up with an admirable courage. Without ostentation, in silence, he concentrated himself on what was ahead. He embodied the desire to keep going at all costs, an unbending desire.

Mevlido leaned toward him.

"Will we arrive soon?" he murmured.

"Forty kilometers more," said Sergueïev.

"Do you want me to take your place?" Samiya Choong asked Sergueïev.

The short dialogue between Mevlido and Sergueïev had brought her out of the comatose abyss in which she had been mummified for the last few hours; all the while they had been driving on a straight and uniform cement track. Her eyelids were glued shut; she was curled up in a ball on her seat. She had asked the question without raising her head.

"In a little while," said Sergueïev. "On the way back."

Every twenty meters, the separation between the slabs of

concrete made the passengers jump. It also shook the spheres of blood floating above the windshield.

"When we have left Mevlido at the border," added Sergueïev. "When he has entered the gate."

"OK," said Samiya Choong.

The tires hissed.

The wind whistled in the chinks of the truck. An elementary melody, continuo.

"OK," she said again, without moving. "For the return."

The shock absorbers creaked.

They could also hear the little metallic pieces clicking, the carabiners used to hold the tarpaulin, defective ball bearings, a piece of chain somewhere in the back.

Tatiana Outougaï got up. She walked, swaying, to the opening in the tarpaulin, above the tailgate. She slid her head outside, and she could be heard vomiting; then she came back to her place and sat down with her legs apart.

In the absence of other noises in the cockpit they might have imagined themselves inside a glider about to land with a cargo of the dying.

A new half hour went by.

Mevlido observed the landscape that now, looking beyond the back of the seat and Sergueïev's shoulders, he could scrutinize at his leisure. When he had had enough of counting the craters made by bombs and the splintered tree trunks, he examined his traveling companions, or counted the marbles, globes, and eggs of blood trembling above their heads.

That man and those women, he finally saw them clearly and not approximately, as had been the case in his bedroom or near the river. In the twilight he observed their raw nudity, their total nudity, their pathetic nudity. Everything was visible. Neither Sergueïev nor the women sought subterfuges or modest positions to hide their sex, their breasts. The women were sometimes collapsed and in disorder, softened by unconsciousness, or curled up upon themselves. Cyanosis spoiled the Asiatic color of their skin, giving them a hue never seen on living organisms. They had both scraped themselves coming down the wall, and, when they had run to reach the truck, they had cut the bottoms of their feet, their ankles. Just before jumping over the tailgate, Tatiana Outougaï had been hit in the stomach by a projectile. The wounds had gotten bigger and were bleeding. The blood ran, escaped, and always according to the same process, it accumulated on one side of the cut until it made a new spherical mass, then the sphere detached itself from its source and began to float slowly, very slowly, toward the ceiling.

An abrupt vision, between two nothings:

- Tatiana Outougaï has her eyes closed.
- She pulls herself upright on the wooden bench, she straightens her shoulders a bit, with a trembling hand she throws her tangled hair back, then, the same trembling hand, she walks it over the wound just beside her navel, feels around for a few seconds, then she places it on the middle of a thigh whose hard, contracted muscles can be distinguished.
- With the other hand, she grasps the edge of the seat.
- Suddenly, she opens her eyes.
- She stares at Mevlido, who is seated across from her, she stares at him with an expression divided between fear and the still-arrogant and disdainful desire not to show weakness.
- Then she closes her eyelids again.

Mevlido wondered how beings fragilized to this point could, after having escorted him all the way to the gate that communicated with the world where he was being sent, accomplish the return voyage. He meditated on the courage of his transporters, on their quasi-suicidal heroism, and on the sense of discipline that had made them accept suffering and sacrifice, without wondering if the cause was worth the trouble or, if they had wondered, without balking, and this rumination on the misfortune of others kept him from pitying himself, when his own fate . . .

When his own fate wasn't very enviable either.

Because, after crossing the last gate, he was going to suffer an irreparable loss of memory and identity, to then be shut up, for a lifetime, inside a foreign body and a foreign mind. A lifetime. Inside a foreign body and a foreign mind. And with no possible consolation, because no certainty about a previous existence would ever come to comfort him. Images would visit him, of course, dreams, nostalgia, or strange intuitions, but he would receive them crudely or furtively, without ever having the keys that could give them a re-assuring meaning. He would gather them inside himself like phantasms, incongruities from his unconscious or his sick brain. And if one day, as Mingrelian had suggested, he crossed paths with a woman also sent on mission by the Organs, he would not have anything special to exchange with her. This woman would also have lost her memory of a prenatal universe. They would stand side by side, chance or fate would associate them perhaps for a few minutes or a few years, or several decades, the remains of instinct would re-inforce their complicity. But at no moment would one or the other find the path of their previous life. He and she, and perhaps he and she together, would be terribly exiled, but without knowing it.

The sky grew lighter. Day was breaking.

There was then a moment when they arrived at a barbed wire gate that coincided with the end of the road. It was not a very imposing barrier: three meters high, well-strung wire but without many barbs, like that used in agriculture rather than at borders.

Behind the wires the roadway had been demolished by dynamite twenty or thirty years before, and it could be seen continuing ingloriously among the plants until a curtain of pine trees. Young trees grew in disorder in the no-man's land between the gates, because for a long time the forest was progressing without anyone giving themselves the trouble to maintain it. Not a single lookout post stood nearby. They were in a place so distant from everything that it had surely been judged unworthy of surveillance.

The truck had stopped.

Sergueïev pulled on the hand brake and remained motionless in the silence, letting almost ten seconds go by before stretching out his arm to wake, on his right, Samiya Choong, who appeared to be sleeping. He touched her shoulder and, at the same time, threw a glance backward, toward Tatiana Outougaï, then he grabbed the steering wheel again and let out a groan of pain.

Tatiana Outougaï was no longer moving.

Samiya Choong opened the door and, hanging on as if in a perilous acrobatic maneuver, got out. Mevlido heard her hiccup, noisily swallow the morning air, warmer than that of the night, then she moved. She walked along the side of the truck. She held herself up by hanging on to low straps. Her hands scraped against the body of the truck. She was walking slowly toward the back. Her breathing had an odd rhythm, she was breathing through her mouth, with the moans and gurgles of a seriously ill person.

"Here we are," said Sergueïev without turning toward him. "Now it's your turn, Mevlido."

"Do I get out?" said Mevlido, to say something.

He went to the tailgate. Halfway, he stopped, hesitated, went back to make a sign of regret in front of Tatiana Outougaï. She was dead.

Then he lifted the tarpaulin, stepped over the iron panel, and jumped to the ground.

Outside, the morning was there, astonishingly pleasant.

Sergueïev's door slammed shut.

Samiya Choong had reached the back of the truck. Sergueïev was approaching. In the pine trees, near the second gate, a cuckoo let out several calls, then was silent.

Mevlido stood, dazed by the night like a clandestine immigrant who doesn't know whether he has been tricked and is waiting for the smuggler's instructions.

"A little farther on, there are some culverts," said Sergueïev.

He pointed to areas to the left of the gate, a hundred meters away, and, more precisely, a curve of damp earth where a slope began, transforming into what must have been a small ravine— a deep ditch, at any rate.

"OK," said Mevlido.

"Only one leads to the place where you've been told to go," said Sergueïev.

"I know," said Mevlido. "I also know that they have numbers on them. But they didn't tell me which . . ."

Sergueïev was swaying a little. He was standing in front of Mevlido, like a fighter in front of his opponent, and he rocked slightly back and forth, according to a shamanic technique, to continue to exist rather than to fight. Beneath his pelvis, the rubbery mass of his genitals swayed as well.

"I'm giving it to you now," said Sergueïev. "Zero zero sixteen."

Samiya Choong had left the support of the truck, and she pressed herself against Mevlido for two seconds, three seconds, against his body, on the left, on the side of the heart, and she took his arm, and he thought she was going to put his arm in a lock to lead him to the pipe number zero zero sixteen. But it was only a spontaneous gesture, like when a sister is saying goodbye to her brother, when she has already said farewell and he's going to leave right away and, once more, she needs to express her affection for him.

She let him go and moved back.

"Tatiana is dead," she murmured. "Don't make our job harder, Mevlido. Go. Don't wait any longer. Disappear as fast as possible."

With a way of moving his legs indicating a certain mental and even physical numbness, Mevlido left the proximity of the truck and walked along the barrier. The earth was heavy, soaked with dew or mist, scattered with half-rotten, half-green weeds. The soles of his shoes didn't slip, they didn't sink in, walking gave him a certain pleasure, and, as it was the last one he would ever have, he had a certain desire to dawdle, to take his time. However, Mevlido still had in his ear the pleading order that Samiya Choong had pronounced. He didn't take his time. And he even forced his pace a bit to reach the drop-off where he must, once and for all, disappear.

He could feel Sergueïev's gaze and Samiya Choong's gaze on his back. The man and the woman had stayed near the truck, but they were still accompanying him. From there they encouraged him, they directed him, they pushed him firmly toward the opening number zero zero sixteen. All together, they continued to be a team.

28

The ditch is scarcely more than four meters deep. The place makes him think of a dried-out canal, at the bottom of a valley. Disturbed by Mevlido's arrival, a crow flaps its wings without squawking, then takes off, gliding over puddles of putrid water that has gathered at the bottom of the slope. Mevlido has seen the bird, but he isn't interested in it. He doesn't have ornithology in mind at this moment. He is standing in front of a sewer exit, in front of an enormous cement tube emerging from the ground, halfway down the slope. Giant numbers are painted on the cement. The last number is partially hidden by the grassy earth, but it is identifiable with no risk of a mistake. It is definitely a six. It's definitely pipe zero zero sixteen.

It's definitely the last gate.

Soon, Mevlido will enter under its malodorous vault and disappear forever, and, as he is living the last archivable page of his existence, the very last line, he swallows a few mouthfuls of fresh air to gain a little more time. One could claim that this brief moment of inaction will be the very image on which this adventure comes to a close.

He stands there, miserly with his movements, dressed, as we know, like a poor hiker. His pullover has suffered during the voyage and, like his trousers, is stained with spots of oily dust, soot, and blood. The hiker has rubbed against dirty walls and wounded bodies.

Near this cement mouth, emitting a thin stream of sewage, Mevlido has an almost normal, if strangely pensive, posture. His hands are hanging loosely by his thighs, like a man listening to the pronouncement of a sentence while reflecting on what will happen next. To the northwest of Mevlido's left shoulder is a graying elevated roadway with a truck parked on it, and, near the front wheels, can be made out two motionless, monochrome silhouettes, without clothes, a man and a woman. They are too far away, what is being expressed on their faces can't be read. If you don't know what came before, it's impossible to understand what they are thinking of. The photo doesn't reveal whether they are there because their car has broken down, or because they are taking a break related to organic needs, like the death, the burial, of a companion, or urination, or perhaps for other reasons still, like for example saying goodbye to Mevlido, or even because they want to spy on him, to make sure that he accomplishes his mission correctly, that he does what he has to do without cheating, that he goes forward once and for all into culvert zero zero sixteen.

Mevlido turns his head toward the top of the ditch and looks at the truck and the silhouettes.

Then he turns away.

The gray of the sky is crisscrossed with mist. The claylike ground lacks poetry, is astoundingly ordinary, with shiny lumps mostly devoid of grass. Mevlido is two steps from the bottom of the ravine. At the spot just left by the crow, opaque pools and tracks of mire too rotten to reflect the sky are stagnating. Nothing can be seen but mud.

Mevlido remains passive three more seconds.

He remains passive two more seconds.

Then he sighs. It's time.

He sets himself in motion.

He doesn't look back, he doesn't try to glimpse one last time, in the distance, Samiya Choong and Sergueïev.

He's no longer thinking about the people he has known.

He grabs the edge of the pipe to get right in front of the opening. He pulls himself onto the end of the pipe, making sure not to slip in the muck.

He pulls himself onto the edge of the pipe.

He makes sure not to slip in the mire.

It's in there that he has to go.

He will immediately lose all his points of reference.

He will go alone, his body very quickly stripped of its flesh and his spirit immediately amnesiac.

And he will walk underground like that for an immeasurable number of hours, he will cross an immeasurable distance, obeying a program etched in the most labyrinthine layers of his being, inscribed there during the sessions of special training. From then on no one will push him or accompany him. He will be alone. He will be absolutely alone. He will be absolutely free, if you think about it.

Like that, he will arrive in the belly of Mevlido's mother.

He will open the womb and close it again behind him, and he will curl up, waiting for what comes next. And he will begin to wait.

Wait.

He will wait for his birth, for example. On that subject, even the Organs can know nothing in advance. They were bluffing, promising Mevlido reincarnation as a good person. In reality the Organs don't know exactly who will be Mevlido's mother, and it will take them years to find Mevlido, to make sure that it's actually him and not someone else, and to try to establish contact with him during his dreams, or even later, during his death throes. Or even later. The Organs will have difficulty finding him in the middle of all the chaos and war. On his side, he won't be looking for them actively. He might imagine them, he might obey or disobey them, but he will never be sure of their existence. Blindly, he will feel his way toward shapes that look like them. Unconsciously, he will stay on a path that, in a certain way, will bind them together, the Organs and him. When he must choose to go one direction rather than another, the weight of instinct will not be negligible, but chance and unforeseen circumstances will always complicate things.

For example, he will be born in Zone 2, in a family of schoolteachers who have abandoned their school and who fight, with the partisans, against the reestablishment of capitalism on the planet. His mother and his grandmother practice shamanism. They will both be taken away by the enemy three weeks after Mevlido's birth and be found hung from a balcony, naked and flayed. His father will be killed a few days later. All over, the egalitarian communities are dismantled and bombed with acid, poisonous snow, napalm. The baby will be taken in by Bolsheviks fleeing the counterrevolutionary troops. He will spend his childhood sometimes in one household, sometimes in another. His successive parents will be Jucapira, Golsh, Ybür, Khalq, surviving Chinese, Koreans. All belonging to the same ideological camp. Most consider themselves to be soldiers who must still fight no matter the irreversible scale of the defeat. All educate Mevlido in the meaning of revolutionary war. In this atmosphere the little boy will grow up, and, when he is an adolescent, he will naturally be found engaged in a Komsomol commando unit. It is there that he will receive most of his political and military training. He will participate in several insurrectional actions, and, when the combats end, he will melt into the columns of displaced persons, beggars, and demobilized soldiers leaving the most destroyed territories of the dark war. His culture will always be that of defeat, of sabotage, of score settling, of violence. His companions disappear one after the other, men and women. Around Mevlido, all the women of his generation have, overall, the same human trajectory as his own. They all meet a tragic end.

Mevlido will then find himself in the immense horde of refugees who ended up in Zone 3. He will be parked with them in the vast machinery of camps and ghettos that take the place of the war there. He will have to construct his survival in a context of genetic mutations, moral turpitude, technological regress, duplicity, and forgetfulness. He will become just one more left behind among all the others. Like many demobilized soldiers, he will end up joining the most disdained of the social structures put in place by the pacifiers—he will join the police.

His fate is ours, that of the subhumans and the vanquished.

And then, as it will for us, the hour of death will come for him.

And then: nothing.

If nothing unexpected happens.

29

I've already spoken about this, but it's not useless emphasizing once again the role it plays in our story. The moon. Its role in our story. Sometimes it illuminated our worlds of shadow, sometimes it darkened them. I'm speaking here in the name of the *Untermenschen* and of everyone else. It rotted our madmen's dreams.

It rotted our madmen's dreams and didn't give a damn.

Under its rays we could often be seen immodestly stretched out without shame, hallucinating, wild-eyed, our muzzles and haunches quivering like lovesick cats, and, while behind our eyelids our ocular globes twitched, we took the moonlight inside ourselves, sweat welling from all our pores and incisors or canines clacking incessantly against each other. The intoxication overtook us, the moon melted into us. It substituted itself for us. Other times we yearned to be with it at all costs. We climbed the interminable dark stairway that separated us from it, and, even if we were far from having reached it, we raved about the pleasures it would soon offer us. In anticipation we began long walks on its cold flesh, or we went to lie down on its immensity, which we imagined to be pure and powdery. For a moment the most demonstrative among us let out gasps of pleasure, but in the end, some force was always at work beneath our consciousness, pushing us to reject it, to separate ourselves from it and even to wish for its destruction as a moon. Maybe we were remembering the warnings that we had received when we were still awake. Maybe we were hearing, even in the depths of our slumber, the shouts of the old women in Henhouse Four who, night after night, called for a popular uprising against the night. In any case, something always intervened and told us to murder it.

AN ATTACK, A THOUSAND ATTACKS ON THE MOON!
IF SOMEONE IS RUNNING TOWARD THE MOON, WASH
    YOURSELF AND KILL THEM!
IF THE MOON COMES NEAR, KILL IT!

In our speeches to the masses, that is, to the dying dragging themselves around Henhouse Four without living or expiring, we accused the moon of a multitude of criminal devastations and insisted on its arrogance, on its monstrous presence above our calamity, without forgetting its ivory-like beauty—so insulting, so discouraging, so obscene. We denounced the sarcasms contained in its silence. We called a mockery its way of invading the places we slept, hopeless or wallowing in the residue of hope's absence. Often we talked total nonsense on the subject, carried away by a verbal fury whose grandiloquence was not to be pacified even when our last audience member had fled. To bolster our claims, we didn't hesitate to repeat the beggars' vociferations, their slogans coming from somewhere else and going somewhere else. We digressed with brio, evoking the catastrophic consequences of lunar radiation on the past and future social environment. Lying on packing crates, the dying heard us without answering. They were distracted, it is true, by the vultures dancing from one foot to the other nearby, ogling their eyeballs for later on. Sometimes poetry slid into our calls for uprising, and sometimes we were content to recite bloody directives. Sometimes we would reason in low voices near the ears of the madmen, a little discomfited to have to lie to convince them. We spoke of vengeance, of confronting misfortune by inflicting irreversible damage on the moon.

Some people—I know some of them—were not content moving their mouths. They launched projectiles in the direction of the moon, trying to split it open, incendiary rockets that according to their instructions should have shrunk it and sullied its light with greasy soot. Most of the time, the projectiles brushed by it without hitting it. They fell back onto the city, onto the sleeping neighborhoods—sleeping or plunged in insomnia with no perspective.

When we set up such operations, we arranged for the damage, which was easy to foresee, to fall on the enemies of the people and the millionaires rather than on the others, rather than on us and our loved ones. We calculated the trajectory as closely as possible, and, even if our ideas of ballistics had some gaps, even if our manufacturers had theories and faces suggesting serious mental derangement, we weren't simply bombing haphazardly. The mortar shells that flew from our launches would finish their trajectory on buildings far from Henhouse Four, very far from the nearby ghettos and camps where refugees, the left-behind, and the left-for-dead, were gathered. The shells didn't explode on the moon, but they hit secondary targets and managed to at least graze the enemy and frighten them. They inflicted brief ravages in the universe of the eternal conquerors, they destroyed a couple of sumptuous apartments here, some private bunkers there: bachelor pads, gentlemen's little love nests, clubs for former genociders, and the business stayed at this level, often with few victims.

We never took credit for our actions, out of humility or out of caution, and also because we knew neither the name nor the slightest bit of the agenda of the organization that employed us. The absence of a signature forbade the ideologues to describe our crimes, which thus escaped publicity. The police toiled at an impasse, and after exploring a few dead ends the sleuths threw in the towel. The police never caught the culprits. Not without duplicity—since in their ranks we had allies—they opened the dossiers and left them empty without closing them for a long time, then they archived them.

The attacks against the moon didn't take place with any great regularity, but they were part of the night, just like the cries of the Bolshevik demonstrators, or the stench of the gulls, or the magical ceremonies for bringing back the dead, or the stifling heat. They belonged to our night, and we approved of them, even if, deep down, we weren't able to think about them intelligibly or even to blindly believe in their relevance.

Because even the least discouraged among us, even the most combatant, already at that time didn't claim to be able to change the course of things. The full moon illuminated the last state of human barbarity before the end, before our end, and, no matter what we might have been able to undertake, it continued to bathe, with its bewitching light, the final calamity. It continued to illuminate the ghettos, the camps, the ruins, the absolute capitalism, the death, our deaths, the deaths of our loved ones. Even the most determined among us could sense the vanity of any action. We knew that the exhausting modification of the climate would continue, that the summer would grow longer, would reach twelve months a year and even more, and that our lives would forever be populated with spiders and death and moments of unconsciousness or semiconsciousness. We could sense that it was unlikely that we would one day see the dawn or the awakening. The attacks against the moon did not pacify us, they didn't counteract our tendency to go mad. But for us, who no longer had any motivation, or any ideological rigor, no intelligence or hope, they gave the impression that perhaps under the surface, maybe, existence might just have retained a hint of meaning.

30

The tram stopped in front of Leonor Iquitos Gateway, then left again.

At the same moment, Mevlido felt a dream rising toward the surface of his memory. Something moved, coming from the depths, with dialogue, decor, episodes, a complete story about which he immediately had the intuition that it might have fundamental importance for him. The dream film grew nearer, but, as often happens, it tore apart at the last moment and was stuck on a lone vision that revealed neither a before nor an after. A naked woman, inside an army truck, was dying. The context was missing. Nothing was left of the trajectory of the dream, of its dramatic ups and downs, nothing was left. Mevlido concentrated on this mental snapshot that was already threatening to vanish. The scene didn't call to mind anything he had lived through in reality or in slumber. The woman's features were hidden beneath long hair that fell in a tangle in front of her face, hair dulled by sweat and darkness. Her body didn't resemble Verena Becker's body.

This dying body. It was not Verena Becker's.

He got out at the Marachvili Gateway Station. The moon was nowhere to be seen. The lamps around the station gave off a subterranean glow. Two other passengers had gotten out of the tram at the same time as himself. He didn't feel like walking in their company. He waited a minute on the platform to allow them to get ahead of him.

He watched them slowly grow smaller and enter Henhouse Four.

Exhaled by Marachvili Gateway, the stench of dirty feathers, mud mixed with shit, and ghetto came in tepid waves.

I'm in front of Henhouse Four, he thought, waiting for these human silhouettes to grow smaller. I feel the weight of the night. One day, I don't know when, I dreamed of a woman agonizing inside a military truck, then I forgot. I can't manage to remember her or the relationship I had with her. Her name has left my head. I left her behind with the others. She is dead behind me like the others. I survived; I am standing on a wobbly block of cement. I'm hardly moving. I'm sweating underneath a streetlight. The weather is gloomy. The nighttime heat covers the landscape with a mist breathable only with difficulty. The smells coming from my home disgust me.

My life is like many others. It is like nothing.

It has no reason to be.

After a moment, he began to walk toward the ghetto.

Two women waited for him under the brick archway of the gate. They were both on the lookout for him, immobile and swallowed up by the darkness, almost side by side, but it was visible that they weren't together. The first one leaned her back against the wall, deformed by a beige overcoat that took all femininity from her and weighed her down. Maleeya, thought Mevlido with affection. He was happy at the thought of going home with her to Factory Street. When he was forty meters away, he gestured to her. She didn't answer. The second woman was sitting on a folding chair. She was wearing glasses with thick lenses whose left earpiece was repaired with duct tape. She stood up heavily and waved her hand in his direction. She had on a very worn winter skirt and a severe blouse that, at the collar, was fastened with the ruins of a frill of lace. Her feet were weighed down by heavy beggar's shoes. When he was closer, Mevlido was hit by her smell. She smelled of old woman sweat and rancid hardtack.

He eyed her with displeasure.

"Cornelia Orff!" he exclaimed. "What a nice surprise!"

The other held out a bony index finger. She shook it five or six times, as if she were scolding a child.

"And the last cell meeting?" she said. "We waited for you."

Mevlido spread his hands apart in a gesture of powerlessness and tried a lie.

"I intended to go," he explained, "but then it started raining. The sewers overflowed on Factory Street."

"I don't remember this rain," said Cornelia Orff.

"The road had disappeared under the water," Mevlido assured her. "It was raining harder and harder. The water was rising."

"You could have braved the elements," scolded Cornelia Orff. "It's not because of a little shower that you should abandon political work."

"We were blocked by the flood," Mevlido defended himself. "You can ask Maleeya. Right, Maleeya? You remember, all that water in Factory Street."

Maleeya had just peeled herself away from the wall. She made the three paces that separated them, came to press herself to his side.

She smiled vaguely. She turned her head toward him. They were back together, she and he.

Mevlido put his hand on her hip.

"You remember, last week?" he asked. "We were looking out the window. It was raining, it was coming down hard. The street was like a river. We couldn't go out."

"The rain," said Maleeya. "The river. It was coming down. We couldn't go out."

"You see?" said Mevlido. "She confirms it. You see, I'm not telling lies."

Cornelia Orff expressed her skepticism with a scornful toss of her head.

"In any case, this time, you won't escape," she said.

"Escape?" stammered Mevlido. "What . . . ?"

"This evening, we'll go together," said the old woman.

"I wasn't told," said Mevlido.

"If you want to be told, you have to come to the meetings," said Cornelia Orff.

She was folding up her chair. She attached a strap to it and hung it around her neck. She was wearing it across her body now, next to her pauper's knapsack.

"Let's go," she said.

"Wait," objected Mevlido, "I can't. I'm with Maleeya Bayarlag."

"And so?" said Cornelia Orff. "The Party has no secrets for a representative of the laboring masses. We can welcome her as an intern or a sympathizer."

"Yes," said Maleeya, "sympathizer."

"Sympathizer with what?" Mevlido said irritably, turning toward her.

"I don't know," said Maleeya. "I love you, Yasar. Everything you like, I like."

A nocturnal bird passed over their heads, stirring the fetid air savagely. They all three looked at each other for a few seconds without saying anything. The bird had disappeared.

"And it takes place where, the meeting this evening?" asked Mevlido.

Cornelia Orff suddenly adopted a conspiratorial attitude. She shrunk down a good ten centimeters and with her nearly opaque eyes scanned the area. She took her time as she scanned it. She was making sure that no informant was spying on their conversation.

"At waste treatment plant number nine," she whispered.

"Number what?" asked Mevlido.

"Nine," whispered the old woman after another look around.

"Number nine, that's where I work," said Maleeya proudly.

"OK," said Mevlido, "that means that we will pass right by Factory Street. We can drop Maleeya in front of the house."

"We're late," said the old woman. "We don't have the time to make detours. Maleeya will come with us, period. We'll cut through Gateway Street."

"That's idiotic," protested Mevlido. "At night there are enormous flocks of chickens that gather there. It makes the street impassable."

"What are you talking about with your chickens?" The old woman became indignant. "In the past we knew how to crush the class enemies. You think we're going to let ourselves be scared by some poultry?"

"They're mutants," warned Mevlido.

"Mutants," said Maleeya.

"Crushing them, we crushed them good," continued the old woman, sneering pensively.

The discussion was over.

They set off.

Cornelia Orff directed the operations.

The streets, most of the time, were empty of light. To show off her knowledge of the city, the old woman began to choose foul alleys that smelled like hallways full of piss, then, when she herself felt near nausea, she began to follow a more reasonable path. Mevlido was holding Maleeya's moist hand and dragging his feet, discontent, a meter from Cornelia Orff. When they took slightly wider streets, she proposed that they move as a procession.

"We must not be afraid of waving our flag," she said with enthusiasm. "The masses must know of our existence. If we show enough conviction, they will elect us as an avant-garde, and they will line up behind us as one man. The moment is favorable, our ideas are moving forward, and the Party has observed, these days, a growth in the fight."

Mevlido shrugged his shoulders. Against his side, Maleeya Bayarlag struggled to keep up. She was panting. She said nothing. Mevlido kissed her on the cheek.

"Don't worry," he whispered, "we'll get through this."

"No," said Maleeya.

"After the meeting, tonight, we'll be together."

"That's why . . . ," she said, without being able to finish her sentence.

"Yes," he said.

"That's why we're done for," she continued, "because we're together."

"No," he said.

"Yes," she whispered, "that's why."

At that moment, Cornelia Orff cleared her throat, then she began to yell out slogans. She knew that neither Mevlido nor Maleeya Bayarlag would repeat them, but she was intoxicated by the idea that she was at the head of a parade that she had started, and she did not turn back, preferring to imagine a larger number of protesters walking behind her. Certainly the proletarian armies weren't unfurling onto the street in an impetuous stream, but, for once, a detachment of solid ideological positions had answered her call. And even if Maleeya Bayarlag was a fragile recruit, even if Mevlido, as a policeman, belonged to a repugnant category, she was not advancing alone down the street. She felt at her back the embryo of a crowd, she was reciting internally the Party brochures explaining the principles of the march forward, the dynamic that tied the avant-garde indestructibly to the masses. And that gave her impressive energy.

> WORKER, SOLDIER, TAKE UP YOUR OLD DREAMS
> AGAIN FROM ZERO! she yelled.
> LOSE YOUR WAY, TAKE UP YOUR OLD DREAMS AGAIN
> FROM ZERO!
> SCREAM AT THE MOON WITH THE LOST!
> TAKE EVERYTHING BACK TO ZERO, GIVE ORDERS TO
> THE MOON!
> IF THE MOON DOESN'T OBEY, KILL IT!
> WORKER, SOLDIER, YOU ARE THE FRAGMENT OF AN
> OLD DREAM!
> GO TO THE MOON, LOSE YOUR WAY, KILL IT!

As Mevlido had feared and predicted, the mutant chickens had invaded Gateway Street, and they were occupying it completely, without leaving the smallest surface open. The flock they formed was grayish, continuous, undifferentiated, and aggressive. By malevolence, but also as an effect of obstinate collective stupidity, the multitude forbade passage. The bodies clucked at knee height and resisted. It was practically impossible to force a passage through them without a fight. Cornelia Orff entered the quacking masses vehemently and began to kick violently in front of her. She was brandishing the folding chair she had been carrying across her body until that point and was using it confusedly, a little like a beginning fencer defending her life with a scimitar. She provoked movements of panic, hysterical flights, and, when the birds surged back toward Mevlido, the majority agitated their stunted wings at chest or face height, amid horrible odors of shit and coarse skin. In a few seconds, Mevlido was drowned in a cloud of hostile feathers and legs. He let go of Maleeya's hand and began to punch blindly. His fists met flying carcasses with hot and incomprehensible shapes. He struggled not to swallow the dust and lice that had replaced the breathable atmosphere. He sensed Maleeya Bayarlag on his right, swinging her arms frantically and swaying. She let out whimpers of disgust he could barely hear.

"Get behind me!" Mevlido yelled to her. "Grab on to my belt! Stick with me!"

He wanted to make his body into a wall to protect her, but she didn't obey him. In the confusion and the darkness he felt that the distance between them was growing.

"Get behind me!" he shouted.

He guessed that they were separated by two meters, then by three or four, then he had the impression that she had flattened herself against the wall and was moving forward with small steps, sheltering her head with her arms. He turned and called to her, but the shadows only grew deeper. Absolutely nothing was visible. At the same instant he was hit by a furious turkey on the back of his neck and pivoted violently to confront again the compact flood of birds. He was covered with down and parasites. The vermin squeaked in his shirt collar. Feathered crests brushed against him, more and more numerous, hindquarters of a nameless ugliness. He couldn't manage to avoid the blows on his stomach and the scratches. Lower down, other poultry were attacking his calves, through the fabric of his trousers, with hostility.

"Maleeya," he yelled again over his shoulder, "I'm here."

Cornelia Orff, at the front line of the group of hominids, didn't waver. She was heroically digging a kind of tunnel through this animal avalanche. She continued to yell strange slogans, all the stranger because they didn't correspond at all with the difficulties she was currently facing. Her voice was sometimes so excited that it covered the din of the chickens.

    FAINT WITH THE DAUGHTERS OF CHANCE! she
      brayed.
    DON'T GIVE UP ON THE DAUGHTERS OF CHANCE!
    EVEN IF YOU ARE NOTHING ANYMORE, PREPARE FOR
      VICTORY!
    BAG YOURSELF UNTIL VICTORY!
    BAG YOURSELF WITH THE DAUGHTERS OF CHANCE!

Then they had broken through the obstacle. Now they had arrived at the end of Gateway Street, almost under the hanging catwalk that linked two building terraces, and that had given its name to the street. The number of chickens was diminishing around them, a sign that they would soon be done with the problem. Cornelia Orff choked and coughed, and, a few meters farther on, she stopped yelling. The march immediately lost its epic nature. Cornelia Orff hadn't given up exercising her leading role, but she was moving forward in silence. She had strained her vocal cords and was having trouble regaining her breath.

"We have to wait for Maleeya," Mevlido stopped her.

The old woman froze.

"Where is she?"

"I don't know," said Mevlido.

They both peered toward the territory they had just crossed. The light was poor, except for the dark gray phosphorescence of the poultry most affected by mutations. The chickens had quickly found their calm again. They had reconstituted a cackling barricade that closed everything off. Gateway Street was a gloomy parade. As there were many perches in the cement walls—mortar holes, windows—not only were the chickens covering the ground, but what's more, they clung to the walls at various heights, up to the first floor where there were multiple stories. Not much could be seen, but it seemed impossible for Maleeya to still be standing in the middle of them. She wasn't there anymore.

"Maleeya!" Mevlido called.

"She must have backtracked," suggested Cornelia Orff, squinting behind the lenses of her glasses.

Mevlido made a bullhorn with his hands around his mouth.

"Maleeya!" he called again.

They stayed still for a minute. Weakly luminescent, the immense flock spread out in front of them, spread out until the far end of the street. The cries had fallen silent. The feathery snow finished falling back down. The smell of rotten bedspread made them want to vomit. Cornelia Orff retched loudly and coughed.

"She's gone," she said.

Mevlido continued to scrutinize the repugnant landscape, in the hope of seeing a trace of some kind left by Maleeya. A bad feeling constricted his lungs and his muscles. He was worried for Maleeya, but he still refused to believe in the worst. Even as a horde, the birds could hardly cause irreparable physical damage, or kill.

"Come on," said Cornelia Orff.

"I wonder what happened to her," murmured Mevlido.

"Come on," repeated Cornelia Orff, "we're going to be late."

Mevlido examined Gateway Street one last time, the thousands of chickens crowded tightly together, that grayish carpet, then, without a word, he fell into step behind the old woman, who had just set off again.

He followed her like a shadow for a quarter of an hour. Despite her age, she trotted along tirelessly. Now the trip went on without trouble. The silence of a sleeping aviary accompanied them. No vehicle ever ventured into this sector of Henhouse Four; they couldn't hear the slightest noise of a motor. From time to time they stepped over junkies, scarcely less harmless than dead bodies, or crossed paths with wanderers in the night, insomniacs who swerved into the shadow to avoid them and who had no intention of picking a fight with them. As to the concentrations of birds, they no longer attained the critical mass that they had in Gateway Street. Upon their passage the flock of birds opened up automatically. They sometimes got pecked, but they no longer had to fight to move forward.

They started down Park Avenue, along a wall topped with barbed wire; after having slipped through a door standing ajar, they were in the territory of plant number nine. The lamps of the avenue modestly lit the successive courtyards full of trash and the brick buildings, with black and broken windows. There was a smell of dirty clothes in the place because they had come in on the side where the rags and irreparable shoes were stored.

"Where is it?" asked Mevlido.

The old woman went between two mountains of disgusting clothes, in the direction of a demolished door, then she stepped back.

"You with the good eyes, do you see 'Sternhagen Block' written somewhere?" she asked.

"No," said Mevlido.

"Sternhagen Block," muttered the old woman. "You should know it."

"I haven't been here often," said Mevlido, "and when I come, I never use this entrance."

"It's in Sternhagen Block," said Cornelia Orff. "If it's not here, it's right next door."

She had lost a bit of assurance.

"I don't see any sign," said Mevlido.

They walked to another building. They had gone deeper into the labyrinth formed by the trash. The buildings all looked alike. They were in ruins. No light shone inside. No one was having a meeting.

"Ah!" announced Mevlido, pointing to the remains of paint above a staircase. "There it is. Sternhagen Block."

"There it is!" rejoiced Cornelia Orff.

"I don't see a meeting," said Mevlido.

The old woman shrugged her shoulders and grumbled. She stood still in front of the abandoned staircase. After reflecting for half a minute, she climbed three steps and went to knock on the door. Rats squeaked on the other side. The knocks echoed. They created a formidable impression of desolation and void, but they didn't scare off the rodents. Cornelia Orff came back near Mevlido. She contemplated the deserted building with a look of reproach.

"I would have sworn it was this evening," she grumbled.

She spread the supports of her folding stool in the form of a cross and sat down on it.

"What are you doing?" said Mevlido, with more fatigue than brutality.

The old woman didn't answer.

"You were wrong," continued Mevlido. "The cell will meet another day. We came here for nothing. There's no sense in staying here."

He sniffed. Dust, rat piss, filth, devastated cloth, rotten leather, rags covered with dirt.

"And besides, it stinks," he observed.

Cornelia Orff cursed his contrariness. She didn't get ready to leave. She had set herself up at the foot of the stairs, in front of Sternhagen Block. She had crossed her arms over her old woman's chest, and abruptly, she was like a rock.

"What are you doing?" asked Mevlido again.

"I'm waiting," said Cornelia Orff. "The Party demands patience from us."

"It's idiotic!" said Mevlido, exasperated. "What are you waiting for?"

"You can't understand, Mevlido," the old woman said suddenly in a bitter tone. "Go away. You are an unreliable element, you don't believe anything, you belong to a repugnant category. You can't understand what the Party asks us to wait for."

31

But no, he thought.

Nothing serious happened.

Having left Cornelia Orff between a pile of stinking shoes and mounds of clothing that had been hardened by rain and guano, Mevlido hurried toward Factory Street. He tried to persuade himself that he would find Maleeya Bayarlag there. She had surely turned around when the confusion became uncontrollable, at the moment when the birds had gone wild. When I was striking out into the mass of birds without being able to take care of her anymore. We hadn't yet gone very far into the flock, and when she saw that she was unable to follow me, she turned back. She must have turned back then. There wasn't a great distance to cross to get to the place we started from, the part of Gateway Street that the poultry didn't occupy. The entrance of Gateway Street. And then she returned to Factory Street. Obviously, that's what happened. She got out safe and sound. She's at home, on Factory Street, on the fourth floor. She is maybe already in bed, or sitting in the kitchen, eating a piece of cake, or talking to the cockroaches, telling them about her day or the hostility of the chickens on Gateway Street. If the water isn't cut off, she's had the time to take a shower to get rid of the avian lice and feathers, and now she is daydreaming, she's resting. Now she feels all right. It's useless to worry, to imagine her still body, no longer reacting, swallowed up under the mutant chickens on Gateway Street. She's fine.

Everything is fine, he thought.

Anxiety made his muscles feel like cotton.

She escaped the danger, he repeated. She's all right.

He didn't take long to get to the bottom of his building. From waste treatment plant number nine to Factory Street, there was less than a kilometer. He climbed the steps without turning on the hall light and opened the apartment door. The light was off, and, out of habit, he didn't reach toward the switch. He walked forward without any particular precaution, took three steps, and froze. He had just glimpsed a shape in the main room. The window lighted it, from behind, and poorly. It was a young silhouette, the body of a girl, slender. It wasn't Maleeya. His heart, already agitated by the rapid ascension of the stairs, began to beat harder.

"Sonia," he said, "it's happened before, me dreaming about this. I open the door, and you are there, in the dark, waiting for me."

"Cut the bullshit, Mevlido," said Sonia Wolguelane.

He stayed in front of the kitchen without going near her. For the last half hour, he had thought pretty much exclusively about Maleeya Bayarlag, and this confrontation with Sonia Wolguelane was too sudden and irritated him. Maleeya had disappeared, something horrible had happened on Gateway Street. The moment was inopportune for him to flirt with the young killer.

He let a few seconds go by. He got his breath again.

"Is Maleeya in the bedroom?" he asked.

Sonia Wolguelane shrugged her shoulders.

He went to the door of the bedroom and stopped. The smell of mattress and mental illness stagnated between the walls.

"She isn't at home," he said. "I'm afraid something has happened to her."

He put his hand on the switch and flipped it. There was a current. Even if the lightbulb in the main room was no more than forty watts, the clear electric light, after so many hours of shadows, at once created a completely shocking atmosphere of abnormality. He immediately wanted to turn it off.

Sonia Wolguelane was wearing a dark blue tunic that went down to her knees, with a very high, very severe collar and long sleeves. Her legs were hidden in trousers of the same color. She had thrown on the table the too-big worker's jacket she would pull on when she went out in the street, that weighed her down and effaced a large part of her charm, helping her pass unnoticed. Of her body, only her hands could be seen, her feet enclosed in sandals, and her knockout's face. She was magnificent. She was looking with her black eyes directly into those of Mevlido. Her gaze shone.

"Can I turn it off?" asked Mevlido.

"Whatever you want," she said.

"I'd prefer to stay in the dark," he said. "There's enough light in the night sky to see each other."

"Yes," she said.

He turned off the lamp. He immediately felt much more at ease talking to the young woman.

"What do you . . . ?" he began.

"I have information for you," she said.

"OK. I'm listening."

"I found a former child soldier," said Sonia Wolguelane.

"Ah. And so."

"It might interest you."

"Bah," said Mevlido. "Was he a gang leader?"

"No. He was part of a column. A totally ordinary child soldier."

"Leave him to those who need to take revenge on him," said Mevlido. "If he was an old gang leader, we would have signaled it to the group. But, as you say, it's an ordinary little monster."

"What group?" asked Sonia Wolguelane.

"You know," said Mevlido, "there is a group that takes care of that."

"Who takes care of what?"

"Of taking them out."

"You know them?"

"Sometimes I talk about them during my self-criticism," said Mevlido. "Sometimes I don't. I don't know their name or their agenda. I don't know if it's one person or many. It's an anonymous military group. They take out the old child soldier recruiters. The old supervisors and column leaders."

"And do you support them?" said Sonia Wolguelane.

"Yes," said Mevlido.

"Me too," said Sonia Wolguelane, "and besides, I thought it was you."

"No good talking about this," said Mevlido.

They stood face-to-face without saying anything.

Sonia Wolguelane came close to Mevlido and pressed herself to him for one or two seconds, chest to chest. He felt her breasts caressing him through the cloth, he could make out the feeling of her nipples against him. It was a way for her to express her complicity. A fusional proximity, removed from any carnal consideration. He understood that there was nothing amorous in the gesture, so he let her do it without opening his arms to hold her, without moving, and, when she pulled away from him, he didn't hold her back. There was nothing amorous in her gesture, but it was delicious and fraternal. Then she moved away.

"I'm sure it's you," she said.

"Think what you want," he said.

She seemed to regret something a little, then she began speaking again.

"The guy has managed to integrate himself here," she said.

"He hasn't gone mad like the others. He's hidden his game. Really quite well. He's opened a telephone station near Leonor Iquitos Station. He survives there, as a shopkeeper and a dealer."

"Alban Glück?" Mevlido was astonished.

"Yes, him. You know him?"

"That guy is a former child soldier?" asked Mevlido.

"Yes. I had serious doubts in the beginning, and then someone showed me proof."

"What proof?"

"Proof," Sonia Wolguelane scowled.

"What kind of proof?" insisted Mevlido.

She moved away. She had returned to the spot she had occupied when, five minutes earlier, he had entered the apartment. Her face was almost invisible. The table once again was between them, a black splotch, on its top the worker's jacket resembling a vile gray corpse.

As she was no longer answering what he was asking her, Mevlido went slowly to the window. He leaned on the sill, wiped away the sweat running into his eyes, and observed the sky. There were a few stars and a lot of clouds. The moon was absent. The neighborhood rustled. On the roof of the house across the street a row of chickens and owls crowded together, side to side, letting out ridiculous coos with regularity.

"For a few days . . . ," began Sonia Wolguelane.

Then her voice choked, and she was silent.

"I went into withdrawal," said Sonia Wolguelane.

"Yes," he said, "it happens."

He turned his back on her. He pretended to be captivated more than anything else by the examination of the constellations. If he made the blunder of moving, of turning around and seeking out her gaze, he knew she wouldn't say any more.

"I slept with Alban Glück," said Sonia Wolguelane.

She had pronounced that with violence, with a tone of disdain that insulted the entire world.

Mevlido persisted in facing the night. He watched the owls on the eaves' troughs, the extinguished streetlights. He didn't move, he didn't turn toward Sonia Wolguelane. Besides us, who don't count, no one could see his face. No one saw his physiognomy suddenly go ashen, as if emptied of blood.

"He's a very slick guy," said Sonia Wolguelane. "He knows the risks he runs, and he is permanently on the lookout. Except when he's sleeping, his defenses go down. He talks in his sleep. You can ask him questions, and he talks without realizing it. He tells you things."

She slept with Glück, Mevlido was saddened.

She slept with that hideous vulture for drugs. I've never held her to me, I've never caressed her and loved her, forgetting everything else. I've never counted her tattoos. I've never penetrated her. I've never licked her, forgetting everything else. We've never lain naked next to one another, inside one another. We've never made love. She's never leaned over me listening to what I mutter during my dreams.

"And so?" he said.

"What?" said Sonia Wolguelane.

"You said he told you things."

"Yes. He was part of the racist columns in Zone 5. He was fourteen at the time. He was at Djaka Park West. He massacred with the others."

Djaka Park West.

He was there when Verena Becker died, thought Mevlido. He massacred with the others. He was with the gang that martyred Verena Becker.

"That's hard to hear," he said.

"I know," said Sonia Wolguelane.

"It's really hard."

"I know."

"But oh well," Mevlido hedged.

He remained motionless in front of the window, leaning on the sill, a little bent over, with his head drowned in darkness and sadness. Then he closed his eyes.

"I'll leave him to you," she said.

For a minute the silence between them took over.

"I'm ashamed of having had a relationship with that guy," said Sonia Wolguelane.

"It's your life," murmured Mevlido. "You don't have to give any explanation. I'm not asking you for anything."

"It disgusts me just thinking about it," explained Sonia Wolguelane.

Mevlido hadn't left the window. He closed his eyes, listened to the night in Henhouse Four. He would have liked to seem, at least from the back, calm and solid like a policeman or a killer.

Behind him, Sonia Wolguelane hesitated.

"It happens, having relationships with whoever," she continued. "Sometimes it's no big deal. But this disgusts me."

Mevlido was moving now. He was coming back to the middle of the room. He stopped near the table. He didn't seem all that calm. Despite the darkness, you could see drops rolling down his forehead, his cheeks.

"I'm going," he said.

"Do you want me to go with you?" she asked. "Glück would be less suspicious."

"No," said Mevlido mournfully, "don't come. It's my business."

They were facing each other, but not looking at each other.

"Wait," she said.

She rifled in the pocket of the jacket lying on the table and pulled out a pistol.

"The clip is full," she said.

"No," said Mevlido, "I'm going to manage without it."

"But with what?" said Sonia Wolguelane. "You don't have anything."

"No," said Mevlido, "I don't have anything."

32

He went out through Marachvili Gateway and headed down Macadam Boulevard. He walked between the tram rails. The cement spotted with oil rasped under his feet. To get to Alban Glück's den, there were almost two kilometers to go. The rails shone under the few lighted streetlamps, and, even in the intervals with no lighting, the rails continued to be visible. The night was sticky with heat. He met with no one. He walked with the stride of an automaton, with moments when he slowed down, like a very tired man or one who had been drinking. He wasn't thinking about anything. He didn't feel any particular emotion. He didn't stray from the rails, as elsewhere the road was full of ruts. On his left, on the border of the ghetto, the abandoned houses exhaled the stench of a dovecote, and, on the right, the buildings formed a devastated rampart with very dark gaps and, sometimes, plane trees or acacias with monstrous branches. No tram was running at this hour. One had the impression of being in an improbable no-man's land, far from any human or subhuman activity. Twenty minutes later, Mevlido reached Leonor Iquitos Gateway. There wasn't a living soul there. The platform in concrete, with its stairway made of three cinder blocks, seemed like remains that the demolition crew had negligently forgotten to knock down. One sole lamp shone in the area. It hung under the roof of the shack in which Alban Glück had installed his communication apparatus. Its rays turned the hundred meters of broken track connecting the station and Leonor Iquitos

Gateway yellow. Despite the late hour, the shop was open. The telephone business means that you stay open practically all the time if you don't want to miss the occasion to earn a dollar or two.

With hours like that, I wonder, thought Mevlido.

He wiped away the sweat running down his face. He wondered suddenly at what time of the day or night the vulture had amused himself with Sonia Wolguelane. The images of their coupling, repressed since his departure from Factory Street, flickered inside him as if on a screen. They were precise, silent, colorless. The sequences followed quickly one after the other. The vulture arched himself horribly above Sonia Wolguelane to enter her. Then quickly he fell asleep, in his sleep he pronounced that horrible confession, then he woke and sat up. Once more, he mounted Sonia Wolguelane. The young woman seemed half-dead, the drugs had taken away all her capacity for action. Alban Glück beat his wings, emitting cries that the image did not reproduce. He moved her about like a doll, he sprawled on top of her and groped her. How, he thought, even to get a fix, had she allowed herself to be manhandled and penetrated by an individual like that? She? Let herself be covered with his viscosity, his viscous ejaculations?

Then he sighed. He should concentrate on what he had come to do.

Cut your bullshit, Mevlido, he thought. You are here to commit murder, after all, not to speculate on the sexual degradation of Sonia Wolguelane. Forget Sonia Wolguelane. It's not because of her that you're going to kill Glück.

He had slowed his pace. He examined the area. Now that he had arrived at the scene of the crime, he regretted not having taken the weapon that Sonia Wolguelane had offered. He had been able to identify it—a pistol whose efficacity he had always admired, a Tokarev from the time of the Second Soviet Union. He should have gritted his teeth and accepted it without any other kind of proceeding. Sonia Wolguelane didn't have to account for how she used her body to him. He had nothing to reproach her with. And no one had asked him to make such a show of his consternation and loneliness.

I'm going to pick something up from the ground at the last minute, he thought. I hope that it will be sharp and not too heavy. A brick would do the trick.

He wiped his forehead again. He took care not to make any suspicious movements.

This Glück must watch the comings and goings around his shop, he thought. I'll find a brick later.

The slate was still in place, hung at eye level.

- Alban Glück's Place
- Last telephonic station before Henhouse Four
- Communication with faraway speakers
- Night service
- Sending and receiving in all languages and all dialects

Mevlido propped himself on his elbows on the plank that served as a counter. The shop was dark. Crouched behind the lunar recorder, the vulture was not very visible among his machines. He had taken apart an electric box, and, without light, blind, he was feeling it out or repairing it.

"Do you recognize me?" asked Mevlido.

"No, why?" said the vulture after a pause.

Without changing his position, he examined his customer through dangling bunches of cables, between generators that the shadow made abnormally massive.

"We saw each other yesterday," said Mevlido.

"I don't remember."

"I made two calls," said Mevlido.

"Possibly," said the other. "Did I make you a deal?"

"Between one and two dollars," said Mevlido.

"It was a promotional deal," said Glück gratingly.

He seemed to be exaggerating the off-putting intonation of his voice. He didn't come forward toward the light. He perhaps preferred to negotiate without interrupting himself, or maybe he mistrusted the intentions of this late customer, who had come on foot and wore a dirty policeman's shirt.

"Ah," said Mevlido, "and tonight, it will cost me how much?"

The vulture Glück stood up. He now emerged from his incomprehensible jumble of machines and shadows. The lamp colored the counter a dusty yellow. The yellow bounced off the plank, lighting the advertising sign and half a meter of space inside the shop. Alban Glück held himself back, in an intermediary zone. It was possible to see his features, a sullen expression on his bumpy face, but one couldn't really see if he had a weapon behind his back. So as not to worry him, Mevlido fixed on him a gaze dominated by fatigue and indifference. He didn't examine the tufts of tangled feathers on the skull he was soon going to bash in. He didn't linger over the folds of the retractable neck that he dreamed of slitting or strangling.

"That depends," said Glück. "What destination is it for?"

Between Mevlido and Glück, the distance had diminished, but it didn't allow Mevlido to attack. I would reach my arm out for him abruptly and close my fingers like a vice around his trachea, thought Mevlido. Yes, that, yes. But then, how to pull him outside to settle the score with him? He will fight and grab on to his counter. He will try to hit me or grab me. Even if he is weakened by the pain and asphyxiation, I won't have enough strength to extract him from his den. If only we were out in the open, in the road, I could hit his head against a stone. But there, we'll be facing each other from opposite sides of the counter. That lowers my chances of neutralizing him.

"I have several calls to make," said Mevlido to gain time.

"For more than three, the house has a group rate," announced the vulture Glück. "Two and a half dollars per call. Do you want the recording erased?"

"Yes."

"That will add another dollar to your total."

"That's expensive," said Mevlido, making a fatalistic gesture, "but OK."

The negotiation was complete. Alban Glück bent to get the telephone, which he had stored beneath the counter. He straightened with effort. His arms were encumbered by an enormous country telephone that looked like a crate of scrap metal. He got ready to set it on the plank. Taking advantage of the occasion, Mevlido stretched his right hand out violently toward the vulture's neck. His fingers closed down on cartilage. He sensed that he had grabbed Glück's trachea and immediately pulled with all his strength. The other fought and dropped his load. The apparatus struck the box where Glück had put his takings for the week and fell to the floor, jingling. Coins scattered over the floorboards with a clear tinkle. Mevlido strengthened his grip. He clenched his fingers frenetically. Glück's throat was scaly and cold beneath his palm, and it was shaken by spasms. Mevlido had grabbed the semirigid pipe that led to Glück's lungs; he compressed it and shook it as if to rip it out. He wasn't paying attention to the rest, the arteries and other components that filled Glück's throat. He leaned back to make himself heavier and to protect himself from his adversary's gesticulations. After having felt around for two seconds, he ended up finding a place to solidly hook his left hand. Now he was anchored in place. Now he was going to be able to hold on until Glück lost consciousness or fell out of his hovel.

Alban Glück was in a bad position. He wasn't trying to breathe or scream, and he began to slap unsuccessfully at Mevlido, who hung on to him with his whole weight. Glück arched his body so as not to slip toward the exterior, as he knew that during the fall he would be exposed to a fatal blow. Before he touched the ground on the other side, Mevlido would have the time to shatter his spine or his skull. He had spread his wings, and he was using them to resist the pull, powerfully stirring all the available air in the shop, sending toward Mevlido clouds of metal shavings mixed with the stench of his feathers, of his sweat.

For several seconds Mevlido had the upper hand like this, then the sweat that ran between his fingers made his hand slip slightly, and his vise grip was less effective. The other took advantage of this to suck in a gulp of oxygen, then he stopped beating his wings and collapsed, pulling Mevlido with him, obliging Mevlido to change position so as not to let him go. He had become dead weight. Mevlido abandoned the good hold that he had maintained until then under a plank of the facade and accompanied the other's movement.

Now his body was thrust forward over the counter, and he was inclined toward the darkness of the shop, his fingers still clenched around Alban Glück's trachea. He stretched along the plank, as if preparing to dive over to the other side, and it was at that moment that the vulture grabbed something from the ground, which must have been there forever, doubtless to respond to possible attacks from marauders. He picked it up and used it immediately. It was a short saber or a machete. Mevlido felt a burning sensation below his elbow. For an instant he was unable to imagine the nature of the wound, then his arm, now soft, stopped tightening around Glück's neck.

The vulture freed himself and let out a raucous cry. Mevlido retreated quickly. He managed not to whimper. Now he was in front of the telephone shop, standing, with a forearm that no longer responded to his orders and hung uselessly. Ligaments and tendons had been severed. Nothing functioned at the level of the joint. The wound took several seconds to begin bleeding. Then the blood came, still without real pain, with sinister spurts.

Glück reappeared behind the counter. His eyes bulged, bloodshot. His bald head was scratched, and he seemed to have a hernia in the middle of his neck. Wings still half-spread, he resembled a demonic creature, like medieval painters depicted in the time when religions made people hope for, after their lives, a better world beyond and a hell. He panted noisily. In his hand the weapon shone with grease and trembled. It was a brush knife.

They contemplated each other without speaking.

Glück had a fit of coughing.

Mevlido was bleeding. The blood flowed more and more quickly. It ran toward the ground. In the yellow light of the bulb, the color of the puddle forming in front of Mevlido was not visible.

"So?" gutturalized Glück, forcing his broken voice, "where was it you wanted to telephone?"

"Djaka Park West," said Mevlido.

Glück grumbled something. He didn't seem very shocked by the memories that Mevlido had stirred. Then he retreated into the shadows of the shop, and only his whistling breathing was audible.

Only that was audible.

His whistling breathing.

Mevlido swayed. The shock of the wound had stunned him. His mind got stuck on little nothings. There was a little muddy rut a bit farther up the road, and he spent several seconds looking at it sideways, as if putting his feet in it or not was of critical importance. Almost dreamily, he watched his blood leave his arm to be drunk up by the ground. He was trying to imagine the damage, to evaluate the depth of the cut. He didn't feel much, and, taking the limited light as a pretext, he preferred not to examine the wound directly. He moved away from the shop a little more. He no longer knew very well where he was, whether the confrontation was over. He had understood that he was no longer in any condition to fight, but, when it was a question of reflecting on the sequence of events, his mind couldn't get in gear. In any case, I've lost the first inning, he thought. Then he repeated that sentence several times. He wouldn't have been able to say whether he liked its black humor.

Alban Glück continued to screech inside his shack. From time to time he ruffled or unruffled his wings. He still wasn't coming out to put an end to the fight. He was in there, among his machines. He let out a regular wheeze. It was impossible to deduce anything about what he was plotting.

Mevlido turned on his heels, went about fifty meters, and took off under Leonor Iquitos Gateway. It was a neighborhood that the inhabitants of the ghetto avoided, I've already said—a part of Henhouse Four that had been seriously damaged after the proclamation of the new society, to the point that it now resembled more than anything a succession of demolished and deserted labyrinths. Mevlido went up to the first intersection, turned right, and leaned against a wall. For a minute he tried to make himself a tourniquet with his belt, then he gave up. The tourniquet refused to hold. He peered at the night behind him to determine if Alban Glück had or had not set out in pursuit. He saw nothing. After he passed through the gateway, it seemed to him that he heard the vulture moving around the hut and closing the planks and the shutter of the facade, as if to close up shop in a hurry. Then the noises stopped. If Glück was on his trail, he was doing it in silence.

Now he had entered the network of the ghetto's unlighted streets. He jogged five hundred meters gritting his teeth, without stopping, his inert right arm dripping blood down his thigh, then he began to falter. The pain had not increased, but it had spread to the rest of his body and provoked in all of his muscles a sensation of terrible exhaustion. The nausea wouldn't let him go. He went another two hundred meters; he repeated to himself that he had to find shelter and hide there until morning. He had to recuperate a little vital energy. He had already lost liters of blood.

He took a little street, then came out onto an intersection strewn with rubble. He no longer advanced steadily. He had practically no control over his balance. He took regular stops to vomit. Nothing came from his stomach but stinking bile. He crossed the intersection and entered a gray street. He walked along phantom facades. Behind them, most of the construction had collapsed. The ruins gave off strong aviary odors, but no bird manifested.

The birds, thought Mevlido heavily. Sometimes they don't exist. They aren't clucking in their sleep, or they're elsewhere.

He was having trouble collecting his ideas. The physical effort and the fight against the pain kept him from reflecting. He knew that he should flee and escape his predator, but the rest wasn't clear. He would have wanted to continue jogging, but he couldn't manage it. His steps were less and less sure. At present, he was making continuous, heavy zigzags.

He looked over his shoulder again. At a distance he couldn't estimate, he saw a hunchbacked shadow. That shadow could be Alban Glück's.

It's him, he thought.

The sentence arrived slowly to his consciousness, as if it had gone through a thick layer of felt.

The vulture Glück, he thought. He's on my trail.

He dove into the entrance of a house and found himself in front of a dark pile of rubble. Several buildings had collapsed one onto the other. A sort of corridor snaked among the ruins. He started down it. He stumbled at each step. Above him were torn walls and extremely black bits of sky. Something took flight near his legs with rapid wingbeats.

An owl, he thought.

He leaned back onto a block of cement. There you are, he thought. You lean against something vertical. You regain your strength.

Blood gurgled beneath his right elbow. The tourniquet had come undone again. He retied it as well as he could and without having any faith in it. Blood was escaping even when he compressed the artery a little higher up on his arm. The cut forearm was no longer anything but a heavy piece of meat traversed by waves; its muscles with no attachments had risen in a ball toward his shoulder and screamed. My muscles are screaming, he thought.

He listened to the night. Someone was coming. Someone was trampling bits of plaster at the entrance of the corridor. Someone is coming, he thought.

He began to walk again. He staggered. He didn't open his eyes very often. To guide himself, he sought support with his left hand. His healthy hand scraped over shards of old wood, spikes of iron, sharp stones. He dragged himself along like that to a spot where the ground was flat and clear for several meters, marking out a sort of stage surrounded by blackish piles. The rubble formed a half crater. It's like it's a little theater, he thought. A little amphitheater with sort of blackish terraced seats. For the final scene. You're going to sit there, Mevlido, he thought.

He pulled himself up a few dozen centimeters onto the first mound of debris. His cut arm knocked about between his legs, showering him with blood again the moment he sat down. He pushed it away, whimpering, and set it next to him on the remains of a wall.

It's fucked, he summed up the situation. In any case, it's started very poorly. But at least there's a free place for the final scene. For one or two people. Audience and actors mixed together.

Here I am, Mevlido, I'm going to wait, he thought. I'm going to wait for it to begin.

He settled himself on his seat.

He was waiting for the stage entrance of Alban Glück.

33

It's not necessary to describe the spectacle that occurred in that place. It was strictly a private showing.

After Alban Glück and his dance of death, several people came near Mevlido to talk with him, to give him advice or to say their farewells. He received them one after the other with a certain detachment, as if he were already en route for the Shambles, already on the bus that should take him to the border, and as if he were waving his hand, looking at them from his seat, through the glass, his mind energized almost exclusively by the trip he was going to take.

- Cornelia Orff was the first to appear. She didn't announce herself by bleating insane slogans. She grumbled in the darkness, she had trouble making her way through the ruins. She was like everyone, like the rest of us; she didn't know the Leonor Iquitos sector well. She trampled on pitfalls of plaster, climbing onto a mound of debris that led her nowhere, turned around, and finally presented herself, gasping with fatigue, at the spot where Mevlido lay. She stood before him and considered without saying anything for a minute, then she lifted over her head the strap that helped her carry her knapsack everywhere with her.

"Here," she said in a friendly voice, a bit forced, "I've put some pemmican in there for you, for the road, and two or three books."

"What books?" asked Mevlido.

"I searched in the storeroom. Djohnn Infernus."

"I thought they were out of stock," said Mevlido.

"There were three left. They're a little damaged."

"OK," said Mevlido.

"The second one has no ending," Cornelia Orff remarked. "It's a fantasy."

"That's all right," said Mevlido. "How much do I owe you?"

"You don't owe me anything," announced Cornelia Orff proudly. "It's a gift from the Party."

"You'll tell them I said thank you," whispered Mevlido.

"I will transmit this," said Cornelia Orff.

"You'll tell them that I will never betray the Party's secrets," added Mevlido.

"They know," said Cornelia Orff.

"I've never known its name or its agenda," Mevlido regretted.

"Those are secrets," said Cornelia Orff.

Mevlido put the knapsack around his neck. He no longer had any problem with his arm, and, really, he felt in good shape to undertake the voyage.

• Half an hour later, Maleeya Bayarlag arrived. She was very out of breath, and she took a long time to approach Mevlido. He saw that she had put on a pink T-shirt under her usual beige overcoat. She was wearing espadrilles whose edges cut into her swollen feet. She had suffered from the walk to find Mevlido. She tried to stay standing on the miniscule stage space where their meeting was happening, but, after a minute, she lost her balance and almost fell. Taking clumsy precautions not to slip, she pulled herself up next to Mevlido and sat down.

"My poor Yasar," she said. "In what a state they've put you."

She drew near him to examine him, and she shook her head for a long time. She didn't touch him. She took care not to put her hands on him, but she breathed on him, and he felt her warmth, her tenderness.

"I called out for you," said Mevlido.

"You called out for me?" Maleeya was astonished.

"Yes, when you were in the middle of the birds."

"In the middle of the birds?"

"On Gateway Street."

"Gateway Street?"

She breathed on him. He felt like pulling her to him and holding her very tightly, but he reflected that she was perhaps afraid of this amorous demonstration, that she would find it incongruous, brutal, and he held back.

"We've foundered," he said, "but at least we've never stopped being together."

"Yes, my Yasar," she said, "we're together in the middle of everything, really."

They both began to laugh.

"I'm going to leave for the Shambles," said Mevlido.

"Well, of course, my Yasar," she said, "I don't know what you could do other than that."

"Take care of yourself, while you wait," he said.

"While I wait for what?" she asked.

"I don't know," he said.

They stayed silent for a moment, then Maleeya stood up again.

"I've made you some pemmican and a cake," she said.

She put the pemmican next to Mevlido, where she had been

sitting, and suddenly she began to search in her overcoat pockets, she patted her hips, the tops of her thighs. She looked devastated.

"But I brought you a cake," she continued. "I had a cake in my pocket for you. But I don't have it anymore."

- An hour passed, and Sonia Wolguelane appeared. She was in the center of the stage, two meters from Mevlido. He had dozed off; he opened his eyes and noticed her presence. The night hid her from him. It seemed that she had already been talking for several seconds.

"He was trying to go back into his shop," she said. "He must have had something he wanted to get. He still had his machete in his hand. I shot him in the kneecaps and at the base of his wings. Then I interrogated him to know where he had left you. I wasn't tender. After the bullets, I used the machete."

"That Glück, we spent part of the evening together," said Mevlido.

"I know," said Sonia Wolguelane, "that's why."

"Why what?" asked Mevlido.

She didn't answer. She was in work clothes, like the Komsomols leaving for communist Saturdays in another time, in the time when there were Saturdays and communists. Her work vest was spotted with blood. She hunted around in it and pulled out two packages wrapped in newspaper.

"Pemmican," she said, "and a pistol. A Tokarev. I thought that you might like that."

"I don't really need it, now," he said.

"You never know," said Sonia Wolguelane.

"And if pemmican gets into the mechanism? Crumbs? It might gum it up."

"No. I wrapped it in plastic. Take it."

"It's heavy," remarked Mevlido, putting the two packets into his bag. "It's loaded?"

"Yes, a full clip."

"So when I fire on the enemy, I'll think of you," said Mevlido.

"Cut the bullshit, Mevlido," said Sonia Wolguelane.

• Then, at the moment when he expected it least, a woman arrived, in traditional Korean clothing. It was a shaman, a *mudang*. She was accompanied by a drummer who immediately sat down, cross-legged, without greeting, and who, after having settled his instrument against his right foot, began to tap on the rim with a short drumstick. The rhythm was a warmup, but already it was precise, mysterious, and strong. The *mudang* walked around the miniscule space several times, paying homage to the spirits of the ruins; she made the gestures of making a pâté of pemmican between her hands, then she stopped in front of the musician, and she addressed Mevlido without looking at him. As he didn't understand ancient Korean, he didn't answer. The *mudang*'s voice rose through the shadow, through the piles of rocks and rubble, touching Mevlido deeply. She sang few notes, but her intonation was overwhelming. The musician played serenely, with an exceptional quality of touch. He struck the walls and skin of his *gutbuk* with the palm of his left hand; the stick he brandished in his right hand had been cut from a tree that was participating in the ceremony with all its dead tree's vigor—a birch tree, doubtless, a birch in the fullness of age. Mevlido received the music and lost all notion of time. It continued to be nighttime in the Leonor

Iquitos neighborhood. The *mudang* sang, sometimes she stooped and stood back up, she moved her arms, but she had too little space to dance, and she preferred to concentrate in her vocal cords all the magic of the moment—in her vocal cords and in her breath. She didn't try to find out whether Mevlido was listening. She didn't look in his direction. She turned toward the musician, toward the black sky, toward the wounds of the bombed facades, toward the mounds of debris that surrounded them. The stage on which she was performing was almost circular; it might be compared to the closed mouth of a crater. In its center the *mudang* lamented and ceaselessly created beauty, something ephemeral and fundamental that only the dead and their like could hear.

Tears ran down Mevlido's cheeks.

He said nothing, he didn't try to engage in a dialogue with the *mudang,* but the tears ran down his cheeks.

- When dawn, if we refer to our biological clock, should have broken, Mevlido ended another period of somnolence. In front of him the confined landscape hadn't changed, a theatrical place surrounded by buildings in ruins and rubble. The *mudang* and her musician had left long before. Mevlido peered into the darkness. Devastation, piles of rocks, here and there an enormous bird perched, immobile. Nothing, exploded walls, twisted beams, windows balancing between two voids. Everything was plunged in thick shadows. On the little esplanade where the *mudang* had shamanized, the ground now looked like it was covered with a layer of liquid, blood or black oil. He tried to think of the appearance it would take on when the light of day increased. His thought was too disjointed to finish.

He sighed, a little vexed now to have to make do with reduced intelligence.

Blood or black oil, he repeated.

At the same time, steps hesitated nearby.

Maybe someone is looking for me, he thought. He imagined hailing the newcomer, but he gave up. The latter was already a meter away and watched him, his face closed, arms immobile by the sides of his body, as if at attention. It was Berberoïan.

"I had trouble finding you, Mevlido," said the commissioner.

"Well, here I am," said Mevlido.

"They told me it happened in Leonor Iquitos. OK. But once in the neighborhood, getting my bearings? Not a chance."

"The best thing, when that happens, is to ask a local," said Mevlido.

"I didn't see a single one," complained Berberoïan, "and it's nighttime. And the rain doesn't make it any easier."

"What rain?" asked Mevlido.

He lowered his gaze again, toward the ground. Berberoïan was standing in a mix of water and mud. The surface was pock-marked. Splashes dampened the bottom of Berberoïan's trousers.

It's raining and I haven't even noticed, observed Mevlido. I don't hear any pattering of drops, I don't feel a drop.

Berberoïan was dripping. His hair was flattened to his head as if it had been soaked in molasses. His policeman's shirt stuck to his body. On his belt was a patent leather case. Awkwardly, he put his hand on it.

"Do you want a weapon?" he asked. "Do you want me to give you my pistol?"

"No," said Mevlido, "I prefer to travel without. In general, I do better with bare hands."

"I forgot the pemmican, I hope you won't hold it against me, Mevlido."

"Bah," said Mevlido.

They spent a few seconds looking at each other. The commissioner seemed more emotional than his subordinate. He swayed back and forth, alternately lifting his feet, as if he were afraid of being stuck in the mud. His shoes splashed.

"Soon you are going to leave," said Berberoïan.

"Yes," said Mevlido.

"Do you have enough to buy the ticket?" Berberoïan worried.

"I think so," said Mevlido.

"I will have you reimbursed, anyway," said Berberoïan. "We'll make it work. We'll dig into the community chest."

"Bah," said Mevlido, "it's not going to break me. At the point where I am."

"If you want, we can walk together to the bus station," proposed Berberoïan. "You don't seem to be in great shape."

"I'll make it. It's not very far."

"It will be time soon. Are you sure you don't want me to go with you?" insisted the commissioner.

Mevlido hesitated.

"I'd rather go alone," he said finally.

"Once in the Shambles, I hope that you will be able to find that woman," said Berberoïan.

"What woman?" asked Mevlido.

"I don't know," said Berberoïan.

They were quiet. The commissioner made a noise in the water with his feet.

"You're the one who knows, Mevlido," Berberoïan said again. "It's you who knows. Not me."

34

The voyage is endless.

The last kilometers are the hardest to travel. Too many bumps. Your mixed-up brain gives up on differentiating between the present and the rest. Evening after evening, because it is thus that the days follow each other, you still ruminate a little on the past or the future, but your cerebral activity has declined so much that you feel like you are permanently dozing. For a long time already you don't even look out the window; you no longer clean it when it is covered with mist and grease. You have trouble being interested in external things, and, inside yourself, the images are dull, conventional, as if created by someone other than you. Interiority escapes you also. You are worn out.

Finally, you approach your final destination. You are still somewhere in Henhouse Four, but the atmosphere of the border makes things less familiar. That's it, yes. Less familiar. Nothing finds an echo in you. The bus has entered the suburbs, it is already taking the long avenues of the Shambles. You are going slowly, the roadway is covered with cinders. The tires crush this crumbly layer with the noise of a millstone. Dust foams behind the windows. You don't glance toward the outside. You have arrived in a very distant world, and that doesn't excite you, provokes no curiosity in you. You don't feel like you're in the skin of a tourist reaching the mysterious country for which he has felt nostalgia since childhood. In what you still tend to call your existence, nostalgia has no role to play.

You feel the knapsack lying next to you, on the next seat. The bus wasn't full, and the seat has remained empty since the beginning, you haven't had to endure chatty or disgusting company on the way. In the bag the reserve of pemmican has greatly diminished. You weren't hungry, but you made yourself eat from time to time, afraid of fainting before it was time.

When you think about it, you have taken care not to arrive in the Shambles in a lamentable state. As often as you had the chance, you shaved and you changed clothes with what you could find at the bus stops, when the driver changed over with a colleague or repaired the motor. At the end of each month the company gave you a new disposable razor and clean underwear. During the long minutes or years that the trip lasted, you were able to keep a little bit of your physical dignity, clean yourself off or dress yourself here and there, for example, in the latrines or under the public tap of such and such a gas station, which the other travelers often neglected doing. And today, if you don't cut a particularly fine figure, you are, after all, still presentable. Your hair and your nails have continued to grow, your clothes have become worn, the fabric cracks with the smallest movement, you look like a mummy coming apart, but you remain presentable. One night, in the sordid courtyard of an inn, you traded your pistol for a patent leather hat. You hide your face beneath it, as if desirous to proclaim your intention of not engaging in dialogue with anyone, but, in fact, the other travelers avoid contact with you. You have realized this more than once. No being gifted with intelligence will enter voluntarily or warmly into a relationship with you. Animals are better disposed to you, but the distance between your intelligence, even if it is diminishing, is enormous.

Animals are better disposed to me, you think.

But the distance between our intelligence . . .

And just at that moment of your reasoning, right there, in the middle of a sentence, you plunge into a vast concrete hall. After a maneuver, the motor hums louder, vomits a last cloud of hot oil, and stops. The bus has arrived at its terminus. You have to get off.

You leave this seat that you have occupied for so long, with for sole distraction your fear of precipices and the unspooling of the shadowy landscape and, every two hundred kilometers, the possibility of going to relieve yourself in the company of the other passengers and drivers, on the roadside, in the cindery stones and the debris of old metropolises.

You are the last to get off.

You walk along the burning side of the bus. The corrugated iron has blackened, as if an hour earlier you had been charging through the heart of an industrial fire. At the rear, a group of passengers is waiting for the drivers to open the compartment where the suitcases are piled up. After all this time the suitcases must have rotted or burned up, but, just in case, they're waiting. Sullen. Silent. You pass by them. You pull your boonie hat down harder over your eyebrows. You breathe in the air, the smell of gas that no air current can disperse. You grow onto the cement platform of the bus station, and you walk away.

You are wearing the beggar's uniform, those dirty rags that have always suited you beautifully.

You move, on your shoulder the strap of your almost-empty knapsack.

Avoiding the traces of motor oil and rusty water, you direct your footsteps toward the exit. A vast, rectangular mouth whose luminosity is blinding. Beyond it the street shimmers. The dimensions of the garage evoke those of an aviation hangar. They are more than is needed, as if, five or six centuries earlier, the architects had predicted an augmentation in traffic that hasn't occurred. You brush by buses cooling off. Several of them have arrived recently. You slip between these almost-consumed wrecks that will take months to lose their smell of the blast furnace, and a team will then come to take them apart for good, like ships. At regular intervals, every fifteen meters, you go around the base of the staircase going up toward a floor where logic dictates that offices and ticket booths would be located, maybe also a commercial arcade. In reality, from up there are coming only shadows and silence. On the lower levels are installed faded zombies, probably candidates for another hallucinatory expedition, left-behinds who imagine they will be able to leave again—to start from zero, to travel in the other direction.

All bus stations look alike, no matter what part of the universe one has run aground in. They have in common the filthy brouhaha, misery, discomfort, gas stagnating at every hour of day and night, but, above all, an atmosphere of serious intellectual degradation, fed as much by the insolence of the employees as by the resignation of the clientele. For those who feel the need, in order to imagine it, of a precise geographical reference, let's say that the place here evokes the bus station in Puduraya, in the middle of Kuala Lumpur, in Malaysia. Puduraya, when one arrived there during the global revolution, at the end of the seventies, for example, from the north, from Padang Besar, Kota Bharu, or Gerik. Such superb names used to appear on maps, like Malaysia, scarcely more than two or three centuries earlier. The place where Mevlido is currently walking recalls Puduraya Station at that time. The same staircases leading to a story about which one can guess nothing, same unbreathable shadows, same feeling of loneliness, wandering, and no return.

Anyway. You have never spent time in Malaysia, and, when you came into the world, Malaysia had disappeared from memory long ago. You freeze on the threshold of the garage, and you look at what you can see of the city: an intersection, a little plaza, a few totally dilapidated houses stifled under layers of ancient dust, and, along the road, black brick walls behind which factories sleep. Not the least sign indicating any commercial activity. Nothing that seems like a haven for voyagers. On the plaza, electric wires run in every direction, from roof to roof, through mixed-up bundles. What am I doing here? you think fleetingly, with no answer. The residential neighborhoods stretch out beyond the intersection, invisible. The Shambles is built on a slope. You're at the edge of a high plateau, and then, after the break, you dive. Giant dump trucks cross the intersection, in front of the bus station they raise a loud cloud of stone dust. The ambiance is that of a mining district, brown and bare is the Sierra that bars the horizon. Two pedestrians slip into the entrance of a street and disappear. They are dressed as in a proletarian republic after the defeat.

You decide first of all to look for a shelter for the night. According to your calculations, the light will decline in two or three hours. I have to know where to sleep, you think.

Five drivers are talking near the door, in front of the caretaker's glass booth. You ask them if they can recommend a place where you can spend the night, a boardinghouse not too expensive for subhumans or travelers. They interrupt their discussion and measure you up with their brutish eyes. You would think they were butchers examining in their stupor a slaughterhouse animal gifted with speech. For a moment, you don't know if they understand the dialect that you have used to communicate with them. It is after all a simple jargon, the general language of Henhouse Four. You have simplified the syntax as much as possible. Camp Blatnoï mixed with Korean, with traces of English and Darkhad.

They look at you silently.

You repeat your question.

- The night
- Sleep
- Not too expensive

Five drivers. One of them obese, another with a red cap, a third with a bare chest, with a denim vest. The others are normal, or at least without any remarkable particularity. They look at you, they all have their mouths half-open.

"It's still talking," says the fat one.

"Incredible," says one of the normal ones, "it's still talking."

"And what is it talking about?" asks the red cap.

"About the night," says the fat one.

"It's talking about the night?" the bare-chested one asks, surprised.

"Yes, it must still believe in night," says one of the normal ones.

"Incredible," says the other normal one, "it still believes in night."

35

You don't wait around with the drivers. Again, you enter the hangar reeking of oil and burned rubber. You find the bus that has brought you to the Shambles. On the cement platform you step over the body of a left-behind. It's hard to tell whether it's a man or a woman. Above him or her, your rags and leather hat seem luxurious. You stop in front of the stairs going up to the first floor. You stay a moment at the bottom of the steps, and, finally, you climb them.

You come out onto a poorly lit esplanade, deserted and full of echoes. On the ground, cement tiles crumble. There is nothing, only concrete pillars and the ground scattered with piss-filled puddles.

At the end, at the extremity of the space, a neon tube helps you get your bearings. You choose that as a goal, and besides, you don't see what other direction you could take. You approach the light. Your soles crush hardened crumbs. Your steps echo in the emptiness. A series of volumes in plywood and iron are lined up, with narrow doors or gratings, something like a baggage check made of bric-a-brac. An amputee oversees the whole thing. He has a baton and looks like an old soldier in rags. While walking through the shadows, you observe the neon and the lockers, the doors, and this one-legged man sitting with his cane next to him. You wonder if he will be in a better mood than the drivers. You hope all the same to get some information from him about where you can spend the night.

The veteran sees you coming.

He is doing his motionless work as watchman. You glance again at the lockers. They are fairly big. After all, perhaps the old man is watching over an establishment that shelters people rather than suitcases.

You approach, you greet the man, but he doesn't welcome you. He doesn't react. His face is rough, the unpleasantness of life has as if forever sealed it in a kind of ferocious frown. You stand before him and consult the available document, the sign nailed behind him. The announcement is written in a language whose characters you can't all identify. You take a long time to translate the main idea.

- Splendid Hotel
- Warm Welcome
- Rooms for the night or for a long stay
- Competitive prices

The only information of which you are really sure concerns the price of the room. It's not excessive. One dollar. You gather from the bottom of your bag the money that was buried there at the same time as the pemmican for the trip. You have three or four bills left. You take one. The guardian pockets it without examining it and, using his cane, points to the door.

You go to the cell you've been given, a cubby hole without a ceiling whose floor must not be more than three square meters. It's narrow; the neon light reverberates weakly there. The furniture is limited to a seat recuperated from the carcass of a bus. There are knife marks on the back of it. The lingering smell of fuel coming from the lower floor is overlain with animal odors, the acrid smell of bodies that night after night collapse here, on this broken-down chair, to sweat in solitude and terror. Graffiti scars the cement, like in a hiding place or in latrines, but there are no illustrations. Only opaque messages. The characters don't look like anything. A few numbers appear in the margin of the texts. Impossible to tell what they are referring to.

When you look for a nail to hang your knapsack from, you see a rat. The animal is not very big, slightly hunchbacked, and frozen against an arm of the bus seat.

Your eyes cross the red cinder of its gaze.

That reminds you of something, you don't very well know what.

Don't make contact with the rats, you think, suddenly. Don't enter into contact with the rats.

Under no circumstances enter into contact with the rats.

Not with the rats, nor with the spiders.

You go out, you leave your cell.

You close the door behind you with the bit of thread that had replaced the lock.

"I've reflected," you tell the old man. "I'd rather stay somewhere else."

The old man asks a question in a gruff voice. You don't understand. You shake your head. You point a finger toward the room. The old man in turn shakes his head. He seems furious that you don't want to stay there. He makes a comment about it, raising his voice, maybe he's afraid of you asking for your dollar back.

"You can keep the dollar," you say. "I have more."

The old man says something else. He grips his twisted cane. He indicates the sign by brandishing his cane.

Of what he says you can't make head nor tail. Trying to avoid a conflict with him, you lean toward the sign and pretend to decipher something that had, until now, escaped you. You nod your head as you read.

"Good," the old man ends up saying. "Room. Good."

"I know," you say. "Good. No problem."

You sway from one foot to the other in front of him. You would like this dialogue to end as quickly as possible.

"No problem," you say. "Good room. But I've changed my mind. Good room, but I'm looking elsewhere."

The old man is now hitting the ground with his stick.

"I have an address," you repeat.

The old man growls a new chain of angry words. You don't understand anything. He taps around him with his stick like a blind man.

"No goodbye," he grumbles. "No room, no goodbye."

"Waddell Street has been recommended to me," you say at random. "It's more central. No problem."

36

In the back of the bedroom, there's not the slightest trace of light.

The house is very small, with three tiny rooms. After his arrival in the Shambles, Mevlido didn't take long to find a place to stay, but he settled in reluctantly, with the idea that he would move as soon as possible. That he would leave the first chance he got. Fatigue, fatalism, and routine took over after that. So he stayed. He lay down in a corner, and for a moment he seemed to be dead. He himself was persuaded that he had finished with existence. Then daily life ran over him like a soothing liquor, and he began to move again. He had already stopped looking for a new house. It's a detached house, mostly in brick, with few openings. It looks out onto Waddell Street, but you have to go down a hundred meters of a disgusting alley to reach Waddell Street. A long hundred meters in an insalubrious trench, smelling of muck. That's where Mevlido has ended up. He is there, he lives there. It's there that he waits.

Now we're exactly the same, or almost. Neither days nor years count for him. Indistinctly, they follow one after the other. When night falls, darkness reigns inside. Then dawn prowls the streets, and a kind of day breaks within the walls. The opposite is also true. Approximate twilight, then night, or the opposite. And so it goes for hours grouped by twenty-something. This is the rhythm of the world for Mevlido and those like him, that is to say, for us.

Mevlido gets up, he feels his way to the chair. The evening before, he folded his clothes and put them on the back of the chair. He finds the chair with no difficulty, then his shirt, his underwear, his canvas trousers whose rips have gotten worse over the recent weeks. Then he bends down. Although he took care to leave them next to his shoes, right next to them, less than ten centimeters away, he can't manage to lay hands on his socks. He passes his hand back and forth over the linoleum. He explores the crevasses in vain. This improbable disappearance leads him to believe that he's dreaming or that he's losing his mind, but he prefers, for the moment, to set aside these two hypotheses. He grabs his shoes with his left hand, he stands up, he piles the rest of his clothes in his arms. He holds the half-dirty rags to him, to his bare chest. Then he stands still for a moment and turns back to the bed.

The bed is empty now, and it could be supposed that it has already lost part of its warmth. As nothing can be seen, everything has to be imagined. One has recourse, evidently, to images suggested by memory. A blanket pushed aside. Rumpled sheets. The bottom sheet that reveals a deformed mattress, just wide enough for one person.

"Don't move," Mevlido says softly, "I'm going to take my shower. Don't get up."

No one reacts in the darkness of the bedroom, no one moves in the bed. Asleep or not, no one murmurs an answer.

"Keep sleeping," says Mevlido.

No voice crosses the darkness in his direction.

He leaves the bedroom.

He takes two steps in the hallway.

He pushes open the bathroom door and drops his bundle to the floor. A muffled noise is heard. The shoes hit the tile at the same time as the shirt. Mevlido suddenly is hit with the smell of the rags in which he has sweated for too many days. He suddenly inhales it. He wrinkles his nose as he opens an armoire where he thought he had stored a change of clothes. His hand doesn't encounter anything. The shelves are empty. For more than a month he hasn't done any laundry. He is several washings behind. In that area, as in many other domains, he is not above reproach.

In the bathroom, the shadows are more pronounced even than elsewhere. No trace of luminosity of any kind. It's always been a closed-off room. Those who have had that experience wouldn't hesitate to say that it's as black as the inside of a furnace.

"Don't get angry at me, OK?" murmurs Mevlido. "I'm going to take care of it, that laundry. You know that I don't like to wear dirty clothes. Me neither, I don't like it. I'm going to soak it right away."

His bare foot comes down on a washcloth. That's a point of reference. It hasn't completely dried from the last time. He goes to the shower. He reaches for the taps with his right hand and opens them. He regulates the temperature and then gets under the water.

The water falls with fits and noisy starts, constant changes of pressure. It is sometimes cold, sometimes slightly tepid. In a place like the Shambles, where the temperature is rather low, taking a shower that is not hot enough in the dark is no picnic. It's a trial for each of us and a trial for Mevlido. He bears it valiantly because he has an accommodating nature and also because, despite everything, he guesses that he's had good luck and that fate could have been more unjust with him. He has long had the philosophy of not complaining, no matter what happens. He tells himself that he could have ended up in a hovel not connected to running water, like many in the sector. He also knows that he could have sunk down further into the mud of unhappiness or of inexistence. He could have lost all contact with reality, for example. And he has the impression that that's not the case. The idea of no longer being in reality often worries him atrociously, but that's not the case. He sometimes remembers things other than dreams. He doesn't remember why he is there, but he feels that he is responsible for an investigation. While the cold water contracts his skin, he frequently has that intuition. That he was sent on a mission. What mission, when, who sent him, he no longer remembers. But that trace persists in his memory. Under the miserable shower, he rejoices at not being a simple brute, to have traces in his mind, anyway, to not moan endlessly, with no idea of his past, like an idiot, in the absence of light. He rejoices to still persist and to be able, when he thinks about it, to be conscious of it.

Once well cleaned, he dries himself and dresses himself as well as he can. It takes him some time to find and then put on his shoes. The walls around him are damp and smell of mold.

"I'm going to make us a tea," he says. "Do you want some tea?"

Once in the kitchen, he opens the window. The opening looks out onto the disgusting alley. Nothing is shining outside. No star twinkles in the sky. There is no difference between the sky and the earth, no line of separation. Eyes open or closed, nothing can be seen. No tree nearby, no building, no relief. The darkness is without shade.

It is neither cold nor hot.

Mevlido breathes a moment at the window. He leans on the cement sill; he fills his lungs. It's an agreeable moment, one of the best moments of the morning. He breathes and he listens. In the next house, someone has turned on a tape player, as often happens at this peaceful hour, before daybreak, before the unfurling of the rays of dawn, which will interfere with everything. The magnetic tape has passed over the heads so many times that it produces more crackling than music, but, even so, only a philistine wouldn't recognize the enchanting melody that Naïsso Baldakchan inserted into the *Second Golden Song* and the *Third*. More precisely, the larghetto of the *Third Golden Song*. Mevlido listens and cries. He cries in time with the music. His tears fall in the darkness without anyone noticing or thinking about commenting, and without sniffs and sobs. Mevlido cries without theatrics.

When the tape player goes silent, Mevlido detaches himself slowly from his immobility and closes the window again, and then he pours tea powder into a pot that contains a little cold water, and he stirs. There's no light in the house, and no flame comes from the stove. Despite all this, the tea made this way is drinkable. It's a bit muddy, and one might regret that there's nothing in the kitchen that could be used to filter it, but it is drinkable.

"It was the *Third Golden Song*," says Mevlido. "Do you remember when we listened to it together for the first time?"

He sips the tea straight from the pot.

"I'll leave it on the burner for you," he says. "Keep sleeping. I'll leave it hot for you, for a little while."

Then he looks for a stool in the kitchen. The stool lay under the table, knocked over, since the night before maybe, or another night. He puts it straight, he sets it near the table, a meter away, then he sits on it.

Then he waits.

He begins to wait again, as he's in the habit of doing, in calm and silence.

He waits for someone to knock on the door and take him away. Or just to talk to him.

Hard to say exactly what is going through his head.

In any case, he is waiting for the sunrise.

37

A little later, the same year, in any case, Mevlido got up from the
stool where he was sitting, then he bent down, got on all fours, and
began to scrape and rummage around under the kitchen sink. The
shadows were even darker underneath than elsewhere. He spent a
moment groping around unsuccessfully among the pipes and old
plastic bottles of cleaning products. Instinctively, he was looking
for a trapdoor on the wall. His hands ended by finding a square
plaque made of something other than brick. He explored the out-
line with his nails. Damp dust had accumulated in the groove,
freezing compared to the warmth of the air.

That trapdoor. It reminds me of something, he thought.

He stood petrified for a minute. He had the impression that
from that image of the trapdoor, memories would come rushing
back. It should remind me of something, in any case, he thought.
As nothing distinct presented itself to him, he began to move things
around again.

I'm going to open that, he thought.

It's a way like any other to get out of the house, he reasoned.
Surely it's the beginning of some kind of subterranean passageway.
I'm going to get in there. If it's too narrow, I'll just have to tuck my
shoulders in a little. I'll just have to shrink down a little. I won't
die from that.

When he had found a handhold, he gripped it and pulled, but
the piece of metal immediately came off, taking with it screws and
rotten wood that was falling to pieces. A heavy waft of air spread
around him. Spores of cave mushrooms had replaced the air, mixed
with the smell of wet earth, sewer gases. The poorly closed bottles

also exhaled gases, sharp smells of disinfectant or lye. He sneezed twice and cleared his throat.

What's the good of keeping up this theater of breathing? he thought. No one is asking it of me. What good is it to pretend to inflate and deflate these ridiculous pulmonary sponges?

He slid his fingers into the craters left by the screws and assured his grip. He wanted to maneuver the cover by shaking it. The plank was crumbling around his thumb, but resisted. He became discouraged and abandoned for a moment all physical and mental activity. Time passed, then he came to life again and doubled his efforts. The sink above his head and the pipes got in his way. On his right, a bag of antiroach crystals had burst. The crumbs crunched under his knees. Finally, the plank broke, the metal hardware that had kept it in its place gave way. The opening, all at once, was clear. It was wide enough. Mevlido slid into it, satisfied that he wouldn't have to shrink his shoulders too much to keep going, and he began to crawl out of the kitchen. He knew that he was dreaming, but that didn't bother him. It didn't influence his behavior. After a few meters, there was enough room to straighten up, and a little farther still, he could start to walk on his posterior limbs, which on one hand allowed him to go faster and on the other reassured him regarding his belonging to the family of hominids. The passage had become a gallery. This ended in a courtyard. He crossed it, and, from there, he reached a covered alley that seemed familiar to him.

- I know this alley, he thought.
- It's an alley that Mevlido has already gone down. Mevlido already went this way to go to Gorgha's place, the female crow, he thought.
- Mevlido, he thought. Mevlido has to go knock on Gorgha the female crow's door.

He didn't succeed in the least in collecting ideas or memories, and he witnessed their apparition and their disappearance inside his skull as if they were monologues dictated by someone else.

I have to go knock on that door, he thought. Perhaps it isn't a decent hour, but, no matter the hour, Mevlido has to knock on that door. He has to make his report to Gorgha.

There weren't even fifty meters left to go to reach the shack where Gorgha lived.

What report? he thought. What do I have to give a report on? And why to her?

Then he was distracted by obstacles. The path was complicated principally by metal carcasses and detritus. The obstacles overcome, he arrived alongside a little house, and then memories awoke within him. But of course, he thought. He came to Gorgha's house from time to time, at night, most often without having told her of his visit in advance. She welcomed him lazily, they chatted for half an hour about banal subjects over a cup of tea or a plate of dried fruit. She didn't light the lamp. Sometimes afterward she would lead him to her bedroom, and they would make love with an almost total absence of desire and pleasure. They made love like two dead people.

They made love. Like two dead people.

When his memory had finished reconstituting the relationship he maintained with Gorgha, he lifted his arm and struck the panel with his cartilage and bones. In the hovel, the echoes developed for a second, then died out, and then nothing else moved. It will take Gorgha a good minute to come here and open up, he calculated. A feeble luminosity opposed the opacity of the shadows of the surroundings. It had as its source the few streetlights burning in Waddell Street, right nearby, or farther on in the city, in places that still benefited from a connection to the electrical system. While Mevlido waited, his gaze wandered over the decor: earthen walls;

tiny, untended gardens; scrub bushes; other doors. After a bend the alley met Waddell Street, and, from the side Mevlido came from, it melted into shadows.

A minute had passed.

What if I knocked on this door again? he thought. If I yelled her female crow's name? Maybe she didn't hear me.

What if Mevlido knocked on this wood again? he thought.

At that moment were the sounds of dragging steps, and Gorgha came to open the latch in the vestibule. Jingling could be heard. She moved a bolt, several chains, she poked about with something like a key in something that must have been a lock. The door opened a crack. Gorgha examined her visitor tiredly.

"I knew it. It could only be you," she said.

Through the crack in the door one could make out her black feathers, the brilliant black feathers of her chest, her unbuttoned top, almost all of her black breasts, of her black stomach, of her black thighs. She was unkempt but magnificent. Her robe was open, hanging to the ground, one of those horrible brownish robes that in the past humans sold at a discount in hypermarkets, in a time when there were hypermarkets and discounts. She wore no undergarments.

"You've come to make your report, I suppose," she said.

She showed no intention of inviting him in. She had not undone the security chain, and she was blocking the entrance. Mevlido danced awkwardly from one foot to the other. In front of the threshold was a slab of slate. The soles of his old shoes scraped on it.

"It's not a decent hour," remarked Mevlido.

"Of course not."

"I wanted to see you. To touch your feathers."

"Cut the bullshit, Mevlido," said Gorgha without moving a millimeter.

Mevlido hesitated. He wasn't swaying anymore, but he was stuck on the threshold, breathless, not knowing very well how to prolong the conversation. To gain a few seconds, he began to breathe again and let out a sigh.

"Since you're here, get it off your chest," said Gorgha. "Make your report. I'm listening."

"I don't have anything particular to say," Mevlido admitted.

"So make it up," advised Gorgha.

"You can make it up?" asked Mevlido. "I can make it up?"

"It's for you to find out," said Gorgha.

He looked at her. She was big for a female crow. They were almost the same height. He launched into a story with neither head nor tail. The episodes followed each other at random. Gorgha listened, or pretended to listen. She nodded gravely at the end of each paragraph. When he had finished, he sighed again.

"And another thing," he said. "I don't know where Maleeya Bayarlag went."

"She disappeared?" asked Gorgha.

"Yes, we were going through the middle of a group of birds. Toucan buzzards, snowy owls, but mostly chickens. Mutants. They were angry with us. They were flying at eye level. We had to fight. We had to make a path through the middle of the flock. Maleeya Bayarlag was walking behind me, but when I turned around, there was no trace of her. She didn't give any sign of life after that."

Gorgha nodded slowly. They observed a silent pause. Mevlido suddenly had the desire to stretch out his arm to touch Gorgha's feathers, to crumple the down at the base of her head, to put his hands in the collar of her robe. They stayed in that immobility full of unsaid things, near one another but separated by the threshold and the security chain—she, Gorgha, in a destitute dishabille, and he, Mevlido, gray with dust, at once heavy and ghostly in the weak light coming from Waddell Street. Other houses stood nearby, but it was obvious that no one lived there. No one was pressing their forehead against a window to spy on their conversation or to evaluate the intimacy of their relationship. It was as if they had been alone in the world, out of sight of everyone, free, outside of any constraint.

"Do you want to come in?" said Gorgha. "I was going to go to bed anyway."

Perhaps because she still didn't open the door to let him pass, Mevlido remained passive in front of her. He didn't answer, apparently plunged in painful reflection, or rather as if the unambiguous proposition she had just made choked him and provoked in him a confusion that he couldn't master, except in freezing and opening his mouth on an empty sound. They were there, face-to-face. It is difficult to say whether sexuality was vibrating between them, reviving old complicity, or if, on the contrary, between them trembled only loneliness, an infinite and irreparable loneliness.

38

Sonia Wolguelane had taken off her dress. I was in the room with her. Three meters separated us, four at the most.

I don't know how it happened, by what magic spell, but we were in Factory Street again, like old times, like the times when we rubbed shoulders in groups whose names and agendas we didn't know, and who encouraged us to shoot mortars at the moon, when they weren't employing us to assassinate enemies of the people. She had taken off her dress, and, as she wasn't wearing a brassiere, I began immediately to tremble from head to foot, impatient to get to the next minute, when I could be intoxicated by her chest, already thinking only of the contact between, on one side, her very young woman's breasts, small and firm, and, on the other, my lips, my hands, the flesh of my fingers, my cheeks.

It was visible that she was used to being naked in front of men, and when I say men, I don't imagine those who aren't like me—I'm not capable of that, and I'm not trying to be—I imagine only those like me: subhumans, cops, murderers at the end of the day, bad elements attached or not to the sixth or ninth disgusting category, refugees from the very beginning, survivors, Bolsheviks or not, Ybürs, escaped Koreans, Chinese who don't even know where to find their country on a map, half-wits. It was visible that she was used to being naked in front of those men. It was, in any case, the first time she undressed in front of me. I hadn't yet taken off my clothes, and my presence in shirt and trousers three meters away manifestly didn't bother her—same with the very bright light coming from the street through the open window, exposing us to the possible curiosity of the neighbors across the street.

She smiled at me beguilingly, conscious of the erotic charge radiating from her shameless posture. She was a total knockout. She was graceful, attractive, imprinted with a laughing magnetism no one could escape. I didn't have the intention of resisting, and I was disarmed, but despite everything, I couldn't help but think that the difference in age between us complicated our relationship, making it almost incestuous, and, on another level, profoundly ridiculous. I had begun to move toward her, but before becoming intoxicated with her I felt overcome once more by an evident fact—we could have been father and daughter. Today Sonia Wolguelane was twenty years old or a bit more, which was the same as saying that the daughter we could have had, Verena Becker and I, was in front of me taking off her clothes and offering herself. In such circumstances it's difficult to get around the sudden shame of being fifty years old, and there was in me a half second of hesitation, then I managed to more or less distance myself from what was bothering me. I bracketed the remains of proletarian ethics that might have gotten between me and Sonia Wolguelane. The only thing that counted, here and now, was the ordinary and natural desire between hominids. It was enough to silence the moralizing chatter within me. It was enough to cynically privilege the purely animal side of the coitus that was about to happen.

Sonia Wolguelane was waiting nonchalantly for the first contact between us and, in any case, between our bodies. She had put her dress on the back of the chair, and she turned her back to check that it wasn't going to be wrinkled, then she came back to face me, upright and supple, slender, radiating well-being, physically perfect.

I paused briefly to observe her in detail and admire her.

- the witchy gray-white of her plumage
- the almost prominent hip bones, still covered enough not to give the impression of gauntness
- the silvery firmness of her breasts, the marvelous mahogany color of her areolae, the elegant points of her nipples
- scars on her, scars up until that point evidently unsuspected, a red scar that clawed the top of her right thigh, then a gash made with a blade under her left breast, another on her stomach, she had been brutalized, she had fought back, she had been wounded several times, at different points, doubtlessly beginning in childhood
- tattoos, near her navel a drawing of a grenade and a star, on her arm two butterflies, at the base of her back and on her left hip several words traced in characters reminiscent of dead languages like Khmer or American
- her black irises expressed a complex-free gaiety, she accepted that I was contemplating her, she approved of my desire for her, she kindly offered me her beautiful living being's beauty, with generosity

- her young living being's beauty
- it was hot, but I didn't see a single drop of sweat sparkling on her smooth, very brown skin
- there was no down anywhere on her body, except on her face, and even there the feathers were almost invisible
- a drop of sweat snaked down the length of her stomach, on her skin the color of raw silk, very light
- everywhere on her body was covered with a smooth down, everywhere on her young seductress's body, a complete knockout, on her chest, her shoulders, her limbs up to the daintiest extremities
- it was hot, and a sheen sparkled over her, accentuating the desire that one might have to soften against her and to lose oneself
- she didn't have a navel, she had no tattoo in the place where she could have had a navel, an abundant growth of feathers of a deeply moving light gray covered her stomach, completely hiding her skin from the base of her breasts down to mid-thigh
- in a past unknown to me she must have belonged to a gang and undergone initiation rituals, cruel rituals, and who knows what semi-illiterate brute had carved under her arm, in the place where pain is hard to stand, a number that brought to mind a concentration camp prisoner's ID, and on her pelvis the number was repeated, in horribly clumsy writing
- she let her arms hang by her sides defenselessly, but I wasn't unaware of the fact that she could use weapons with those arms, that she knew how to kill with a club or knife with those hands, and still she seemed more fragile than muscled, more loving than warlike

- and besides, her gaze shone and invited me, it drew me toward her without a shred of irony, without thinking ill of me, without letting on that we could have been father and daughter

I paused briefly. To observe her in detail and admire her. Already I had come close to her.

Then, without a word, I went to brush the tips of her nipples with my mouth. My hands were damp. I didn't want to impose my perspiration on her, the dampness of my palms, whose disagreeable abundance she might not appreciate and which she would probably associate with a mental imbalance or morbid anxieties which to tell the truth I didn't have. The body has no secrets, skin is a crude tissue with no surprises, for millions of years we have known and archived that in each one of us; all the same, I didn't want to present myself in the unflattering light of dampness and haste. I lowered myself, put two fingers into the elastic band of her underwear and slid it down her legs. As this last piece of clothing reached her ankles and I helped her out of it, I had my face buried between her thighs. I've always had a problem there. It's a place where the little feathers take on a texture on the tongue that I find unfortunate, even detestable. The barbs come off easily, and they have a smell that's hard to ignore, and suddenly I have between my palate and uvula a nearly nauseating collection of threads. I moved my forehead and nose through the feathers, I buried myself in them, closing my eyes and letting out a gasp of pleasure that Sonia Wolguelane immediately echoed. I felt her take my head in her hands and guide me. Leaving aside my memories of bad experiences, I began to obey her suggestions. I was beside myself, tumescent to the last degree, aroused, continuously sighing like an animal in rut. I had forgotten my misgivings about cunnilingus. Sonia Wolguelane writhed against me, above me. I was floating a bit outside of reality and the passage of time, as if infinitely enchanted by the present, not asking myself whether I was crouched in an uncomfortable position, entwined with the legs of a girl who could have been my daughter, licking little feathers and fumbling around in them with my chin, with the tip of my tongue, with all of my available facial muscles.

"Come here, Mevlido," said Sonia Wolguelane, all at once pulling me upward.

I emerged.

I was covered with saliva, with sweat, and with cyprine, and I felt the urgent need to take off my clothes and penetrate my partner's body as quickly as possible. Sonia Wolguelane gave me a salacious wink and opened her mouth in a little laugh. She had grabbed my shoulder, she released me to let me take off my shirt, then she took a few steps and disappeared behind the bedroom wall.

I was standing. I took advantage of the moment alone to run my index finger between my gums and the bottom of my tongue, where a repulsive little ball of filaments had formed. I gagged.

I unbuttoned my shirt as fast as possible, unbuckled my belt, and began to attack my shoelaces.

"Come here," said Sonia Wolguelane again.

I couldn't see her anymore. She had a weary voice.

I took about twenty seconds to untie my shoes. They were tied with twine whose unorthodox knots had to be undone. My hands were trembling.

"I'm coming," I said.

I was very near the window, and I could see, in the apartment across the street, a *mudang* in ceremonial dress, prepared to dance so that the dead that have been shown to her go back to their world and cease to meddle in the affairs of the living. The musician who accompanied her was settling his drum against the arch of his right foot. Neither one nor the other was looking in my direction.

The sky was black.

I had a pang of emotion.

At that instant, the drum was struck for the first time.

I hurried to rejoin Sonia Wolguelane in the little bedroom. I was finally naked. I had only one idea: make love to Sonia Wolguelane, unite myself with her. Understand through what orifice she wanted me to enter her, and enter her. My hands were wet; I wiped them clumsily on the bed and lay down. I felt like I was drenched. I began to crawl toward her, on the mattress. I felt that I was crawling with my whole body and going toward immense happiness. I was crawling toward Sonia Wolguelane.

"Cut the nonsense, Mevlido," said a sleepy voice in my ear.

I had closed my eyes; it seemed to me that the sexual euphoria was going to be even more intense. The voice made me open them. I didn't do it right away. I imagined the bedroom plunged into darkness. I thought about happiness.

The drum beat.

"That's just nonsense, Mevlido," repeated the voice. "Stop. We just did that."

I opened my eyes.

There was in the air an odor of rancid oil, as often was the case in Gorgha's house, as she liked to smooth her feathers with a grease that she claimed was aromatic, perfumed with musk. Around us, the darkness was absolute.

"I was just dreaming of you," I said.

"Bah," said Gorgha, "you're just talking bullshit."

"We were making love," I said.

"Come on, Mevlido," said Gorgha. "Go back to sleep. Enough fucking for tonight."

The drum beat.

"Do you hear?" I asked, after a moment.

"What?"

"A drum. A *gutbuk*."

"Where?"

"I don't know. In the street."

"No," said Gorgha, "there's nothing to hear. Go back to sleep."

39

"And now, do you hear?" asked Mevlido.

"What?" said Gorgha.

"The drum," I said.

We were concentrating on the noises. They were infinitesimal. Something in the darkness indicated the imminence of twilight: we were nearing morning, or evening. In Gorgha's house, the air wasn't moving. Nor were we. An omniscient narrator or even a spider from its web would have doubtless guessed us to be dead of asphyxiation or of dual loneliness, or fainted after an excess of pleasure, still mixed up with our animal residue, with the stagnant stenches our bodies had produced around us, with residue of excretion upon us, and, inside us, the dark memory of rasping wings, torn membranes, mucus membranes exhaling their last dew before torpor. We were lying on the bed, immobile. We were listening.

The drum was beating.

"A ceremony for the dead," I murmured. "A man is tapping on his drum. A *mudang* is dancing and reciting a chant."

"Bah," said Gorgha.

"I recognize the rhythm," I said.

"But no," said Gorgha, "it's a guy at the end of the street."

"A guy."

"Yes," she explained, "a madman. He's hitting bits of metal, walls. It depends what's within reach. He's mad with fear. It's his memory that has driven him mad. He's tapping on things to get away from what's weighing on his memory."

"How do you know, do you know him?"

"No. But I've been given information about him. He participated in the third extermination. He was a child soldier during the atrocities."

"Ah," I said, "a child soldier. And he has a name?"

"It appears that he's called Alban Glück."

"Ah," I said, "Alban Glück."

Gorgha fell silent. I let a quarter of an hour of silence go by, then I got up.

"Where are you going?" she asked.

"I'm going there," I said.

"Where?"

"Over there," I said.

I heard Gorgha behind me, smoothing a wing, stretching it slowly, then folding it. The bed was not wide. She was getting comfortable now that I had left my place empty.

I headed to the bathroom. The tap let out a hiccup but didn't spit out a single drop. I insisted, screwing and unscrewing the handle. Nothing came.

"There's no water," I protested to Gorgha.

"It's been cut off since yesterday," said Gorgha.

"I need to wash," I said.

"Don't go," said Gorgha. "Don't go out. Stay here, you'll get washed up later. It will come back."

"What?"

"The water," said Gorgha.

"When?" I asked.

"What?" Gorgha made me repeat myself, since the wall between us absorbed certain vowels.

"The water, when will it come back?"

"I don't know," said Gorgha. "Stay with me, we'll wait together."

The drum was beating at the end of the street. Muffled beats, barely audible, but audible. Alban Glück was afraid. He was tapping to unencumber his memory.

"It will come back next month maybe," Gorgha reflected.

"Bah," I said.

"Stay here," insisted Gorgha. "Why are you going there?"

"I have to go," I said.

Reluctantly, I abandoned the idea of cleaning myself, and I began to gather my clothes. They were scattered without any logic in the shadowy chamber. I pulled on those I could find as well as I could.

Then I left Gorgha's house.

As it benefited from indirect lighting, the street was not compactly shadowed, and, as the minutes passed, the light got still better. The sky was changing from pitch black to dark gray. A day was beginning. I was walking with very small steps, trying to make the least noise possible, mind a little numb but nonetheless conscious that I was going to try once again to commit a murder. Absorbed by the outside air, the echo of the knocking was practically imperceptible. Perhaps also, Glück, having heard a door open and close a bit higher in the alley, had decided to make himself scarce.

As I walked cautiously along the facades of one-story hovels, sometimes with untended gardens or twisted gates, I heard Glück's music again. It was an elementary solo. The percussionist's hands sometimes hit the ground, sometimes a wall. The ground was hit with the palm, the wall with the fist. The rhythm didn't vary. A piece of metal hanging from a nail bounced when Glück knocked on the wall.

The sounds became clearer and clearer.

I was getting closer.

Alban Glück's place was a low construction, apparently without an opening other than the one to the street. In the shadows, it seemed like an artisan's storage shed or a large garage. A shutter of corrugated metal remained unmoving halfway up the doorframe. When the neighboring house had crumbled, the collapse must have deformed the supports or the guide rails, forever blocking the metal curtain.

I examined the premises for a few moments.

Child soldiers have always horrified me, even before they martyred Verena Becker. In the police training rooms, where they taught us to manage the most hateful situations, the confrontations with child soldiers were always seen as the worst. Their attacks or their responses to attacks had something unpredictable and dishonest about them; hand-to-hand combat with them was dirty. They were formidable adversaries, capable of a baby's laughter at the moment they were trying to hit your vital organs, and adept in techniques that guaranteed a lengthy agony for their opponent. Abruptly, I recalled the atmosphere of those special training sessions, the heat, the lack of ventilation, the smell of the straw of the tatami mats. I had once more in my ears the shouts of our instructors, who reproduced with distaste the cunning of adolescents drunk on savagery: their child's sobs, their deceptive cries for help. I didn't have the time to wonder in what circumstances I had received this instruction, in what real or dreamed world, and why, and when. The images were there, sprung from nowhere, and, instinctively, I knew that I had no power over them and that they had no more permanence than memories of a dream. They could disappear as suddenly as they had appeared.

I had begun to reflect. I had neglected all combat practice for a long time, and I was going to fight. Alban Glück was a former child soldier. My chances of neutralizing him were mediocre.

Stop thinking, Mevlido, I thought. Stop contemplating the images passing through you. All of that risks complicating your job. Don't measure the horror of what is to come. Put an end to your scruples and enter into the action. Don't think about the rest anymore. Don't let thoughts and disgust take away your last strength.

Then I ventured into the building.

The action immediately unfolded. That put an end to my scruples.

Alban Glück was sitting at the back of the garage, near a jumble of planks and old parts of gates, slabs of corrugated iron. At the second I appeared in the door, he interrupted his percussion concert and rattled the metal with rage to dissuade me from entering. Of my silhouette he must have seen only the legs, lit from behind. I bent down to get past the obstacle of the metallic curtain and stood up immediately on the other side. Now I was in Glück's house. While the echoes of rattling died down, I heard him retreat toward the place where he cowered to sleep. His gestures were sharp, he reacted aggressively to my intrusion, and to begin with, he threw in my direction a pair of pincers that he had picked up from the ground. The tool went on to hit the shutter half a meter from me, provoking a thunderous din. A rain of rust pattered down on my skull. It was dark, but my eyes were sufficiently used to the darkness to see what needed to be seen. I was watching all of Glück's movements, nothing surprised me. Terrorized, two rats ran along the wall. They ran as fast as they could. They suddenly turned around and came back to hide behind a crate full of empty bottles. They would have liked to hightail it for the street, but my presence prevented them.

Don't have any contact with those animals, I thought in a flash.

Alban Glück changed location. He had jumped into a corner and got a hold of a machete. He was suddenly motionless, hunched over, on guard in that dark corner of his lair, all concentrated strength and menace. He showed no mental weakness, and what could be seen of his posture showed on the contrary that he was a tenacious adversary, wary and ready for anything.

Trickery would be necessary.

"What's gotten hold of you, Glück?" I asked in a frightened tone. "You don't recognize me?"

I hadn't moved since the pincers had fallen next to me. We were separated by a half-dozen meters. It's not much, and it's a lot.

"It's me, Ogoïne," I continued. "I didn't come here for us to tear each other apart."

I had made up a name at random. I wanted to disconcert him without losing the initiative. He had made the mistake of not rushing at me immediately, which had allowed me to get used to his space.

"What are you thinking?" I said. "Calm down. You're scaring me."

I shook my head, spluttering, as if preoccupied more than anything with getting rid of the bits of rust irritating my face.

I was actually looking for a weapon. On the ground were several metal carcasses, broken sinks, and cement slabs that I would have had great difficulty picking up to fight. This debris didn't suit me. The pincers could work as a projectile, but we were no longer at the stage of throwing things in each other's faces. I moved toward the place the rats had crept into shortly before. In the crate were glass containers, some jars, a few bottles. If I threw myself to that side, I'd have the time to grab a beer bottle and break it to transform it into something dangerous.

"Go ahead, put your knife away," I said. "We're not going to fight."

I leaned over to clean off my hair.

"I have a message from the old lady for you," I added.

I brushed off my head without sparing the gesticulations,

like an inoffensive person would have done. Then I stood up and stayed still again. Nothing in me showed a desire to fight.

Glück stayed hunched over. He seemed to vibrate. He had intended to uncoil himself, to rush at me and to cut me down, but the clues I was giving him one after the other upset him. He hesitated. First, one always hesitates before destroying a messenger whose message you don't know. Second, unknown people had been introduced into his present life and forced his memory to work. Ogoïne. The old woman. His memory was working with no result, and that necessarily created an imbalance in him.

His age was absolutely unknowable. From nostalgia perhaps of the years when he had been an actor in a nightmare, he wore a mask of rubbery material that resembled human skin, a pale mask, expressionless, with a grotesque rodent's muzzle from which sprouted fake whiskers, very thick and stiff. The eye holes pulled on his eyelids and made him look like he had pig's eyes, almost immobile, near idiocy. A curly wig of synthetic fibers covered his skull, in a color that the shadows rendered undefinable. It was easy to imagine this hideous puppet leaning over Verena Becker, playing at hurting Verena Becker, my dear little Verena, frightening her and taking away all of her hope.

It was my turn to be troubled by what my memory brought to the surface. I had begun to wander down private paths. I had begun to think of something else besides combat. Alban Glück observed this and attacked.

I felt him leap.

Without looking at him, I threw myself to the right, toward the crate I had seen. In my path were metal grates and cinderblocks lying on the ground. I had to make a detour, I zigzagged, and, after four steps, I realized I was turning my back to Glück. I no longer had time to change tactic. I was no longer thinking. I put my hand out toward the bottles. The present broke down into violent intuitions. My back toward Glück, in a position of weakness, I leaned over the glass containers. Behind the cage, the two rats, disturbed again, ran in the direction of a safer shelter. I heard Glück put his foot on an iron plate. I'm not left-handed, but I had grabbed the bottle in my left hand. I had just closed my fingers on the neck when Glück got to me. He hit me full force. I stopped breathing, and, as I spun around, I broke the bottle against the wall. I couldn't see the shape of the piece of glass in my hand. I didn't know if what I was holding was going to be effective. Glück was already bringing down his machete to shatter my head or shoulder. I was turning around. As I couldn't retreat farther, I matched his movement. I got past his guard without running into his blade. I don't know why, after what secret signal, I suddenly had the ease of an expert. The lessons I had received during those training sessions were finally paying off. The lethal blade was whistling by three centimeters from my flesh, and I was moving with a self-assuredness my instructors would have been proud of. Everything happened in a very short time, hardly more than a third of a second. The pieces of the broken bottle still hadn't reached the ground. I nicked Alban Glück's wrist and brought the shard upward again with force to slice the inside of his elbow. It was now or never that I would discover if my improvised weapon had the qualities I was hoping for. The glass cut like a razor.

I heard a physical reaction from Glück. He didn't scream, but his body let out a sigh of surprise. The pain hadn't reached his consciousness yet. I knew he was dropping his machete, and I continued the arc of motion I had begun a fraction of an instant earlier. Now I could see what my knife looked like. It was a vicious kris that must have sliced through everything in its way in Glück's arm—tendons, nerves, and arteries, down to the bone. I let it come out from under Glück's shoulder, I pointed it toward the mask and planted it in the mask. Alban Glück collapsed onto me. I pulled my glass dagger from his cheek and bent down to avoid his left arm, which was trying to get hold of me. The crate tipped over under Glück's feet. The machete fell. Glück now fell to the floor howling in pain. He immediately bounced up to get away from me and was rolling around in the scrap metal. He was getting near the door. I picked up the machete, caught up with him, stood over him to keep him from running away into the street.

Now I could catch my breath.

The shadows hid many of the details. I couldn't see any blood; I couldn't see the tear in Alban Glück's rubbery face. Alban Glück was crawling in a spiral on the ground, screaming. He threw a fistful of dust at me, then gave up confrontation and stopped spinning in circles. He occupied himself with compressing the wound on his right arm. His left hand gripping his elbow, he sobbed with rage and suffering, but, as his mask was still in place, his carnival physiognomy seemed impervious to it. Beneath the mask his cheek had been horribly gouged. Beneath it flowed blood and tears. The wig hadn't slipped either. I stood over Alban Glück at my full height, disappointed at not having killed him at once and at having to lean over him again to finish him off. Now that I had time to examine the situation, I realized that, instinctively, I had preferred to tear his face apart rather than cut his throat and thus end him more quickly. I had prolonged his life so that he could witness his own death, I had wanted to wound him in such a way that his agony would not be too quick. I had had this torturer's impulse.

Useless to try to hide it from myself. I had had this torturer's impulse.

I didn't feel any compassion for Glück, but, at the same time as the desire to make him suffer before his death, a discourse of shame was taking shape inside me. Fatigue and disgust invaded me. Finish it as fast as you can, I repeated to myself. Don't let yourself be tempted by barbarity. Don't dream of making him suffer, of making him afraid, don't abandon him without giving him the coup de grâce.

I still couldn't manage to determine Alban Glück's age. Underneath his mask, he could have just as easily been fifteen years old or two or three times as much. His voice whined like a child's that hadn't yet changed. As I wasn't hitting him, he moved away from me. He was writhing on his back. He tried to drag himself out of my reach. He had reached a pile of scrap iron, and he was now showing his intention of returning to a vertical position. He leaned on what had been a gas can at some point. He leaned his back against the remains of a radiator. His size was scarcely that of an adolescent. He's not even fourteen, I thought. He was one of those who organized the torture of Verena Becker twenty years ago, but he's not even fourteen. Not finishing him off right away would be criminal, I thought. It would be an insult to proletarian morality.

Respect proletarian morality, I thought.

Alban Glück had pulled himself back to standing. He was leaning on an unstable pile of carcasses, heavy objects. He was raving, hiccuping, with sobs terrible to hear. He was speaking a language I didn't know. From time to time he stopped compressing his mutilated arm and grabbed, without conviction, a piece of metal that he tried to throw at me. Rust flew in every direction. I was two meters from him, but the projectiles didn't reach me. Ribbons of blood now flowed from his wounds, and, under his mask, he had begun to choke.

Finish off this Glück, I thought. End this, proletarian morality or not. Who am I to respect a morality or to betray it?

Glück fought against suffocation. He began to shake in all his limbs, then the trembling died down. He was still far from his last breath. He raked the air with his left hand, looking for a piece of pipe or a metal blade.

Don't make Glück undergo an agony as monstrous as that he inflicted on Verena Becker, I thought.

Or rather, yes, I thought. Frighten this Glück before you finish him. Dance with him and his death a little. Who am I to be or not to be a torturer?

I approached him with the machete. I could very well reflect on proletarian morality, I didn't have a good idea of how this was going to continue, after all.

40

Mevlido bent down under the metallic shutter to pass through the opening in Alban Glück's building, and he left that place forever. It was visible from his movements that he wanted to avoid wasting time, and yet he paused briefly. He gave off the impression that he was accumulating gases clumsily to inflate his chest and that, after that, with the same awkwardness, he expelled them. The air of the alley had the coolness of dawn. The building's door was stuck halfway down, and the light was weak, but on the ground could be seen detritus, shards of glass, and part of Glück's body.

Then Mevlido staggered into the light of the early morning. He was going toward the end of the street where there was a bit more light. He was reciting syllables that didn't have the ability to make words. Physically and intellectually, he had sunk very low. He was thinking of only one thing: cleaning himself off. He wanted to wash. He brushed by me without noticing my presence. It's impossible to deny that he looked like a murderer. It's impossible to deny that he looked like a murderer who had had trouble finishing the job.

He continued to brandish a repugnant machete, and when he realized it, he threw it over a fence into a garden where burdock was growing. Then he walked the last part of the alley. He seemed not to believe in anything. His shirt and a leg of his trousers were black with blood. He wasn't looking behind him. No noise came from the garage where Alban Glück lay.

Mevlido felt horribly dirty. He was. He couldn't stand the smells of murder that he was carrying with him, the smells of dirty feathers, shattered arms, spasms in the scrap iron, the stench of wigs stained with brains.

I have to get clean, he thought. He came back to that thought obsessively, and, outside of that, he was incapable of making a sentence or a memory. I'm going to get back to the street, he thought. Get into a building, look for water. I'm going to get under a tap and eliminate this filth.

He came out onto a road whose name he didn't know. Waddell Street or Factory Street, he thought. Or even another street. For all the importance that could have.

Find a place to wash, he thought. That's the main thing. Outside of that, nothing counts. Names, language, images—nothing counts.

In the street the movement of the very early morning hour was beginning.

There was a little oily smoke nearby. A cafeteria was opening its doors. Someone was sautéing rice in sizzling oil.

A bird took off from a roof, letting heavy droppings fall to the ground.

The lamps, where there were lamps, were still lighted. They indicated here and there someone's presence. I have to avoid the inhabitants, thought Mevlido. Whether they are alive or dead, it's better for me to avoid them.

He slipped into the first opening he came upon. It was the entrance to a small building, an ordinary entryway, with a panel of mailboxes that the spiders had taken over years before, and also with cables and fuse boxes encased in a sticky layer of dust. On the ground, puddles of dark water stagnated. A fluorescent tube agonized above the first steps of the stairway, adding a touch of pale yellow to the shadows. The staircase hadn't been swept for months.

A staircase, thought Mevlido. I'm going to go up, avoid the inhabitants, force a lock if there's a lock to be forced. I'm going to look for a shower if there is a shower. I'm going to put myself under it. I'm going to rinse myself from head to foot and then steal clothes if there are clothes. I'm going to get rid of all this dirt. It has to go. The rest doesn't count.

When he had arrived at the fourth floor, he leaned on a door handle, and it opened. The apartment was one of great poverty, with rudimentary furniture. It was made up of a bedroom without windows and a room looking out onto the street, with a kitchen that served as a washroom as well. Mevlido made the rounds to make sure that the occupants were absent. The examination took him three seconds at most. Spider webs covered the walls of the bedroom. The bed was rumpled and dirty; it looked as if it hadn't been used for several days. In the kitchen, the pantry held a plate of indistinct scraps that two cockroaches were ogling, tempted by the scent but frustrated to not be able to get through the grating.

He undressed completely and maneuvered the tap sticking out over the shower drain on the floor. The water began to run over his hands, then splashed below, scattering drops around. He let it splash his legs, then he entered the ceramic container and crouched down. The tap was attached a meter from the floor at the most. The pipe let out with regularity a thin, twisted stream of water where sometimes a silvery reflection shone. Mevlido put under it sometimes his arms and hands, sometimes his head, which he tipped back so that the ignominious substances impregnating his hair didn't run into his mouth. The water laboriously dissolved the stiff and encrusted filth. It took time, but it did it. Around

Mevlido's feet it murmured and accumulated, forming thick bubbles, bubbles with an almost grainy texture that flowed toward the drain and refused for a long time to burst.

The pipes vibrated, sometimes coughed up liquid mixed with sand, but the water continued to drip onto Mevlido and to wet him, and, progressively, it delivered him from the concrete traces of the night. That's the main thing, he thought. Clear away the traces. Clear away the traces once and for all.

From time to time he opened his eyes. Around his ankles the water was still far from being transparent. The bubbles had thinned, but they remained brownish. From their perch at the pantry, the cockroaches observed him without saying a word. He himself didn't address them either. He remained crouched in the shower. He tried not to see, at the entrance of the kitchen, his clothing soaked in blood and pus, drenched in black humors. He looked beyond them, the main room had a chest, two chairs, and a table and, behind them, the distorted rectangle of the window. The sky hesitated between gray and black. He received this on his retinas without understanding. Quickly, his eyelids closed again. He had no desire for images.

That's how Mevlido remained all day, under the tap, his eyes generally closed, his mind inert. The time that passed didn't count. Only the water.

Afterward, in the same place. Mevlido had just finished his shower.

He considered his clothes with horror. They were blocking his way. He stepped over them like you would step over a dead animal and began to search for something to wear in the apartment. Besides the sheet, the bedroom held nothing that could have covered his nudity. He came back into the main room, rifled through the chest, and pulled out a pair of trunks and jeans that fit him, as well as a plastic bag containing a pair of sandals and a blue-and-gray-checkered shirt. I know this chest, he thought. It's the chest where Maleeya puts our things. And this shirt, he continued. I know it too. It's Yasar Bayarlag's shirt, which Maleeya kept piously, in memory of him.

He only put the shorts and trousers on at first. He hesitated before the chest, before the not-very-worn, almost-new-even shirt, then he put it on without buttoning it. The sandals had also belonged to Yasar Bayarlag. They were in his size.

And now? he asked himself.

He remained standing in that room. On the course he should follow his intelligence told him nothing. He weighed the pros and cons meditatively without being able to form the least solid idea. His memory gave him unstable fragments, names with no explanation, which seemed like certitudes and then immediately disappeared.

Night had returned in the apartment and over the city.

Night is here, again, he thought.

A drum had begun to beat somewhere nearby, a Korean *gut-buk* like those played to speak with the dead.

He had the intuition that he was dreaming. Nothing allowed him to know whether that intuition was based in fact. In any case, even if I'm dreaming, I'm in reality, he thought abruptly.

He headed to the window. It was from the house across the street that the drum could be heard. It was also on the fourth floor.

There a ceremony calling up the dead had started. The apartment was lit by several bulbs. Mevlido saw the singer, who was passing in front of a lamp. She was turned three-quarters toward the street. Then she continued her movement and slipped out of sight. That *mudang* looks like Linda Siew, thought Mevlido. The resemblance is striking. He would have liked to examine the features of her face with more attention, but already a wall was between them, and for a moment, only her arm, from time to time, appeared. A green sleeve could be seen with multicolored ribbons attached to it, and a rather thin hand, which the effort of the dance gnarled. The whole thing moved in a sweeping motion when she sent toward the ceiling or toward the outside objurgations in witch's language. The ribbons accompanied her song. They wound about and floated, they took time to take an earthward direction. It grasped, it attracted, it spoke a language that only the inside of your bones could understand. The *mudang*'s voice was acting also, a voice that came from the dark depths of the body and that, despite everything, was melodious and calming. The drum beat, in tension, in relaxation, in tension, in relaxation.

The *mudang* reappeared in front of the lamp. She was beautiful.

She reminds me of someone, thought Mevlido. Linda Siew or someone else.

The name existed inside him but didn't open up onto any memory.

I don't know who this Linda Siew is, he thought again. The best thing would be to go to her and interrogate her. Whether or not this *mudang* is Linda Siew, she will maybe have something to tell me.

In any case, I have to go over there, he thought again.

He still hadn't buttoned Yasar Bayarlag's clean shirt over himself. He did it, buckled his sandals, and left the apartment.

He went down four stories, reached the street, and crossed it.

Already he was inside the building across the street.

I know what I'm going to ask her, he thought. I am going to ask her to tell me where Verena Becker is right now.

This other name, like the previous ones, evoked nothing for him.

He walked down the corridor of the entrance. The staircase was shadowy. He started up it. He constantly ran into birds as big as dogs, who scattered at the last moment, rubbing their wings and their beaks against his legs. The hall light wasn't working. The number of steps changed from floor to floor. Soon he didn't know what level he had ended up at. On the landings were no doors. He froze. He was seeking a point of reference by following the echo of the voice and the drum, but he could no longer hear anything. No *mudang* was lamenting anymore over the fate of the dead and the living, trying to confuse the two to come to their aid. Slogans had been scratched into the plaster of the wall. He began to decipher them, then he remembered that he couldn't read them, because the stairwell was submerged in darkness. Anyway, it's not very important, he reasoned. If I'm not dreaming, I've gone mad. I've seen worse.

"Yes," he murmured, "I've seen much worse."

All around him the birds opened and closed their wings. They piled up against each other to avoid contact with him, and they didn't squawk. Much lower, in the street, life went on. A junky and a beggar woman were arguing at the intersection; someone was sweeping in front of a porch; at the entrance of a restaurant, the diners were exchanging pleasantries. The sounds came to him clearly, but as if after having been filtered by a long distance. Whether or not he liked it, the exterior was far away.

He pulled himself up to the next floor, and, when the birds he had disturbed had calmed down, he explored the landing by feeling his way around. His fingers only met resistant webs, in funnels or burrows. They tore apart with a silky noise that you needed stoic nerves to hear without screaming. Nausea forced him to give up. He sat on a step and wiped the sticky threads that had clung to his hands on the edge. What good was it to wash? he thought. Then he remained a long moment without doing anything.

A long moment. He dozed.

He was sitting.

The stairwell was almost silent.

"I'm thinking of you," he murmured.

Around him the extremely dense shadows shivered, moved by the unexpected sound of this human voice. There were only, to receive it, spiders and giant owls, sleeping, at every level between the ground floor and the attic.

"I'm thinking of you," repeated Mevlido in a low voice. "I miss you. I will think of you. Whatever the end is."

He had paused.

He couldn't put a woman's picture on the shadow behind his utterances. There was no picture. Names came to him. Sonia, Verena, Maleeya, Linda. My dear little Verena, he thought randomly, in a kind of mechanical outburst. The names told him nothing. He didn't succeed in finding out whom he was thinking about.

41

He was sitting among birds and spiders, surrounded by darkness and silence. He was sitting among the beasts. His thoughts were running out of his head, less and less precise. He wouldn't have been able to cite a single one of the women's names that had visited him a little earlier. He could no longer explain his presence in this place. Behind the walls, there was no noise. The building was uninhabited. After an hour or two he noticed that he had slept for an indefinite period of time, maybe an hour or two or a little more. His mouth hung open; his head was heavy. His muscles ached. He had no memory of the rest. Concerned that he not get trapped in an unknown place, he began to descend in the direction of the ground floor. Giant chickens and toucan owls that came up to mid-thigh shook their feathers out nearby. Some of them slapped against his knees. Their wings were powerful. Others, frightened by his movement, preceded him, jumping from step to step, and, when he was in the building's entrance, they scattered into the night, squawking.

He paused on the threshold, dazed by amnesia, interrogating the dark street. The place became confused with others.

Maybe I have already lived through this, he murmured. Or a variation. Under my name or Mevlido's name or another's. Or it will happen later. Or never. Maybe it will stay in the forgotten form of a dream. What good is it to untangle what is before and what is after? Because I ended up in the bottom of the Shambles, what good is it to make the effort?

He looked at the street. He had the intuition that he lived somewhere in the Shambles, but he didn't remember where or since when. I'll end up finding something familiar, he thought.

The street was sloping. He went up it.

It was a street of spiders. It was followed by another, then by a third, still worse. It was raining most of the time, with intervals of burning night. It was dark, and besides, there were no windows in the place that Mevlido had found to stay. He hadn't returned to his little house near Waddell Street and, on the contrary, had come back to live in the bus station.

At the time, I had evacuated my mind of everything that had happened at the moment I had fought with Glück, explained Mevlido to whomever would listen to him, when he had begun to speak again—and when people or living beings were listening. I had washed all of that off, I didn't want to touch that pain again, those dregs. Instinctively I had returned to the bus station, in one of the nooks guarded by several cripples who took shifts twenty-four hours a day and all looked alike. The dividing walls of my cubbyhole and the wall covered with graffiti ran with water, drops rolled down, carrying over their surface the remains of cloth and black mildew. I had, very high above me, the flickering presence of a fluorescent tube that had been resisting power outages forever. I curled up as well as I could on what served as a seat or bed, and I closed my eyes when the moment came to feign sleep. The door, half a meter from me, closed thanks to a greasy cord whose knot came undone during my absences. I rented this room by the month, for a moderate price, a dollar and a half. I had to negotiate credit, but, seeing that I was installed there in a quasi-definitive way, the cripples had decided not to ask me for anything anymore. The weeks passed, and my clothes little by little acquired the appearance of shiny scabs. The infirm men who looked after the little rooms spoke to me only to reprimand me. Several ragged men like me lodged next door, but they were in such a state of prostration that it was impossible to form any kind of relationship with them. They went out from time to time to curl up on the steps of the stairs that went down from the first floor to the bus garage. They sat there, in the middle of the smoke of burning tires and gasoline. The drivers scolded them, the rats attacked them and ate their feet up to the calf muscles. They didn't react. For my part, after a period of inertia, I ended up going through the doors of the bus station. They were open, and I was allowed to come and go. It was raining, the sky was permanently swollen with ink. I walked in the city for hours, standing in the middle of the road to get the most out of the rain. When I came back, my clothes were clean. As if I had been closely observed and as if these excursions had been an occasion to test my capacity of resistance to internal loneliness and to the absence of meaningful events, I was soon recruited to the Party. I swore not to betray the Party, and, here no less than elsewhere, I won't say by what methods contact between us was established. But one day I knew that I was again in the service of an organization whose names and goals I didn't know. The radius of my movements outside the bus station grew. The Party confided small missions in me. From time to time I went to empty a pistol cartridge onto a precise target, in general on someone of whom I learned afterward that he deserved to have been pumped full of bullets, but sometimes also I was asked to assassinate a poor person like me in every way, which I did out of respect for discipline, but with distaste. I came home exhausted. Above my head the fluorescent tube fluttered a message in a milky Morse code to which I didn't have the key. As if it were a question of confiding the details of my adventures in just anyone, I invented, in a low voice, nightmares that I told to the spiders—always present—and to the rats, when they were there. My stories didn't interest them, I realized from the fixedness of their reddish gaze, which suddenly became insulting. Very quickly I seemed to have exhausted the main idea of the narrative, and I was silent. Other times, lacking anecdotes, I deciphered the graffiti left by the occupants of the cubbyhole before they disappeared, sounding them out. Besides the numbers and obscenities, there were some exclamations whose echoes in me took time to die out, as if one day, in another place, I had already heard and understood them:

- THE ANIMALS HAVE THEIR ANIMALS!
- THE INSANE HAVE THEIR INSANE!
- THE BIRDS HAVE THEIR BIRDS!
- THE ASSASSINS HAVE THEIR ASSASSINS!

I went to make a solid knot in the piece of cord that closed my door, and I sprawled insomniacly on my seat, in the silence of the night, in the fetid humidity of the night. The wall dripped, the dividers dripped, the fluorescent light weakened until it became a moistly phosphorescent stem, then relighted, blinking. I closed my eyes. Through my eyelids the electric light continued its vacillations.

I opened my eyes again. The night hadn't changed, the light was the same. The cord was untied and no longer held the door closed. I must have lost consciousness for several minutes. A rat had entered the room and sniffed who knows what behind my seat. I got up, I went out, I went to ask the time from one of the lame men. He didn't answer me. I listened to the low sound of the motors, the bestial interjections of the drivers. When morning was near, I crossed the desolated space of the first floor, I went down to the garage where the buses were maneuvering, and I went out into the city.

Weeks went by. Armloads of weeks. Years. Some passed without leaving the slightest memory behind them. Some were years of spiders, others weren't.

And so passed Mevlido's death, that is to say, mine.

42

Then one morning. A morning or an evening. In the course of one of Mevlido's sempiternal wanderings inside the Shambles. We find Mevlido that day. Mevlido, or someone who is close enough to me to be me and to have the same name as I do.

I had crossed a street and had gone into the entrance of a building. The place stunk. The night was falling. I had pressed on the hall light switch, on the off chance. Lamps had come on in the stairwell, and I had begun to climb the stairs, but, on the second floor, the light went out. I hadn't been able to find another switch. My hands scraped the empty walls without success. My fingers got caught in spider webs. We were in a year of spiders; I think I already mentioned that. The webs were numerous and very resistant, but they weren't stretched across the hall and didn't keep me from moving forward. I began my ascent again. Having arrived at the fourth floor, I sat down in the dark. There was a regular pounding in my head or on the other side of the wall. I had wanted to sit down to listen to it. I have already experienced this, I thought. Something was there, close by, beneath my consciousness. I've already experienced this, I don't know when, I thought. In any case, it was in the past.

There was a knocking on the other side of the wall. A man was playing a beat on a drum. A *gutbuk,* I immediately thought. The man was producing a beat on a drum set up vertically, with a skin at once sonorous and melodious. Someone, behind that wall, was trying to calm the dead. A *mudang,* I thought. She's calling the dead; she's dancing for the dead and the living and calming them. I wonder whom she is dancing for here, I thought. I like this rhythm, I thought. I was sitting on the steps, my ear now glued to the wall.

And if it happens that I know this *mudang,* I thought.

A harsh melody could be heard, a Korean voice with tragic power that made me shiver. It was a monotone call, sorcerous, pronounced on only a few notes, with from time to time a momentum that made you think of a solitary song facing cliffs, facing narrow passages, facing absolute despair, facing mountains. The drum accompanied the singer, with a broken rhythm that made one desire immediately to join the music without ever again pretending to breathe or even really breathing. An *uga,* interpreted to perfection, I thought. I got up. I explored the brick with my palms. The spiders had moved out of reach, their ruined traps now sticky rags. The tips of my fingers stopped at a groove. The brick was interrupted in a geometric, rectangular way. It outlined a small door. I know this kind of opening, I thought. All I have to do is pass through it to end up on the other side. It's just like a door or a trapdoor. It's enough just to open it. I have practice with that, I thought. I have that experience. It's enough to push, to slide, or to pull, and then you go into the emptiness and go forward. It's not too hard, I'm going to do it, I murmured.

On the other side of the wall, the tapping of the drum didn't stop. The *mudang* had grown silent, but now she began to sing again. She had a rocky voice, enchanting, expansive. I shivered again. I love that voice, I thought. I have to go to it. Whether or not she's talking to me, I have to go to that voice. There's an opening, after all, it's not a great feat to get to the other side. I spent several minutes running my hands over the bricks and the grooves surrounding the brick. The wall didn't give way. I've already had the occasion to live or to dream this, I thought, scraping the wall with my hands. I don't know how, after that, a little cast iron door appeared under my digits. It was cold. I looked for the bolt that would allow me to open it. I was on the opposite side from the latch, as if getting out of a blast furnace or a simple wood stove. After a few efforts, the metal plate moved. I slid through the crack.

It's exactly what I thought, I murmured. All I had to do was get to the other side of the wall to change place.

I crouched immediately in the shadow. The room was illuminated by a weak bulb. The windows were open, and from the street, at the same time as a warm, humid air, came a little extra light. Nothing escaped me of the apartment or its occupants. The *mudang* was magnificent. She had long black hair that she had tied together in a braid that swung back and forth when she shook her head. Her face was ageless, of great delicacy, light, with brilliant eyes, slightly almond shaped, with scarcely visible brows and a thin mouth. One could see with each movement the vigor of her body, the caressing softness of her skin. She was wearing an unbelted green dress, a green that the poor lighting didn't allow to be fully appreciated but that must have been deep jade or *shocking green*. Linda Siew, I thought immediately. I know this witch. I know her voice. I know her beauty.

Linda Siew, I thought. I was too filled with emotion to move. An eternity in amnesia, and suddenly, here I had the certainty of a memory. I had been able to name this woman. I had recognized her. Finally my memory was useful for something again. I set myself to sitting in my corner, at the base of the wall, dazed.

The minutes passed. I witnessed the ceremony. Linda Siew's accompanist had his back turned toward me. He had white clothes, a traditional hat, gray gaiters. He was providing without stopping the rhythm onto which were grafted the song and the calls, the moments of silence and of dance. When Linda Siew spoke or sang, her voice filled the space. The room was of medium size, and the officiants had pushed the furniture in front of the kitchen door to make space. Visible on the table were several ritual objects and a ball of cloth tied up with twine to make a crude doll. It was lying on its side; its head had only an approximate relationship with a head, and most of its limbs ended poorly. I know that silhouette, I thought immediately. I know its name. It's Mevlido.

It's Mevlido that the *mudang* is talking to, I thought. Indeed, the *mudang* approached the table and bowed toward the figurine. She was talking, she was chanting again, she was declaiming something in the direction of the ball of cloth, she waved her hands in space, she danced. For a moment I observed her practice, admiring the grace of her gestures, the depth of her intonation, the beauty of the lines traced by her body, then I had nostalgia of a real contact with her. Watching her like this, passively, was not enough. I could try to understand what she's saying to Mevlido, I thought. If she's asking questions, I could try to answer, I thought. Linda Siew sang in a mix of Korean, magical Blatnoï, and Ybür, and, when she turned toward Mevlido, I grasped the main idea. She was saying to Mevlido that he needed to talk, that speaking was indispensable, especially in his case. Especially in my case, I repeated internally. She asked Mevlido to put an end to his mutism, she asked him about his life, about his birth, about what had happened before and after his death or at other moments of his existence. She wanted Mevlido to explain why his destiny had been so different from the predictions, why he had developed so poorly, why Mevlido's destiny had imitated that of the global revolution, made bad choices, idiotic crimes, psychotic distortions, stagnations and monstrous betrayals. She reproached the Mevlido rag doll for not manifesting himself, she preached to him, sometimes on the contrary, she tried to cajole him so that he would react.

I can do my self-criticism, I said abruptly, from my shadowy corner. My voice was hoarse, garbled. I don't know any answer, I said, but I can explain the mistakes and the impasses. The Mevlido rag doll did not relay my intervention. Linda Siew continued as if I had not made the smallest sound. She dipped her fingers in one of the bowls that had been placed on the table and threw drops toward the ceiling, drops toward the floor, drops toward the shadow where I remained. I didn't get anything, I said. The drops didn't reach me, I said. She went toward the window and undulated in place for a moment. I can do my self-criticism, if you want, I proposed again. Linda Siew paid no attention to what I was stammering. The sounds that filled my mouth didn't reach her.

She took a few steps in front of the window, then she returned near the Mevlido. She grabbed him and shook him, and after a moment she let him go, as if disgusted. One of the cords used to make the Mevlido's stomach had come undone. The Mevlido had lost a bit more of his human form. In reality he was reduced to a handful of ribbons and rags put together as if at random. Linda Siew now listed names above it. Maleeya Bayarlag, I heard. Verena Becker, I heard. Linda Siew, I heard. Samiya Choong, Tatiana Outougaï, I heard. There were others. The list was long. Each name opened a long chapter of memory within me. The drum beat after each utterance, immediately fixing these memories in me. I don't remember everything, but I remember chains of emotions, episodes tied together, images. I remember, I thought. I knew these women. They disappeared or they are dead, I thought.

If you want, I can accuse myself of their horrible deaths, I said. I should have shared the pain of their horrible deaths; instead of that, I was absent, they faced their deaths alone. The drum beat, Linda Siew's voice articulated the names of the dead in a solemn tone. Sergueïev, I heard in the middle of the list. Yes, Sergueïev too, I said. There are men too. Yasar Bayarlag, I heard. Yes, I said. He too. The list is endless, I said. I feel intimately tied to Sergueïev and to Bayarlag, to them too. Their deaths took place, mine, no. Men and women, we were together sometimes on one side of death, sometimes on the other, but only I got out safe and sound. If you want, Linda, I can accuse myself of that. I am a foul larva. No one has survived around me.

Linda Siew continued to sing. She wasn't listening to me. The drum beat, the rhythm, was very beautiful, simple, with regular breaks. The Mevlido was slumped on the table beside the magic bowls. He wasn't listening to me either. I've also killed people, I said. I'm not sorry. But if you want, I can accuse myself of their deaths too, Linda. I can always insert them somewhere in a self-criticism, I only have to invent a few details and some patronyms here and there. The *mudang* continued to dance and sing without turning toward me. From time to time she bent over the Mevlido and shook him. She admonished him or spoke to him tenderly according to the phases of the ritual. I preferred, evidently, the moments when her approach was soft. The Mevlido didn't move.

I began to yell to attract the *mudang*'s attention. If you want, Linda, I can talk, I howled in her direction. I have enough memories again to make it all up, Linda, I screamed.

She didn't hear me. She left the table. She had left the Mevlido on the table like a dirty piece of clothing. Now she was facing the window. Her green dress rippled and floated. Her black braid swung back and forth over her back. Her face was darkened by the trouble of establishing a dialogue with the Mevlido, with the dead and with the living who didn't answer her. She respected the rhythms of the drum to move or say words. The bulb in the ceiling lamp lit her poorly, and, under that light, I found her marvelous.

I have enough memories again to lie, I insisted. You can interrogate me, Linda.

The officiant still struck the vibrating skin of the *gutbuk*. The scene seemed not to have to end. I didn't feel myself to be in my normal state; it was like I was intoxicated by the flood of recollections in my memory, and by the music. Linda Siew continued to dance.

I'm ready, Linda, I said.

Is it all right if I call you Linda? I asked.

She didn't hear me. She didn't speak to me. She continued to dance.

I remember everything, I lied. Everything is all right, I lied.

I stayed in my corner, a little outside the action but conscious at least of having found enough memory again to be able to choose, if the need made itself felt, between lies and silence. It was exactly as if I had remembered everything.

PART VII

43

Summer arrived, an nth summer. It resembled the preceding seasons, the spring and the winter that had already been torrid. The days passed slowly, each more bituminous than the others. I was stifling. To the heat was added the absence of sleep or nightmares. When the dawn's gray light appeared, I went out into the street with no goal but to end a vain and troublesome quest for sleep. At the smallest change in atmospheric pressure, sandstorms blew up. Ripped from the neighboring mountain, crumbs of coal mixed with the silica, transforming the air into a dark yellow cloud that reeked of sulfur and sulfides. These odors stagnated in the refuges where I ended up after hours of wandering. Those who breathed had to permanently confront a sensation of disgust and burning. You would have had to move through the streets with glasses and a mask. Not having the means to acquire that kind of material, I had sewn pieces of cloth onto the brim of my old leather hat. Under such gear, there wasn't much oxygen. I stumbled, I lost consciousness, I liquefied. Streams of sweat soaked my rags, and when, back in my cubbyhole or elsewhere, I took them off to wring them out, bitter, very black humors ran out onto my feet.

That morning, I was moving forward in the muddy light, against the wind. The wind roared, onto my clothes hailed thousands of impacts. Between the gusts could be heard birds' cackles, the sighs of *Untermenschen* or of the dead: the ordinary music of the Shambles at twilight. I took a dozen steps, I stopped, I began to walk again, I stopped again. The wind, the sandy shadow, and the noises made the streets identical. I moved forward with my arms held out in front of me, my nostrils and eyes closed, because the dust got into the openings in my cloth shield despite everything and irritated me.

An hour earlier, while everyone was still sleeping in the bus station, I had dreamed that Gorgha was making an appointment with me. I had thought I understood that it was to establish a connection with the Party heads, but already I wasn't very sure of that anymore. On the off chance, I was now going toward the place she had indicated. A bus wreck.

A bus wreck before an intersection. Gorgha had also mentioned Waddell Street.

In front of my face, the protective curtain came undone. I brushed myself to get rid of the soot that had accumulated on me, and I opened my eyes. The landscape had grown a bit lighter, the coal powder in the air wasn't blocking my sight anymore. There was a bus carcass a hundred paces away. It was leaning a bit to one side, and a fire had made it lose its paint. It was a sinister old carcass. One scarcely wanted to approach it, still less to go inside.

Obey the Party, I thought.

Someone trustworthy told you to go there, Mevlido, I thought. So you're going.

Whether Gorgha ordered you to do it in a dream or some-where else doesn't matter, I thought. You're not there to speculate on the oneiric existence or not of the Party or on what that does or does not imply, Mevlido. You're going there, period.

I took up my march toward the wreck again.

The wind had calmed.

Under the soles of my espadrilles the metallic dust squeaked.

The black dust had formed hills of a satiny appearance that softened the angles of walls. Behind the facades, anything alive was asleep or silent.

I first walked around the vehicle unhurriedly. It had burned long enough before that it no longer gave off the stench of fire. Although it had no tires, the wheels must be able to allow a move-ment in the case of absolute necessity. The windows had all been broken. Even if some rows were missing, a few seats could still be seen inside. The rear door had disappeared, and, in the front, un-hinged and twisted, the door almost totally blocked the passage. A man was at the steering wheel, in a position that made you think more of napping than of driving. He was rigorously immobile, as if tarred there since the last fire and forgotten. I tried not to look at him, I felt that I didn't have the right to surprise him in the ob-scenity of his sleep or death. The wind had left a layer of soot on him that increased and blurred his stature.

It's not with him that I have an appointment, I thought.

A passenger was sitting in the second row and waiting. With that one, yes, I thought. That's my contact. It's me he's waiting for.

I pulled myself up into the bus by the rear door. The whole vehicle moved slightly and creaked, then stabilized. The steps were covered with tarry dust. I sank into it up to my ankles. The inside of the bus had been devastated by the flames, but there were still a few spots that weren't destroyed. I went to sit on an empty bench, a meter from the passenger. The man was of a size comparable to mine. From shoulders to toes, his silhouette was enveloped in a greasy duster. He was wearing on top of that a very dirty leather hat. His face was protected by a dirty undershirt he had fixed around his head with a piece of twine and in which he had cut two holes for the eyes. Behind these holes, his eyelids were closed. I think he must have heard me coming, but he was pretending to sleep, maybe because something about me displeased him, and he insisted on greeting me with a demonstration of sulkiness.

I wedged myself into my seat and kept quiet. If I had had a newspaper at my disposition, or even any scrap of paper whatsoever, I would have pretended to be buried in my reading, but I had had nothing like that in my pockets for several years, and I had to resolve to look straight ahead with a morose attitude. The heat and the bad smells had concentrated inside the vehicle. I felt like a toxic gas was flaying my throat. I had a coughing fit. Alongside me the metal side of the bus was covered with spider webs. The webs had been abandoned by their inhabitants, and the wind had swelled them with coal. They formed pouches ready to burst, and, when I coughed, they trembled.

I continued to spit and wheeze for a minute or two. It was also a way of breaking the ice. The passenger could no longer ignore my presence. He turned toward me.

"That isn't your shirt," he said, in the tone of someone picking a fight.

"I know," I said.

"It's Yasar Bayarlag's shirt," said the man.

He threw his hands suddenly behind his head, untied his mask, and took it off. I saw then his big, angular face ravaged by wrinkles, with light, piercing, inquisitorial eyes. I immediately had the intuition that we weren't going to have an easy relationship.

"A blue shirt, checkered," he said, refusing to look me in the eyes. "I remember quite well. The jeans and shoes aren't yours either."

"I had to borrow them," I said. "Maleeya Bayarlag had stored them in a chest. She didn't want me to touch them. I was obliged to put them on. I didn't have anything else."

The man shrugged.

"All of that is mine," he said.

"By what right?" I retorted. "Maybe you're Yasar Bayarlag?"

"Yes," said the other man, "Yasar Bayarlag. Does that bother you?"

I let out a confused, animalic noise. I was in shock. The man had no reason to lie to me. He corresponded to the portrait that Maleeya Bayarlag had provided me of her Yasar. According to Maleeya's version, we were physically fairly close, he and I, and this man, in fact, resembled me.

It did bother me, yes, to stumble, without transition, upon the person with whom Maleeya had never stopped confusing me.

"You want me to give it back to you?" I proposed.

"To give what back to me?" he said heatedly.

"Your shirt," I said. "Do you want me to give it back to you?"

"No," said Yasar Bayarlag, "you've messed it all up. What do you want me to do with that rag?"

I made a fatalistic gesture.

"And besides, I don't steal from the destitute," he added. "I don't belong to the gang of capitalists."

"Me neither," I broke in.

"That's all I need," he said sternly.

There was a gust of wind. The street began to crackle again. In the bus the soot moved. The metal supports cracked around us as if the carcass were suddenly being dragged violently. Near the motionless driver, who knows what was clicking obstinately. The bits of cloth that I had attached to my hat flew off. They struck the carbonized dashboard, then were sucked outside. Everywhere the spider webs were trembling. Then the wind grew quiet. The noises died out.

"Do you know why you are here?" asked Yasar Bayarlag.

"Someone said something about a meeting," I said.

"You know with whom?" said Yasar Bayarlag.

Brutally, on the ceiling, a pouch of spider silk tore open. The coal dust fell onto the front of my shirt. My nose and sinuses stung. I began to cough again. Yasar Bayarlag examined me with a disgusted attitude. I withstood his gaze.

"With the Party," I murmured with a parched voice, "if it still exists."

"With the Organs," Yasar Bayarlag corrected. "Deeplane is looking for you. He wants to see you."

I was clearing my throat.

"Deeplane, you remember?" asked Yasar Bayarlag in a doubtful tone.

"That rings a bell," I said.

"He wants to see you," repeated Yasar Bayarlag. "You should see each other shortly, if everything goes well. If there are no surprises."

"Bah, what surprises?" I said.

Yasar Bayarlag was quiet. He shook the undershirt he had been using as a mask, then put it back on like a balaclava, making sure that the holes were more or less in front of his eyes. Now he pulled his hat back down over his skull again so that everything stayed in place. He hid his arms in his coat again and slouched down as if to go back to sleep. Scarcely the smallest bit of human could be seen of him. With his coat streaming with soot and this getup substituted for his head, he had taken on the appearance of an anonymous *Untermensch,* poorly dressed and angry. He was no longer making the effort to turn toward me. He wasn't even watching me from the corner of his eye.

I began to wait.

"You're still there, Mevlido?" he suddenly asked.

"Of course," I said.

Beneath the dust that covered my skin, drops of sweat swelled, and, from time to time, they trickled down.

"A surprise," he said. "What did I tell you?"

I made a doubtful face and muttered a vague commentary.

"Hurry up and get out of here, Mevlido. There's going to be an attack."

"An attack against whom?" I grumbled. "What kind of attack?"

"Hurry, I'm telling you," he insisted.

I got up from my seat and examined the surroundings. The street seemed deserted. The wind had not risen. The particles in suspension formed brownish strata that floated softly downward. No one was coming toward the intersection. The landscape was as peaceful as could be. In the bus the driver hadn't moved a millimeter since just now.

"Good God, Mevlido, do you understand what you're being told?" Bayarlag grew angry.

"And the meeting with the Organs?" I asked.

"This place is going to blow," yelled Bayarlag. "Get out of here!"

I sensed all the urgency in his voice and ran toward the rear of the vehicle. I don't know why, during the two seconds that that movement took, I saw my own movements as those, precise and frenzied, of an insect or something worse yet. Mentally, and even physically, I had the impression of having slid fairly low on the biological ladder. Then I got a hold of myself and threw a last glance over my shoulder. Behind me, everything looked normal, like in a black-and-white photograph showing a war scene hours or days after the disaster.

Everything is normal, I thought. Everything is normal, and it's going to blow. I have to get out of here.

I got down and got about ten paces away.

Now I was leaning against a wall, and, my feet buried in the soot, I was wondering what I was going to do, when the bus jumped very slightly.

Immediately, the smell of carbon and chlorine spread through the street. No noise had rung out, not a single flame had reddened the image. I neared the bus again. A thick smoke was just escaping from the windows near the driver. As if from the top bulb of an hourglass, a stream of ash was running from the roof to the ground, forming a small cone on the sidewalk. I stuck my head and shoulders through the rear door, then, not seeing any danger, I got back inside the vehicle. Yasar Bayarlag was no longer sitting. He was lying in the middle of the aisle. His duster was ruined and wrinkled but continued to hide his torso and limbs. As for his undershirt, if it was still covering his head, hiding his face, it had changed color. It was all sticky with blood. The hat, itself sliced to bits, had rolled toward the driver's feet.

I approached the suffering mass. I was trying to get the least scrap of information possible about what Yasar Bayarlag had endured, about what his flesh, his viscera, and his bones had become. I looked furtively at the duster and, farther on, next to the gearshift, the hat with its oily tears. I looked at the square, dull back of the driver. The driver hadn't escaped the attack, but, from where I was, I didn't notice anything special in his posture. Compared to a little while before, he was just a little more bent over his steering wheel.

"Is that you, Mevlido?" asked an exhausted voice.

"Yes," I said.

I wasn't trying to meet the gaze that perhaps subsisted still, behind the holes in the undershirt.

"Take care of her," said Yasar Bayarlag.

"Yes," I said, "I'm going to wash it, iron it. It's still salvageable. I'm going to clean it thoroughly."

"I'm not talking about the shirt," gurgled Yasar Bayarlag.

I let out a silence.

"Don't worry," I said after a moment.

"It bothers me to leave Maleeya with you like this," gasped Yasar Bayarlag. "I know what you're worth. We all know. You're not worth much."

"Bah," I replied.

"But I'm leaving her with you anyway. All the others are dead. You're the last one. I'm counting on you."

I leaned over Yasar Bayarlag to decipher what he was whispering, then I got back up. It seemed to me that he would never again pronounce a sentence. I had heard the last, and, all of a sudden, the idea of silence overwhelmed me. His, mine, silence in general. I filled my lungs like before a sob.

"I don't know where Maleeya is," I said. "I know that she was counting on me, and I messed that up too. She was behind me, on Gateway Street, a place where the mutant chickens form an impassible barrier. They make a compact flock, and, when you try to make a path, they start flying at the height of your stomach and face and spread feathers and avian lice around. It becomes impossible to go forward. I was going with Maleeya to a Party meeting. During all the years we lived together we scrupulously respected the instructions of the Party. For my part, I have barely ever betrayed proletarian morality, and only in dreams or, at most, when sleep had abandoned me and not betraying it was too complicated or impossible. I always obeyed the Party's instructions no matter what the circumstances, whatever the instruction and whatever the Party and its agenda. It was very dark. Maleeya was following me; I had told her to grab on to my belt so as not to lose me. The birds were throwing themselves at us, spreading the stifling smell of a henhouse. I had to push them away like a boxer. We had gone through Gateway Street so as not to get to the meeting late. Cornelia Orff was leading the way. We had formed a parade. Maleeya was right behind me, then she disappeared. She was backed against the wall so as not to be submerged by the flood of poultry. Then she disappeared as if the birds had buried her. Which birds? Mostly hunchback chickens as heavy as dogs, toucan chickens, giant owls, giant gulls, giant phosphorescent guinea fowl. They rushed at us beak first. Once the obstacle was passed, I called out to Maleeya. She didn't answer. I called out to her several times in a very loud voice. She didn't answer. She didn't give another sign of life. I always took care of her since she began to have mental problems, that is to say, since always. I know that I'm not worth much, but I tried not to let her go under alone. We were together in the midst of animals and men, in the middle of the night, in the middle of the noises made by the *Untermenschen* and the old Bolshevik women of Henhouse Four."

I couldn't shut up. At my feet Yasar Bayarlag was no longer breathing. He had uttered a last sound, and then he had thrown backward what was bleeding under his undershirt and what must have been the remains of his head, then he slumped down under his duster, moving for the last time what must have been the remains of his flesh.

My mouth continued to move without stopping.

"We were together in the middle of the heat," I said, "beneath the rain, for the years of spiders and the years of sleep, for the years of twilight, then the years of a violent moon and the years of amnesia. We were together in Henhouse Four in the midst of our calamity."

A gust of soot cut me off.

Sweat beaded underneath the dust that enveloped my body. It flowed underneath it without showing itself.

The wind had picked up again.

44

The sandstorm. It had picked up again. The gusts projected burning puffs, like bullets.

Outside, everything had grown darker. Between the houses filtered bits of yellow fog, and, after the intersection that opened up thirty meters from the bus, the scenery stopped. Nothing was visible beyond that. Under the assaults of the wind, my shirt tore apart. My hat protected me little. I felt it leave my skull and disappear. Torn from ragged people like me, scraps of clothing flew in the middle of the dust. Ruins of cotton, rectangles of furry canvas were constantly hitting me on the back, the neck. I began to pant, then I gave up. Sometimes I managed to be quiet, but most of the time I no longer had the strength to interrupt the fragments that manifested on my tongue. In reality I had only one desire, to curl up in a corner and never speak or move again.

Something had begun to bang on the side of the bus. A hand, perhaps. The hand banged, then stopped. The noise had a certain regularity. I gathered myself together above Yasar Bayarlag and his corpse, in front of what was left of Yasar Bayarlag. I was inspired by that rhythm; I took refuge inside that rhythm so as not to be submerged. The wind howled, then calmed down, then began again. Hard flakes hailed down upon the nearest bench. Fistfuls of dusty material came in by one window, went out by another, swirling like smoke. In the street a dark flour collected in moving dunes. The hammering against the side of the bus didn't stop. I had remained standing over Yasar Bayarlag. I didn't know what movements to make. I wondered out loud, unintelligibly, if we had entered a year of attacks, after having so long endured years of spiders and years with an intermittent or intense moon. I muttered a few unfinished sentences on the subject, then I observed the silence again. Threads of soot slid along my neck to the top of my chest. I felt them running toward my stomach. I had noticed a bench in the back. Are you there, Mevlido? I thought. The best thing would be for you to go crouch or sit down there.

I backed up four or five meters. My espadrilles made no noise. All around, the wind howled. The back of the bus was invaded by an abundant layer of black particles. I dusted the seat off clumsily and sat down. On the ceiling the spider webs were only fragile pouches. When one of them burst, its contents spread over me. I had put myself in a position that allowed me at once to rest and to oversee the whole interior of the vehicle. I thought again vaguely of my appointment with the Organs. Yasar Bayarlag's corpse had not left the vehicle. Of Yasar Bayarlag's prone body nothing could be made out. The spilled blood had been drunk up by the soot. From where I was I could see practically nothing living. I could think of the victim without being obliged to imagine the horror of his torn flesh, pierced by shards of bone. The duster moved under the wind's influence. One of the sleeves rose as if an arm inside were moving, communicating instructions or a farewell, then fell back.

- I didn't answer these beginnings of communication.
- I preferred to try to doze off. Sleep overtook me, then left me.
- On the side of the bus a hand was tapping out a rhythm.
- Time passed with no point of reference.
- The wind roared with a low, monotone voice.

Sometimes I plunged into a sort of dreamless nothingness, then I emerged without being able to say how long I had lost consciousness, half a second or three hours. Something continued to bang against the metal, the chassis. I felt my sweat dripping. It made a subterranean path under the shining, oily black soot that currently enveloped me but didn't emerge on the exterior. I remained motionless at the back of the vehicle. On the other side of Yasar Bayarlag lying in the aisle was the driver. His heavy silhouette was bent over the steering wheel. The fire or the black space had caramelized him in a position that made you think of someone fighting against sleep. His clothing had been converted into a carbonized envelope that grew thicker hour by hour under the arrival of new layers of ash and dust. Outside, the deserted street disappeared under the coating of ash brown, under the crackling covering and the shadows. No one was visible behind the windows of the houses, no human or animal or intelligent presence. I had the feeling of being very alone. I continued to meditate on the attack without being able to decide whether it had already taken place or whether it was still going to happen. I wondered if there had been other victims whom I hadn't yet seen, individuals in fragments or in ashes whom I hadn't yet noticed.

- No one brought an answer to my questions.
- Pieces of shoes or shirts blew through the space quickly, like wandering, filthy flames.
- Something knocked on the metal like on the skin of a drum.
- Yasar Bayarlag's corpse disappeared under the soot, then a raucous gust cleaned it, and, at once, the process of burial began again.
- Sometimes there were moments of total darkness.

- Sometimes I opened my eyes, sometimes I closed them.
  In both cases, the scenery was the same.

Several hours had already passed like this when a woman appeared in front of the destroyed front door. She slid in sideways, with a graceful slowness of a dancer or a gymnast. She took care not to hurt herself on the shards of metal and the hinges. Her skin was pale. She wasn't wearing any clothes. She was about thirty years old; she looked magnificent. As soon as she pulled herself up onto the step, her hair began to swirl and tangle around her, around her naked body.

Linda Siew, I thought.

She is coming to calm the dead, I thought. Those whom the attack has disfigured mentally and physically, or, if the attack is for later on, she is coming to console the living who are going to replace the dead.

She is coming to dance the ceremony of the *gut*, I thought. She is coming to sing and dance the *uga*. The knocking against the side of the bus is a shamanic drum.

I freed my ankles from the soot that imprisoned them, and I got up. The *mudang*'s back was toward me. I knew those curves, the arch of that back, the length of those legs. I knew the bluish black of that hair. Linda Siew had drawn near the driver. She leaned toward him, she touched his arm and put her lips near the nape of his neck, near his ear. I suppose she was talking to him.

The driver sighed.

"Do you want me to take the wheel?" asked Linda Siew.

"No," grumbled the driver, "later. After the attack."

So the attack hasn't taken place yet? I thought.

"The attack hasn't taken place yet?" I asked.

The wind blew. There was a moment of total darkness, then the light came back, weak and oily. I stepped over Yasar Bayarlag's corpse. No one noticed my presence. Linda Siew was pressed against the driver. She was clearly leaning over him. Her left arm and hair were now lying on his shoulders and neck. It was a gesture of complicity, an affectionate embrace. Linda Siew was resting for an instant and giving her companion a little of her life force. Each one gave a little of their strength to the other. It seemed to me all at once that I had already experienced a comparable scene or witnessed it, but, so as not to complicate the moment, I tried not to allow any memory to rise up inside me.

"You're exhausted, Deeplane," said Linda Siew.

"And you?" replied the driver.

"And him?" asked Linda Siew. "Do you think he's going to come?"

"This time, there's a chance," said the driver.

I took two more steps toward the front. I had the feeling they were talking about me. I couldn't believe that the driver's name was Deeplane.

"He shouldn't be far now," said Linda Siew.

The drum beat against the outside of the bus.

"I'm here, Linda," I murmured.

I wanted to brush against Linda Siew's naked back or hip, to get her attention, but I held back. I didn't dare.

"I'm not very far away, Linda," I said again.

My words didn't reach her.

"I can call you Linda, can't I?" I asked, raising my voice vainly, because my voice could not cross the distance that separated us.

"I have the impression he's getting closer," said Deeplane.

Indeed, I hadn't stopped getting nearer to Linda Siew and Deeplane. I should have been able to fall on them and touch them now, but I still couldn't make up my mind. I was afraid of feeling them crumble in my arms or shake me off violently or gesticulate for me to get away, like when you feel a big spider or insect on your bare skin.

In the shadows whistling with the wind, Linda Siew embraced Deeplane fervently, and, all the while holding him to her, she watched what was coming toward the bus, the deserted crossroads, the black clouds, the half shadows traversed by dust, the windows behind which no witness could be spotted. Then she stood up. Stirred by the breath of the wind and sullied by the assaults of soot, her hair twisted around her and tangled. She stayed glued to her companion to peer at the dawn light. Deeplane and she were waiting for me to emerge in front of the wheels.

"I wonder what shape he will take," said Linda Siew.

"We never know ahead of time," said Deeplane. "He will maybe take the shape of an insect or a rat. Or worse. Everything depends on the dream in his head at the moment of meeting."

Linda Siew's hair beat against the black coating that covered Deeplane's face. She had begun to sing again. I believe the words were meant for me. I believe that she was asking me to come forward without thinking about anything whatsoever.

I would have liked to have made contact, but I made no move to do so.

45

The novelistic corpus of Mingrelian is not exclusively consecrated to Mevlido and his catastrophic mission among the hominids. It's abundant, it numbers in the tens of titles, and its fields of interest are varied. Certainly Mingrelian's best works are those that discuss the Mevlido affair and the associated developments, and, as the years pass, it's visible that this subject is more important to the author than all the others. When Mingrelian writes of Mevlido, he immediately gives to his story a tone of affectionate nostalgia, a benevolent color not justified by the events, something like an assumed tendency to indulgence. "Total and painful complicity," evaluates Deeplane in a handwritten note accompanying the *romance From Our Collaborator in Henhouse Four.* "Between the narrator and his character, there is, alas, not even the thickness of a cigarette rolling paper," adds Yokog Gans, also a reviewer of the reports transmitted to the Organs.

Mingrelian met Mevlido in the training center, when he was doing special training for Action Branch, and, during the thousands of hours of training, an authentic camaraderie brought them together forever. At a certain point Mingrelian could have taken Mevlido's place and left in the same conditions, in the same direction, on mission for the same failure. That proximity is palpable, that close brotherhood. It is evident when Mingrelian reconstitutes Mevlido's distress or dreams and when, as a teller of tales, he accompanies Mevlido in his confusion and sadness. Mingrelian inhabits his character without trouble. No psychological barrier stops or impedes him. No self-censorship makes the fiction painful for him. Mingrelian is a brother for Mevlido, and, over the course of the writing, there is between them not the smallest mental or physical difference. They have the same profile, the same morality, the same loves. Mingrelian takes Mevlido's side, and, from the first unexpected events that condemned the mission, he is dismayed not by the Organs' failure but by what happens to their agent on the ground. In the majority of the episodes he refuses to take any other lens than a subjective one. He is like us: first dismayed by the inexorable failure of everything, then unable to resolve to accept that we and our loved ones are the victims. When he chooses Mevlido as the hero of his fiction, it is obviously his own, Mingrelian's, portrait whose painting he undertakes.

About twenty works signed by Mingrelian have Mevlido's fate and directly related themes as their subject. All these volumes are preserved in the Organs' library, to which access is free, but no one borrows them or consults them. The hierarchy read over them once, then they were archived, and after that, neither the ordinary public nor intelligence experts ever presented themselves to open them. This loss of interest is hurtful to Mingrelian, but after the first few texts, this became established as a feature of the work, and Mingrelian, as a creator, finally resigned himself to it. The disinterest of the readers could be explained by the abuse of adjectives and the neologisms with which he studded his texts, as well as the syntactic overload, the baroque or lyrical collages that make them unreadable. We might also appeal to a certain change in fashion. Mingrelian's art, influenced by post-exoticism, plays with uncertainty, incompletion, blurring opposites, nothingness. These concepts, momentarily popular in Action Branch and even beyond, did not survive the strategic changes in the policies of the Organs. They became obsolete, although Mingrelian had adopted them as an immutable literary base. They were perceived as being part of an outdated aesthetic and too difficult to understand. To sum up, Mingrelian's books were ordered by the Organs, but, even while recognizing their good qualities, they never attributed the least importance to them.

No one ever asked me my opinion, but, because I'm here, I will take advantage of the opportunity to give it. We love Mingrelian's books. We loved them from the first, and we have never been disappointed by their way of describing the world. We love these collections of theatrical sequences, these *entrevoûtes,* these *romånces* of which the most beautiful tell of Mevlido's ending, a soldier lost from the beginning of the mission that had been entrusted to him, and his impossible meeting with Deeplane, the officer of Action Branch who sent him toward disaster. We have our preferences and our prejudices, we rank *Oisals* and *Attacks on the Moon* above the others, but, deep down, we don't think of any one of these books without feeling a little surge of tenderness. As Deeplane pointed out about the relationship between Mevlido and Mingrelian, we are tied to these books, all these books, by a total and painful complicity. Between us and Mingrelian, as between Mevlido and Mingrelian, there is not—alas! Yokog Gans would exclaim—the thickness of a cigarette rolling paper.

The character of Deeplane is complex; from story to story he evolves from a monk-soldier figure, incorruptible, rigid, and distant, to the figure of an individualistic dissident who resists his superiors, refuses to accept Mevlido's sacrifice, and insists on respecting at all costs a word given fifty years earlier, just before Mevlido's transfer. Deeplane promised Mevlido that Action Branch would try to recuperate him after his death. When the Organs question this perspective, when they end up losing interest in the fate of their agent and choose to abandon him, Deeplane opposes them. In *One of Mevlido's Loves, Departure for the Detachment,* and *Today We Assassinate,* Mingrelian tells how Deeplane mounts several operations of exfiltration of which the Organs don't approve. Like the rest of the undertaking, these operations fail one after the other.

Mevlido was programmed to be incarnated as a baby human, but the incarnation took place at a calamitous period of human history, even more calamitous than the others, because it marks the beginning of the prolonged death throes of the species. The generalized dark war is the only concrete perspective for a community whose behaviors are aberrant in practically every domain. Everything is drifting permanently toward the atrocious and unacceptable, nothing is rational, models of analysis no longer apply. The Organs are incapable of predicting the development of the situation, and they imagine that an agent on the ground will be able to harvest decisive information. In reality, nothing of what had been planned by the Services and their Action Branch goes as planned. Perhaps because the voyage in the black space has traumatized or weakened the embryo, the process of reincarnation completely escapes the Organs' control, and, from the moment Mevlido is born, his life does not respond to the demands that had been imprinted on him in the course of innumerable training and education sessions. It is governed by a gloomy, cruel logic that seems more than anything to correspond to the paroxysms of a nightmare. Besides a few oneiric traces, almost nothing subsists of the special education that should have made Mevlido a creature on a mission among the hominids, a being apart. Starting at birth, Mevlido is a human as limited and indecipherable as the rest of his species. The backdrop of Mevlido's childhood and adolescence is only extermination, flames, columns of refugees, a proliferation of mutant species, chaos. Mevlido's adult life is a blind march, the traversal of a society of misery and idiocy. Very rapidly, the Organs observe that contact is disappointing and difficult, that Mevlido's collection of intelligence is too thin, too random, lacking any relevance. Mevlido betrays all the hopes placed upon him. Once washed up in Henhouse Four, Mevlido is in such a state of spiritual destitution and dilapidation that the Organs cross him off the list of their active agents. The question of sending another agent on-site, with the mission of supporting Mevlido, is buried, despite Mingrelian's reports, which insist on the possibility of maintaining an extrasensorial liaison with Mevlido, and Deeplane's point of view, seeking by any means to avoid abandoning his protégé.

It's also because the Organs are proceeding with a fundamental strategic change. After centuries of negative experiments the Services are theorizing the disappointment provoked by hominids and imagine a rapprochement with more promising and resilient species like arachnids. This spectacular reversal is combated by certain influential officers like Deeplane, but the opposition is in the minority, and, at the time Mevlido is living as a somnambulist in Henhouse Four, the Organs are already making plans destined to solidify, long term, an alliance with several hordes of terrestrial

spiders on their way to dominance. Deeplane argues with his superiors, he emphasizes how the spiders' behavior doesn't coincide on
a single point with the altruistic and collectivist bases of the proletarian morality, which should be used to build an ideal human
society. The hierarchy accepts the debate, it listens to Deeplane's
plea and publishes his contributions, but, at the end, it relieves him
of his political responsibilities. After a few years Deeplane can be
found in a department of minor importance, a department dedi-
cated to the oneiric observation of birds.

Out of recognition for past services rendered, he is allowed a
certain freedom and initiative. He still has a small technical team
under his orders. It's with the support of certain members of that
team that Deeplane organizes several operations that adopt as
their task to find, contact, and try to recuperate Mevlido.

"We know," writes Mingrelian in *Rendezvous on Waddell
Street*, speaking in Deeplane's name, "that we won't reach Mevlido
before his death, we also know that our chances of extracting him
after his death and before he disappears completely are slim, and
even very, very slim. But we are going to dedicate our strength
to that. Mevlido as he presents himself to our eyes today, when
we close our eyes and dream of him, is a devastated subhuman,
a wreck with no reason for being and no future. We are going to
do everything we can to go to meet him and extract him from this
nightmare where we have imprisoned and mired him, and, even
if we don't succeed in bringing him back with us, for example,
because our organic levels don't coincide, or because he refuses
to accompany us, or even because we will ourselves have lost too
much energy during the voyage, because we ourselves will have
become in our turn devastated subhumans, scum with no reason
to be and no future, dead men who have run out of dreams—even
if we don't succeed to bring him back fraternally with us, we will
do our best to give him something, to get him into an image of love

and peace, an image in which he will have the illusion of being able to continue his death otherwise than in solitude and shadows. We will do that, we will try to do that no matter the price and even at the cost of our own existence, because for us faithfulness to our word is not a vain idea, because we have a morality—because, despite the humans, the idea of the proletarian morality is not an empty idea, because on Earth all is lost and because, despite everything, we have no faith in the spiders."

46

In his two best *romånces* about Mevlido, *Attacks on the Moon* and *Henhouse Four,* Mingrelian tells how Deeplane, after fifteen years of fruitless tracking, succeeds finally in reestablishing contact with Mevlido. We see Deeplane at the controls of the carcass of a bus, with no motor and no wheels, exactly the kind of vehicle made for advancing through the black space. The bus goes slowly through the Shambles. The city is darkened by a storm of coal sand. Something horrible has just happened or is going to happen, an attack, a hostile action meant to generate fear, doubt, and uncontrollable suffering. Deeplane was for a long time surrounded by flames during his voyage in Mevlido's direction. His carbonized flesh has hardened, it has combined with the soot and grit carried by the wind, and now Deeplane looks like a big, round animal, black and cadaverous. Nevertheless, he's holding up. This time, his rendezvous with his former subordinate, the former agent Mevlido, is going to materialize. He is sure of it, and he is holding steady in the driver's seat. The bus moves forward, sliding imperceptibly the length of streets that the storm blurs and makes indistinguishable one from the next. On the route Deeplane is taking, there is Factory Street, Gateway Street, Park Avenue, Waddell Street, and many others. None is truly familiar, none is unknown. All of them are more or less inscribed in Mevlido's memories or in ours. The passengers of the bus have difficulty imagining that the vehicle might be moving. Several get in or out along the route without noticing the slightest change in the scenery. Most of them are in such an advanced state of biological or intellectual distress that they would be incapable of saying whether the attack had already taken place, whether the fire is happening now or the metal had cooled off long ago, whether the bus is moving, whether they are surrounded by other *Untermenschen* or humans or animals. They don't understand either at what moment of their existence they are situated, before or after their memories, before or after their death throes, during their deaths or much later. They only know that they have ended up in the Shambles, and this indication is enough for them. The number of these passengers varies, because Mingrelian, in the course of his narration, sometimes places them inside the vehicle, sometimes takes them out. Mevlido, obviously, is among them, but one could also include Yasar Bayarlag, whom a fatal blast has taken to pieces and annihilated; Gorgha, the female crow; as well as Linda Siew, who is helping Deeplane in his undertaking and transmitting her *mudang*'s energy to him as well as she can. Someone was thrown from the vehicle during the attack and is knocking on the frame or on the side panels to signal their presence or to fill their own silence. All of them, men and women born of comparable animals, are dressed in rags or have nothing or almost nothing on their skin. Linda Siew, for example, is naked. She is beautiful. She resembles Verena Becker; she isn't exactly the same height, her hair is blacker, her skin has a glow or a texture that doesn't immediately evoke that of Verena Becker, she doesn't have the same way of being comfortable in her naked femininity, but she resembles Verena Becker. Mevlido, at first dozing in the darkness and smoke, advances toward her. He walks down the aisle of the bus, and he goes toward her, toward the place where she stands, to the right of the driver. It's the moment when contact is finally established between Mevlido and Deeplane.

Mingrelian hesitates here. He doesn't like to end so many ordeals with a single episode. Neither *Attacks on the Moon* nor *Henhouse Four* is an adventure novel. He has recourse then to the post-exotic technique of "narrative fluttering," notwithstanding, unappreciated by the Organs—who demand certain answers—and hatefully criticized by the adepts of official literature, who see in it yet another insult to their theory of fiction. As if the dark wind of the narrative were, at that key moment, incapable of finding a satisfying direction, the story folds back on itself bizarrely, gathers itself up, ready to rebound once more, and suddenly trembles upon itself. Three versions will thus coexist, independent and inextricable, three sequences born of the same narrative clay with which Mingrelian skillfully fashions an unfortunate ending for his tale, as well as, for his hero, an unfinished eternity.

- In the first of these three series of images, Mingrelian shows Gorgha, the female crow, the companion of Mevlido's bad nights, the ambiguous partner often poorly accepted, or accepted reluctantly. Perhaps because of this parasitic presence, contact with Deeplane is again thwarted. Linda Siew and Deeplane are sucked out of the vehicle, and Mevlido, whether he will or no, must in turn sit behind the steering wheel. Projectiles penetrate what is left of Mevlido's body. The traveling conditions become worse. The lens loses all clarity. Only Gorgha seems capable of surviving the nightmare.
- Then Mingrelian engages in a reflection on the extinction of humanity and on the species that is called to take its place on Earth. He describes the flow of mil-

lions of years, the transformation of the landscape into dust. When he wakes Mevlido, the world is definitively dominated by the spiders. So all life has not disappeared; on the contrary, a stable and peaceful civilization is in place. On Park Avenue, under the lunar light, only waste treatment plant number nine remains. The remains of the bus have been dispersed long ago. With the shamanic help of Linda Siew, Mevlido enters the plant. We know he will die there. *Attacks on the Moon* is the only one of the two *romånces* in which Mingrelian has the courage to accompany his character in his interminable descent toward nothingness, the only one of the two books in which he forces himself to narrate this new stage in exhaustion and death. *Henhouse Four* doesn't develop that, and this sequence stops at the moment when Linda Siew helps Mevlido to pass through the booth behind which he will join waste treatment plant number nine. In reality, after that, Mevlido enters the plant, and Maleeya Bayarlag is in the courtyard, sitting on a folding chair. She is sorting rags. She doesn't react with astonishment to Mevlido's appearance in front of her, and, like in old times, she confuses him with Yasar Bayarlag. Often collected in anthologies as an example of disaster humor, a theatrical moment develops, incongruous and painful: psychically nonexistent, Maleeya speaks to Mevlido, calling him Yasar, while Mevlido addresses Linda Siew, giving her the name of Verena Becker. During this conversation, Linda Siew fades into the darkness and doesn't appear again. Maleeya Bayarlag suggests to Mevlido that he lie down in the rags that will soon be sent off for incineration. Mingrelian describes that—

Mevlido's ultimate burial in the middle of the scraps and waste bits of cloth, beneath the inexpressive gaze of the spiders.

- The third sequence has Deeplane appear again. Mevlido and Deeplane come out of a narrow passage, in all likelihood a furnace. They come out onto a light street, in a city that resembles neither Henhouse Four nor the Shambles, and we understand it as an intermediate place between dream and reality, belonging to the universe of Verena Becker. Mingrelian until that point had not broached that foreign universe—no more than he had wanted to bring up that woman, out of respect for Mevlido. Mingrelian is convinced that Mevlido and Verena Becker's reunion does not concern the Organs. It has no place in a report destined for the Organs' archives. For the same reasons, doubtless, Deeplane retreats. The meeting with Verena Becker, for whom Mevlido had had nostalgia throughout his whole existence, and, also, well before his birth and well after his death, this meeting is finally about to happen. Mevlido will clandestinely enter one of Verena Becker's dreams, an image where he will forever be in Verena Becker's company. Even if incomprehensible human echoes can be heard there, the image will be silent. And above all, there will be no more before-the-image or after-the-image.

"There will be no more before-the-image or after-the-image," writes Mingrelian in a commentary. "Mevlido will finally be frozen in an unmoving destiny, in the only form of the catastrophe that he would have wanted if anyone had ever asked his opinion, in a destiny from now on without story or speech, in a destiny where no one will ask the question of his insignificance, of his misfortune, of his political irresponsibility, of his belonging to the Party, of his relationship with the human race, of his morality, of his fidelity to Verena Becker, of his criminal ruminations, of his perception of reality, of his dreams, of his loves, of his deaths."

Of my criminal ruminations, I felt like adding, of my perception of reality, of my loves, of my deaths.

47
Dwarf Birds

The bus floated in the direction of the intersection, pushed at once by the wind and an indescribable force from black space. In reality, it went at a snail's pace, and often it even remained immobile during inexplicably long halves of a day or an hour. I wasn't impatient, but sometimes I wondered if I was going to arrive anywhere. When the wind wasn't blowing too hard, I got down from the rear of the bus and walked the length of the bus to stretch my legs. I sunk up to my knees in the warm ash and residue. Above me, the windows spat out clouds of dust. The heat had not abated. It made the image flicker and dazed me. These expeditions led me to the front of the bus. I didn't go farther for fear of getting lost. I raised my head. The celestial vault resembled a flooding river that had exchanged its waters for kerosene. Lower down, near me, the front of the bus creaked. Where the windshield would have been, the glass was missing. Behind that nonexistent facade, I saw Deeplane at the controls, obese and unidentifiable because of the layers of soot that had accumulated on him. He made no movement to wipe his face, for example, or his eyes; as if crumpled over the steering wheel, he peered at the route, at the dirty shadows. I was in plain view, a meter from him, just in front of the wheels, but he didn't see me. Next to Deeplane, Linda Siew sang softly or danced, according to the phase of the ritual she had reached. Her hair, whipped up by the wind, scratched at the emptiness around her or came to beat against Deeplane's shoulder when she in turn leaned over to peer at what was coming. She didn't see me either. She wore no clothes, and the dust did not attach itself to her skin. I already said it, but I'm saying it again here: she reminded me of Verena Becker. I felt nostalgia at the thought that it was up to me to speak to her and to act as if she were in fact Verena Becker and could hear me. I hesitated in front of the demolished front door, then I regained the rear of the bus and again I went back in to sit or crouch inside, no matter where, on an empty seat or below one.

Then horrible black dunes began to foam up all along the street, with a noise of ocean swells and dark hail. Fortunately, I was not wandering on the sidewalk. The air was full of particles that looked like cinders. I protected my eyes with what I could, the remains of clothing, my eyelids. The storm lasted about ten minutes, then, without transition, the gusts lessened. In the street a sepulchral calm established itself, and in the vehicle could be heard fits of coughing and throat clearing, because, during the worst of it, two or three new passengers had come in through the windows or the rear door. I removed from my face the coal that had hardened onto it and took stock. I had lost consciousness for a time. I had changed place; I was now sitting just behind Deeplane. Beyond his shoulders, which the sediment had made monumental, I could see the junction where we were going to enter Waddell Street or Park Avenue. I had in my mouth nauseating, granular smoke. I spit it out, wheezing. Linda Siew was also wheezing. She had interrupted her magic chant, and, between two painful breaths, she was confiding something to Deeplane. She had the intonation of a dying woman. Someone else, nearby, was fighting against suffocation. I turned my head. Upright, a meter away from me, stood a familiar silhouette. Gorgha, I thought, without really knowing whether this meeting brought me pleasure. I got up and slipped through the shadows with the intention of joining her. Her crow-black feathers had lost their impeccable luster, their well-groomed appearance, they had dulled, but Gorgha kept her magnificent air of a magnificent female bird. She coughed, closing her eyes. I drew near to her and held out my hand. Against my palm her plumes moved. Just underneath them her flesh had contracted slightly. I had touched her lower abdomen.

"Cut the bullshit, Mevlido," she sighed, without prying her eyes open, "if you think it's the time for that."

"I'm glad you're here," I lied. "Lately I had thought that you had gone, and we wouldn't see each other again."

I opened my arms, we held each other close. Gorgha regained her breath little by little. She accepted to nestle against me, but I felt her reluctance. She didn't relax into my arms. She didn't relax more than in the past. There had always been between us organic misunderstandings of which we were conscious but which we preferred not to inflame by expressing them in words.

In the bus, no one was coughing anymore. People either were no longer breathing or had adapted to a milieu of which no component furnished them with the means of life. At any rate, there weren't many people. A ragged woman was sitting at the back, immobile; another was lying across a bench. Yasar Bayarlag lay in the aisle, totally buried. We were all in rags. We all reeked of broiled garbage.

"There was an attack," I said, embracing Gorgha.

"Of course not," said Gorgha. "It's the wind. It's just the wind that blows on the Shambles, a sandstorm. What are you talking about with your attacks, Mevlido?"

"Bah," I said.

"What are you talking about?" she repeated.

We remained several minutes without talking. I was ashamed

to press Gorgha to my chest heavy with soot, to the remains of Yasar Bayarlag's shirt, now ignobly filthy and torn. Against me, Gorgha stiffened. Perhaps she thought of me as a physically odious being, with whom intimacy was problematic. I didn't know how to neutralize her disgust. Her tousled feathers did not soften at my contact, her breath was tense, raspy. Something about me horrified her. I began the conversation again to put up a good front.

"You hear?" I asked, "someone is playing a *gut* rhythm. There must be a *mudang* around here, a *mudang* singing the *uga*."

"I don't hear anything," whispered Gorgha. "You're talking bullshit, Mevlido. You only talk bullshit."

"No," I said, "there's definitely a drum, a *mudang*. I know her name. Her name is Linda Siew. Do you see her? The naked woman standing next to the driver. She looks like Verena Becker."

"I don't see her," said Gorgha.

I almost told Gorgha to open her eyes, but I held back. It's true that it was impossible to see much, even at a short distance, and that in the air hostile dust was floating. And besides, my presence in front of her was perhaps the reason she preferred to remain sightless.

"She's singing the *uga* so that the dead enter into contact with the living," I explained, just in case.

"What living, what dead?" said Gorgha, shrugging her shoulders.

I didn't add anything. I was concentrating on the ceremony going on. In her exhausted voice the *mudang* continued to repeat and repeat the melody, concerned that the song reach its intended audience at last—dead, living, or others. I had the impression that I didn't belong to any of these categories, but, in any case, I managed to catch a few notes. A lot more conviction was needed to hear the drum, hit without force and, most often, with mistakes in the rhythm.

"Deeplane is looking for you," announced Gorgha suddenly.

"I know," I said.

"No, you don't know," said Gorgha.

She writhed against me. In the shadow, her dark eyelids had no color. They were obstinately closed. She twisted and turned with the noise of feathers, she moved her shoulders as if to disengage from my embrace or to get rid of an excess of oily dust or heat. I loosened my arms. Immediately, she moved half a step away.

"I have something to transmit to you from him," she said.

I glanced at Deeplane. He was still at his steering wheel, enormous as a statue sculpted from dark clay. He was peering at the route. He wasn't moving.

"I'm listening," I said.

"It's about Verena Becker," said Gorgha.

"Ah," I said, "finally. The Organs are finally taking an interest in her."

"First instruction," continued Gorgha without listening to me. "It's useless to hope to rejoin Verena Becker anywhere but inside one of her dreams."

"I know," I said.

"No," said Gorgha, "you don't know. For too long you have been out of touch with Verena Becker's worlds. You never dreamed together again since she found herself surrounded by child soldiers. You would feel foreign, you would not like her dreams anymore. Second instruction. You will be the only one to know that you are together inside the same image. She will not even suspect your presence. She will continue her nightmare with the sentiment of absolute loneliness. You will be of no help to her."

"That's harsh, as an instruction," I pointed out.

"Bah, even before this, you weren't any great help to her," observed Gorgha. "Third instruction. Don't complain. Don't complain about luck, or the strategic changes in the Organs, or about Deeplane. Accept anything whatsoever from fate."

"I know," I said, "resign yourself to anything whatsoever, whatever happens."

"That's all," concluded Gorgha.

She was panting. Her head fell back to one side as if she no longer had any strength in her cervical vertebrae.

Coal-filled dust undulated above us like a burning cloud, carrying smells of burned motor and sulfur.

I began to cough again.

Less than two meters away, Linda Siew was dancing. Her hair tangled in the black wind, snaking around her like a bunch of algae. She danced without solemnity and as if for herself. When she turned toward us, on her stomach was suddenly visible a wound the size of an awl punch, bleeding. A black thread trickled down to her waist, toward her pubis, reappeared on the inside of her thigh. Then she pivoted, and we saw her back, skin dulled by the stream of grains and powders. Her features grown ugly from suffering, she continued to sing and to speak the *uga*. Her broken *mudang*'s voice could be heard, shattered, again and again putting music to words made for the dead or for those who were trying to survive as the dead.

She's been shot in the liver, I thought.

"I don't know whether the attack has already taken place," I murmured, approaching my head to Gorgha's. "In any case, we're being shot at."

"Of course not," said Gorgha.

Something came in the window, hummed briefly, then came to rest in the seat next to her. The casing rattled over ten centimeters away, a pouch of soot burst and suddenly spilled its powdery black contents.

"And that?" I said. "There's an attack on us, on the bus."

"Of course not, no one is attacking us," said Gorgha. "It's just that we're crossing the intersection. It will calm down when we've crossed the intersection."

"There are bullets flying everywhere," I said.

"Stop talking bullshit," said Gorgha. "What are you talking about with your bullets? What bullets? They're tiny birds, mutant mynah birds. They are flying at a phenomenal speed without looking out for obstacles. They're blind."

In the shadows Linda Siew caught her breath between two phrases. I was trying to imagine what would happen if, instead of talking with Gorgha, I stuck to the *mudang* and Deeplane, if I embraced both of them to melt into their group, to join them organically; but this idea didn't succeed in becoming an image, and I remained with an empty mind, listening without acting to the tired and courageous voice of Linda Siew and watching Deeplane's enormous back. We had reached the intersection, but we would have needed a navigation expert to realize that. By intervals, little black masses chirped at our arrival. They went through space and immediately pierced our flesh or the seat cushions, or they smashed against metallic obstacles with the crack of a shooting gallery.

All at once the chassis of the vehicle jumped. The metallic carcass around us trembled, and, a fraction of a second later, everything grew calm.

"An attack," growled Deeplane in Linda Siew's direction. "Stay strong."

Linda Siew was no longer singing. I saw her lose her balance and be slowly thrown onto Deeplane. She tried to slow her fall with her two hands, with her knees, she tried to grab on to the dashboard, on to Deeplane, but her hands grasped nothing, and her limbs seemed no longer to obey her. There had been no deflagration, no breath of air or flames, not even the brutal stench of nitrates, but the *mudang* and the driver were fighting as if they were captives inside an explosion. They had these kinds of hopeless gestures. Around Deeplane the shadowy envelope was becoming undone. It had, until that point, tripled the real volume of Deeplane's body, but now it broke apart and detached itself from its underpinning, revealing Deeplane's real silhouette, his old warrior-monk appearance, an incorruptible combatant. Now we could see the ascetic physiognomy that we had always kept in our memory and that here was ravaged by fasting, devoured by asphyxiation and the sorrow of having once more failed in the search for Mevlido. The pieces of carapace seemed heavy and compact as coal, and, instead of turning to dust, they fell heavily to the ground. Linda Siew was enveloped by a wave of dust, and she was already no longer touching the ground. She was suspended a few centimeters from the floor, as if dislocated, disheveled, and she swayed like that for several fractions of a second and maybe even in Deeplane's vicinity, then she was sucked with him toward the side window, and both of them began to slide inexorably toward the outside. The outside was calling them, the outside wanted to swallow them up. They contorted themselves like drowning people near the surface. They tried to conquer their inertia, to grasp each other's hands so that they could be together at the end, to end together, but, stunned and mentally dislocated, they didn't succeed. Deeplane's fingers felt at random toward Linda Siew's torso, and suddenly they found her collarbone and wrapped around the bone. It was not an elegant handhold, and it must have been painful, but like that, despite everything, they had managed to come together. They continued their trajectory toward the street, and, slowly, they disappeared.

Mineral or organic waste rained down onto the dashboard.

I turned toward Gorgha. She still had her eyes closed.

"No one is driving the bus anymore," I said.

"Take the steering wheel," said Gorgha. "Replace Deeplane."

"I can't do it," I said.

"I'll help you," said Gorgha.

I went to sit on the seat that Deeplane had left empty. First, I had to clear it of a mound of coal-like material. The idea of sitting on the debris that had been more or less part of Deeplane was distasteful to me. I settled down on it against my will, grabbed the wheel, and stared ahead at the route. Nothing much was visible beyond a few meters ahead. The black powder that covered the road was of an immeasurable thickness. The wind planed the surface, creating here and there little spots of fog or smoke. Our gaze didn't go as far as the houses. I leaned toward the opening on my left, anxious to discover if Deeplane and Linda Siew were still nearby. There were mounds near the vehicle, dirty dunes, but no footprints, no sign of a fall or crawling.

"We'll soon be beyond the intersection," said Gorgha.

"And then we'll enter Waddell Street?" I asked.

"I don't know," said Gorgha. "You have something planned on Waddell Street?"

"No, nothing in particular," I said.

I sat back upright on my seat. Gorgha was next to me, her eyes still closed, her legs slightly apart, wings half-open to keep her balance. Her plumage was disheveled, and rancid odors radiated from it. She now looked miserable, with the appearance of an old, unappealing crow. In her place, shortly before, the naked *mudang* had stood and danced. If I'd had to team up with someone at the controls of the bus, I would have preferred that it be with the shaman, Linda Siew.

We headed between two walls topped with barbed wire. I didn't recognize Waddell Street. It seemed to me that we had just entered Park Avenue instead. That meant that we were going in the direction of waste treatment plant number nine, where Maleeya had worked. I bent over the steering wheel to bring my head closer to our route and to get any clues on the route we were following. The greasy wind, black and torrid, beat against my face. I couldn't make out anything decisive.

Then, again, whistling noises zigzagged around us. I had the clear impression that, for the blind birds, I was a target.

"Do you hear that?" I said to Gorgha.

"Yes," said Gorgha, "a drum. A *gut* rhythm. There is a ceremony not far from here."

"I don't hear anything," I said.

"Then what are you talking about?" asked Gorgha. "What bullshit are you still talking, Mevlido?"

"It's whistling," I said. "I get the feeling that we're being targeted."

I was finishing that sentence when something throbbed against me and pierced through my torso. I let out a moan.

"What's wrong with you?" asked Gorgha.

I felt a microscopic mynah bird beating its wings in my blood, inside my chest. I don't know if it was getting comfortable or if it was thrashing about to enlarge the tunnel in whose depths it found itself.

"It just missed my heart," I said.

"What?" Gorgha inquired.

"A bird," I said. "It's collapsed one of my lungs. And now it's wriggling about next to my right ventricle."

"Bah, it's been a long time since your heart has beaten," Gorgha philosophized. "Since the very beginning, it hasn't beaten."

"What beginning?" I asked, disappointed to observe Gorgha's insensitivity regarding me.

The mynah was frolicking about. It didn't peep, but I could hear splashes, and miniscule jumps, and rustling wings, and pecks, its blind joie de vivre, its insouciance, its wriggling.

48

Black Spiders

Once past the intersection, the voyage lasts a long time still. Hours and more. Hours or millennia. Impossible to know. Time passing gets bogged down, night is permanent. Infinity coagulates in the somnolence of the travelers. The bus continues on its trajectory. It is driving, for better or for worse, on Park Avenue, alongside the factory, but old age infiltrates it and gnaws at it. It becomes more and more fragile. One lovely evening, after having hit the edge of the sidewalk, it breaks up. In the shadows the metallic parts scatter. They immediately begin to decompose, they peel off without losing any time, but it would be necessary to count to 767,767 several times before the debris would truly blend in with the dust. The axles, the brakes, and the steering wheel are the pieces that most resist degradation. For innumerable decades, when nothing solid remains near them, they resist, then, in turn, they vanish.

During this time, Mevlido is camping not far from an axle that has buried itself in front of the factory gate. He is not animated by a great desire for sociability, and he doesn't form any relationship with those who find themselves on the ground in his company, but he doesn't feel any hostility toward them, and, fundamentally, the survivors of the bus form a sort of little group clearly distinct from the other residual elements and soot. There are two or three in the same situation, including Linda Siew, Deeplane, and he, Mevlido. They can't be observed restlessly exploring the ruins around them, no, and they are even characterized instead by an absolute inertia, but rare among them are those who have abandoned the prospect of reaching the gate of waste treatment plant number nine. They don't know if the number nine refers to the plant or the waste and if, once they get in, they'll be treating or being treated, but the idea remains. Without moving in any meaningful manner, they are camping, all two or three of them, near the axle, in the calm, black landscape, in this image of a motionless city, so motionless that even the idea of an attack seems to have been withdrawn permanently.

Then the axle disintegrates, and they are left with no points of reference. Everything is still. Neither wind nor tide comes to bother the terrain, the hills, and the dunes of dust. The moon, which had long been absent above Henhouse Four and the Shambles, has made its reappearance. It is illuminating the world again. It is in the sky, high above the horizon, and not moving anymore.

On the zoological level, the world has changed its foundations. During the long parenthesis when the moon was hiding who knows where, the status of humanity did not stop deteriorating. One can still today dig up here and there individuals who still possess enough language to explain that they descend from a lineage of hominids, but, in reality, the reign of humanity is finished. The Organs, for once successfully, have invested their strength and their hope in a more understandable and less barbaric, less suicidal, less unbalanced species. The spiders are currently administering the ruins of the planet. They also claim a kind of humanism, and, even if it's true that they eat their sexual partners as soon as their eggs have been fertilized, there can't be found among them, as the millennia pass, the least theorist of genocide, of preventative war or social inequality. On Earth, at present, slavery, refugee camps, chaos, mass murder, and humiliation no longer occur. The hominids and their murderous practices, the hominids and their cynical discourses, are no longer anything but a memory. The dominant species never raises the question of happiness or misfortune, which means that, in a certain way, it's been solved.

The moon came back, and it's not a bad thing. Its disk shines constantly above the landscape, in the same place, which guarantees pale light and faces no matter the circumstances and the hour of day or night. The landscape is as it already was in memory, rich in a great variety of tones of gray, black, and white. The faces are ours. The street knows a permanent warmth. On one side are crumbled, indistinct buildings and, on the other, the wall that designates the factory's perimeter. The spirals of barbed wire that used to top it are broken in places, hanging to the ground, forming confused bunches in which are slowly rotting rags or very old canvas that no one has bothered to reconstruct. Near the gate or elsewhere the spaces corresponding to missing bricks are inhabited by spiders, representatives of a giant and rotund species. Now that the wind no longer blows, they remove the soot that swallowed or even blocked up their dens, and, that task accomplished, they put out some of their feet and remain motionless, observing the street below. They have the same attitude as the idlers and dreamers we used to know, and, if the question had been asked, they would surely have answered that they descend from an interminable lineage of hominids and that proletarian morality consists, precisely and fundamentally, of taking the air at their window when their work has been done and the weather conditions permit it. On this subject the Organs made sure that the ideological rupture between the two species was not unfathomable. It's even possible that, in certain breaches in the wall, one or two heroines are cleaning dust off themselves while thinking of their flawless fidelity to a Party of which they neither know nor reveal the objectives, the secrets, the importance, the structures, the methods, the founding date, the probable allies, the medium- and long-term strategies, the immediate program of action, or the name.

Here we are.

And here Mevlido opens an eye. He is sitting askew atop a little hill, less than ten meters from the factory gate. The moon is lighting the remains. Beneath the silky film that covers the iron doors can still be seen the posters that the old Bolsheviks pasted there before exiting the stage, in the hope that one day an intelligence won over to their language will see them, for example, Mevlido's intelligence, or ours.

> IF YOU LIVE ON AFTER YOUR DEATH, WAIT FOR
> ORDERS!
> CROUCH DOWN AND COUNT TO ZERO!
> FORGET THE SPIDER IN YOU, GO WITH THE NAKED
> WITCHES!
> CLIMB TO NOTHING AND THEN TAKE OFF YOUR RAGS!
> WAIT FOR DREAM ZERO ZERO SIXTEEN!

No noise troubles Park Avenue. From time to time the spiders push out of their living space the coal-like filth that has accumulated there, provoking little, black, extremely fine cascades.

Then, right nearby, Linda Siew gets up. She spends a day or two brushing her skin and hair, getting rid of their impurities and their ashes. Finally, she leans over Deeplane, she murmurs to him incantations or a few sentences. Deeplane is incarcerated in an enormous carapace that gives him an almost spherical appearance. One could imagine underneath a sort of microscopic chrysalid soup, or maybe think that Deeplane inside has kept his original silhouette, his shape of an incorruptible wanderer, persevering at pushing through adversity, black space, or the difficult intersections of the Shambles, or one might decide that that granular ball no longer contains form or consciousness of any kind.

Despite the magical insistence of Linda Siew, Deeplane doesn't answer. Linda Siew moves her hand at the height of what might be a part of Deeplane's back and strikes the hardened layer imprisoning him. She breaks it. Into the opening she puts her arm up to the elbow. She's looking for Deeplane's skin.

"I've been watching him for a while," murmurs Mevlido. "It's been a while since he moved. I think it's over."

Linda Siew pulls out her arm. She stares at the person who just spoke to her, that is to say, Mevlido, that is to say, me.

"Is that you, Mevlido?" she asks.

"Bah," I say.

Less than half a meter separates us. Now that the *mudang* has cleaned off the dust and combed her hair again, her nakedness has never been so enchanting. She found her beauty again, simple, vertiginous. Under the milky moonlight, it looks like she just took a shower. She's an extraordinarily beautiful *mudang*.

She looks like Verena Becker, my dear little Verena.

The *mudang* takes a step and slowly draws alongside me. She is up to her knees in dust. My head is at the height of her stomach. I wrap my arms around her legs. Her body is like the rest of the universe, warm and calm. We receive together the energy that shimmers down from the moon rays. Time passes.

"Get up," says Linda Siew suddenly. "Now the path is clear."

She is out of breath. Her voice trembles.

"What path?" I say.

With an imprecise gesture, she points out the factory, the slightly open gate.

For hours we crawl toward the gate. The soot that covers the road seems not to have been disturbed for millennia. Everything is asleep under a crumbly layer that threatens to break at any moment. On all fours, exhausted, scarcely bigger than the spiders watching us, we move forward very slowly. The spiders are watching us. There are many of them. We move ahead very slowly. We are nothing any longer. I head toward the opening in the gate, but Linda Siew stops me.

"Through the window, Mevlido. Not through there."

"I don't see a window," I say.

The *mudang* shrugs her shoulders.

You look so much like Verena Becker, Linda, I want to add. Like Verena, my dear little Verena. Can I call you Verena? Does it bother you if I call you Verena rather than Linda?

I don't say anything. We have drawn near the right panel of the gate, and, now, we're in front of it. The metal has rusted deeply but hasn't lost its structure to the point that one could go through it by reducing it to dust with a blow of the head or fist. Silk threads ensure the cohesion of the surface in the places where the blisters and lacelike formations indicate holes. Underneath the invisible silk threads, there are the remains of a proclamation. Only an exclamation point and two words are legible. I try to decipher them. It looks like a number written out in letters, in obsolete characters: zero zero sixteen.

"The window is there," whispers the *mudang*. "That's where we're going to go through."

She puts her hand on the poster and pushes. The spider webs break, the paper crumbles, and an opening becomes visible. The edges are irregular and sharp, they shine like mournful blades. If it's a gateway and I venture in, it will be difficult to escape slitting my throat.

"You think so, Verena?" I say. "Are you sure?"

Linda Siew pushes me without answering. She guides me. I feel her hand trembling on my shoulders, and, when I try to turn to look at her, I already feel against my neck the warmth of the iron tearing into me.

49
Verena Becker

"I warn you," said Deeplane, "they martyred her."

"I know," said Mevlido.

"No, you don't know," said Deeplane. "They tortured her, they raped her, they played with her body in vile ways, they left her for dead. During the night, she crawled over blankets and mattresses soaked with blood. The soldiers had piled their victims up on them, it was a former dormitory. She slipped under the mattresses and didn't move for hours. The next morning, the soldiers kept dragging the bodies of those they'd massacred the night before to that place. They are under the control of international organizations; they've been taught to hide their traces in the cases where the butchery has reached unacceptable proportions. They poured gasoline over the bodies so that everything would disappear in a fire, but, as they were in a hurry to leave and their boss was badgering them, they weren't being careful with their work. Verena Becker was able to escape the flames. She was able to pull herself from the furnace. The soldiers weren't far away, but they were no longer watching what happened in the burning building. She then wandered between the lines for two days and two nights. By a miracle she wasn't used as a target, she didn't have her legs blown off by a mine. But it's as if . . . you know, Mevlido, she got out of it, but it's as if she didn't get out of it alive."

"I know," said Mevlido.

"No, you don't know," said Deeplane. "She is immobile. She no longer opens her eyes, and besides, now, she is blind. When she sleeps, her sleep is like death. The world she inhabits is no longer ours. Supposing you still want to be with her one day, it will only be in a dream."

"I want to do that," said Mevlido.

"I warn you," said Deeplane, "she won't recognize you. Once you have slipped into one of her dreams, you will have to be content with watching her from far away. It's out of the question for you to establish any contact with her. It will be hard for you. Will you be able to stand it?"

"I'm ready," affirmed Mevlido without hesitating.

"So let's go." Deeplane was becoming agitated.

The shadow had given way to night. No lamp was lighted. Deeplane thrashed about, fumbling in the darkness. The space had the appearance, the echoes, and the smells of a furnace. A furnace or a cellar. Mevlido opened his eyes wide without being able to see anything, and suddenly it seemed to him that he could make out a club in Deeplane's hands. He backed up against a wall and bent down. Against his hands he felt a metallic plaque that he would have had to force open to get through the wall. He closed his eyes. His mind was totally inert. Everything was the same to him.

After several grueling operations, because disengagement almost always looks like a vile execution, Deeplane got Mevlido to the other side of the curtain. They began to advance wordlessly, feeling their way along a hallway. The walls crumbled when they leaned against them. A sharp smell of burned coal dominated. It was aggressive and difficult to stand.

"As long as we haven't arrived at the end of the hall, it's better not to breathe," advised Deeplane.

"Is it far?" asked Mevlido.

"Don't worry about distances, Mevlido," whispered Deeplane. "Distances don't count. Just think about going forward, and above all, hurry a little more."

"I feel like an insect scampering around in the darkness," Mevlido remarked, "an insect or a spider."

"Yes," said Deeplane. "Unfortunately, here, there is no difference."

When they had reached a door, Deeplane opened it with a blow from his shoulder. It was a cast iron door whose only handle was on the outside. They found themselves in an alley, a bottleneck between the rear facades of two buildings. The atmosphere was gray. There were rotten vegetables and a dirty puddle on the ground. The daylight wandered over it all with no conviction. The entrance to the street was signaled by a trash bin with no lid. On the other side the city hummed.

"I'm leaving you," said Deeplane. "Watch her. Don't try to speak to her. Whatever happens, don't intervene."

"Understood," said Mevlido.

"I can't do any more," said Deeplane.

"I know," I said.

"No, you don't know, Mevlido," insisted Deeplane.

He was standing next to me. I heard his halting breath, then he moved another step away. I wasn't watching him; I was examining the place we had just left. I was looking for the passage. I was looking for a cast-iron plaque, a handle.

No opening pierced the wall near which we were standing. In cast iron or any other material, there was not the smallest door. It was as if our bodies had just traversed the bricks without having been stopped by the material obstacle. As I examined the surface we had come through, I heard a metal panel screech on its hinges inside the building, then abruptly slam.

"Thank you for everything, Deeplane," I said, turning toward him.

But he had already disappeared.

Already, Deeplane has disappeared.

Deeplane. He disappeared. Now I am walking in the direction of the urban hum. I walk around rotten cabbage, a rat's corpse, rags. I don't know why, I take care not to brush against the two gray walls that tower over me, pierced by tiny barred windows, with air ducts and exterior pipes from which hang bunches of dust. After the container, the gallery opens onto an avenue darkened with pedestrians. I stop an instant before integrating myself into the passing horde. I would like to understand what form I exist in here, in this place where, if one analyzes Deeplane's elliptical remark, there is no difference between humans, beings with six legs, and those possessing eight. I try to count my limbs, I would like to arrive at a reliable result. I get confused and give up. I have in my mind the vital minimum: my name, Mevlido, and the name of the woman I love, Verena Becker, and a small certitude—from this moment on, I am moving about in the dream of the woman I love.

The crowd spreads out on all sides.

In a crowd, wherever you are, there is always a man alone or a woman alone. It might be you, and it's often you, but sometimes it's someone else. It depends on the mood of the crowd more than on yours. And here, in the human tide coming and going, thick, heavy, it's Verena Becker who is alone.

It's difficult not to lose sight of her. There are too many people. I'm in danger of being crushed and knocked over at any moment. But here I am talking about myself—let's not talk about me. It's her dream, Verena Becker's dream, my dear little Verena, and I don't claim to play the smallest role in it. Here she is again, twenty meters away. She just entered a procession of women who occupy the avenue and chant in rhythm. They chant, they repeat terrible slogans, and yet their faces remain impassive. It's as if they are covered by a mask. Even their eyes seem dull. No passion sparkles there, no anger. Only their voices show an intense emotion, made up of anxiety and an inexhaustible hatred for the enemy.

Young, old, dressed in black rags, the women walk forward in close ranks, forming chains. They march quickly, brandishing neither banners nor flags, and they launch ahead of themselves threatening slogans, with little variation, that come one after another like waves. After each series of protests, there is a second of abrupt silence, a second of waiting, suspended, when everything stops breathing, a moment when the idea floats that what has been formulated with violence will manifest soon, in very, very short order. Then the women remember inside themselves, all at the same time, that no revenge turns out well, and they come back to earth, in the middle of the street, together, a knot of despair in their throat, draped in the rags of mourning dresses, in tattered coats, and the cry begins again. Verena Becker, my dear little Verena, immerses herself for a moment in this tide, hardly more than a minute, then she abandons it. Even when a crowd becomes a collective organism thinking only of combat or speech, there is always in it a woman alone who remains alone. Verena Becker has quickly lost all desire to agglomerate herself with the rest, and, if she opened her mouth slightly, it was without repeating the slogans that were being roared next to her. The exhortations of her companions awake nothing in her, no rage, no sentiment of urgency and almost no sympathy, as if they were being expressed in a foreign language. She doesn't understand any longer the use of calling for the punishment of the enemy if the call is not followed by an immediate thunderbolt strike. Marching, proffering curses, this is what helped her in the past to convince herself that she wasn't made entirely of nothing. Today she believes the contrary. She moves away from the procession.

Now she is wandering in the middle of the onlookers, on the sidewalk. In a reflex of old militant solidarity she accompanies the group of women for another fifty meters or so, then she tears herself away, down a cross street. The slogans burst forth behind her again:

NAKED SHAMANS, NAKED LITTLE SISTERS, LEAVE
  YOUR FLAMES, BE REBORN, STRIKE!
LEAVE YOUR FLAMES, BE REBORN, STRIKE!
BE REBORN, STRIKE!

In the narrower street where Verena Becker is walking the people press against each other in herds. My dear little Verena moves forward obliquely in the middle of the throng, struggling to maintain her direction. Sometimes she is taken in a direction that she didn't choose, often she goes sideways, or she has to go back four or five meters. I am thinking about the happy days in our past together, in Zone 2, during the only year that wasn't a year of defeat, when we would walk, Verena Becker and I, through the dense Chinese multitudes of Mongkok, at the end of the day, physically lightened by the fatigues of a martial arts training session, in the time when Mongkok hadn't yet been flattened and could be the destination of a voyage. But here the affluence seems much greater than in the working-class neighborhoods of Zone 2, where already the influx of refugees and survivors metamorphosed the streets. Verena Becker presses herself against a wall, and the current tears her off it and pulls her farther away. She doesn't have the strength to resist. Now she has her back against a door. Next to her shoulder is a dirty window. She stands on the threshold of that place—maybe a little shop, an abandoned artisan's workshop, maybe a simple, sordid lodging house. She feels worn out, almost incapable of moving, of filling her lungs with air, of remaining vertical, in balance.

The demonstration is getting farther away. The slogans echo along the buildings. They are still intelligible.

BEFORE BEING REBORN, ONLY THE FIRE, BECOME
  THE ONE WHO BURNS!
ENTER THE STRANGE IMAGE, BECOME THE ONE WHO
  BURNS!
WHEN YOU HAVE BURNED, TAKE OFF YOUR CLOTHES,
  BE REBORN, STRIKE!

So as not to fall and no longer to have to suffer the rubbing of arms, the pressure of arms and stomachs, and also the breath, the eyes that look through her or turn away quickly, turn away from her as if she were an unacceptable creature, Verena Becker seeks the handle of the door against which she is leaning.

The handle offers no resistance.

She opens the door and goes into the house.

The place has for its only lighting the feeble luminosity that filters through the little window. Cardboard boxes are visible, piled up as if for moving, metal shelves, debris. The shelves are empty. The smell that dominates doesn't permit one to say whether the place is inhabited. It's the smell of winter in poor basements, where the mildews and the left-behind come and go at their leisure. Behind the boxes a second dark room can be made out.

"Is anyone there?" asks my dear little Verena.

She closes the door. Immediately, the hubbub coming from the street lessens. Verena Becker repeats her question. The damp walls absorb her voice. No one answers. No invitation to make herself at home comes from the back room.

"Here I am, it's me," murmurs Verena in a mournful tone.

She listens.

"I came," she says again. "I'm waiting for you."

Verena stays there a minute, just at the entrance of the place, immobile, then she grows braver. She takes off her mask. She was actually wearing a mask until that moment, like the women just now, not a gas mask, nor a carnival mask, but a more subtle mask, of an ochre transparency that barely changes the face, that changes it slightly into wood, the mask that it's best to put on when you don't want to expose your wounds to an audience, the mask behind which solitude and fear are more tolerable in the middle of the crowd: your face is impassive, even the eyes express no passion; no matter the suffering, no tear runs down your cheek. She takes it off noiselessly and takes a few steps, heart beating, underneath a fluorescent tube that doesn't work; she brushes past the cardboard boxes, she moves through this narrow space that smells like the urine of small animals and cellar mushrooms.

She goes to the second room. It's a windowless bedroom, with a little camp bed, a table, a hot plate, a chair, a sink, a toilet, a central lightbulb. One could stay there, imprisoned or sheltered, for centuries. Verena Becker lights the lamp. A cockroach runs along the base of the wall, takes refuge under the bed. She doesn't recognize me. She sits on the bed. The bed frame barely creaks. The sheets have marks of rust or blood, but they're not really dirty.

The lamp lights this cell and, beyond, the disorder of cardboard boxes and the debris strewn about the floor. After a moment, Verena, my dear little Verena, presses the light switch to find herself again in what she now prefers, the shadows, away from everything. I hear her put her mask back on.

She stays seated for a quarter of an hour on the bed, not doing anything, reflecting. From my point of observation, under the bed frame, I can no longer see her. I can sense that she's moving slightly. I suppose it's because she just took between her fingers a little lock of hair and she is twisting it against her right temple, fascinated by the tiny rustling noise, tranquilized. It's a habit she had. I can no longer see her. I'm not even trying to look at her anymore. I don't need to; I remember her features perfectly. I'm sure she is still beautiful. I'm sure she is very beautiful.

We listen to what continues to go on, in the street, outside. I don't really know where we are, if it's outside or inside the world or someone. We listen passively to the tumult of steps and voices. On top of it suddenly is superimposed the rumor of slogans, which becomes more and more clear. The women's demonstration is winding through the neighborhood and, at the moment, getting closer.

I would like to talk to Verena Becker, to my dear little Verena, to whisper a few words to her or to signal to her, but I know it's better not to, even if I don't know exactly what harm would come of that for the two of us. I remember Deeplane's warnings. Making contact is out of the question. Whatever happens, try not to intervene in the dream of the woman I love. So I freeze in my corner, under the bed, eyes closed.

The demonstrators are plunging down our street now, occupying the street. Let's say that it's Waddell Street to say something. The window is shaking. The vibration can't be heard in the middle of the clamor, but, doubtless, the window is shaking.

I have no idea what Verena is thinking right now, my dear little Verena, but at least there's this: the two of us, in the solitude, together, we are imagining that the window is shaking, and we are listening to the phrases that the women are reciting together. I don't know whether we like them, I don't even know whether we understand them. But we are together to hear them vibrate within us:

LITTLE SISTERS DRESSED IN FLAMES, UNDRESS
   YOURSELVES, STRIKE!
NAKED LITTLE SISTERS, LEAVE YOUR FLAMES, BE
   REBORN, STRIKE!
LEAVE YOUR FLAMES, BE REBORN, STRIKE!
BE REBORN, STRIKE!
STRIKE UNTIL THE END, STRIKE!

A UNIVOCAL BOOK
Drew Burk, Consulting Editor

Univocal Publishing was founded by Jason Wagner and Drew Burk as an independent publishing house specializing in artisanal editions and translations of texts spanning the areas of cultural theory, media archeology, continental philosophy, aesthetics, anthropology, and more. In May 2017, Univocal ceased operations as an independent publishing house and became a series with its publishing partner, the University of Minnesota Press.

Univocal Authors

Miguel Abensour	Félix Guattari	Lionel Ruffel
Judith Balso	Olivier Haralambon	Felwine Sarr
Jean Baudrillard	David Lapoujade	Michel Serres
Philippe Beck	François Laruelle	Gilbert Simondon
Simon Critchley	David Link	Étienne Souriau
Fernand Deligny	Sylvère Lotringer	Isabelle Stengers
Jacques Derrida	Jean Malaurie	Sylvain Tesson
Vinciane Despret	Michael Marder	Eugene Thacker
Georges Didi-Huberman	Serge Margel	Antoine Volodine
Jean Epstein	Quentin Meillassoux	Elisabeth von Samsonow
Vilém Flusser	Friedrich Nietzsche	Siegfried Zielinski
Barbara Glowczewski	Peter Pál Pelbart	
Évelyne Grossman	Jacques Rancière	

ANTOINE VOLODINE is an author and translator who has to date published forty-eight novels in French under various names. Several of his books have been recently translated, including *Solo Viola* (Minnesota, 2021). He has won many literary awards, including the prestigious Medici Prize for *Terminus radieux*. His works, incorporating elements of speculative fiction and the fantastic, make up a unique universe that the author has termed the "post-exotic," which draws on sources as diverse as Buddhist and shamanic traditions and Soviet history.

GINA M. STAMM is associate professor of French at the University of Alabama in Tuscaloosa, with a research focus on embodiment and the environment in surrealist and speculative writing, particularly from the perspectives of posthumanism, ecofeminism, and queer ecology.